THE STONE OF ZOHELETH

THE SERPENT'S STONE

by

Eileen Polsky

And Adonijah sacrificed sheep
and oxen and fatlings by
the stone of Zoheleth.
I Kings 1:9

Copyright © 2000 by Eileen Polsky

All rights reserved. No part of this book shall be reproduced or transmitted in any form or by any means, electronic, mechanical, magnetic, photographic including photocopying, recording or by any information storage and retrieval system, without prior written permission of the publisher. No patent liability is assumed with respect to the use of the information contained herein. Although every precaution has been taken in the preparation of this book, the publisher and author assume no responsibility for errors or omissions. Neither is any liability assumed for damages resulting from the use of the information contained herein.

This is a work of fiction. Names, characters, places, and incidents either are the product of the author's imagination or are used fictitiously. Any resemblance to actual events or locales or persons, living or dead, is entirely coincidental.

ISBN 978-0-7414-0478-7

Published by:

Info@buybooksontheweb.com
www.buybooksontheweb.com
Toll-free (877) BUY BOOK
Local Phone (610) 520-2500
Fax (610) 519-0261

Printed in the United States of America

Published November, 2012

OTHER WRITINGS BY EILEEN POLSKY

Back To The Future Of The Past
Talley Ho! To The Preterist Frontier We Go!
One Weak Link
Kaddle County Mystery
(Above titles hold the preterist viewpoint)

House of Edwards. S.F.
Short Stories
Weaver Of Words / Poems and Prose
A Visit With Angels

COPYRIGHT 1997 by Eileen Polsky

All rights reserved. No part of this publication may be reproduced in any form without the written permission of the author, except for brief quotations in critical reviews or articles.

My deepest appreciation to JoAnne Gerety and all the staff of Holy Ground Ministries.

Ms. Eileen Polsky is to be congratulated for her writings. The novel "Zoheleth" is a fine volume, well written, and teaches as it goes. It is a real page-turner. May it be a blessing to all those fortunate enough to read this well researched book.

Rev. Arthur Melanson
The Joy of the Lord
A Christian Radio Ministry
Audubon New Jersey

Zoheleth

CHAPTER ONE

The year is A.D. 67 and the month is June. Marcus Severus' journey by caravan was slow from his home in Antioch to the area of Jotapata, a province of Rome, now under siege by the Roman legions.

Marcus is on his way to join his father who serves in the cavalry of the Syrian Auxiliary. After leaving the caravan, he traveled by foot until he saw in the distance the Roman camps. Pausing to shade his eyes, he scanned the view of the city of Jotapata atop the high cliffs. It was said their heights could make a grown man faint when looking down. His heart was pounding from the heat as he climbed the path up the hillside, and dust from the sun-dried earth itched his bare legs leaving his dark skin an ashy color.

The shouts of soldiers and the sounds of racing horses were coming close. In a moment of panic he leaped behind a boulder and the hard ground met his face.

The galloping horses kicked clouds of dust into the air making him choke. He tasted blood on his lips and felt the gash on his cheekbone. His hands were scraped raw and he lay panting waiting for the sounds to fade.

The boulder was perfect to place his back-pack against and use for a headrest. His mind drifted home and he visioned his mother's tears as he said good-bye. His elder brother, Nicator, hugged him and said he was glad to be rid of him. Of course he was kidding, but it hurt. His thoughts were abruptly interrupted when someone spoke.

"You'll get trampled upon if you stay here any longer."

Marcus jumped to his feet and faced an elderly man in a white robe.

"Are you all right, young man?" he asked.

"Yes, sir," Marcus answered. "I'm here looking for my father."

"And who is your father?" asked the man.

"His name is Sabinus Severus. He's with the Syrian Auxiliary."

"Then you must be Marcus?"

"How did you know?" he asked, feeling certain the man was a friend and not one of the Jews who burned the villages of his relatives.

"Your father was expecting you yesterday," said the man. "He asked us to watch for your arrival."

"The caravans were delayed by a down-pour," Marcus informed.

"I'm Joseph Abtolim, a physician," said the man. "I treated your father when he was wounded."

"My father wounded?"

"Nothing serious. But you look like you could use my service. Come, let's walk."

"Will you take me to my father?" Marcus asked hopefully.

"After I cleanse that nasty cut on your cheekbone."

"But I'm all right," he complained as he reluctantly followed Joseph.

Outside the tent Marcus was given a basin of water in which to bathe. He splashed his face and arms, then poured the remaining water over his legs and feet.

Inside the tent, Joseph administered to his wound.

Marcus seated himself on a folding chair next to a table and watched Joseph making tea. He hated wasting time with the physician. His cheek burned and his hands stung as he lifted the metal cup. In the tent, he saw a cot in one corner and numerous scrolls neatly tucked into small openings in a wooden cabinet. Boxes of herbs were on a shelf, and wine skins hung on the wall. Joseph spoke.

"Is this your first time away from home?"

"I'm fourteen, and I want to be a soldier."

"I see," said Joseph as he poured more tea.

"Where's my father?" Marcus persisted.

"I'll take you to his regiment after you've eaten." Marcus gulped down the tea. He waited for Joseph. "My father and I will kill the Jews who burned the villages of our relatives in Antioch."

Joseph arched his brows. "By all means then, let's take you to your father." They left the tent and Joseph called out to a young man with a splint on his leg. "Philip, meet Marcus, the son of Sabinus."

Philip limped toward them. "Welcome, son of Sabinus!" he said as he greeted him with a firm hand shake. "You're as tall as your father."

"You know my father?"

"Ah, yes. We did battles together." Philip smiled and asked Joseph what he could do for him.

"Can you get us two good mules so I can take Marcus to his father?" Joseph asked.

Philip hobbled away and soon returned with the mules. "Will you need me to escort you?" he asked. "It will be past sun-down by the time you start back. Please, allow me to go with you. You'll be entering enemy territory."

"Philip, if you insist! But you ride your own horse and not a mule." They left the camp area and headed up hill. Marcus found any attempt to make the beast move faster was in vain.

"Why must Philip ride so far ahead?" he asked Joseph.

"We might meet with danger. Some of the renegades have been stealing mules from the riders."

"What good can Philip do with a wounded leg?"

"Marcus, Philip is a Roman soldier," said Joseph. "On horseback he needs only a sword!"

They rode slowly, while overhead the pale gray clouds blotted out the sun but it gave no relief from the indomitable heat. Marcus' black hair hung in damp ringlets beneath his soiled turban.

The mules grew more stubborn as they plodded up rocky embankments. Joseph stopped and dismounted when he saw Philip returning.

"I'll ride on and search for Sabinus," said Philip. "You and the boy stay here."

Marcus was impatient, but while waiting he looked

Zoheleth

up to the cliffs of Jotapata and was astounded by their majestic heights. They appeared like miles of rocks rising from the ground and towering over the countryside. Suddenly he gasped.

"Look!" he shouted and pointed upward. "People are jumping off the cliffs."

Joseph looked in the direction. "Good Lord!" he cried. "They've chosen suicide rather than surrender to the Romans."

Marcus covered his ears to block out the screams as he witnessed women and children being forced over the cliffs. His heart pounded, and he wondered how people could do this.

Shouts of protest rose from the soldiers as they looked on in disbelief. When the screams faded, Marcus lowered his hands.

"Who are they?" he asked.

"They're Jews who have turned against Roman authority," Joseph answered. He was saddened.

Marcus saw Philip riding toward them. "Did you find my father?" he called out.

"He's on his way," Philip replied. He looked at Joseph and commented, "Governor Gallus should have defeated these arrogant troublemakers while he was in Jerusalem."

Marcus was curious and asked, "What happened with Governor Gallus?" He noticed Joseph became silent and refused to speak on the subject, but Philip was more than willing to talk.

"Cestius Gallus had orders to put down an insurgency in Jerusalem, but for some unknown reason he retreated." Philip glanced at Marcus and continued. "By retreating he lost the rear division of his Twelfth Legion."

"What!" Marcus was in disbelief. "Gallus is the governor of Syria. Our people of Antioch favor him. What caused him to lose part of his legion?"

"When he left Jerusalem, a group of rabblerousers followed him and destroyed the legion's rear division."

Zoheleth

"In Antioch, it can take weeks or months before we learn what has happened in other cities," said Marcus.

"Gallus' retreat cost the lives of the Roman garrison stationed at the Tower of Antonia in Jerusalem." Philip went on. "Emperor Nero learned about the defeat and dismissed Gallus. He ordered General Flavius Vespasian as Gallus' replacement."

Joseph broke his silence. "Some of my people have decided to go against Rome."

Marcus felt his blood drain. He just learned the physician was a Jew. He walked away and stood near Philip. It was then he caught sight of his father.

Sabinus' black skin glistened and his lean body looked small on his stallion as he brought the beast to a halt.

"Father!" Marcus cried out joyously. Sabinus jumped down and hugged his son.

"Marcus, my boy. You gave us a fright when you didn't arrive yesterday."

"Nothing would keep me from being by your side, Father," Marcus smiled widely.

Sabinus turned to Joseph. "How are you doctor?"

"Busy with your son, as you can see."

"What battle were you in?" Sabinus laughed as he examined the wound on his son's cheek. Marcus fixed his gaze on his father.

"When can we leave?" he asked.

"Son," said Sabinus, as he removed his helmet and wiped his forehead. "That's what I want to talk to you about."

Marcus knew something was different. "What's wrong?"

"Nothing is wrong," Sabinus replied as he avoided his son's searching eyes. "I've had a long talk with Joseph and he has agreed to keep you with him."

Marcus felt his heart sink. He tightened his lips and shrugged his shoulders. "I came to be with you,"

"I know why you came," Sabinus addressed him. "I'm allowing you to remain, but there are conditions."

Zoheleth

Marcus kicked the dust with his sandals. "What are the conditions?" he groaned.

"Joseph knows you can read and write. He has offered to allow you to help him with his medical records. In exchange, he will teach you the art of his skills."

"But father, I don't want to be a physician," he protested. "I want to be a soldier, one like yourself."

"The battlefield is no place for my youngest son," Sabinus announced.

"Would you say the same thing to my brother, Nicator?"

"You're not being fair," said his father. "You know Nicator is unable to join the army, or have your forgotten he's lame?"

Marcus was crushed. Had his father blamed him for what happened to his brother? How could he face his mother if he didn't avenge the deaths of their relatives? What about Martha, his childhood sweetheart? They promised to marry when he finished his training and became a soldier. He clinched his fist and reeled about to face his father.

"You're the one who's been unfair!" he challenged. "You permitted me to come here. Why?"

"Because I didn't want to see my son join a group of bandits in the hills. That's exactly where you would have wound up if I allowed you to be on your own."

"But Father," he moaned. "I want to serve Rome."

"You're now in the service of Rome!" Sabinus snapped back. "You've been given an order. Either obey it or you can leave Jotapata immediately."

Marcus fought to conceal his emotions. He straightened his shoulders and looked directly into his father's eyes. "Father," he said bravely. "I'll serve Rome!"

Sabinus mounted his horse and spoke firmly to his son. "Serve Rome well!"

Marcus was stung. He watched tearfully as his father rode off. He turned and glared at Joseph, finding it hard to hold back his anger.

Zoheleth

"Don't be unhappy, young man," said Joseph. "Your father is concerned for your safety. You'll get training as a soldier while you're here."

Marcus lowered his head to hide his despair.

Philip rode up to him and waited while he dried his eyes.

"Marcus," he said. "How game are you for a fast ride back to camp?"

Marcus heaved a sigh and forced a smile. "I'm game!" Philip reached down and lifted him onto the back of his horse.

"Joseph, I'll double back for you," Philip informed. "You take the mules and I'll drop Marcus off at your tent."

Joseph nodded and watched the two ride off. He thought how nice it would be to have a young lad for company. It would be like having a son. A son which he never had. He planned to set up another cot in his tent for Marcus.

The sun slipped behind the cliffs of Jotapata, casting a cool shadow along the path. The lonely physician rode slowly back down the trail, leaving the despairing cries of Jotapata behind him.

CHAPTER TWO

THE FALL OF JOTAPATA

The Roman general, Flavius Vespasian, rode to the foot of the hills of Jotapata with his elder son, Titus. He was extremely irritated by the direction the battle had taken. The rebellious Jews held an advantage from the higher position on the cliffs. The enemy taunted the Romans for days with their abundance of water while he had to ration his men's water supply.

The Jews hung dripping wet cloths over the cliffs which plagued the Romans. The battle raged for forty days in a constant bombardment of stones, arrows, and fire missiles from both sides.

Vespasian's soldiers grew weary from fighting and losing ground. It appeared that the revolutionaries had their own general who outsmarted the Romans in every move.

With such miserable conditions, Vespasian proposed a strategy. If he could find their leader, it would put an end to the battle. He knew the insurrectionists depended on the strategy of their general. It was time to find the enemy's general and destroy him. He called upon the service of the Syrian auxiliary.

"Men of the cavalry!" he shouted, as they came to the call for action. "You who stand by to serve Rome. Put an end to this madness. I'm asking you to keep our armies and our Caesar from being demoralized."

The Syrians raised their hands with loyal salutes. Vespasian continued. "I need a man to get through the enemy lines. A man clever enough to capture the Jewish general."

One Syrian soldier, a slender but strong man, rode his horse to the front. His black skin and dark eyes glistened as he stopped in front of Vespasian.

"General!" he saluted. "I'm your man!" His

comrades hailed him.

Vespasian looked in disbelief. The soldier appeared to be no larger than a lad in his teens, but he noted his presence held the respect of his Syrian comrades.

"Your name, soldier?" Vespasian asked.

"I'm Sabinus Severus of Antioch, sir."

"Your confidence assures me you will accomplish my order," said Vespasian. The Roman general held back a smile. "Do whatever you must, but I make it clear. I want their general!" he commanded with determination. "Bring the Jewish general face to face with me!" His horse strained and reared. He pulled its reins and added, "Bring him alive, if possible."

The Syrians, with their horses' hooves wrapped in leather for protection, trotted the layers of stones. The men broke out in loud war-shouts as they moved upward toward the enemy.

The Jews of Jotapata saw them advancing and showered the Syrians with arrows. But due to a sudden change in the wind's direction, the arrows fell short of their targets.

Sabinus thanked the gods and took it as a good omen. He rode like lightening ahead of the men. His high spirits gave courage to those who followed. When they could go no further on horse-back, they abandoned their horses and went the rest of the way on foot.

The Roman soldiers, when seeing the Syrians joining the battle, regained hope. The wind change gave them an advantage they hadn't had in the past seven days. But the wind change was bad news for the enemy. The Jews were aware of the oncoming disaster when seeing the Romans gain footing and now able to do close combat.

The Jews who knew the outcome lost heart. It was time to retreat, or jump the cliffs as their fellow Jews had done.

Sabinus left his division and disguised himself in the garments of a beggar. He slipped secretly into the nearby caves in search of the Jewish general. While keeping a low profile he came upon a weeping woman seated outside a cave's entrance. He reached down and touched her shoulder to question her. His garment opened and revealed his uniform. When she saw his uniform, she froze in terror.

"I'm not going to harm you," Sabinus assured her. "I'm looking for the leader of this sedition. Can you help me?"

She lowered her head and wailed loudly. Sabinus feared she might give him away with her words in another language. He understood nothing she said, but tried to comfort her by kneeling down beside her. She seemed to gain her composure and pointed to another cave.

"General Josephus!" she moaned. "I curse him to heaven for the death of my only son!"

Sabinus signaled two of his men and they entered the cave the woman had pointed out. Inside they found the Jewish general, Josephus. He surrendered without issue, but his group of constituents had already killed themselves.

Vespasian was notified that the Jewish general had been captured. It was the turning point in the battle. The remaining Jews had lost their general and their spirits were dampened. They were captured and placed in chains.

Sabinus rode ahead with pride as he led General Josephus in chains behind him. He pranced his horse in front of Vespasian and Titus who were waiting to see the defeated leader of the Jewish revolt.

The Roman soldiers wanted the leader's head on a pole, but Vespasian rode calmly to meet Sabinus, the hero of the day.

"And where is the scoundrel who defied Rome and her legions?" Vespasian shouted.

Sabinus dismounted and brought forth General Josephus. The frail slender prisoner moved gracefully forward in chains. His head held high and his dark eyes glaring directly at his Roman conqueror.

Vespasian exchanged glances with his son and pointed to Josephus in unbelief, saying, "Is this the founder of the war?" he smiled widely. Titus was amused by his

Zoheleth

father's keen-wit and unsophisticated manners. The troops laughed as Vespasian joked.

"I can pardon a dog for barking," he snickered. "But this? A scant of a man who brings half of Rome to send his people to their death?"

Josephus remained aloft with his head held high before introducing himself as Joseph ben Mattathias. "I'm both priest and general of the Jewish army!"

Vespasian, a brute of a man, frowned. His round face hardened from wars, belied a gentleness behind his dark eyes. "Your title doesn't impress me," Vespasian laughed, then ordered his men to send him with the other prisoners to be executed. The prisoners protested loudly when hearing the death sentence.

"Wait, Father!" Titus pleaded. Vespasian was puzzled.

"You challenge my command?" he questioned resentfully.

"Please, father. It's important." Titus' words carried an urgency. "You must hear this man out and spare him!"

Vespasian knew the Jews admired and trusted their priest, but his son? He wondered if the Jewess, Queen Bernice, had influenced Titus. He had listened to her once and found her delightful, he thought. She was a beauty, but he knew her loyalty was with her people and not with Rome.

"Why do you want me to spare one who has slaughtered our men in every surrounding city?" Vespasian asked Titus.

"They say he's a prophet," said Titus. "It is rumored he has made an interesting claim, so I heard."

Vespasian drew in his lips and shook his head. He looked suspiciously at Josephus. "Speak to me, prophet!" he ordered while frowning at the small man before him.

The Jewish general lowered his eyes, as though he was praying before responding to the command. His long light brown beard flowed in waves about his chest. His features were thin and his nose too large for his face. He raised his hand as he was about to speak.

"Hail Caesar!" he said firmly. The prisoners were astonished by this, but the Romans pounded their shields with their swords.

Vespasian grunted in disgust. He rolled his dark eyes upward and removed his helmet to wipe his balding head. He waited for his soldiers to cease their noise.

"Yes," he said in a boring tone. "We hail Caesar Nero."

Josephus looked at him sternly and raised his voice. "You don't understand. It's you who will rule the world. You will be emperor of Rome! You, and your sons to follow."

Vespasian had to bring silence to his soldiers. He smiled slightly and looked down at the small man.

"Thank you, little man, but it won't free you!" He ordered the prisoners to be sent to Caesarea.

Titus rode next to him until they pulled their horses to a stop at the side of the road.

"Father, how can you be sure Josephus is lying?"

"How can you be certain he isn't?" he answered with a question. "Don't concern yourself. I'll spare his life." He gave Titus a wink. "I remember Queen Bernice's advice. I'm no fool to kill a man whom the people believe to be a prophet." Titus was satisfied.

After the Fall of Jotapata the legions of Rome marched to the outskirts of Caesarea. They camped and awaited orders from Rome.

Joseph, the physician, shared his tent with his new apprentice, Marcus. The lad was sleeping while Joseph wrote in his journal.

Zoheleth

The year is 67.

I, Joseph of Alexandria, rode back to camp from Jotapata. I grew weary from the long hot journey there and back. At the age of sixty, I wonder how long I'll be able to keep up with the Roman battles. At times I wish I had returned to Alexandria, but I chose to help the wounded. There are too few army physicians with any skill of surgery. We are stationed near Caesarea, and Marcus has asked each day how long we'll be here. I see his disappointment when I have no answer. I know he would like to be with his father, but he's been a good help to me and follows my instructions faithfully. I think he's homesick. I wish he would make a friend.

We are now six weeks waiting for word from the emperor of Rome. There's news of more trouble in Jerusalem, but Vespasian can't move on the city unless he's given orders from Rome.

My last visit to Jerusalem was during the religious feast days. I heard talk about a sedition. Although King Agrippa tries to keep things under control in Jerusalem, there are those who are set on war, since the fall of Jotapata.

I didn't expect to be caught up in all this, but here I am.

Joseph rolled the scroll of his journal and put it aside. He reached for fresh papyrus to write home. He wanted to send word to his workers to not expect him for a long time. There was no urgent reason to return since the house servants were capable of managing the estate.

He missed home and his servants who became his only family after his father died. He was wealthy enough from his inheritance to build private houses on the estate for his workers and their families. Some of his servants had served his father, who was a physician. These servants had families of their own by the time he had grown up.

He sat back and remembered when he was a lad.

Zoheleth

One of the servants walked him to school every morning. Came the end of the day, his mother would meet him and walk him home. When he entered medical school, the same servant rode to the school to bring him home on visits during his breaks. He sighed deeply and momentarily felt homesick like Marcus. He told his devoted servants what was happening in Jotapata and how he feared the outcome from the disruptions.

He worried about the future of the Jews, especially those who chose to become followers of Christ, as he did. The holy city was anything but peaceful lately. He knew the Jewish resistance were far from wanting peace with Rome.

He recalled the words of the Lord telling people to flee from the city when they see it surrounded by armies. (Luke 21:20). Jesus warned of the destruction on those who hated him. He opened the letter of John's Revelation and read silently. He wondered if this was the time Jesus would return with vengeance and the wrath of God? (Rev. 11:18)

CHAPTER THREE

THE INFIRMARY

Marcus shared the tent with the physician. His cot was opposite a small writing table with an oil lamp. He examined the pots on one side of the wall where green shoots sprouted. He poured droplets of water on the plants. Small boxes with dried herbs lined a shelf. Nothing was familiar to him but he paid attention to Joseph as he grounded leaves in a stone bowl, then, added oil to them. Joseph placed the mixtures in containers he carried in a long wooden box. He slung the strap of the box over his shoulder and motioned Marcus to follow him.

They walked into the infirmary. Marcus felt a chill when hearing men crying out in pain. He looked at one soldier's skin scorched by fire darts. He stood helplessly watching Joseph remove the linen wrappings from the soldier. Seeing puss oozing from the wounds made him gag.

"This will be one of your duties," Joseph informed as he applied a salve to the wound. "You must use a gentle touch when applying an ointment." He turned and saw a shocked expression on the lad's face.

Marcus gasped. "I can't do that! I don't know how to help all these men."

Joseph looked with understanding. "Just think of each man as though he were your father in need of your help. Would you turn your back on him?"

Marcus drew in his breath. He felt sick from the smell of the ointments, the burned flesh, and the vomit. The words of Joseph made him ashamed. He made an effort to overcome his feelings and joined in helping the physician. His thoughts of being a soldier were vanishing when seeing more wounded men than he ever dreamed.

Joseph worked long hours in the infirmary. Marcus watched every detail as the physician cared for the wounded.

"Are you the only one to do this work?" he asked the physician.

"I've trained a few slaves belonging to the Romans," he replied. "I also have Philip to aide me, and now I am grateful to have you by my side." His statement made Marcus more humble as he followed him to another soldier pleading for the doctor to give him something for his pain.

"How will you stop his pain?" Marcus asked.

"I have an opium mixture which will give him relief. I administer it only to the severely injured." He lifted the soldier's head and let him drink the potion.

When the two were about to leave the infirmary, Philip met them.

"Calling it a night?" he asked.

"I think so," said Joseph. "If you need me through the night, come and wake me."

"I'm sure you can sleep the night through," he smiled. "And, Marcus, be ready for a long day tomorrow."

Marcus liked Philip. He admired his strong muscles and dreamed of being that strong. He didn't favor the way the Romans wore their hair, since he and his brother allowed their hair to grow long. Philip was tanned from many years in the sun and his smiling eyes showed warmth.

"Marcus," said Philip. "At sunrise be ready for some exercise and practice with a sword." Marcus lit up.

When they arrived at their tent they heard soldiers singing and celebrating, while others cursed the Jews for the long hot days of battle. He heard the soldiers exchanging stories as they carried the armor of their dead comrades.

"Don't expect to get much sleep," said Joseph. "The soldiers celebrate for many nights when they have a victory." Marcus removed his sandals and sat on the edge of his cot. Joseph gave him smoked meat and bread, and soaked leaves in water to make a drink. After a few hours the soldiers' talking grew less, but he could hear some soldiers' laughter. It was good to hear men laughing. He had finished writing the names of the wounded who were treated in the infirmary. Joseph taught him how to spell the medications he had to record. When he finished the reports he handed them to Joseph.

"You did a good job. Why not go outside?" he suggested. "You might get to meet a few friendly soldiers." Marcus did so.

Joseph joined him later and they rested under the stars. The breeze was cooling and many fires glowed throughout the camps. Later, in the tent, Marcus rested on his cot. He had just dozed off when he heard a voice. Joseph opened the tent and welcomed Sabinus.

"Father!" shouted Marcus as he jumped from his cot. "Are you well?" His father greeted him and assured him he was well.

"Son, how was your day with the wounded?"

"An experience," he answered, half awake and trying to smile bravely.

"I'm sure you'll be a good assistant to the doctor." Sabinus turned to the physician. "I'm afraid I bring some unwelcome news."

"What is it?" asked Joseph.

"We have marching orders for tomorrow."

"Why so soon?"

"There's an uprising in Jerusalem and we may be called upon. Vespasian thinks it's necessary to move the wounded to the hospital in Caesarea."

"The men won't like that," said Joseph. "But I'm aware of the complications. An army can't travel far with wounded men." Marcus hoped his father would change his mind and allow him to go with him.

"Father," he interrupted. "Will I be allowed to go with you?"

Sabinus shook his head. "It would be impossible, my son."

"Why, father?"

"You have your option, Marcus. Or have you forgotten?" Anger rose in Marcus when he heard his father's disapproval. Was he to do the work of a slave the rest of his time in the service of Rome?

"I haven't forgotten my oath to Rome," he said despairingly. His father smiled and asked him to walk outside with him. Marcus eagerly went with his father.

"Son, I have no idea where I'll be going," he sighed. "I expect you to follow my orders and do what the physician may ask of you. I want no bad reports when I return."

Marcus nodded. This wasn't what he wanted to hear. He made a commitment to his father and to Rome and he had to follow it. He hated every day of his dreadful life. Sabinus took him in his arms and hugged him tightly.

"Make certain that you write to your mother and your brother," he requested. Marcus promised he would, as his father said good bye.

Marcus returned to the tent and found Joseph praying. He heard him mention the name of Jesus and wondered if the physician was a member of the strange sect which worshiped a dead man. He crawled into his cot and covered himself. Joseph dampened the lamps and the darkness softened the outside noise as he drifted off to sleep.

Before dawn, they ate a scant breakfast and then hurried to the infirmary. Some of Marcus' chores included cleaning chamber pots, feeding the injured and washing soiled linens and bleaching them in the sun. He liked feeding the injured because it gave him time to hear their battle stories.

"Good morning, Cadet," said Philip as he entered the infirmary, limping slightly.

"Cadet?" Marcus smiled.

"Are you ready for your combat training?"

"I don't understand."

"You're with the Roman army and you must be trained to use a sword. It's army regulations that every man, boy, slave or merchant, who follow the legions, must be able to defend himself against an enemy raid."

"I wasn't aware," said Marcus, who was filled with anticipation.

"Come with me," said Philip. "We'll join the cadets on the training field." They rode on his horse and reached

Zoheleth

the area where the men and boys were in mock battles with wooden swords. Marcus was introduced to his opponent, a cadet close to his age. He laughed when he held the sword made of wood.

"It feels like a toy," he jested.

"Don't make lightly of it," Philip warned. "You have a worthy opponent facing you." Philip gave the boys their signal to start.

Marcus' opponent appeared to think him to be an easy prey, but Marcus astonished him by his agile maneuvering. To him this was game playing, as he avoided each thrush from his make-believe-foe.

"Ah!" he teased. "You think I'm not trained in the art of self-defense?" His opponent jumped back when the tip of the sword hit his chest.

"My father taught me with a dull-edged weapon!" Marcus declared, as his strong dark legs sprung him up and around like a top. He laughed as he plunged his body forward and knocked the sword from the cadet's hand. When the lad reached down to retrieve it, Marcus took advantage and used his foot to push him off balance. The cadet landed on his rear and his face turned red from the unexpected defeat.

"Good thing it wasn't for real," he kidded, as he reached down to help his comrade regain his footing. Both boys laughed heartily. The next stage of training was wrestling. Marcus excelled once more.

"You're like your father," Philip praised him. "I can see you've been trained well." Marcus felt a surge of pride for the first time. He returned to the infirmary with Philip where they found Joseph moving the wounded.

"Joseph," called Philip, "you should have seen Marcus with a sword. He rendered his foe useless."

"Perhaps the two of you could render yourselves useful here," said Joseph. "I need your help."

The badly wounded and the severely ill were placed in carts hooked up to oxen. The other wounded were able to ride mules.

"We must make haste," Joseph said. "The injured should get to the city hospital before the heat of the day."

"Have you seen my father this morning?" asked Marcus.

"Not this morning," Joseph replied.

"Why are the soldiers destroying the camps?" he inquired.

"They always do," said Joseph. "It prevents the enemy from settling into a ready made city." Joseph looked over the area. "We're heading to Jerusalem," he sighed, "a city which holds my countrymen."

"Too bad your countrymen have turned seditious," Philip said.

Joseph stood in a moribund state for a moment. "I'm not in favor of what the Romans are doing," he began, "but I can't agree with the unscrupulous Jews who have turned riotous."

"Why aren't you with your people?" Marcus asked.

"I was in the holy city when Governor Gallus retreated. I remained to aid the wounded."

Joseph looked into Marcus' dark eyes and added, "As a physician, I made a vow to the Lord to help the sick and the wounded." Marcus glared at him. He didn't hate the physician, but he didn't want to like him.

"Do you serve the Roman gods?" he asked.

"I serve the Lord Jesus Christ only!"

"Wasn't he killed for creating trouble?"

"He was crucified by those who hated him."

"Why did you leave Jerusalem?"

"Because Jesus warned when the city would be surrounded by armies, its destruction was about to take place" (Luke 21:20-23,32).

"There are no armies surrounding the city," Marcus noted.

"There will be, Marcus." said Joseph. "The Roman army is heading there and will in due time destroy it."

"I've never been to Jerusalem," said Marcus. "I heard it's beautiful. Why do the people want to fight against the Roman army?"

"I'm not proud to say it, but my people were wrong to go against the tax collector, Florus. Governor Gallus was sent to settle the problems and when he thought all was well, he left. Unfortunately, Florus, the tax collector, had the Roman garrison at the Tower of Antonia killed. The garrison was there to protect the people of the city."

Marcus thought for a moment. "Is it true the walls of the city are impregnable?"

"We depend on the strength of the walls to protect us against invaders."

"So why are you afraid the city will be destroyed?"

"Our Lord warned his people to flee from the city."

"Why would you flee if the walls are so strong?"

"A good question. It is just the opposite of what we usually do when trouble arrives. But we must obey the word of the Lord" (Mark 13:14).

Marcus saw tears in the eyes of Joseph and it made him feel guilty. He ceased questioning the physician.

The Roman legions were packed and ready to leave the area of Caesarea. Philip and Joseph took down the tents and packed the carts with the doctor's possessions.

Marcus rode a mule and Joseph drove the cart while Philip rode his horse. Philip kept watch on the physician and Marcus as he led the way. The merchants were behind them and the traveling was slow due to all the equipment being moved.

Marcus worried about his father and never lost his desire to be with him. Joseph dreamed of seeing the holy city once more, and Philip dreamed of being with his men to do battle again.

CHAPTER FOUR

GOVERNOR CESTIUS GALLUS

It was the twelfth year in the reign of the Emperor Nero when Gallus held command of the Roman Twelfth Legion, known as the "Thundering Ones".

In the year A.D. 66 Gallus was given orders from Rome to settle disputes between the Jews and the Roman appointed procurator, Gessius Florus.

Gallus entered the city of Jerusalem with his legion. It was a hot day in August and he was annoyed from the long journey from Antioch. When he entered the gates of the city he was met by a high priest and a few elders of the community each coming with their complaints.

"Where's Florus?" he demanded while remaining on his steed. He wondered why Rome didn't choose men with some honor to gather taxes. He bellowed again. "Find that greedy mongrel, and bring him to me! We'll hear what he has to say." His tired eyes scanned the area as he waited for his men to locate Florus. Soon they returned with the procurator.

"Well, Florus, we meet again," said Gallus. "No doubt you'll plead that the Jews have treated you harshly."

Florus grinned and the gap in his front teeth added an expression of malice. He looked up at the governor and replied.

"Greetings, Governor," he bowed slightly from the waist. "Surely you're not believing all the lies you've been fed by these rebellious people?" He wiped the sweat which rolled down his face.

"I want the truth!" Gallus shouted. "What have you done that Rome sends me with my legions to settle?"

Florus frowned. "What are the charges?" he asked smugly.

"The charges?" Gallus mocked. "The charges are excessive cruelty!" He pulled the reigns of his horse and leaned over and spat at the feet of Florus. "The Jews have complained of your miserable presence and have informed me of your undeniable orneriness!"

Florus went silent.

"Speak up! You wretched excuse of a man." Gallus bellowed. He watched Florus compose himself as the Jews stood staring at him.

"Forgive me, most excellent Gallus," he replied slyly. "But it was not I who created havoc among the Jews," he lied while shifting from one foot to the other.

"Not you?" Gallus said sharply, as he gave a long fierce look. His heavy body felt weary and he wanted to settle the problem and return to Antioch where his wife and family waited.

"Allow me to read this letter from the Jews in Caesarea." He opened a scroll, and removed his helmet and blotted the inside with a rag. His large hands held the scroll open while he read aloud.

To the Governor of Syria.
Cestius Gallus.

We, of the Jewish community of Caesarea, have lived in peace for a number of years. Our people have built a synagogue adjacent a property belonging to the Greeks of Caesarea. We made an offer to buy the grounds that lead to the front of our place of worship. Since we could not come to terms with the Greeks, we paid Florus a large sum to be an arbitrator for our people. Florus accepted the gold with his promise to bribe the Greeks. He rode off with our gold and neglected his oath to do right by us.
We sent ambassadors of good will to remind him of his duty, but he arrested our ambassadors. He managed to incite the Greeks to come against us and out of their animosity toward us, they performed a pagan sacrifice directly at the front entrance to our synagogue. The Greeks then began construction on a building which would block the entrance to our synagogue completely.

Zoheleth

Gallus paused in reading. He glared at Florus to see his reaction. Florus began to protest, but Gallus raised his hand to cease his speaking any further. He read on:

We. the Jews of Caesarea, protested this act of building, and pleaded with Florus to demand it be stopped. He ignored our complaints and threatened to murder the whole lot of us. We were shocked when we saw him cut down our people and slaughter them as though they were common criminals. This made all the Greeks turn against us on orders from Florus.

Gallus continued to read:

The Greeks came down on us to silence us forever. We who have escaped, send word to you and pray you will vindicate us. Bring justice to our people.

We plead with you, as governor of Syria, to look into this matter. These outrageous obscenities put upon our priests and elders can no longer be tolerated.

The news of Florus' scandalous acts upon us has reached Masada. The hot-blooded youths in Masada are eager to avenge us. Rome must put an end to Florus!

Gallus rolled the scroll and was fuming. "I'm not reading the names signed to this complaint," he stated. "I want some answers to this outrage. Speak up man!"

"Governor, am I on trial?" Florus asked with contempt.

"This is not a tribunal, fortunately for you. But the charges against you are serious," he said.

"It's the rebellious Jews who have caused the uprisings," Florus accused. "You know how hateful they are toward all Roman authority."

"No more idle talk!" Gallus ordered. "I find you offensive with your opinionated remarks. You obstruct Rome's leadership by acts of violence, in the name of our mother country." Gallus felt his anger rising as he continued to reprimand Florus. "How dare you," he pointed at Florus, "you who likes to exercise the power of a king. You don't even have the dignity of a slave."

"Please, Governor," Florus pleaded. "Listen to me. You must hear the truth. If you don't believe me, then hear it from Juncundus, my Master of Horse."

Florus motioned Juncundus to come forward as he introduced him to Gallus.

"He can tell you how we tried to quell the tumult by removing the pagan sacrifices in Caesarea, but the Greeks were being assaulted by the Jews," he lied.

"Say no more!" Gallus commanded. "Write your reports and I'll consider how to deal with you after I've read them." Gallus turned his horse and started to leave the city, but the Jews lined themselves like a wall to prevent his departure. He felt their hands grabbing his feet while others held his horse at bay. He and his men were surrounded by panic-struck people. They pleaded with him to protect them from Florus.

"People!" he cried out in an effort to silence them. "I promise you Florus will not offend you again." He hoped this would satisfy the elders and the priests. He heard the Jews murmuring and one priest spoke out.

"What about the outlandish demands Florus makes on us? He steals from the poor. He doesn't stop at taxes. He tries to rob our Holy Temple! What are we to do?"

Florus mounted his horse and rode closer to Gallus. The crowd became unruly and Gallus could see he was not convincing the people or the priests. He fixed his gaze on Florus and demanded. "Is this true what they're saying?"

Florus denied it by shaking his head wildly. "These people are embittered toward Rome," Florus persisted. "They don't want to pay their taxes to Rome." His statement enraged the Jews. Gallus tried to settle them. His soldiers saw the growing hostility of the people. His army surrounded the general. The horses nudged the people to move a safe distance from the governor.

"People of Jerusalem!" Gallus entreated. "You must honor the emperor's rulings. You are subject to pay the taxes placed on you." He saw they were not pleased with what he said. He glared down at Florus while he continued.

"If you have a problem with the procurator, then I will ask Rome to appoint another." This seemed to be what the people wanted, but it troubled the procurator, Florus.

The crowds began to disburse and Gallus called to Florus. "You and your men better come with me."

Gallus figured by removing him from the city it would prevent the Jews from taking the law into their own hands. They departed from the city. Once outside the walls, Gallus stopped along the roadside to talk with Florus.

"Go easy on the Jews, if you want to keep your title as procurator," he suggested firmly. "Be aware if Rome gets word of this trouble, it could mean you'll stand trial for misgovernment. You could find yourself banished!"

Florus fell silent and made an effort to hold back his anger. Gallus knew him well enough to feel he wouldn't follow his orders.

Before they parted, Gallus made him promise to stay out of Jerusalem until things calmed down.

Florus gave his word.

CHAPTER FIVE

GESSIUS FLORUS

Governor Gallus and the Twelfth Legion were now headed in the direction of Antioch. Gallus hoped his orders to Florus would be followed.

Gessius Florus licked his wounds after Gallus left. He hated the rebuttal from the governor. His anger and humiliation had to be avenged. He planned with his men how they would have their day with the Jews. He rode slowly toward Jerusalem with his trusted companion, Juncundus. He was fuming over the accusations made against him and planned his revenge.

His small army waited a quarter mile outside of the walls of Jerusalem.

"Juncundus," he said as he motioned him to ride closer. "How easy it would be to come against the Roman garrison at the Tower of Antonia?"

Juncundus smiled. "You have plans?"

"Yes! We can start an uprising in Jerusalem to distract the garrison from their station."

"That will give our men pleasure," said Juncundus. "Gallus can't protect the Jews all the time."

"Tonight, we can put our heads together and plot our way," said Florus. "Once I convince the people to allow us inside the city, your men will head to the Tower and slaughter the garrison."

"What if Gallus hears about it?"

"I think I have the answer to that," said Florus while rubbing the stubble on his chin. "I have an idea on just how to use Gallus in our plans for the uprising in the city."

The two traveled until they met with their party. They made camp far enough from the city as night began to fall. Florus wanted the watchmen on the walls of the city to think he was keeping his distance as warned by Gallus.

"Men," he said, as they gathered. "I've done my best to get you gold. You've seen my efforts and how they have been curtailed by a few so-called pious men in Jerusalem." His men nodded as they waited to hear what he planned.

"I wish to reward you personally for your loyalty. If you go along with my plans, you'll have all the gold you need!" The men wanted to cheer but he motioned them to keep it low.

"I promise," he continued, "within two days you will be rich men."

"Show us the way," one said. "Let us kill those who have treated you badly." Florus smiled and inwardly was rejoicing the day was coming when he would repay the Jews for their vicious reports to the governor.

"No need to kill without probable cause," he added. "Remember the Roman rules that we must not attack without cause. But if the Jews invoke an incident and we are attacked first, we're permitted to kill on the grounds of preventing a civil uprising." His men were in agreement.

Drawing on the ground, he designed his strategy. "We will strike the upper market first," he recommended. "You'll meet with opposition, and when this happens, you will kill every Jew who stands in our way." The men appeared a bit uneasy with this.

"Do you mean you want us to kill their holy priests?" asked one man who seemed superstitious.

"I said, you kill everyone!" Florus commanded. "Whether they're priests, old men, or women." He knew their hunger for gold would win, but first he had to give them enough wine to bring them to one mind.

While his men enjoyed drinking, he finished writing on a small scroll and sealed it with hot wax. He heard his men bragging how they would spend their spoils. He knew he had inflamed them with his impious desires.

"Juncundus," he called softly. "I need you to do a favor." Juncundus came promptly.

"I'm at your service, sir."

"You have a brother in the legion of Gallus, is that

right?"

"Yes, sir." Juncundus answered. "He's with the Twelfth Legion."

"I need you to fulfill a special mission. No one is to know. Do you understand?"

"You have my word," Juncundus struck his chest with his fist in a salute of loyalty.

"Ride all night until you reach the camp of Gallus and give your brother this message I've written."

"I think I can accomplish that," Juncundus said. "Knowing how tired Gallus' men are I'm sure they're resting by now."

Florus gave him a small bag of gold. "Give this gold to your brother and tell him there's more where this came from." He smiled as Juncundus tucked it into his sack. "I know the men of Gallus haven't been paid lately. This should be in our favor. Also, inform your brother to destroy the scroll after he reads it!"

"Will this help us in your plan?" he asked.

"Let's say it's impossible for us to succeed without your brother's help." Juncundus saluted again as he mounted his horse.

"Go now, my friend," said Florus. "Join me tomorrow outside the city." Florus watched him ride into the night. He then joined his men and drank with them. They were all in a good mood as he filled them in on his plan.

"I want you men to know in order to get the gold in the temple, you'll have to slaughter the priests. But first you must kill the garrison stationed at the Tower of Antonia. No one must be allowed to escape to get outside help. Do you understand?"

"We'll serve you well, Florus!" they agreed.

"Tomorrow" Florus continued. "I want half of the cavalry to remain outside the gates of Jerusalem. This will show the Jews I mean no trouble by leaving half my men outside. Juncundus will lead you."

"Why can't we go in?" asked one.

"Just hear me out," said Florus. "I will get the priests

Zoheleth

and the elders to go out to you. They will expect your peace offering." The men grew quiet.

Florus smiled and went on explaining his plans. "I will insist the priests make peace with me by saluting my men stationed outside. They will salute in good faith, but you will not return the salute."

"What will that do?" asked one man.

"By not returning the salute, the priests will consider it an insult. They will learn they have been tricked into leaving the protection of the city walls."

His men began laughing. They now understood the strategies of Florus.

"And, if anyone speaks against this procurator, which I'm sure they will, you have my orders to slay them. Juncundus will then lead you into the city to join me." They raised their drinking cups and cheered. He knew they were ready for action.

"Tomorrow, in the afternoon, while half of you are stationed outside," he began, "I'll be inside when the Jews will be closing their markets to prepare for the feast days." Florus lifted the wine cup to his lips. "They will never suspect anything to happen with only half of my men with me," he smiled and drank. "Once I create an incident, the priests will protest to my presence in the city. When this insurrection occurs, my men with me will cut down the Jewish resistance." The men listened intently to all his plans. Florus continued to instruct them.

"When we strike the protesters, then the elders and the priests will plead for mercy. That's when I offer them my conditions and send them outside to you."

His men went on drinking late into the night. He lay on his sleeping blanket and heard the men rehearsing their orders late into the night. He was pleased with the moment as he lay under the stars. He thought about the letter he sent with Juncundus. It contained instructions to pay a few men to turn traitors to Gallus.

He counted on the Jews to send for Gallus to return and settle matters once and for all. It would take Gallus time to get back to Jerusalem, and when he enters, he will realize a number of his men have turned against him. The letter held a promise of more gold to those who stirred up trouble with the Jews while Gallus is in the city.

Florus had no intentions of sharing the gold from the temple once he had it. He didn't care what Rome did when they learned about it. He would make sure the blame would fall on Governor Gallus.

As for himself, he and Juncundus would be well on their way out of the country with the gold from the temple. Everyone knew that the Jews had a portion of the temple where they kept as a bank. The wealthy as well as the average citizen, trusted their gold to the temple. He could live a wealthy man and as far as his men were concerned, what could they do?

The camp grew quiet except for the distant sounds of men snoring. The wine dulled their senses and he wished he had allowed himself to get drunk.

THE REVENGE

It was mid-afternoon when Florus entered the gates of the city with half of his men. He noticed the people avoiding him as he rode directly to the market place and suspiciously eyed the markets. The Jews were closing before sun-down to prepare for their feast days.

He showed no sign of evil intent which gave the Jews a false security as they continued their work. Florus couldn't forget the insults received from Gallus. He would make the Jews pay for their idiocy. He motioned his men to block the narrow alleyway.

"You men know what to do," he said in a low voice. "We'll send these arrogant Jews to meet their God!" His men slowly got into position and waited for Florus' signal. He turned his horse around and galloped straight into the market place. With his sword, he deliberately knocked over a merchant's stand, scattering the wares to the cobble-stone street. The crash startled all. This act was his signal.

The Jews were outraged and began cursing him vehemently, and with impaired judgment they retaliated by throwing garbage at Florus.

He raised his sword and signaled his men to take over. He removed himself from the scene as the front division rode in and destroyed the markets. The Jews screamed in protest.

The horses reared as though they resented the senseless killings of the men, women and children who came in their paths. Florus watched his troops rampaging, and then ordered his middle division to raid the houses nearby.

"Get all the booty you can!" He was now ready to ward off the men who were headed toward the gates to escape. The more he killed the more insensitive he became to their desperate cries.

"Complain to Gallus, will you!" he shouted and

mocked them as he struck them down like dogs, showing no mercy.

The Roman garrison at the tower were alerted to the disturbance and they ran with their swords raised but found themselves surrounded by Florus' men. Florus shouted his orders to kill every man in the garrison.

"Get to the Tower of Antonia!" he commanded. His men rode through the bloody alleyways. The horses legs were stained as the animals trotted over the slaughtered victims. The Tower of Antonia was now under siege. The remaining soldiers could no longer defend the Tower or themselves. The surprise attack was unprecedented.

Florus' men returned with the news that all the Roman garrison were killed. What they didn't know was that one Roman soldier escaped.

The elders of the upper city came running and the priests followed. Florus was amused by the horrified expressions on their faces. Many of the respectable Jews prostrated themselves to the ground and wept bitterly. Florus smiled.

"What have we done to deserve such violence from you, Florus?" wailed one elder while on his knees.

"Why have you murdered our people and the Roman garrison?"

Florus was filled with hatred as he listened to them plead for mercy. Not all were willing to beg. One priest rose up and stepped forward.

"You'll pay for this!" he dared to threaten the procurator.

"And what are you going to do?" Florus laughed at the priest raising his fist in the air.

"We've sent for King Agrippa," the priest warned.

Florus laughed at his boldness. "Do you think King Agrippa will be here today?" he said mockingly. "I happen to know he's in Egypt. How long do you suppose it will take him to get here?" Florus watched the priests' expressions fade into despair.

From a distance he noticed King Agrippa's sister

being led by a group of elders who were bringing her to him. He knew of her beauty and heard of her cleverness in dealing with public relations. It pleased him to see how her people were expecting her to be their answer.

"Florus!" she cried out as she ran toward him. "I beg you to stop this madness."

He smiled and his eyes didn't miss any portion of her beauty. She was tall, slender and graceful. Her dark hair neatly rolled in the back of her neck, and her body shaped the way men desired. It might give him much pleasure to see just how far she would lower herself for her people. She bent down and removed her shoes to present herself barefoot in supplication.

"Queen Bernice," he nodded slightly. "Tell me why a queen presents herself in such a lowly manner?"

"Florus!" she cried out, looking directly into his eyes. "What is this violence you have perpetrated."

"Where's your beloved brother?" he taunted as he looked about. He saw her glaring through her dark eyes, but she was able to hide her fear elegantly. "You know, dear lady, with the tip of my sword I could end your lovely life this moment."

She showed no signs of alarm but continued to prod for an answer. "What have you done to my people?" she demanded in a royal manner.

"What makes you think I have to answer to you?" he replied. Did she think her beauty would be more persuasive than gold? He enjoyed toying with her in front of her associates.

"You'll answer to Agrippa," she reminded him. "I've sent him word of this violent action of yours."

"Now isn't that just like a woman," he answered.

"I warn you, Procurator," she flared. "You'll pay dearly for this."

"Enough!" he shouted and raised his sword and threaten her. She fled back to the palace in fear for her life.

Unnoticed by Florus, men took to the roofs of the houses. They began heaving heavy stones. Florus sped with

Zoheleth

his troops to get out of range from being struck.

"We must act quickly," he said to his men. "Allow the priests and the elders through!"

"People of the city," he shouted while raising his hand in the air. "You have dishonored me. My duty is to serve Rome. I've been appointed by Rome to collect taxes. You have given me problems but I'm ready to offer your priests and elders a means for a peaceful settlement."

The elders and priests waited to hear what he might propose.

"If you want peace, you must do as I request."

"Please," cried one priest. "Tell us what to do to stop this bloody massacre."

"Now you're regaining your senses," Florus said. He was ready to set his plan in motion. "You will take your priests and the elders as well as the prominent citizens and go outside the gates."

"Why would you have us do that?" questioned an elderly priest. Florus ignored the man and continued to order them. "You will honor and salute my two cohorts waiting outside the walls for your gesture of peace!"

The majority became unruly and were reluctant to do what he asked. They complained and cursed the choice. He waited until the priests calmed the people.

"People of Jerusalem," one priest called out. "If we don't cooperate with Florus' demands, our country will be pillaged and our temple profaned." They were forced to go along with the wishes of Florus. They went outside the gates while Florus remained inside. Hundreds of followers decided to go along willingly to salute Florus' troops. They wanted to regain peace in the city so they could celebrate their feast days.

Florus heard the shouting outside and he knew it was time to ride to the temple. He wondered why Juncundus hadn't arrived, but there was no time to waste. He rode carefully through the crowds but unbeknown to him, there were those who were one step ahead of him. Suddenly he found himself blocked by Jews from every section of the city. He was trapped!

"Juncundus!" he shouted over the maddening screams from outside. Where was Juncundus? Where were his cohorts? Had they deserted him? A cold chill ran through him. He turned his horse and sped to the gates of the city. Protesters followed him on foot. When he got to the gates he saw why his men were unable to enter the city.

When the gates opened, there was a pile of bodies blocking the entrance. It was a human wall of dead which prevented his troops from getting inside the city.

When his men saw him, they dug out a path through the bodies so he could exit.

The Jews shouted for him to get out. But he turned and informed them he had to leave some of his men because there was no garrison at the tower.

"I'm taking the rest of my men to Caesarea," he told the people as they jeered him.

Juncundus met him. "Forgive me, sir," he said. "We had no idea the people would attempt to head back to the gates before we could kill them."

"How did it happen?" he asked Juncundus who was spattered in blood.

"We followed your instructions but the Jews panicked. Those trying to get back inside the gates, fell and blocked the way. A wall of people formed."

"Have you heard from your brother?" asked Florus.

"He's agreed to do what you asked, sir."

"That means Gallus will be coming back to the city. Just what I wanted." Florus smiled pleasantly at his friend, Juncundus. "We can slip in after Gallus arrives and get to the temple." Little did Florus know that he would never get back inside the city of Jerusalem.

CHAPTER SIX

AGRIPPA

The ship from Egypt docked and King Agrippa stepped ashore. He was met by a courier on horseback who delivered a letter to him. He opened it and found it was from his sister, Bernice. He was troubled by what he read.

"This informs me that Florus has raised considerable problems in Jerusalem. Do you know anything about it?" he asked the messenger.

"I know there was a disturbance, but how bad? I don't know."

"I want you to ride to Governor Gallus and tell him what's happened."

"It's been done," said the messenger.

"Good! As soon as my army is off the ship," he said, "we'll ride to Jerusalem immediately. In the meantime I'll write to the Senate of Rome and inform them of Florus' acts of insubordination."

Agrippa's private army was ready to ride when a courier from Antioch caught up with him. The message was from Gallus who promised to make haste to Jerusalem.

The news put Agrippa at ease. Gallus would be there in Jerusalem and they would settle whatever the differences were between the Jews and Florus.

The courier from Antioch rode along with Agrippa.

"Tell me, young man," Agrippa addressed him. "Was Governor Gallus enjoying the horse races at Antioch?"

The courier smiled. "Governor Gallus likes the races too much. He's never happy when he must sail to Caesarea then march to Jerusalem."

After several days of traveling Agrippa reached the gates of Jerusalem.

"Hail King Agrippa!" came the shouts from the crowds running to greet him. He nodded politely in their direction as he rode forward. A deputation of leaders and priests welcomed him and reported their misfortunes.

His heart was troubled when he learned how many widows were lamenting their dead, and shocked to see the market place in shambles. Widows threw themselves at his feet when he dismounted. They pleaded and wept over the miseries they suffered from the procurator, Florus. He forced himself to listen while his eyes searched desperately, looking for Bernice.

"Where's my sister?" he called out. "Is she safe?"

One priest answered. "She's hiding in the palace. She risked her life for us," he added.

Agrippa handed his horse to a soldier and he headed toward the palace. He hurried over the blood stained stones and shook his head in disgust. People followed him, informing him of the horror which took place. He stopped a moment and fingered his trimmed beard. His hand traveled across his lips as he outlined his mustache with one finger.
He was a man who kept his barber busy with his appearance. He liked having his wavy hair neatly groomed and resting on his broad shoulders. He felt he was somewhat irresistible to the ladies and was delighted in learning how many women found him so. While he walked through the crowds he would see young ladies blush when he smiled and bowed to them.

"Agrippa!" girls called from the rooftop and showered him with flower petals. Another swooned when he was near and sighed. "He's beautiful."

Agrippa loved all the admiration. He laughed as the girls graveled to touch him. "Smile for us, Agrippa," one golden haired girl cried out. It was times like this when he wished he weren't king of the Jews, but it did keep him from browsing.

He pushed his way to the palace with the help of his men. Still the ladies clung to his hands, kissing them passionately.

At the palace he was greeted by the guards as he asked. "Where's my sister?" The guards helped him away from the people.

Bernice heard him calling and she came racing from her bedroom.

"Agrippa!" she squealed with delight and ran with her arms outstretched to him. "Thank God you're here," she said as she hugged him, kissing his beard and his cheeks.

He laughed and lifted her off the floor. "Are you gaining weight, my pet?" he kidded.

"Stop it, beloved brother. Why do you tease me so?"

"Because I love you so!" He was happy to be home with her.

Agrippa never grew tired of seeing her lovely face. She was notoriously beautiful, he thought, as he put his hand to her cheek and gently kissed her mouth.

"Have you been crying?" he asked. "Your eyes are swollen."

"Brother," she sighed, "it's been a nightmare. I couldn't tell you in the letter. You must come and see for yourself what's been done to our people."

"Little sister," he laughed. "You have no concept of politics. You must learn to be indifferent with those who desire riots." He put his arm around her and they walked to the garden.

"Now, talk to me," he said softly.

"Agrippa, I was in fear for my life," she began. "I'm fortunate to have escaped Florus' sword."

"You're exaggerating," he laughed.

"Agrippa, how dare you!" she gasped and stepped back. "How could you? I warned you of Florus' treachery."

"I'm teasing you," he said. "I've heard enough complaints for the day. Come, we'll examine the damages."

They left the palace and walked to where the slaughters took place.

"The young men tore down the cloisters leading to the temple," she informed. "And people began stoning Florus to keep him from robbing the holy temple. He was forced out of the city."

Agrippa listened to the long list of accusations and he

felt badly about his subjects, but he couldn't condone any act of violence against a Roman procurator.

"The people appear ready to wage a war," he said to his sister. "We must avert a war no matter how much pressure is put on our people." He saw his sister glare at him.

"Are you condoning Florus' actions?" she accused. "Do you think the people destroyed their own market place?"

"I don't think that at all," he defended. "Don't think I favor the actions of Florus or the actions of our people." He saw her expression soften as he tried to explain his viewpoint. "I'll call a meeting tomorrow in the city," he announced. "But, dear sister, I want you to appear on the roof of the Hasmonian palace."

"On the roof of the palace?" she questioned.

"Yes!" he insisted. "I'm concerned for your safety."

"Then you do expect more trouble?"

"I'm not certain what will take place when I exercise my authority."

"Oh, Agrippa," she cried. "I'm afraid for you."

He remembered her as a child, whenever frightened, she clung to him. He looked into her dark eyes and saw the same child.

"You must do as I say," he continued. "We are Roman aristocracy even though we are Jews. We represent Rome. This is a political issue and must be handled as one and not dealt with by emotions."

Bernice let go of his hand and nodded in agreement.

The following morning, Agrippa called an assembly of men. He looked to see if Bernice was on the roof top. She stood waving a blue sheer scarf so he would see her. Knowing she was safe he could address the men.

"People of Jerusalem!" he began. "I stand here among you and have witnessed your suffering."

He looked compassionately at his people and spoke loudly.

"I must remind you that all Romans are not unjust."

The people hissed him and a few cursed him.

"Hear me out," he pleaded. "You men have brought this on yourselves. I pleaded with you to keep the peace

Zoheleth

while I was gone. Rome is too powerful to oppose." His statement infuriated the men.

"Down with Florus! Down with Rome!" they shouted. For a moment he feared they would turn on him.

"Let me call to mind the countries who opposed Rome. They were ruined and now are ruled by Rome. You can't go against Rome and expect to win!"

"We don't want war with Rome." one man shouted. "We want Florus banned from Jerusalem."

"Fair enough! But as your king," he said, "in order to serve your needs I must have your full cooperation. You know the temple holds much riches from the donations of foreigners. Rome has given us much!"

"And Florus wants it all in his purse!" shouted a priest.

"I know what he has done. But what you have done is not right. You must repair the damages and rebuild the cloisters you have destroyed." There was silence. "I must order you to start the repairs today. Remember you're under the protection of Rome, and we must pay Rome her dues. We are her subjects!"

Some young men picked up stones to strike him. His private army closed him in.

"Agrippa, our king!" shouted one respected citizen. "Beware! Word about Florus has reached the zealots in Masada."

Agrippa was startled. Masada held a group of zealots who went hand in hand with the sicarii, men who were political assassins. He had to send a messenger to Masada and plead for them to allow him to settle the peace in Jerusalem.

He waited to hear from Masada and by early evening his messenger returned, but the news was not good.

"What is it, brother?" asked Bernice

"I'm afraid we're too late," he let the letter slip from his hand. "The zealots and the sicarii have murdered the Roman garrison stationed at Masada. They're on their way to our city."

"My Lord," Bernice gasped. Agrippa asked the messenger if he could tell him more about Masada.

"How bad is it there?" he asked.

"I fear the worse. The priests of our temple now refuse to make sacrifices for Nero, the emperor of Rome."

"Who dares to do this?" he demanded.

"It's one named Eleazar, my king. He's a new priest, but he favors the zealots and the sicarii."

Bernice was nearly in tears. "What are we to do?" she moaned. She thought for a moment and excitedly said, "I know what I can do!"

Agrippa was surprised. He turned to her and was willing to hear her out.

"Allow me to go to General Vespasian," she said above a whisper. "I hear he's stationed only a few days from here."

"And what good will that do?"

"I can inform him of the conditions and he might bring soldiers to help you keep order in the city." Agrippa knew she was serious.

"Perhaps it is a good idea," he agreed.

Bernice was relieved that he had no objections. "I'll travel with my guards," she assured him. "No one will suspect anything unusual if I leave the city. You must remain here. I'm sure Gallus will arrive soon."

"Where in God's name is that man?" Agrippa complained. "I've got to keep the situation within our territory. If Rome hears about the uprisings, we will be under their siege."

"I know Vespasian will not inform Rome," she said. "He's a good man."

"Then go to him right away," said Agrippa. "Leave the city to me. Just get us some help." He shook his head in despair and added, "I can't believe they killed the Roman garrison at Masada. What will happen when Rome learns of the slaughter?"

Bernice departed. Agrippa walked toward the temple. He was glad to see the young men beginning to rebuild the cloisters around the temple. He could relax until Gallus arrived, if he ever arrived.

CHAPTER SEVEN

THE PHYSICIAN

Before the battle of Jotapata, Joseph Abtolim, the physician, had traveled from Alexandria, Egypt. Although he was a Christian, he made a yearly visit to Jerusalem during the feast days. He entered the city with his small caravan before the noon-day heat. He rented a stall for his mules and went in search of an inn where he could stay.

"Joseph!" a voice called to him. He turned and saw Drusus Macer coming toward him. "Welcome to Jerusalem," said Drusus.

"God be with you, friend," Joseph greeted him. "Can you tell me what has happened? I see the market place in shambles."

"Friend, we had much trouble," Drusus sighed. "I fear there will be a serious revolt in this city," Drusus expressed his concern.

Years back, Joseph had met the parents of Drusus when they came to Jerusalem to hear Paul of Tarsus. The family were Greeks who came from Bethoron. Joseph joined their caravan on the trip homeward. Drusus, who was just a boy, took ill. His father pleaded with him to administer something to his son. Joseph used a mixture of herbs and remained with the boy until he recovered completely. He remembered the evening when Drusus was strong enough to stay up late. The boy had asked him about the teachings of Paul of Tarsus. Joseph went over all the writings of Paul. It was not long after, the lad became a Christian.

Drusus interrupted the thoughts of Joseph. "Did you know it was Florus who destroyed the market place? He has caused problems in Jerusalem."

"I did hear some news on my way here. Is it true that he instigated the massacre of the Jews in Caesarea?"

Zoheleth

"It's true, my friend," said Drusus. "My Greek brothers were incited to kill many Jews at their synagogue."

"What a sad thing to happen," said Joseph.

"The whole nation of Jews are now infuriated over the incident," Drusus informed. "In revenge, they ravaged the Syrian villages and burned them down, leaving many homeless and dead."

"What happened to the rioters?"

"It is said that many fled to the cliffs of Jotapata."

"Where's the scoundrel, Florus?"

"I don't know, but I know he used the Greeks to his advantage. I'm certain he paid much to have a few Greeks incite a riot in Caesarea."

"Did any Jews escape Caesarea?"

"I heard that many of them fled to other towns, but the Jews living in those towns turned against them and wouldn't allow them to enter."

"What! You mean they turned against their own people?"

"They were fully armed when the escapees attempted to enter the town."

Joseph shook his head in disbelief. "How awful to think they might have killed their own people who needed refuge."

"My guess is they feared retaliation from the Greeks and the Romans." The two walked along the city streets.

"Is there any news from Alexandria?" Joseph asked.

"The news is not good, I'm sorry to inform you. The Greeks living in Alexandria, after hearing about the incident, turned against the Alexandrian Jews."

Joseph worried about his home and his servants.

"Where are you staying?" asked Drusus.

"An inn, if there's a lodging open."

"Come with me," Drusus offered. "We're meeting at the house of Cornelius Rufinus."

Joseph thought for a moment. "Where have I heard that name before?"

"You don't remember when you were in Rome at the

time when Paul of Tarsus was arrested."

"Yes, I remember that."

"You saved Cornelius' life," Drusus reminded him. "He was the lad who was left for dead in Emperor Nero's arena."

"Ah!" said Joseph as he recalled the horrible scene. "Someone brought me a bloody child, half dead. I still see that red-haired boy who was torn from his shoulders to his small feet." He lowered his head. "It's a scene I'd rather forget. Nero disgracefully amused himself by having Christian children covered in fresh animal skins, then, setting the wild dogs on them in the arena."

"Cornelius has never forgotten the physician who nursed him back to life," said Drusus, as he put his arm around Joseph's shoulder in gratitude.

"I never thought the boy would live," Joseph admitted. "How the boy's face was not disfigured is a miracle. I stitched every part of his badly torn body. What a painful memory." He thought for a moment. "I think the reason the boy's face was untouched, it was down in the sand after he lost consciousness."

"That could be," said Drusus. "You know he lost his parents in the arena, along with many Christians. But you're the one who saved his life."

"That, dear Drusus, was the Lord's workings!"

"Amen!" Drusus laughed. His smile was bright against his tanned skin and a firm jaw set into his square face. His dark eyes seemed to hold a spark of joy as he spoke. "Let's get to Cornelius' house before sundown."

Joseph glanced in the direction of the Jerusalem temple. Its golden doors brightened the surrounding walls. He loved the sight of the temple which Herod the Great embellished. A pang of sorrow came when he thought of the words of Jesus. He said the temple would be destroyed (Matthew 24:2).

"What a beautiful sight," he remarked to Drusus as he pointed to the temple. They paused to admire its structure. Joseph shook his head. "Herod took over forty years in its construction."

They walked until they found a produce stand. The stands near the upper city hadn't been destroyed by the men of Florus. Their stalls were filled with plenty of grains, barley, fruits, vegetables, dates and figs.

"I'm buying some Judean wine," said Drusus. "Cornelius asked me to bring it along."

"Well," said Joseph. "I can't pass this bakery without taking some treats to our host." He pushed goats aside to get to the stand because they roamed loose through the market place. Young boys picked up baked goods left by women who brought their unbaked dough to the Bakers' oven. The boys got paid to do this.

Drusus came back grumbling. "Everything is taxed by the Romans," he complained, "from the cattle down to the smallest portions of land."

"I guess you could say Rome is both robber and protector," Joseph laughed. "It does maintain order, even at a cost," he added.

"If you ask me," said Drusus. "I think Jerusalem is the envy of every tax collector. The Jews tolerate the high taxation, as long as the people can worship their God in peace."

"Peace?" Joseph questioned. "All the outward signs read peace, but I sense that underneath there is a spirit of uneasiness. I see too many men meeting in secret as we've been walking." Drusus scanned the area and pondered.

"I wonder what mischief they're up to? If my calculations are right, they're planning an uprising."

Joseph agreed. "It could be that they don't understand the messianic prophecies of a new kingdom. They may think by destroying Rome's control over them, it will open the way for God's kingdom to be set up in Jerusalem."

"You and I know differently," said Drusus. "Jesus said His kingdom was not of this world." (John 18:36)

"You're right, but remember how many didn't believe that Jesus was the chosen one. They think the

Kingdom of God is a piece of land here on earth."

"I know what you're saying, physician," Drusus paused a moment. "Things haven't been right since the execution of James, the brother of Jesus."

"It was an unjust act accordingly to the law," Joseph empathized. "Jesus warned how the blood of His saints would be avenged" (Rev.6: 9-10).

"We had some of our followers return to Judaism, and go back under the law," Drusus informed.

"That's sad, but they were not there when Thomas fell to his knees and worshipped the risen Christ."

"How would that have changed them?"

"Look at it this way. Jesus would have been a sinner to allow anyone to worship him. But Thomas called him Lord and God (John 20:28). Jesus had to be God incarnate. Do you see my point?" Drusus nodded in agreement. The two walked in silence for a time.

"Have you heard of the sicarii?" asked Drusus.

"Yes. They are known as political assassins."

"I learned they have spies throughout the city."

"Has it come to that?"

"I must warn you not to speak in public against the zealots or the sicarii. You'll find yourself dead should they walk beside you."

Joseph gasped. "Have they killed anyone?"

"Yes," said Drusus. "But no assassin has been caught."

Drusus leaned closer to Joseph. "These sicarii, after they have cut the throat of a Roman sympathizer, mingle among the peasants. The people in Jerusalem live in constant fear."

"This is a strange story," Joseph admitted. "I hear of the Jews fearing the sicarii, and Florus, that Ionian Greek. I know the Christians are in fear of the Romans. But the zealots, with the sicarii, fear no one."

"You have summed it up nicely," Drusus laughed.

"I fear God," said Joseph. "I fear that God's wrath is about to fall on this city." He lowered his head and sighed.

"Your fears are justified, my friend. Now let's hurry, we're close to the house of Cornelius."

Zoheleth

CORNELIUS

Joseph and Drusus resided several days at the house of Cornelius. Christians came from the upper portion of the city of Jerusalem to come to the house meetings.

The letters of Paul were read daily while the group prayed for the safety of those in the city being attacked by the sacarii.

On the third evening of the Christians' secret meeting, there came a knock at the door. The group fell silent until Cornelius signaled it was one of them.

"We're cautious when meeting," said Cornelius. He smiled nervously and ran his fingers through his red hair. "The Emperor Nero sends spies to find our whereabouts."

The memory of Nero and the arena burned in his mind. He witnessed Christian children like himself, being stripped naked and made to wear fresh animal skins. He could feel the blood running down his arms and legs after the savage attack by the wild dogs. He could hear the screams from other victims. Even his own screams he heard until he blacked out. His dreams still terrified him and caused him to wake up in a cold sweat. Joseph broke into his thoughts.

"I didn't know that Nero was still seeking out the Christians."

"Many Christian men, women and children were murdered by the Romans after the soldiers found where the Christians gathered," Cornelius said as he motioned a friend to open the door.

A young woman dressed in a hooded cape entered. Her eyes scanned the room and she stared at Joseph.

"He's one of us," Cornelius assured her. "He's the doctor I told you who saved my life as a boy." Cornelius turned to Joseph. "This is Ravenna, the daughter of the high priest, Samuel." She smiled at Joseph.

"Why the urgency?" Cornelius asked her.

"There's trouble in the city," she announced as she

Zoheleth

removed her hood, showing a thick crop of dark hair tightly braided. Her face was pale in the lamp light, but her skin glowed with a softness. Joseph noticed her clothes were finely designed and she displayed an expensive taste in jewelry.

"Someone must get word to King Agrippa to call for reinforcements in the city," she announced.

"What's happened?" Cornelius asked as he blinked rapidly.

"It's the sicarii. They have killed several leading men in the city who let it be known they would not support an uprising against Rome." Her lips trembled as she spoke. "You know how radical the sacarii can be. And now the zealots have set fire to the house of one of our priests for resisting their offers." The guests were astonished by the news.

"Can you tell us more?" Cornelius asked when seeing her state of mind. She composed herself in order to give them more bad news.

"When the people saw the priest's house on fire, they ran to put out the flames but without warning the sicarii struck them down!" She began shaking. "Then," she continued, "the zealots ran to the Archives where all the records of debts are filed and set fire to the place. Now there are no records of debts which the poor owe."

Cornelius stood for a moment thinking, He gently stroked the scars on his arms, then, announced to the group. "Brothers, it's time for us to fight! We must put down these zealots or flee the city!"

He looked at Ravenna and asked. "What are the majority of people with the zealots choosing to do?"

"They seem to be in favor of going against Rome," she sighed. "The poor are rejoicing now that they are free from all their debts. Since the records have been burned, they are now siding with the zealots."

Joseph nodded his head and spoke softly. "Brothers, it seems the rebellious ones have won the support of the poor people, at least for now."

"Yes," Cornelius replied. "They don't know what's in store for them. Let's see for ourselves. Those who want to come along, we can leave tonight."

"You will get word to Agrippa?" asked Ravenna.

"We'll inform the guards outside his palace, if we manage to get there unseen."

Some men returned to their families. Those who chose to remain armed themselves with weapons.

Joseph refused to accept a weapon when handed one. Cornelius turned back to Ravenna.

"You must get your family out of the city," he warned, "they're in danger of being robbed and killed."

She nodded and understood the warning. "You think they will come into our area and do harm to my father?" she asked.

"If they have already burned the house of one priest, they'll seek out the wealthy to feed their poor who follow them. You're father is a priest and you must act now!"

She placed her hood up and left the house.

Cornelius turned to Joseph. "Ravenna must keep her belief in Jesus a secret. Her father would disown her."

"I understand," said Joseph.

Six men left the house of Cornelius, including Drusus, Joseph, Cornelius and three others. They walked through the dimly lit alleys of Jerusalem.

Shouts could be heard in the distance and violence seemed to permeate the night air.

"Joseph, you need not come with us," said Cornelius. "I don't want to see anything happen to you."

"I'm going along," he said. "But I fear in your effort to protect the Christians, you might instigate a worse problem."

"We must do something to warn our people," said Cornelius. "Even the priests no longer help us or follow the laws of God."

"Leave vengeance to the Lord," Joseph stated.

"But the priests have grown heartless toward the poor. They rob the widows and the orphans," he declared.

Zoheleth

"If you take the law into your own hands then you are no better than those you accuse," Joseph stated. "Remember the words of Jesus. He warned the Christians to flee from the city when they saw the armies surrounding it. (Luke 21:21). Rome will send an army to put an end to the sedition!"

Cornelius stopped suddenly. "He's right, brothers," he replied. "We're too hot-headed. We could be walking right into the mouth of the beast."

"What can we do?" asked one man.

"We can go to our brothers' houses and warn them to leave the city. I think serious trouble is on the horizon."

"Better conceal your weapons, or you could be taken as one of the zealots," Joseph warned.

"The others can go," said Drusus. "I'm staying with you, Joseph. You need protection."

The group separated. Drusus reached to relieve Joseph of his medical box.

"No, Drusus," he resisted. "I've carried this box for years. Tonight is no different."

The two stayed close to the walls while moving toward the sounds of shouting. They could hear men yelling out. "Down with Rome!" and, "We'll come against the Roman swine!" Others shouted, "It's time to fight!"

Joseph saw them with their swords raised, and he noted they were drinking. The poor were cheering the zealots for freeing them from debt.

Suddenly from out of the darkness into the light of the fires, where the groups stood, came an old man, lamenting.

"Woe to you, Jerusalem!" he cried in a painful voice. "You who have killed the prophets. You who have killed the Christ!"

It silenced the group for a moment as they watched the man come into view. His white robe and turban took on a glow in the light of the torches. His white hair and beard were stringy and his dark eyes wild looking.

He glared at the people and repeated his message while pointing an accusing finger at the group.

Zoheleth

"He's loose in the head!" shouted one bystander. They picked up stones and struck the old man to make him flee. Joseph watched the man fall to the ground with blood running down his wrinkled face. The old one struggled to crawl away from the crowd.

"Come, Drusus," said Joseph. "I must attend to the man." He hurried through the darkness to reach him. After caring for his wound he asked him to join Drusus and himself.

"Thank you, stranger," said the elderly one. "I can't go with you. I must try to bring these people to their senses."

"They'll kill you! Joseph predicted.

"I don't fear death," he sighed as he rose to his feet. "I'll be with my Lord."

Drusus carried the man into the shadows away from the rowdy group. "Stay here until you feel stronger," he said. "That's an ugly cut on your head." They left him.

Drusus suggested they find a place to stay for the night. Joseph agreed and suggested the crowds may cool down when they must prepare for tomorrow, the Feast of the Tabernacles. "Let's pray they feel differently tomorrow," he said, doubtfully. The two searched for an inn to rest for the night.

CHAPTER EIGHT

GALLUS RETURNS

The day after the events in Jerusalem, the Jews prepared booths made from branches where they would spend the next seven days. They ate their meals within these shelters on the days known as Sukkoth.

Early that morning, Governor Gallus arrived in Jerusalem with the Twelfth Legion. He was met by King Agrippa along with his personal guards to usher in the governor.

"You came at a good time to negotiate with the Jews," said Agrippa. "It's the Sabbath and they might not be in an angry mood."

Gallus sweated as he rode next to Agrippa, his round face wet and red. He pointed ahead and remarked, "We might not get the opportunity."

A group of men having sinister expressions ran up to them with threatening gestures.

Agrippa smiled and said with confidence. "I doubt if they'll fight on the Sabbath." His smile faded when suddenly without cause, the group attacked the Twelfth Legion.

Gallus' face registered shock. Agrippa himself was stunned when he saw the priests in on the assault. These priests had ceased their worship to join the zealots in the fight. Agrippa tried to bring order, but was forced to disperse his men and take cover.

"You priests!" he shouted. "How can you do this on a holy day?" They ignored him.

Gallus knew his legion was in trouble and he called to Tryannius Priscus, his camp prefect. "Take the cavalry into the middle of the group and stop the resistance!" he ordered. Priscus was successful in striking down many of the rebellious youths and causing the crowds to scatter.

The zealots, when seeing Gallus' strength, fled the

suburbs and headed to the temple. Gallus halted the chase and had his legion camp in the upper city next to the palace.

"Station your men here," he ordered Priscus. "I want men on watch all night. We can't allow these rioters to attack us again."

"As you say, General," said Priscus. "I doubt if they will return. We put a good scare into them."

Gallus nodded, but inwardly he didn't trust Priscus because he knew him to be on friendly terms with Florus. He checked his men through the night and noticed Priscus watching him. He wondered why his camp prefect kept looking toward the temple.

For three days Gallus suspended all operations. He was willing to give the rebels enough time to forsake the desire for an uprising.

King Agrippa, after the attack on Gallus, road through the streets and found a man aiding a wounded soldier of the Twelfth Legion.

"Who are you, sir?" he asked.

"I'm Joseph Abtolim of Alexandria. I'm a physician."

"Joseph of Alexandria, I'm King Agrippa and I thank you for aiding a wounded Roman."

"It's my duty to aid the wounded," said Joseph after administering to the soldier.

"Joseph, I have a servant who lies near the palace wall. He's been injured. Would you attend to him?"

"I'll go immediately," said Joseph.

"I must tell you that he's a Christian," Agrippa admitted. "I take it that you are one, also."

"I am," said Joseph as he picked up his medical box and started walking.

"There will be trouble in the city, physician," said Agrippa. "Tell your fellow Christians and any who desire safe haven, they may enter my province, Pella."

Joseph smiled. "Thank you, and may God bless you, King Agrippa."

Joseph found the servant and administered to his

Zoheleth

wound. He then went in search of Drusus who, in turn, went to seek Cornelius so they could spread the good news from Agrippa. Many Christians and peaceful citizens in the city took the opportunity to leave Jerusalem and head to Pella. They would return when things were settled in the holy city.

On the fourth day, Gallus noticed Priscus talking with several men of the cavalry. He had a suspicion there was treachery among them. Could they have been bribed to instigate trouble? He wondered.

Late that afternoon, Gallus came back to where his men were camped. He took a head count and found a few of his cavalry not accounted for. He noted that one was the brother of Juncundus, Florus' Master of Horse. It was then that one citizen came running to give him the bad news.

"Governor Gallus!" shouted the elderly man. "Some of your men dared to go into the camp of the zealots. They were killed!" He immediately summoned his private guards.

"Did you hear that a few of our men from the cavalry instigated an incident?"

"Was it Priscus?" asked one officer.

"How did you know?"

"I recall Juncundus coming to our camp and visiting his brother. Later, I saw the brother talking with Priscus. There was an exchange of items. It could have been gold."

Gallus was filled with indignation and suspected more treachery from within. He ordered some of his trusted men to act upon the killings by the zealots. The news came back that these men were also assaulted. He had to act quickly to change the course of events.

"Get our legion to the temple and set fire to the gates!" Gallus ordered. His men forged forward with torches, and the zealots saw that the temple gates were to be set afire. They panicked.

Gallus' threat had worked. He called his men back, but remained concerned about the temperament of the people, especially the zealots.

"Men! I fear we have some traitors among us," he

reported. "Should another attack occur, I fear we may have to get out of the city in a hurry. I have no idea how many of our men have turned against me!"

"Where's Agrippa and his men" questioned one of his officers.

"I've heard nothing from King Agrippa, which tells me he's in the same predicament as we find ourselves. We must make ready our leave!"

"Commander Gallus!" shouted one officer. "Who are the traitors? Let us end their miserable lives."

"One among us pledged himself to Florus, but he and his accomplices have been killed. Priscus is no longer among us, nor the brother of Jucundus."

They marched toward the gates of the city to depart. Once the cavalry neared the gates they were surrounded by zealots who sprung from hiding. They rushed in and killed many of the cavalry and the men of the infantry.

Gallus fought fiercely to get his men through the gates and once outside he raced the remaining legion toward their encampment at Gibeon.

When they arrived and were about to settle, Gallus was astonished to see the defiant zealots had followed them. It was at Gibeon where Gallus lost the rear division of the Twelfth Legion.

The Jewish zealots took the Roman ensign for booty, and made off with the war machines which Gallus' rear division had to leave behind.

He knew when Emperor Nero received the news of the event that he would no longer be in command of the Twelfth Legion.

CHAPTER NINE

EMPEROR NERO

In the palace of Rome, the Emperor Nero was extremely distressed by the news he had just received. He paced the floor shouting obscenities.

"What kind of an idiot is Governor Gallus? How could he lose the rear division of the Twelfth Legion?" His plump body shook with rage. "And to learn that our Roman Ensign has been taken by a handful of arrogant Jews. How dare they do this!" he ranted.

"What am I to do?" he asked the messenger. "First it's the Christians and now a bunch of riotous Jews to contend with." His fury increased the more he thought about the reports he had just received. He called to his Imperial Guards and ordered them to send for his scribes.

He addressed his private bodyguards standing idly by. "Who can I send to replace that good-for-nothing Gallus?"

"My Emperor," said one guard who bowed slightly. "If I may speak?"

"Speak out!" Nero demanded. "If you have anything sensible to say."

"There's a veteran general who has won over thirty battles for Rome," said the guard.

Nero stopped pacing and grew solemn. He needed to know if anyone was good enough to take control of Rome's legions. How was he to remember all the generals and commanders in the service of Rome? He never had to concern himself about the uprisings among the Jews, the Germans, the Celts, or any nation which dared to challenge Rome.

"Our Roman armies have been invincible, until this fiasco." He stomped his foot and clinched his fist. His anger burned as he watched the water clock drip away the time.

He searched for answers and turned to the guard who offered his suggestion.

"We've many commanders in Rome," he grumbled. "But since you think you know who is best suited to protect Rome and her provinces, then give me your opinion."

The guard bowed and stood straight to face his emperor. "He is Flavius Vespasian! One well fitted for honorable duty to the Emperor of Rome," he informed.

"Vespasian?" Nero repeated as he squinted his eyes. "Flavius, where have I heard that name?"

"My Emperor," said the guard. "He has a brother, Sabinus, who holds office in Rome."

"Ah! Now I remember," Nero lied. "You were right in thinking Vespasian would be my choice."

The guard stepped back and bowed again.

"Send for him!" Nero ordered with the flip of his hand. The guard left to carry out the emperor's command.

The other guards stepped aside allowing a young boy to visit the emperor. Nero's boy-lover came dressed in a light purple gown with flowing scarfs hanging from his shoulders and draping to the floor. His feet were in golden slippers and his long hair adorned with flowers and ribbons.

Nero dismissed the private guards and told them to wait outside. They joked among themselves and made common slurs against their emperor.

"I heard he had the lad castrated," one guard whispered to the other. "Is it really true?"

"It's true," the other answered. "I've seen him caressing the boy like you would a woman."

"How long do you think we'll be standing outside the door?"

"Until he's finished with his lover," said the guard.

After a time Nero called out. "Guards! You can enter now!"

The men filed back into the palace room.

"Can anyone tell me more about General Vespasion? I need to refresh my memory."

"My Emperor," said the head guard. "General

Vespasian's recent victories include Jotapata, Sepphoris, and Japhia. All have surrendered to Roman authority under his leadership. He's captured the Jewish general, Josephus."

"Josephus?" Nero questioned. "Never heard of him." He gazed into the eyes of his lover. "I'm impressed with Vespasian's conquest. Let it be known in Rome that I appoint General Vespasian as commander of the legions of Rome!" He turned to his lover, looked into the young eyes of the lad, and whispered.

"You, my loved one, are the envy of every woman."

The lad smiled sweetly as Nero caressed his hand.

"You sit beside the emperor of Rome. A place where no woman can hold."

The guards looked away in shame. One spoke in a whisper. "The Emperor dishonors himself and all Rome."

Early the next day, Nero waited impatiently for his special messenger being escorted to the emperor's private chambers. He felt his hands sweating and his stomach churning. He tried to sit calmly at his desk, but he was too nervous.

"Your Majesty," said the guard at the door. "Your messenger is here."

"Bring him in!" he ordered. He waited for the guard to leave and then asked, "Have you news from Spain?"

"My Emperor," the man said apologetically. "Your agents haven't returned from Spain. I fear they have been killed."

Nero jumped to his feet. His eyes widened in fear. "Killed?" he questioned. "You worthless scum! How dare you suggest my agents have failed in the service of their emperor!" His knuckles turned white and he bit down on his lip. He wondered if his plot had failed? If so he could be certain there would be retaliation, and he would be a dead emperor.

Nero hated Galba who was a threat to Rome and the emperor himself. He paced the floor aimlessly while thinking about his future.

"Where's Galba now?" he asked.

"He's in Spain, my lord." The messenger trembled.

Nero had sent assassins to Spain to end the life of Galba. If the assassins were caught, they would be tortured until they revealed who sent them. Or, he thought, it would be easy for them to betray the emperor and pledge themselves to Galba in return for leniency.

Nero ignored the messenger who watched him pacing the floor. Tears filled Nero's eyes and sweat rolled down his face. What could he do? he asked himself. If only his mother were here. She would tell him what to do.

"Alas," he sighed openly. She could no longer comfort him. He, who was a mother-killer, and now was about to be a target for someone else, the Spanish Galba.

He dismissed the messenger, and stood alone in his palace room.

"Justice from the gods," he said softly as his eyes turned to the ceiling. "May they be quick." The thought of Galba entering Rome was too much for his poetic heart and his melodious spirit.

Suddenly he heard men running through the corridors of the palace. A guard's voice shouting with urgency.

"Emperor! We've news from Spain!" the guard called and waited to be summoned forward.

Nero felt his heart leap. Surely his plan was successful.

"Good news?" he asked hopefully as the guard entered.

"My Emperor, I'm sorry to inform his Excellency that Galba is on the march from Spain."

Nero's blood drained. His heart beat rapidly and he cried out. "Will Galba enter the city of Rome?"

"Galba claims an attempt was made on his life by the Roman Emperor. He's let it be known that he intends to retaliate," the guard added.

Nero trembled. He felt the room spinning and he crumbled to the floor. When he regained his senses, his guards were holding him upright.

"Let go of me!" he ordered. He felt weak as he tried to stand. "Oh, gods of Rome, what can I do now?" he moaned. "Galba is such a ruthless man."

Nero blotted the sweat from his face. "Galba will invade Rome. I must do something to stop him!"

His guards remained silent as he went on. "I've held the throne of Rome since I was seventeen. I'll not allow that old Spaniard to take it from me!" He raised his fist and stood in a dramatic pose as though on stage.

He wondered if his guards suspected him of plotting to kill Galba? His fears heightened when he thought the Senate of Rome might learn about his plot, they could declare him as a public enemy. He dismissed his guards, and slumped into deep despair.

The following morning, he was filled with new courage. He had designed a plan to solve everything. He would give a party that evening and invite his devoted friends. Friends who had received favors from him through the years and now it was time for them to return some favors. With wine and women, he would serve their pleasures, for they liked living big at his expense. He would present his plans and pray they would go along. The promise of gold and land could miraculously change the course of events, if they could be persuaded to help him retain his position as the emperor of Rome.

THE EMPEROR'S PARTY

Nero's elaborate party was not like any other affair he had arranged. The guests were served exotic foods brought in from foreign countries. He hired both males and females to dance naked and spared no money when it came to entertainment.

His few devoted friends were honored by sitting at his table. After a few hours, his conversation led to the reason he had invited them. He chose a few to confide in, and expressed the possibilities of Galba's attempts to overthrow Rome.

"What would we do if such a thing happened?" he asked those near him. They seemed unperturbed by the idea while they laughed and drank his wines. One guest lifted his goblet and declared.

"We'll make war with fat old Galba if he enters!"

"But how would you divert him from entering the city?" Nero asked slyly.

"Make sure he has no sympathizers in the city," one guest suggested. "There are too many Gallic men in our city who would be willing to join forces with him."

Nero stiffened. "I encourage you to debate on how you would settle this before Galba arrives." He lifted his wine cup to toast. "Drink up, and speak up!"

"I say we get all the Gallic men drunk and dump them in the Tiber," one man boasted and the guests roared.

Nero grinned. He aimed to protect his rule in Rome. Even if it meant killing all who opposed him.

"Who needs the Gallic?" shouted one guest as he fell over a lounge. "Feed them to the licker fish in the Tiber."

"I think you have answered the problem," said Nero. "What must be done is to have all the Gallic residents in Rome killed." He waited for their approval. A silence fell over the room and smiles vanished.

Zoheleth

"Does anyone understand my strategy?" Nero inquired. Some of the guests nodded, but others turned a deaf ear. He looked around and saw them whispering. Others made lame excuses to leave the palace.

"You people of Rome!" he shouted. "Do you want a Spanish ruler?" His question stunned them, and they started talking and drinking again.

"This is a serious matter," he impressed. "If the Gallic residents are not here to join Galba, then the old man will turn away and leave Rome."

"Save us from Galba!" yelled one man. He stood up and toasted the emperor. "My comrades," he implored. "If Galba conquers Rome it will be our death sentence, because we are close friends to Emperor Nero."

A sudden soberness came over the guests. Nero saw their expressions change. He knew they feared what would happen if Galba did enter. He wanted them to be afraid, but above all he wanted their loyalty.

The guests began to disburse and talk outside the palace. They spoke secretly among themselves, and feared for their lives and for Rome, if Nero's plan back-fired.

"What if Nero follows through with his plan?" asked one friend to the other.

"I fear for the future of Rome. But Galba is not as blood-thirsty as Nero."

"I know what you mean," said the first friend. "I have several friends who became Christian sympathizers after seeing how Nero ordered children to be eaten alive in the arena. This emperor is worse than a beast!"

The guests went their separate ways.

Inside the palace, Nero was uneasy seeing his trusted friends leave earlier than usual. These parties lasted for nights, but tonight only a few remained, and they were too drunk to move. He looked them over and thought, perhaps none were really his friends.

For three days the city of Rome engaged in a bloody rampage. Nero ordered the merciless killings of the Gallic residents. His secret agents who hungered for gold, made certain that every Gallic was killed.

Word reached Galba about the killings of innocent Gallic people in Rome. He grew more determined to end the worthless life of the lunatic, Nero.

Messengers arrived at the palace and informed Nero of Galba's rage over the slaughtering of the Gallics.

The closer Galba got to Rome the more disturbed Nero became. He couldn't sleep at nights and swore he heard his mother calling him.

One night he awakened in a cold sweat from a nightmare. He visioned those he killed had come alive to torment him and drive him to insanity. He saw the wife he kicked to death while she had a child within her.

Thousands of faces flashed in front of him. The faces of Christians being eaten by wild beasts and their screams were haunting him. He couldn't make them go away. He heard the chilling sounds of naked humans covered in oil and tar and used as torches for his garden parties. He and his guests would eat and drink as the horror went on before them.

He sat up in bed and tried to think of something pleasant, but the scenes from the fires of Rome tortured his mind. It was he who gave the order to burn the city. He wanted to make a new city. Why did the people become enraged against him. He had to blame the Christians.

"Those awful Christians," he groaned aloud. "I was thinking only of Rome. I had to rid the city of the scum."

He jumped out of bed and paced the floor pounding his fist. "Was Rome grateful to him for weeding out the low class? These people stunk the alleyways," he complained aloud. He convince himself that it was all for the good of Rome. Didn't he conduct a fire-fund to provide for the Roman families who were left homeless?

Two nights later he was awakened by shouting outside the city. He heard people in the streets cheering. He was sure Galba had been turned away but then he heard the crowds shouting Galba's name. Fear struck him like a snake and he stood paralyzed by his bed. He began to cry and whimper like a baby. He had reached a point of frenzy.

"The living will want me dead," he shouted madly. "Even the dead want me dead! Who will come to my aid?" Hot tears rolled down his round face. He called to his slave, but to his disgust, the slave ran in terror. He then reached for his dagger and tried to plunge it into his heart. His hand trembled and the dagger fell.

He bewailed his fate. "I can't even end my own life," he cried out desperately. Why was it easy to see others die at his command? Why couldn't he face death bravely?

His heart pounded wildly when he heard the footsteps of soldiers running in the corridors of the palace.

"Epaphroditus!" he shouted to his secretary. "Come quickly! Help me! I beg of you."

His secretary came running to his master and found no guards outside the emperor's door. He pushed it opened and ran in.

"What is it, my Emperor?" he asked and fell to his knees in front of Nero.

"Where are my Imperial Guards?"

His secretary lowered his head. "I'm the only one who remained, my Emperor."

"Traitors! All of them!" He shouted and wept at the same time. He looked down at his lowly secretary.

"Dear Epaphroditus. You are my faithful one. I can't plunge this dagger into myself. You must do it!"

His secretary trembled when the dagger was placed in his hands. Nero saw the fear in the eyes of his faithful one, and he pleaded once more.

"I beg of you. Look at your emperor. Don't allow me to be abused by my enemy. I now give you my last command. Kill me!"

The sounds of Galba's men grew closer.

"We can escape, my Emperor," suggested Epaphroditus, as he clung to the dagger.

"There's no time!" Nero cried bitterly and collapsed into the arms of his secretary.

Zoheleth

Nero felt the sharp tip of the dagger enter his throat. He twisted in pain and fell to the floor grasping his neck. The hot blood ran through his fingers as he struggled to meet death.

The doors flew open and Galba's men burst into Nero's bedroom.

"Where is he?" one thundered loudly as he held his sword high.

"You're too late," said Epaphroditus. "See my emperor's eyes gazing into a place where you can't go."

"Is this your emperor?" the soldier asked scornfully. He looked down at the fat body with blood flowing through his curly hair.

The secretary nodded and went on talking about his master. "I remember my emperor from when he was a child. He was born into the Domitian family nine months after Emperor Tiberius died."

"Too bad your master didn't die along with him." The soldier sneered.

"You didn't know him like I did," he defended. "He was a poor boy until his uncle, Emperor Claudius, adopted him. Nero was ten at the time."

"I don't need a history lesson," said the soldier. "General Galba can celebrate now that the beast is dead!" He placed his sword back in its sheath.

The secretary spoke softly to his master as though not to disturb his sleep. "Your mother planned that you would one day rule Rome," he sighed as he held Nero's hand close to his face.

The soldier laughed. "You forget how he had his mother assassinated."

"Rumors! All rumors," he declared.

"Remember this rumor, old man," said the soldier. "His mother welcomed the final blow to her womb which had cradled a snake!" The soldier turned and left the room.

Epaphroditus stared pitifully at his master.

"They all hate you, my Emperor. But I know you have served your purpose on the stage of life. The gods forgive all evil deeds of those who have been deified on earth."

He wept over his master and gently placed Nero's hand over his dead heart. His last wish for his beloved master was for the gods to lead him safely beyond since they knew Nero was a god.

CHAPTER TEN

THE EXODUS

Across the sea from Rome, the city of Jerusalem held frightened people who began abandoning their homes.

The roads to Pella were thick with caravans burdened down with the possessions of the owners. Some traveled with push carts, others with back-packs, and many used donkeys for the trip.

Thousands of Jews and Christians fled Jerusalem after learning that King Agrippa offered them santuary in Pella. They had to flee the city for their own safety.

Joseph, the physician, Drusus, and Cornelius were among those departing after the riots broke out in the city.

"How will Pella hold us all?" Cornelius asked Joseph as they rode side by side. "The people are endless who seek a refuge in Pella."

"I'm sure the Lord will fill the needs of the people," Joseph said while riding behind his small caravan. He knew the people would want to return to their homes later, but he was certain they would have little to return to since the rioters would rob every vacant house.

Drusus was riding his horse and talking with Joseph. "There are some of us who don't care to settle in Pella," he informed. "They're going to Ephesus. I've given it some thought and decided to join them."

Joseph asked his reason.

"There's more opportunities in their cities since commerce flourishes there."

"You have chosen well," Joseph smiled. "Ephesus needs fresh Christians like yourself."

"You're in agreement?" Drusus was surprised.

"Go! my friend. May God watch over you." He watched Drusus join those headed in a different direction.

Cornelius trailed behind Joseph. The physician

Zoheleth

announced his plans to go to Jotapata and not Pella.

Cornelius was irritated. "You should stay with the caravans," he replied. "The people may need a physician. I heard there's an uprising in Jotapata and I understand the Romans are doing battle with the Jews who set fire to the villages in Syria."

"They'll be many wounded soldiers who could die without a surgeon," Joseph reminded him.

"That's Rome's problem!" Cornelius shot back. "The armies have their doctors. Why must you go?"

"They have doctors, yes, but they have no Christian healers."

"Then allow me to join you," Cornelius offered. "You shouldn't travel alone."

Joseph thanked him. "You must remain in Pella. The people will need a house church and you must establish one."

"We're going to return to Jerusalem when the riots are settled," said Cornelius. "The Romans will arrive and settle the people there."

"Have you forgotten what our Lord said?" Joseph asked earnestly. "Not one stone will be left upon another in Jerusalem. He told the daughters of Jerusalem not to weep for Him (Matt. 24:2) but for themselves and their children (Luke 23:28). We were also told by Jesus that this generation would not pass away until all these things take place" (Matt. 24:34).

"Do you think this is the time Christ will return?" asked Cornelius.

"The signs of His return have begun," Joseph stressed. "John, the apostle, speaks of the beast in his writings" (Rev. 13).

"Just who is the beast?"

"John uses Hebrew numerology. It's the Kabbalistic method which dates back to the ancient prophets who addressed it as the Gematria. In Hebrew, Nero's name is NRVN KSR. We don't use vowels and his name adds up to 666" (Rev. 13:34).

"You're serious?"

"Yes, put Jerusalem behind you. The Holy City will be destroyed, and Nero, the beast, will die."

"This is more than I bargained for," Cornelius sighed. "All my possessions are in Jerusalem." He hung his head and pondered. "I never realized the meaning behind the numbering system which John presents in his writings."

"Stay in Pella and spread the Gospel so others will find salvation in Christ," Joseph encouraged.

"You have my word, Joseph," said Cornelius. "I'll do just that. I believe you and I believe the words of Christ."

Joseph knew Cornelius was disappointed about not returning to his home in Jerusalem. He feared many would suffer the same sorrow.

The caravans were east of the Jordan River, and Pella was not far off. Joseph felt sorry for Cornelius, but he also felt that God spared him as a child from the jaws of the wild dogs for a reason. Perhaps this was God's reason?

He motioned to his caravan driver that he wished to ride next to him and allow the donkey to walk unburdened. He said farewell to Cornelius and his caravan headed to Jotapata.

They camped under the stars that night, and early the next morning he could see the cliffs of Jotapata in the far distance. Joseph wondered what he would find once he arrived. He was a lonely man without a family, and he needed to serve others with his skills. He also needed to share the Gospel with those in whom he came in contact.

The Christians were his family after many of his old Jewish friends deserted him once he followed Christ. He was fortunate the servants of his household became Christians. He did miss them, but as soon as the wars throughout the cities were settled, he would sail back home to Alexandria.

CHAPTER ELEVEN

ANTONIUS OF ASHKELON

Jewish forces were forming their armies in different regions of the Roman provinces. With the defeat of Gallus in Jerusalem, the zealots grew bold and began attacking the cities garrisoned by the Roman soldiers.

An army of rebellious Jews marched to Ashkelon, located below Joppa off the Mediterranean Sea.

Antonius Salo, a Roman commander of the cavalry, was stationed in Ashkelon when the watchman sounded the alarm to prepare to defend the city.

Antonius hurried to the tower. He saw in the distance thousands of armed men heading to the Ashkelon's gates. He alerted the cavalry for an attack.

Antonius was a fair skinned man with hair bleached white from the sun. His physique was like a gladiator and he was blessed with a charming smile.

"Romans!" he shouted. "We have some daring Jews who desire to treat us as they did Governor Gallus. Shall we teach them a lesson?"

The troops cheered and clashed their swords against their shields.

"Antonius!" his men shouted. "Lead us to victory!" He smiled and signaled from his horse for them to follow.

With the thoughts of an oncoming battle a twinge of excitement stirred him. It gave him a rush of adrenalin as he raised his sword over his head and in a circular motion rode full force ahead.

"Let's put these peasants beneath our feet!" he urged as he ventured forward.

The earth shook under the hooves of galloping horses as they cut loose. The horses of a cavalry were as brave as their riders. They never feared a battle.

The gates of Ashkelon flew open and the steeds raced

Zoheleth

ahead raising mounds of dust as they sped to the open fields, competing with each other, for that was the nature of the war horse.

Antonius' strong legs tightened against the sides of his steed as they advanced swiftly on the Jews. The invading army had little chance to move from the hooves of the horses as the riders slew the rebels.

The enemy tried dismounting the Roman soldiers, but were amazed to see they never broke rank while riding.

Swinging swords struck down the impetuous young men who came against well trained soldiers.

Antonius signaled to surround the enemy in a familiar pattern. Another group of men were to separate and allow enough space so the horses could turn back.

While the enemy were attacking the phalanx of his division, he signaled his men to retreat and ride away as defecting. They did so, and turned with a fierceness that confused the enemy, who had little understanding of Roman military tactics.

The division appearing to retreat, raced back attacking the Jews who floundered wildly with little strategy. The Romans kept the enemy in a constant state of alarm.

Death was thick over the grounds leaving the area stained in blood for miles. The battle lasted until sunset. The dead spread across the land like a bloody blanket.

A few of the enemy escaped. Antonius didn't pursue them.

"Victory!" he boasted as he and his men raced back to the fortress of Ashkelon to celebrate.

The night was spent in drinking and dancing. The men laughed and made love to their woman. The people roasted oxen over the fires and the wine flowed like the blood of the enemy.

Antonius was a hero to his men. The women of Ashkelon ran to embrace him and kissed him. He loved all the attention. He hoped his heroism would not go unnoticed by Rome. His dreams for advancement with the Roman officials would be highlighted by today's victory.

Several days later, Antonius was shocked to see the enemy who escaped mustered up more men and returned to Ashkelon.

His spies from the city, went outside the perimeters of Ashkelon and waited for the band of cutthroats to fall into a trap. The Romans were given orders to allow no man to remain alive.

The cavalry ambushed the brazen youths who dared to return with more forces. The entire group were massacred. Ashkelon settled back into peaceful living.

A few days later, a messenger of Rome rode to Ashkelon carrying a request from General Vespasian.

Antonius read it and called his men. "I have a message from Rome!" he announced. "The Emperor Nero has appointed Vespasian to be commander of the Roman Legions." His men sent the word back to the men in the rear. Antonius waited. "We have orders to march to Caesarea right away!"

The cheering was loud and the men of Ashkelon were as pleased as Antonius.

"We'll march at dawn!" he announced. This is the dream he held in his heart for years. He knew he had a future with Vespasian, who was notorious for his great victories in battles. He wanted to make a name for himself.

The gods now favored him and he promised to sacrifice to them before they marched.

"Oh, god of Fortune," he prayed softly. "Keep me as one of your favorites."

THE AMBUSH

The soldiers from Ashkelon marched two and a half days when they were suddenly attacked by a band of thieves hiding in the surrounding caves.

The Romans were outnumbered and fled for shelter in the nearby caves. The cavalry forced their way and broke through the ambush to get on higher grounds. Antonius fought to protect the flanks, but was thrown to the ground when his horse was wounded. He struggled to his feet and clung close to the side of the cliff. His sword ready to strike.

His life would have ended but for the bravery of one soldier who lifted him to the back of his horse. They sped away.

Inside the cave, Antonius commenced to design plans for their escape. They were trapped and robbed of food and water. They had to remain inside the cave and share one skin of wine.

"How far do you think Vespasian's legions are from us?" Antonius asked a scout.

"We have traveled twenty miles a day," he calculated. "I would say we're within a few miles of Vespasian's camp."

Antonius saw the expression of hopelessness in the eyes of his men.

"Vespasian must have scouts somewhere within the area." Antonius reasoned. "Before daybreak, I'll take six men and search for his scouts."

"You'll need more than six men," one officer noted.

"With less men we can slip out without being seen. The thieves will sleep at some hour and by the sounds of their laughter I would guess they're drinking our wine."

"They'll expect us to make an escape and will be waiting out there," the officer insisted.

"Your archers will prevent the thieves from exiting.

Zoheleth

Take note that we're on higher cliffs. Keep us covered should we come under attack."

Antonius picked his bravest to accompany him on a daring mission. One man offered to ride ahead to distract the thieves. Antonius refused his offer because the thieves knew the area too well.

"Each man keep your distance behind me," he instructed. "Make it appear that I'm alone."

"It's too dangerous!" uttered one soldier. "We should stay close in case we're forced to do battle."

"Listen!" Antonius insisted. "One of us must get through to Vespasian. The others will be safe in the caves until we can get help."

His men were quiet, but they understood his explanation. Antonius knew if one man was caught, the other could go in a different direction to distract the thieves. They might not know the number of men trying to break through. Confusion was the name of the game.

The Auxiliary of Syria had scout duty through the night, and when dawn came Sabinus suggested they return to camp.

When the sun rose, Sabinus scanned the hills one last time for any signs of bandits spying on the Roman Legions. He was ready to leave the area when he noticed movement in the distance. Thinking he came across a nest of bandits he halted his men.

"Wait here," he ordered as he rode cautiously forward. When he approached the boulder he saw a Roman uniform and a soldier slouched over a horse.

Sabinus used caution in case it was a trap. The horse's reins hung loose and Sabinus knew the rider was in trouble. He waved his men forward.

"We have an injured Roman soldier," he called out. "There must be more of his company. Look for them!" he ordered.

His men found two others wounded and without horses.

"Who are you? And who is this wounded man?"

Zoheleth

Sabinus asked one soldier.

"We're from Ashkelon," he said. "He's Antonius Salo our commander. He's been badly wounded."

"What are you doing out here?"

"We're to join Vespasian," said one as he limped along. He informed Sabinus where the remaining soldiers were hiding. Sabinus sent his troops to rescue them.

"Where are the thieves ?" asked Sabinus.

"They might have fled when seeing how close you were to their lodgings."

"We must get your commander medical help," Sabinus said. "Ride with one of my men."

Sabinus rode ahead, and led the horse which held Antonius. This pale soldier was barely alive but hung onto the mane of the horse.

The sun rose high and a comforting breeze followed. Sabinus thought how Vespasian would credit him and his men for rescuing the entire cavalry of Ashkelon.

Rome favored the Syrians for their excellent riding abilities. He and his men were known for their skill in using a bow and arrow while riding a horse. The archers were proud men who boasted their skills and won many metals for never missing a target.

While Sabinus rode slowly in respect for the suffering Antonius, he thought about his own life in the Auxiliary. He had spent twenty three years in the service of Rome. In two years, he and his family would receive Roman citizenship. This was his dream for the future. He visualized honors awarded to him and with his savings he would breed race horses when he retired.

Ahead of him was the outline of the Roman camps stationed outside Caesarea. Soon he and his men could rest. His noble deed would be recorded in the books and his men would celebrate this memorable event.

THE INFIRMARY

Sabinus arrived at the infirmary. He dismounted and tethered the horses.

Marcus caught sight of him and came running to greet him.

"Father!' he shouted joyfully and offered his help.

"I've a badly wounded soldier," said his father. "Where's the physician?"

"Joseph saw you coming and he's on his way."

They eased Antonius off the horse and carried him inside the infirmary. Joseph hurried to the scene.

"Who have we here?" he asked. "I know of no battles being fought."

"His name is Antonius Salo," said Sabinus. "He and his men were ambushed. The command was on its way here from Ashkelon when they were met by thieves."

"Get him on the operating table," Joseph requested. "We must stop the bleeding."

Antonius groaned when he was moved. He held his side where the blood trickled through his fingers.

"That's an ugly gash," Joseph noted. "You've lost a lot of blood, soldier. But I think I can fix you."

Marcus heated the searing rod in the flame and handed it to the physician. Joseph forced a leather belt into the mouth of Antonius. "Bite on this, son."

Marcus tied Antonius legs down to the table, and Sabinus held the soldier's arms when the cauterizing rod hit the wound. Smoke rose and the smell of burnt flesh always made Marcus sick.

Beads of sweat rolled down the face of Antonius, before he passed out. Joseph used catgut to sew the muscle together while his patient was unconscious.

"Marcus, hand me the linen thread. I'll sew the skin closed and pray for the best."

Marcus learned to admire the physician's skills and was impressed by the kind treatment Joseph gave to the wounded. He never saw Joseph allow his emotions to rule when faced with the worse scenarios.

"Do I see a shaven face?" Sabinus teased his growing son. Marcus smiled and touched his chin.

Antonius was moved to a cot in the back of the infirmary. Marcus covered him with a heavy blanket.

"He's your patient," said Joseph as he looked at the soldier. "He'll sleep the night away."

He and Marcus washed their hands in wine and Marcus cleaned the instruments by running them through fire. He wiped them with wine and placed them on a metal tray and covered them with a linen cloth.

Sabinus patted his son on the back. "You take good care of that soldier," he requested.

"I will, father."

"I'll stop in later to see how the rest of the wounded are fairing." Sabinus left the infirmary.

The following morning, Marcus did the rounds in the infirmary. He made notes on the wounded and the sick. Some soldiers suffered dysentery problems due to drinking dirty water. Others were treated for cuts, breaks, and exhaustion.

He found Antonius sitting on the edge of his cot.

"Good morning, Ebony," said Antonius as he smiled at the boy.

"Ebony?" Marcus repeated. "My name is Marcus Severus, son of Sabinus. I'm the medical assistant, and it was my father who saved your life!"

"Well, now," Antonius made an effort to smile, as he held his hand against his wound. "From now on, Ebony, will be my name for you."

Marcus took an immediate liking to Antonius.

"You look brighter this morning," he said. "Yesterday you were as white as the linen cloth that drapes you."

"So, it was your father who rescued me."

"Yes. My father is a brave man. He's a commander in the Syrian Auxiliary!"

"Well, Ebony. Your father has a fine son."

Marcus smiled, and commenced to examine the area where Antonius was wounded. He checked if there was any blood seeping through. The bandages appeared clean. Marcus was impressed with Antonius' clear blue eyes against his pure white skin. He found him shockingly handsome with fine broad shoulders and thick muscles.

"You could pass as a Greek god," he kidded. "Is the god -of -war, hungry?"

"I could eat a live goat!" Antonius chided.

"I didn't think gods got hungry," Marcus teased.

Antonius groaned when he tried to stand. "I didn't think that gods got injured."

"Our physician has given orders for you to remain in bed at least seven days."

Antonius lay back on the cot. He put his arms under his head and stared at the tent ceiling.

"Some god," he sighed. They both laughed.

CHAPTER TWELVE

NICATOR SEVERUS

Antioch, the capital city of Asia Minor, was several miles from the home of Sabinus Severus' family.

Nicator, the elder brother of Marcus, was on his way to the city of Antioch to meet the courier with the mail from the Roman army.

Nicator's mother waited for her son to return with news from his father and his brother, Marcus.

The ride was slow since Nicator chose to ride an ass. The beast was not like the race horses he exercised each day at his father's farm. His body swayed with the stride of the animal as his legs dangled over its sides. He scanned the road and noted strangers in alcoves praying to their gods. He stopped once and offered a prayer for the safety of his father and his brother.

Nicator longed to be with his father, but with an injured leg he couldn't enlist. His leg didn't hurt all the time, he thought. Some days he could walk without a stick but after a time the old injury began to pain him.

He entered the city gates of Antioch and jabbed the sides of the beast to hurry it along. The animal made an effort to go faster but then relaxed to its usual pace.

He enjoyed coming to the city and was proud that he was named after its founder, Seleucus Nicator who was a general of Alexander the Great. He was also proud that he knew the names of the city's gates. One was the Cherubim Gate leading to the Street of Herod and Tiberius. The other was the Daphine Gate. The Iron Gate was one above the citadel. He remembered the Middle Gate near the theatre of Caesar, and the Eastern Gate which led to the Forum of Valens. There were other gates but they slipped his mind.

He admired the beautiful Palace of Antioch, and recalled that once he had visited the circus in the same area.

Zoheleth

His father brought him here many times when he delivered horses. Antioch was noted for its horse races and some owners now trusted Nicator with their prized animals.

The city held many Jewish residents since the time of the Selucid rule. These rulers brought the Jews into the city for political reasons, as well as, commercial ones. The religious Jews turned against the Antioch Jews, when learning that to become a citizen of Antioch you had to worship the pagan gods.

Antioch became the refuge for many foreigners including the Amonites, the Egyptians, and the Assyrians.

Nicator came to the mail stop and dismounted. The dispatcher arrived early and Nicator greeted him.

"Do you bring us news from Vespasian's troops?"

"There's a letter for you, Nicator," said the dispatcher as he reached in and withdrew a small scroll.

"My mother will be happy to know there's news." Nicator stopped talking when he heard someone call him.

"Virgil?" he shouted out and hobbled toward his friend.

"Meet me by the aqueducts," Virgil pointed. "I'll be right with you."

Nicator waited and the two greeted each other with warm affections.

"I sent my servant to hire a horse for me," said Virgil. "We can ride together. I've lots to tell you."

"It looks like Rome agrees with you," said Nicator looking somewhat envious. "I see you've even chosen to look more Roman by shaving your face smooth."

Virgil gave a broad smile. "And you, Nicator, look like you've sprouted since we last met."

"And darker," Nicator laughed, as he often did referring to his own black skin from the Syrian side of his father's family. "Tell me about Rome."

"You did know Emperor Nero is dead?"

"Then it is true?"

"It's true," said Virgil. "Galba rules Rome, and who knows who will rule it by the time I return to law school."

Zoheleth

He rested his books on the stone seat by the aqueduct. "I'm home on a short break from school but I still need to study. I tell you there's too many things in Rome which keep me from my studies," he laughed.

"How will we be able to stand you?" Nicator jested, "Especially after you become a lawyer?"

"I may become a lawyer, but I'll still be me. Now I know you want to hear all the juicy stories."

"Give me all the dirty gossip you've heard," said Nicator. Virgil shook his head.

"First, about our new emperor, Galba. He's not much better than the perverted Nero."

"You're serious?"

"The city is constantly in civil disruptions."

"What's the dissension?" asked Nicator as he studied his friend's strong features. Virgil was a handsome young man with a high forehead and light brown hair. He looked Roman, but he was from the line of Alexander the Great. Nicator laughed when he saw him flirting with the young ladies being escorted to the water well to fill their jugs.

"Galba," continued Virgil, "He's as corrupt as Nero. He's old and fat and sloppy. He's in his seventies."

"What!" Nicator was surprised.

"The fat pig loves men his own age." Virgil pushed a fig into his mouth and kept talking. "His men are drunkards, and he never punishes them for their scandalous acts on women." Virgil broke out laughing and finished by saying. "Or on men!" Nicator laughed with him.

"Here comes my transportation," said Virgil as he watched his servant leading a horse toward them. Virgil raised his brows and shouted his disapproval.

"What do you bring me?"

His servant's face turned red. "Master, it's the only one rested enough for your trip."

Virgil shook his head in disgust and took hold of the reigns.

"This poor old nag makes me feel I should be carrying her," he complained but smiled forgivingly as he tapped his servant on the head."

"Do you want to stay in the city?" he asked his servant.

"Thank you, master. I'll find a better ride for you tomorrow and bring it to your home."

"Make sure it's alive," Virgil joked.

"What was that all about?" asked Nicator.

"If he makes me miss my boat back to Rome, I swear to sell him in the market place. He knows I need a fast animal, and he knows I'll wait until the last minute to leave my family."

"If you have any problems," Nicator offered, "I can let you use one of the racing horses in my charge."

"Good idea!" Virgil smiled.

The two headed back by a narrow path leading to the village. The peasants used that road instead of the Kings Highway. The robbers knew those who traveled it weren't worth the effort to rob. Most of the peasants traveled with cargos of the sweet waters from Antioch. The same waters which Alexander the Great said tasted sweet as a mother's milk.

"I heard about the Jews burning down some villages," said Virgil.

"My uncle died in the raid when he defended his home," Nicator said with bitterness. "I'm not at ease with the Jews."

"I'm sorry," Virgil said. "I understand why Rome stepped into the picture. They must stop the groups of Jews turning renegades. I guess my family was lucky not be raided."

"Marcus pleaded with my father to allow him to join the army and avenge our people," Nicator informed.

"How's Marcus these days?" Virgil inquired. "I know you would like to be with him for the same reason."

"Marcus writes more often than father," Nicator smiled. "He complains how he hates the chores as a physician's aide. It makes me laugh when I think it had to be my father who ordered him to do the work of a medic.

Zoheleth

Father was against him joining the army. I would be there if my leg wasn't damaged."

"Does your leg trouble you much?"

"Only at times. I'm able to work with the horses and we hired men to tend the farm."

They rode side by side when the path widened. Nicator thought about his injury and tried not to be angry with Marcus, but at times the memory of the accident haunted him as it did right now.

He recalled as a boy, Marcus was playful around a high-spirited race horse named Seluce. The horse owners rented stalls from Sabinus, and Nicator was taught how to care for the animals. He remembered seeing Marcus in the stall and he had loosened the reins which held Seluce. The memory made him sweat. He could hear his own voice yelling to his brother. He saw the horse rearing and knew the animal would make a dash for the open fields.

Nicator felt his heart racing as he relived the event. He ran to the stall and pushed Marcus from the steed's front hooves as it leaped forward.

"What are you thinking about?" Virgil interrupted. "You look to be miles from here."

"Not miles, just years. I was thinking how I fell to the ground after pushing my brother from the path of the horse. I still feel the hooves when they came down on my leg."

"I didn't mean to bring back the bad memory," Virgil apologized.

"It's all right. I did save my brother's life. It could have been his head crushed instead of my leg."

"Whatever happened to the horse?"

"The horse suffered a greater injury," Nicator sighed. "My father thought I was dead and he rode wildly after Seluce." Nicator wiped sweat from his face. "I guess I was knocked out. But what I did see was my father clubbing Seluce to death and taking his dagger to slit the throat of the animal."

"Of all the gods in Rome," declared Virgil. "Why?"

Zoheleth

"He thought the horse had killed me," said Nicator. "Later I tried to tell him that it was not the fault of the horse, but I saw his dagger dripping with blood and I burst out crying."

"So he killed a valuable race horse?"

"Yes. The owner didn't sue because Seluce had done harm to a human. There was something in the man's religious laws. The Jews have some strange laws."

"You were fortunate not to have been killed," said Virgil as he stopped and let his horse graze.

"My father replaced the animal. It cost him plenty along with my medical expenses."

The sun was lowering when the two reached their village. Virgil promised to visit Nicator before he left for Rome.

Zoheleth

THE LETTER

Adana, the mother of Marcus and Nicator, stood watching Nicator as he came waving a scroll.

She was still in mourning for her brother who was killed in the Jewish raids on the Syrian villages.

Her husband, Sabinus, and her son, Marcus, were a constant worry to her.

"Hurry, Nicator," she called as she seated herself in the chair her husband had made when they were first married. "Open the letter," she pleaded. "Read to me and tell me they are well."

Nicator stood near the window and read. His mother never learned to read or write. Even when he tried teaching her she was too busy.

Adana was proud of her son's ability to read. It was her husband's brother, Crates, who taught them. Crates was a scribe who taught the children of Roman aristocracy.

"Listen, mother," said Nicator. "Marcus writes this letter."

Greetings: My family, from Marcus Severus.
Father wishes you well and we are fine. To write this I had to mix water with gum as writing fluid.
I found some clean papyrus and I use a sharpened reed as a pen. I guess you wonder what I do each day since I'm not permitted to fight.
Some of my duties include keeping records for the physician. I record the events and who has been injured and what medications they receive. I also record those who have died. We, in the service of the emperor of Rome, are never without duties. I go to mock battles each morning and do exercises to keep fit.
Joseph is kind. Although he's a Jew, I find him interesting. He follows a strange religion called Christianity. I listen to

him read what he calls the Gospel but I don't understand its meaning.
I've been taught how to find plants and herbs for his formulas. He laughs when I pick a few weeds by mistake. I know how to brew Syrian Hyssop into a tea and use the hairs of the plant's stem to prevent coagulation of the blood.
We use a wild gourd mixture to relieve stomach pains.
In the crevices of the rocks I dig for a plant called Hebane. The plant is used as a narcotic and Joseph keeps it locked away so it won't be stolen.
I want to tell you about one strange plant. It's called the Mandrake. Joseph said many women soak the plant in wine and believe it has magic to help them conceive children. The doctor said the plant acts as an aphrodisiac to promote fertility. He said there's an ancient folklore mentioned in a Jewish book called Genesis (Gen. 30:14).
The fascinating thing about the plant is its roots which resembles a human.
Working in the infirmary is not what I dreamed of doing, especially since we get so many wounded soldiers.
I administer Ladnum juice to those who suffer from dysentery. The plant is imported from the Isle of Cyprus.
The new commander of the Roman armies is Vespasian. He's favored by the legions. I think he's a great leader. We have a woman in the camp. Her name's Bernice. She's the sister of King Agrippa and she came to appeal to Vespasian. She requested his help to settle disputes in her Jerusalem. Joseph thinks we'll be going to Jerusalem.
Nicator, this part of the letter is for your eyes only. I hate it here. I want to fight but you know father refuses to allow it.
I hate seeing wounded soldiers. I hate emptying the chamber pots and cleaning all the dirty utensils. The physician is strict when it comes to items being clean. I'm dog tired at the end of day.
Please tell Martha I think of her daily. I can't write to her as you know. Her father would learn of it and she would be punished.

    Nicator finished the letter and his mother asked to

Zoheleth

have it. She wanted her friends to read it to her.

"Mother," he said. "You can have the letter after I've read it in the square to the men." He saw her eyes fill with tears.

"You come back with the letter," she requested as she kissed him. He couldn't allow her to hear how unhappy his brother was.

Nicator finished reading in the square and was headed back to the house when he remembered Martha.
She always wanted to hear news about Marcus. Her family had strange ideas about soldiers and didn't want their daughter to marry one.

Nicator recalled when Martha and Marcus were small children. He laughed how they adored each other and there was no one in the world but them. He thought Martha was a silly girl and he teased her just to anger Marcus. He liked her golden hair and fair skin. She looked so pale next to Marcus. His younger brother was tall and stocky. His skin a burnished bronzed like their mother. Marcus had a round face and an impish expression when he smiled. He, on the other hand, was short like his father and slender. His features were fine and his skin dark like the Syrians.

He got the idea to tell his mother how Martha insisted on keeping the letter. He would write to Marcus and tell him to send another letter as soon as he could. This would cheer their mother.

CHAPTER THIRTEEN

THE LEPER

Rome's legions camped at the borders of Caesarea and waited orders from Rome. The soldiers collected their pay, a task which often took four days to complete.

Vespasian selected groups and gave them permission to visit the city of Caesarea. He knew the men wanted to spend their earnings on gambling, drinking and loose women.

Early one morning, the watchman at the post sighted a man coming toward the camp. The stranger wore the garments of a leper.

"Halt!" he shouted. "Come no closer if you value your life, Leper!" The man removed the wrappings from his hands and striped himself of the garments to reveal his Roman uniform.

"Identify yourself!" the guard ordered.

"I'm Metilius of the Roman garrison in Jerusalem." He stumbled to the ground. A guard ran out and took him directly to the general's quarters. When inside, Metilius fell to his knees at the feet of Vespasian. He revealed how his comrades were slaughtered.

"The Roman garrison at the tower of Antonia have been killed by Florus' men!" He went on. "I played dead, and when the coast was clear I slipped out of the city to seek help."

Vespasian saw the soldier was exhausted. "This man needs medical help," he said to his guards. "Take him to the infirmary and see that he gets food and wine. Find a change of uniform for him. Later we can talk."

Joseph examined Metilius, and Marcus got food and wine along with a dead soldier's uniform. Metilius explained that he dressed as a leper to keep from being killed on the road.

Zoheleth

Vespasian wanted to learn more from Metilius. He was troubled because he couldn't make any moves on his own. He groaned and complained how he was forced to remain on the outskirts of Caesarea.

Metilius was escorted to the command tent.

"What happened in Jerusalem?" Vespasian asked.

"The zealots are crazy wild, and the conditions grow worse as the young men forge weapons to come against the Romans."

"They're a bunch of fools!" Vespasian sneered and struck his fist against the palm of his hand. "We can't attack Jerusalem, yet I'm ordered to send troops to Joppa where there's an uprising. Rome refuses to send orders to come against Jerusalem! It doesn't make sense."

"Why has Rome not given orders to move on Jerusalem?" Metilius asked.

"We don't know the reason and nobody in Rome knows what to do. Nero is dead and the latest news is that Galba has been killed!"

"I can't believe this," said Metilius. "Who's ruling Rome?"

"You won't like hearing this, it's Otho. You know what that will mean?"

Metilius shook his head. "What will happen?"

"The Senate will take forever to get Otho to send orders to us."

"I'm sure Rome has been kept informed about the uprisings throughout the provinces," said Metilius.

"I've men sailing every day to take the news. I don't know how long Rome expects us to remain idle."

"I heard Agrippa's sister came here. Is it true?"

"She's here now. I won't allow her to return without us escorting her. I'm waiting for Agrippa to arrive."

"Is there anything else you wish to ask me?"

"No, Metilius. Get some rest in the infirmary."
He dismissed him.

Vespasian felt alone and needed to talk with someone. He thought about Agrippa's sister and decided it was time to pay her another visit.

When he arrived at her tent, her guards ushered him in. He saw her resting on large colorful cushions and nibbling figs from a golden bowl. He glanced around her tent and found it attractively decorated. He breathed in the tantalizing aroma of jasmine.

"You look concerned about something, General," she smiled. "Please seat yourself and have some wine."

"It's your people," he sighed as he sat down. "I think they grow fond of death." She shook her head slowly.

"I regret the conditions in Jerusalem," she said softly. "My brother keeps me informed." She paused. "I understand your concern but the priests have a lot of control over our people. It's my belief that they will hold matters at bay."

"I can't agree with you," he answered as he swallowed the wine. "We have a lone survivor from the Roman garrison."

"You do?" She was surprised.

"He informs me the people are determined to align themselves against Rome."

Bernice raised her brows. She motioned her servant to pour more wine, and her dark eyes stared at him. "I fear they have little chance of doing that. This is all Florus' doings. He enraged the people."

Vespasian wished he could stop talking about these things and relax and enjoy this lovely woman.

"Well," he sighed. "Florus set them up for the kill, if you forgive my saying so." He drank the next cup of wine slower. "I'll take care of that pig-eyed moron when I meet him," he threatened. "I've informed Rome of his antics and Florus has seen his last days as procurator!"

"General, why not allow me to order you a light meal and try to relax a bit." Bernice smiled gently.

"I'll have to pass that up," he groaned as he held the goblet and looked at his reflection. He touched the scar over his right eye and thought he was once handsome. Now he saw his hair thinning and many wrinkles in his face.

Bernice put down her goblet. "My brother writes

he's on his way to join you," she informed. "Now, I would consider it an honor if a certain gentleman with warm brown eyes, would enjoy the meal I'm trying to entice him with."

"Ah!" he laughed and for the first time blushed. "It's been a long time since anyone addressed me as a gentleman. It would be such a waste not to enjoy this evening. I accept your offer."

She raised her goblet and toasted him. "Rome will honor you for your victories. I honor you for your triumph in Jotapata."

"You give me too much credit," he smiled. "My son, Titus, deserves the triumphs. He put down a revolt by the Galileans," he boasted. He wanted to talk about the battles, but this was a woman. He liked talking with her. Although she was not designed to think like a man, she had a good mind. His thoughts drifted to Caenis, his mistress. He met her after his wife died and they fell in love. Caenis was a wife to him in every way but in name.

"And where is this Titus you so proudly speak about?"

"I await his return," Vespasian replied. "You'll meet him soon."

"I'm looking forward to it," she whispered as she watched him eating and drinking. The evening passed swiftly and Vespasian thanked her for her generosity.

Bernice remained awake long after Vespasian left. She walked outside and stared at the stars. She missed her brother. She missed a husband. She longed for strong arms to hold her. Arms that were her age and not like the old men she had been made to marry.

She began humming. Something stirred within her as though she expected an eventful moment to change her life forever.

THE ROMAN SENATE

"Senators of Rome!" Marius Gratus addressed the house. "Rome is at the mercy of the gods of fortune be it good or bad."

One in the Senate rose and answered, "It's been bad most of the time if you ask me." There was laughter.

"We, as Senators, are to do what?" Marius asked. "We have suffered civil upheavals since the death of Nero. Granted, we thought Galba would be a relief as emperor. Never did we expect to witness his head on the end of a pole in front of the Forum."

"Killing Galba was the only good thing Otho did when he entered Rome!" shouted one from the back of the Senate. The men broke out laughing.

"Senators, please," Marius pleaded. "This is serious. We have another dead emperor! Who expected Otho to kill himself when Vitellius threatened war on Rome?"

Marius, a middle aged member of the house, waited for the murmuring to die down so he could continue. "We knew nothing of Vitellius' desire to avenge the death of his friend, Galba," he paused for a moment. "Who knew that Emperor Galba had sent for Vitellius to join him in Rome? Galba wanted to appoint him as second in command." Marius paused. "Look what has happened. Aulus Vitellius is now emperor, and a vindictive one at that."

An elderly senator stood up. "Does anyone want to be the next emperor?" he asked a consul. The House of Senate was amused.

"Who is Aulus Vitellius?" asked a junior member. Marius raised his hand to bring silence.

"You, as well as others, know little of him," said Marius. "The man holds no great victories, but he does command our legions in Germany."

"I know this Vitellius," stated Calpurnius of the

Senate. "It's too bad he doesn't have old Emperor Tiberius to help him!" Some snickering was heard. "Nor does he have the degenerate, Caligulia, to play games with!"

Again Marius had to bring order to the house. "Senators!" he shouted. "This is important! We must address the issues we're facing."

Calpurnius walked out and took the floor. He received an applause and politely bowed in an amusing gesture.

"Senate! I'll tell you what we're facing," he announced as a hush came over the house. "We have a perverted son of a traitor!" A gasp came from the members.

Calpurnius was one of the Conscript Fathers. Originally the *"fathers"* were selected patricians of the Roman aristocracy established by the Kings of Rome. Later the plebeians were included. Plebes were the Roman citizens.

Calpurnius, due to his ancestral background, was highly respected among his peers. He stood tall with white hair trimmed close to his head. His toga shone bright in the sunlight as he raised his hand in the air to address the Senate.

"Hear this! Fathers of Rome," he bellowed. "Lucius Vitellius, the father of Aulus, our newly claimed emperor, was accused of high treason against Rome!" There came deafening shouts of protest from the members. He waited for the noise to die down.

"That's no secret," Marius defended. "His father died before it could be proved a falsehood!"

"Tell us, Marius," Calpurnius challenged. "What saved the son from being put to death because of his father?"

Marius stiffened and looked at the grim faces in front of him, but he kept his determination to control the Senate.

"Check your memory," answered Marius, trying to hold back his anger. "The son, Aulus, was not in Rome at the time you speak about." The senators frowned but Calpurnius smiled and said menacingly, "He was not around, because, my friend, he was on the Isle of Capreae among the male prostitutes catering to Emperor Tiberius' sexual fantasies."

The Senate's laughter could be heard in the street. Marius was embarrassed. He felt his face getting flushed but he held his stand.

Calpurnius looked at him sympathetically and stated, "We mean nothing against you, Marius. We want to inform you about the type of man who calls Rome his empire!"

Marius heaved a sigh. He watched Calpurnius turn back to the Senate and continued to speak.

"You see, the way Lucius Vitellius gained such prestige among the emperors was through his young son, Aulus, who gave up his chastity to Emperor Tiberius." He paused and went on to say, "Aulus gave himself to Tiberius to secure his father's advancement in public office."

Marius raised his voice and interrupted Calpurnius. "Perhaps his father is the real perpetrator of his son's situation?" He hoped the Senate would think differently about Vitellius. "Rome needs a strong hand," he added. "If Vitellius has the support of this Senate, then Rome can get on with the business of ruling the world."

"Well put!" someone shouted.

Marius moved on to say. "I'm sure we can't hold Vitellius completely responsible for what happened in his youth. Can we?"

Calpurnius was outraged. He spun around and faced Marius. He raised his fist in the air and declared. "We don't need another moron as our emperor. I say we declare Vitellius an enemy of Rome!"

"You have no legitimate reason to do that," Marius shot back. "It could be misconstrued as treason!"

"I'm not implying treason against the emperor," Calpurnius defended. "But I think all of us should be made aware of something. What Vitellius was subject to as a youth we can't hold against him." He paused and glanced around, smiling slightly. "But I plead with you, Senate of Rome. We must consider what he has done as a responsible adult!"

The members became silent. Marius could hear

himself breathing. He felt he was losing ground and had to release the floor to Calpurnius, who went on with valor.

"Vitellius was given a prediction that he would one day be emperor," Calpurnius declared, "he went about to make the prediction come true." He held the Senate's attention and they leaned forward to hear him. "The prediction was given to say if Vitellius outlived his mother, then, he would become an emperor."

A grumbling rolled through the House of Senate, but Calpurnius wasn't finished. "Vitellius wasn't willing to wait for the gods to bring about the prediction. When his mother suddenly took ill, he, the scoundrel, made certain that no food was administered to her. She finally died of starvation."

The Senate was shocked. One senator stood up and shouted. "Vitellius has no right to live! And, no right to be emperor of Rome!" Calpurnius won his point. Marius tried once again to express his view.

"Gentlemen of the Senate," he addressed them. "We should think on this before planning any attempts on the emperor's life." He saw how inflamed Calpurnius had made the Senate. Marius insisted on gaining back the floor. He begged them to come to order, and to cool down before deciding on the murder of the emperor.

"I suggest we make sacrificial offerings to the gods first and consult our priests on the future of Rome. We can't be hasty in creating a riot. There are those who favor the new emperor."

After much dispute, the Senate agreed. Marius had won this round after pointing out the need for stability by saying, "Rome needs peace, not civil disruption nor another murdered emperor. The gods of Rome will insure us an honorable emperor, one who will meet with our approval!"

He witnessed a change in the Senate as he convinced them to wait for a sign from the gods before taking a violent route.

The Senate were now on their feet applauding and cheering Marius who smiled and gave a long sigh of relief.

THE SPY

A courier met the Roman ship as it docked and he waited for the messages from imperial Rome. He rode fast to Caesarea to deliver the scroll to General Vespasian.

Vespasian broke the imperial seal and opened the letter. His guards stood waiting to hear if it held marching orders.

Vespasian looked away from his guards. "The news is not good," he revealed. "The emperor Otho has killed himself."

His guards were in disbelief.

"I can't understand it," Vespasian said out of exasperation. "Rome sits in dung and wonders why she comes up stinking. The emperor, Otho, has ruled ninety five days and is replaced by Aulus Vitellius."

A wave of restlessness moved through the camp. The Roman legions were known as fighting machines and Vespasian knew they wanted action. An officer of the guards approached him.

"When do we fight?" he asked forcefully. "Does Rome expect us to learn how to knit?"

"Just hold on," Vespasian reasoned with him. "I understand your dilemma," he admitted. His officer shook his head in doubt.

Vespasian merely added. "Why we are forced to sit and try to hatch eggs is a mystery to me as much as it is to you." He smiled in a humorous manner as he crumbled the letter. "We've had three emperors in eighteen months," he groaned. "There's not one who remained long enough to change his underdrawers. Galba is dead! Otho is dead! And now, a weak usurper by the name of Vitellius has crowned himself the emperor."

While he addressed his guards, another dispatcher rode into camp with a message.

"Now what?" he uttered in disgust while opening the mail. "Great gods of Rome! It's Joppa again!" he cursed aloud. "I'm ordered to send troops to settle another Jewish uprising."

He motioned the courier and the dispatcher to follow him inside his tent where he ordered wine and food. They listened as he growled about conditions around him.

"Damn them! They're a rancorous lot!" His wine spilled while swinging his hand. "I've sent men to settle their puny little quarrels. Now we have Jews who have turned pirates. I swear by the gods if I could get to the head leader I'd tear him apart. In what location of Joppa is it this time?" he asked the dispatcher.

"General, it's off the shore line. The groups who have turned to piracy are cutting off the supply ships from Egypt carrying a shipment of corn for the Roman armies. The Jews have robbed the corn shipment. And they..."

"Enough!" Vespasian interrupted. "Spare me the details." He reached into a barrel holding his maps. He spread one open and examined the surrounding areas of Joppa. "Commander," he said while pointing to the map. "I want forces to march to Joppa tomorrow. Use this route and see if you can trap the self-appointed pirates before they reach the waterways."

When his commander left, Vespasian composed a letter to Rome and expressed his condolences about the loss of the emperor, with tongue in cheek.

When alone, he limped to his bed and removed his sandals. His foot throbbed where he received an injury and it was swollen. He called his private guards.

"I want to speak with Metillius," he ordered.

"He's helping in the infirmary," answered a guard.

"Good! I'll get two birds with one arrow."

"Sir?"

"Help me to the infirmary. This foot is biting. Have my horse brought to the back of my tent." He mounted and rode with two guards to help him off his horse when he reached the infirmary. He was a proud man and wouldn't

Zoheleth

allow his soldiers to see his inability at this moment.

"Where's Joseph of Alexandria?" he bellowed and limped into the tent. "Wake up, physician!" He laughed when he saw the strange expression on Joseph's face.

"I'm here to serve you, General," said Joseph. "But may I ask how?"

"It's this confounded foot," he moaned in an effort to advance his step. He noticed the young lad behind Joseph. "Is this your assistant?" he inquired.

"Yes! This is Marcus, the son of Sabinus who rescued the Roman soldiers from Ashkelon."

"Ahaaa!" He smiled broadly. "Son of Sabinus, I'm pleased to meet you." he smiled broadly and nodded. "Your father will return from Joppa soon. I'm sending fresh troops there."

"That's good news," said Marcus.

"What's the problem with your foot?" asked Joseph.

"First, I must talk with the fake leper you house."

"You mean Metillius?" Marcus laughed. "I'll get him, General."

"Physician," Vespasian grinned. "Now see if you can do something for this ornery foot. It brings back painful memories of Jotapata."

"I'll wrap it but you should remain off it for a few days," said Joseph.

"Impossible!" declared Vespasian.

"Then, I can build up the area with a cushion to relieve the pressure."

"Do it, my friend. I've heard about your healing powers. I'll give a token to your gods."

"I have only one God," said Joseph. "He doesn't accept tokens, but He will accept a prayer."

"Whatever!" Vespasian laughed.

Metillius entered and saluted. "How can I be of a help, General?" he asked.

"I want you to go to Jerusalem," the general announced. "I'm asking you to serve Rome as a spy! You are good at disguising yourself. Am I correct?"

He made Metillius laugh. "I'm at your service."

"Good. Make arrangements with a group of merchants. Dress as a traveler and allow your beard to grow." He pulled back when the physician touched a tender section of his foot. "Let me know who are the ones choosing to be the enemy of Rome." Joseph searched for a map "I'll show you the underground tunnels for your escape, Metillius." Joseph pin-pointed them out.

"Get garments from the merchants and remember to be mute." Vespasian added and dismissed Metillius.

"Come, and share wine with me," said Joseph. "Give me the latest news on Rome."

"Rome," Vespasian sighed. "Our mistress is in much distress, I'm sorry to say."

"Is Emperor Otho well?"

"As well as he'll ever be." He winked at Marcus. "Otho is no longer among the living." This stunned Joseph, but Marcus held back a laugh. "Vitellius now rules Rome."

"Wasn't he close friends with Emperor Caligula?" Joseph tried to recall.

"If you can call them friends," Vespasian replied. "It was Caligula who caused the injury to Vitellius' leg."

Marcus felt a pang when he heard what was said. He thought about his brother's injury.

"How was Vitellius hurt?" Marcus inquired.

"When they were young lads, they ran chariot races," Vespasian began. "Vitellius was the better driver and Caligula knew it. In one of the races, Caligula used a gore-horse chariot. Vitellius didn't suspect anything until they raced. He received a badly damaged thigh when the spikes cut into his wheel. He was thrown from his chariot and run down by Caligula."

"How awful." Marcus sighed.

Joseph thought for a moment before he spoke. "I think Vetillius was married."

"He's been married twice," Vespasian answered.

"I believe he has a son." Joseph added.

"That's right! He has a son who can barely speak

without stammering," Vespasian replied as he punched his stomach to release a belch. Marcus had to smile.

"Would you like more wine, General?" he asked.

"No thanks. I must get back to work. When your father returns, I'll see he visits with you."

"Thank you, General." Marcus smiled and saluted Vespasian. The general returned the salute and gave a hearty chuckle.

Marcus offered to help Metillius pack his items. "I wish I were going with you," he admitted. "I've been here for two years learning medicine."

"You're a lucky young man," said Metillius. "It's an honor that Joseph thinks you worthy."

Marcus never looked at it that way. "I guess you're right," he said as he watched Metillius leave the infirmary.

"May the gods protect you, Metillius."

"May they protect you, also. I'll return soon."

Later in the day, Joseph told Marcus that Antonius was being sent to Joppa.

"Why send him so soon?"

"He and his men will replace your father's men."

Marcus had mixed emotions. He and Antonius became good friends after working together in the infirmary. They spent the nights in Joseph's tent while Antonius drank wine and told war stories. Antonius filled Marcus' life with laughter and excitement.

"Now I'm going to lose my best friend," he cried.

"Marcus," said Joseph. "Losses are what army life is all about." Marcus turned away in silence.

CHAPTER FOURTEEN
JOPPA

Antonius and his men arrived in Joppa late at night. They slipped into the city unseen. By the looks of things the residents had been drinking and celebrating the departure of the Syrian Auxiliary. No watchman was sober.

In the morning, the men of Joppa discovered the Romans inside the city. They panicked and fled to their ships anchored off shore. Antonius pursued and in two days the pirates were defeated. It was an incident which ended in a tragic loss of life. Vespasian was sent word on Joppa.

King Agrippa arrived at the Roman camp. He brought supplies for the army which included food and fighting equipment. It was his way of prompting Vespasian to aid him against the uprisings in his precincts.

While Antonius rode back to Caesarea with his cavalry, he thought how his conquest in Joppa would come to the attention of Rome. He was anxious to receive a reward. When he arrived at the camp infirmary with his wounded, he was greeted warmly by Marcus.

"Ebony!" Antonius laughed. "You see before you a god of war."

Marcus was happy again. "Tell us what happened at Joppa," he pleaded.

"I must report to Vespasian first," said Antonius. "He'll want an account of everything. Where's the doctor?"

"He's checking your wounded."

"I can't believe what I'm hearing," Antonius broke into a wide smile. "You, sounding like a man! And what's this?" he tickled his chin. "Is that a beard you're trying to bloom?" Antonius raise his arms to ward off the blows as Marcus punched him playfully. Joseph entered and greeted Antonius coolly.

Zoheleth

"Have you seen the general?" he asked Joseph. "I have my reports for him."

"I believe he's in conference with King Agrippa," said Joseph. "Vespasian has asked Marcus and myself to take the reports on the events at Joppa."

Antonius frowned. "In that case, since both of you will be taking care of the wounded, I'll go to my quarters and freshen up."

"Will you come to our tent tonight?" asked Marcus. "You can tell us then all that happened."

"Is that an invitation?"

"Yes," Marcus replied.

"And what about you, doctor? Am I welcome tonight?"

"I'll be happy to take your reports tonight." Antonius, on his way out shouted. "See you tonight, Ebony!"

"Are you angry with Antonius?" Marcus asked when seeing the physician's disapproving glance.

"Your friend seems to detach himself from the horrors of killing," Joseph complained as the two headed to care for the wounded from Joppa.

"I think Antonius takes the battles as a game."

"Wisely put, young man," Joseph smiled. "And now I need your assistance."

Antonius arrived early evening and Marcus had readily placed out bread and wine for his friend.

"I've heard some reports from your wounded about Joppa," said Joseph. "You're fortunate not to have suffered more injuries. God was with you," he added.

"You foolish old man," Antonius blurted out. "The gods of fortune have favored me!" He glared at the doctor and found it hard to hide his resentment. He hated the Jews with a passion, and Joseph was a Jew.

"Tell us what happened," Marcus begged. "I want to hear every detail of the battle."

Joseph began writing as Antonius related the events.

"We stood on the shore where the enemy had made

their escape from the city. The pirates rowed out far enough so our missiles would fall short." He paused to finish his wine. "It was difficult in the sand to get our projectile machines set up for stones. We had no way to fight them from where we stood."

"How did you fight them?" asked Marcus.

"We could do little without boats of our own. We waited and held back firing on them. We couldn't waste our ammunition."

Marcus stared somewhat confused. "Did the enemy fire at you?"

"They did," he replied as he held out his empty cup. "Now for the exciting part." Marcus refilled his cup and smiled with pleasure. Antonius made life as a soldier an exciting adventure as he boasted about his conquest.

Marcus wondered if he didn't fabricate a bit.

"We watched the pirates making disgusting signs at us," he shook his head. "They cursed us in several languages and laughed at our helplessness. But when the sun began to sink the entire scene changed. A fierce wind arose and blinded our eyes. It whipped and lashed us with powerful gusts."

Joseph stopped writing and looked up. "That was a Black Norther," he informed.

"We had all we could do to keep our footing. We saw the pirate's ships tossed around on the waves." He stared at the oil light as it flickered. "The sea and wind were so wild that their ships were dashed against the rocks. Their ships broke into splinters. I knew the gods were with us."

"Go on, Antonius," Marcus encouraged.

"The men in the boats were tossed out and flung in the air." He made gestures with his hands. "Their boats were like toys and the Jews were drowning." He grinned and looked at Joseph. He knew his report irritated the doctor. "We were drenched from the rain," he continued. "We could only watch the violent attack by nature. Those who tried swimming ashore were met with our swords. The poor devils were killed instantly." Sweat ran down his face from the wine and the heat of the lamp. He wiped his forehead, and noticed the physician's eyes moisten.

"What else do you have to report?" Joseph asked.

Antonius grinned. "It was not a pretty scene seeing the bodies smashed to bloody pulps, and the sea stained red. What else would you like me to say?"

"Since you have wounded men, did you capture any pirates alive?" Joseph asked hopefully.

"Whoever the sea left alive we killed!" he bragged. "By morning the wind died down and the sea withdrew. The shore was draped with carcasses." He wrinkled his nose and added. "By noon, we couldn't stand the stench from the bodies. We left them to rot in the sun."

"Did any Jews escape from you?" asked Marcus.

"I think some in the city ran in the direction of Galilee. They stole a few of our horses for their escape." He frowned as he remembered. "I know the report won't look good on my record, but we were fighting nature and some horses broke loose in the storm."

"You said you killed all the Jews!" Marcus turned belligerent.

"I told you that during the storm some escaped."

"Then, how many did you kill?" he insisted. Joseph looked at him in horror.

"You! Young man!" he said abruptly, glaring at the lad. "Don't be so eager to see blood. It might be your own blood one day on the end of a sword."

Antonius laughed loudly. "I know how you feel Marcus. You want revenge. Don't worry you'll get it." He finished his drink and left the tent.

After a long silence, Marcus said he was sorry for what he said and the way he acted. Joseph nodded and said they had to finished writing the reports of the day.

"Why was Antonius upset about losing some horses?" Marcus asked.

"For a Roman soldier to lose a horse is a serious offense. Especially as a leader of the cavalry."

"But it wasn't Antonius' fault. The horses fled

because of the storm." Marcus defended his friend.

"It was his place to know. A horse is a valuable asset in battle. Soldiers have been put to death for not keeping watch on their horse."

"I think he should be decorated for bravery."

"There wasn't much of a battle, Marcus. Vespasian knows about Antonius' victory at Ashkelon, but everything else has been nothing but blunders."

"Blunders?"

"Antonius disobeyed every order a Roman soldier has been taught. He didn't permit his cavalry to rest. The horses were tired and so were his men. Remember they snuck into the city at night. They should have surrounded the city at night, then at dawn, they would have prevented the pirates from getting to their boats at the shore. They could have fought on land and won!"

Marcus refused to comment, instead he decided to write to his brother. In the letter he told Nicator he had no stomach for real battles. He said working with Joseph he saw another side of war. He asked how Martha was and complained how Nicator had not given him any word from her. He wrote how he depended on his brother to be the one to get a message to her. He reminded Nicator he wanted to marry Martha if she still felt the same.

Tiredness settled in and he rested back on his cot. He tried to sleep, but his dreams were filled with bloody waters with missing limbs floating to the embankments. He woke in a sweat. His dream had headless men walking the shore, and others searching for their hands and missing arms. When sleep did come it was not restful. Only at the sign of daybreak, did he feel safe.

CHAPTER FIFTEEN

THE MEETING

Vespasian was annoyed when he heard there were escapees from Joppa and he was more annoyed when learning that they escaped on Roman horses. He knew the horses were stolen due to lack of surveillance. In the eyes of Vespasian, there was no reason to reward a man for his failures.

King Agrippa was now his immediate concern. The provinces under Agrippa's authority were being overrun by rioting Jews intent on over-powering the Roman rule.

Vespasian, Agrippa, and Titus prepared to march on Gamala, one of Agrippa's troubled provinces. Vespasian took four legions consisting of five hundred soldiers plus the cavalry. It was his hunch that the men who escaped Joppa would join forces with those in Gamala.

The first day they traveled fifteen miles before setting up camp. Titus knew they had at least four days journey ahead before reaching Gamala. Agrippa allowed his sister to travel with the troops for protection. Titus desired to meet privately with Agrippa's sister. Bernice had her own guards, but it was safer to be escorted by foot soldiers assigned by Vespasian. Titus slipped away from camp with his personal guards and headed to her quarters. He hadn't stopped thinking about her since first seeing her in Caesarea. As he approached, he was met by two of her guards.

"Whom shall I announce is calling?" one asked.

"I'm Titus, son of General Vespasian." The guard bowed and stepped back. "I will inform my mistress you're here."

Titus dismounted and handed the reins to his guard. He began pacing the ground while waiting. The longer he waited, the more his heart raced and the more he felt that he was making a fool of himself.

Zoheleth

"My mistress will see you." The guard led the way. He entered her tent and hoped to be alone with her. He had given his men orders to remain outside.

She pulled across a drape and entered the section where he stood waiting.

"Greetings, Queen Bernice," he bowed, and caught his breath when seeing her beauty. "I do hope the escort of our Roman guard serve you well." He found himself struggling to make it appear that his visit was merely out of Roman courtesy. His face flushed as she walked closer to him. She motioned her servant to pour wine.

"I'm delighted to meet you, son of Vespasian," she smiled in a teasing way. "Please join me with some cooled wine."

"Thank you," he whispered, as he took the golden cup which she slowly handed to him. Her dark eyes were enchanting in the glow of the lamps.

He felt her fingertips touch his hand and linger. "Excuse me for staring," he said somewhat ashamed when she noticed. "I've heard of your beauty, and now I see it for myself."

"Such adulation," she replied, "And you, dear Titus, are more handsome than I dreamed."

He drank the wine in an effort to stop shaking. His hands grew more unsteady as he stood before her.

"I wasn't trying to flatter you," he stammered. "I'm being very truthful." He finished the wine.

"I see you resemble your father." Her voice held an admirable tone. "But I must say your boyish face is a thing of beauty."

He could barely control his longing for her when she touched his chin. "I find that dimple rather amusing. Do any of your gods have dimples?"

He laughed and seated himself where she joined him. Her servant refilled his cup. He knew she didn't believe in Roman gods, because she worshiped the God of the Jews.

"Have you taken a good look at our gods?" he smiled. "If you have, you've noticed that some are beyond human beauty, and some are plain hideous."

"I think I've just looked upon one that is not hideous," she answered discretely. "Is there anything you need help with?" she inquired. "I'm more than willing to familiarize you with the practices of my people, as I have done with your father."

"You and your brother have been a great help."

"Then I take it this is more of a social visit?" Her words seemed to melt into his mind as he sat staring into her eyes. He felt helpless in front of this woman of extraordinary beauty.

"Somewhat social," he answered. "I'll be traveling in a different direction after tomorrow," he informed.

"Oh," she murmured, as she moved her cup past her lips. He watched her like a schoolboy, and wished he was the cup touching her mouth.

"My father will travel with your brother to Gamala. Together they'll put down the insurgents there."

"It's devastating to Agrippa," she sighed softly.

"It'll be settled soon," he assured her. "I trust that you are not thrust into the middle of an unhealthy situation," he added. "I'm concerned for your safety." He rose from the seat and offered his hand for her to rise.

"Aren't you the darling," she smiled sweetly and stepped closer to him. Looking into his dark brown eyes, she added, "I do believe you mean it."

He put down the goblet and fought to keep himself calm in her presence.

"As soon as I complete my mission," he said hastily. "I'll join my father, and your brother, at Gamala."

"I'll be looking forward to the day," she replied almost playfully. She was close enough to him that he could smell her perfume. Her body was touching him, and the fullness of her sent a shock through him. She raised herself on her toes and put her hand to his cheek, then, gently kissed the side of his mouth. He couldn't move as he tasted a droplet of wine from her lips.

"May our God watch over you, son of Vespasian,"

she whispered before stepping back.

He grabbed her hand and gently kissed it.

"Until we meet in your homeland," he bowed. He left her tent, and his heart pumped wildly in his chest. He looked back and saw her standing in the light of the doorway. She waved and sent a kiss through the air.

He wanted to walk all the way back to camp so he could dream of this evening. He wanted to sing under the stars for the rest of the night. His heart was filled with joy. He was in love with a goddess.

His men had to remind him it was a long journey back to camp. He heard them laughing and knew they guessed he had taken the fall, but no one dared ask. He mounted his horse and gave his private guards a run for their lives.

She stood in the doorway of her tent until she could no longer see his outline. She held the hand he kissed. She didn't want the evening to end as she gazed to the heavens. She thought the stars were unusually bright this night. Bernice felt like a young girl who had just fallen in love. Was this the joy that made her sing that night not so long ago?

STACKED HOUSES

Titus and his men were on route to Galilee. Vespasian and Agrippa were now in Gamala, the province of which Agrippa held rule. Agrippa was unable to get back into the city since the sedition broke loose. He stationed part of his army outside Gamala. He complained to Vespasian.

"After I settled things in Jerusalem," he said. "I came to Gamala only to find a revolution had broke out in the city. I was blocked from entering. My men have tried breaking through these walls for the past seven months. General, you can see how discouraged the men are."

"Let's allow your men some good drinking for the night. They'll perk up with seeing our re-enforcements."

Vespasian and Agrippa made plans on how to target the city walls.

The morning sky was a bright blue and a few clouds touched the tips of the mountains. The rising sun glared into the eyes of Agrippa and Vespasian as they sat mounted on their horses and surveyed Gamala. The soldiers were now formed in squadrons awaiting their orders.

Agrippa admired Vespasian. He saw a man of bull-like strength. His wide neck and broad shoulders displayed thick muscles from years of fierce battles.

"I grow tired of all the devastation," said Vespasian as he turned and glanced at Agrippa. "The towns we rode through should have been filled with children playing, instead we find the roads lined with the bodies of old men and women."

Agrippa shook his head. "I've seen babies left to die, and young girls slaughtered and evidence of rape. I don't understand what has happened to this world."

"I had to stop Titus from desiring to bury the dead," said Vespasian. "You never know when the soldiers lay down their weapons to dig, they could be attacked."

Zoheleth

"I understand," said Agrippa. "I must warn you about this city we are confronting. Gamala is one of the strongest cities in my province. It was at one time under the command of the Jewish general, Josephus."

"Ah!" Vespasian smiled. "He's my prisoner."

"Yes, you know the people of Jerusalem have turned against him? They believe he sold out to the Romans by allowing himself to be captured."

"I guess he has a fondness for life!" Vespasian laughed. "Let's ride closer to the walls of this impregnable city." Vespasian surveyed the land surrounding Gamala.

"The soil looks rich from here," he noted.

"Rich it is," Agrippa boasted. "We have plantations of fruit trees as far as the eye can see." He pointed south.

"How many people would you say live in Gamala?"

"On the level of fifteen thousand," Agrippa replied.

The general shook his head. "How sad," he sighed. "There's no sound of merry-making at this harvest time. No feasting or singing. Your people have no reason to celebrate. Why would they forfeit their joy in order to subdue the Romans?"

Agrippa had no answer. He moved his horse next to the general. They rode to a hill overlooking Gamala. He thought about his allegiance with Rome. He was appointed king of the Jews as his father before him, Herod Agrippa I. He was seventeen when his father died, and too young to take control of his father's territories. Later, Rome gave him a kingdom after his uncle died, Herod II, who was the king of Chalus.

Agrippa was favored by Emperor Nero, and was appointed as high priest of the temple in Jerusalem, a position which he held with great pride. It was not long after, that Nero enlarged Agrippa's domains outward to Galilee. The cities included areas of Perea, Pella, and Gamala.

Vespasian interrupted Agrippa's thoughts. "I see a spot where we might approach the city." He pointed out the area to Agrippa.

Zoheleth

"There's trenches dug out to impede any access."

"There must be a weak spot," said Vespasian. "How about persuading your people to surrender? They surely see the power of our forces."

Agrippa thought for a moment. "I can make the effort," he replied. He motioned his men. "Cover me. I'll try talking some sense into them."

He approached the walls and shouted to the watchman and offered them a chance to surrender and save Gamala from destruction. Their answer came in a barrage of stones. Agrippa heard the people cursing him for joining forces with the Romans and declared him their enemy.

Vespasian rode to Agrippa. "Looks like they'll insist on challenging Rome!" They encircled the outer walls to decide their next move.

"I see houses built on steep slopes," he said to Agrippa. "What mysterious force keeps them from falling down on each other?"

"That remains a mystery," Agrippa smiled. "Have you come up with any ideas?"

"We'll start with earth works," Vespasian declared. He instructed his army to fill in the trenches and all the ravines. The work was completed within hours and he inspected the embankments for stability.

"Bring the siege engines into position," he ordered, "and press on with the siege!" The Roman legions worked feverishly to make ready the way for the battle.

Agrippa sent one of his men to spy on the city. He knew the man was a respected resident of Gamala. He offered him much gold after he agreed to help.

When the men inside the city saw the siege machines, they ran outside to keep the Romans from stationing the engines. Vespasian signaled his men to use the stone-projectors and shower the enemy. It worked. The battering rams were at three locations. They were set into motion and fiercely plunged against the stone walls.

The iron ram's head took the blows repeatedly until a portion of the wall gave way. The enemy sent down a steady

Zoheleth

hail of stones on the Romans, but an appointed group of soldiers used shields to protect the men operating the rams.

The soldiers broke through the wall and stormed the city. The men of Gamala fought off the Romans, but General Vespasian continued sending fresh troops to overwhelm the insurgents by volume.

The enemy retreated to the upper portion of the city. The Romans never fell back, which was a mistake.

Vespasian viewed every move his troops made and suddenly he cried out.

"By all the gods of Rome!" he cursed in anguish. "My soldiers!" he screamed.

Agrippa was shocked by what he saw. The Roman legions were at a disadvantage. It was a nightmare for any general to witness. The men of Gamala had the best advantage on high to assault those below.

"My men will never make it up those slopes!" Vespasian shouted. In disbelief, he watched his men forging their way upward, while the enemy sent them to their death as they slipped down the steep passages.

"Damn!" Vespasian yelled. "The men have no room to retreat! Why don't the soldiers behind them stop forging upward?"

"Look!" Agrippa shouted. "The soldiers are taking refuge on the roofs of the houses."

The general thought it was a good move, but what happened next shocked Agrippa and Vespasian. The houses couldn't hold the weight of the soldiers and began collapsing. They gave way like water bursting through a dam, and the houses above took the houses below. The cavalcade of houses brought the soldiers down with them and buried them beneath the rubble.

Agrippa prayed to the God of the Jews and the general called on his gods. He watched his men die in the ruins while others suffocated from the dust that rose like a volcanic ash.

Vespasian, in his fury, kicked his horse to a gallop. He summoned more men to follow him into the city.

Zoheleth

"Romans!" he shouted while he sped to the walls. "Shield yourselves and get out of the city! RETREAT! RETREAT!" he ordered his men trapped inside Gamala. With his sword high over his head, he took no precautions for his own safety as he forged onward.

The foot soldiers positioned their shields in the formation of the "tortoise" and marched. They were a walking wall with their shields knitted closely together that nothing could penetrate. They continued until they rescued the remaining soldiers and brought them outside the ramparts. Vespasian fought valiantly with the calvary. He thrashed the attackers fiercely and made them flee.

The senseless loss of men lay heavy on the heart of Vespasian. The spirit of the Romans were dampened when they learned how many of their comrades had died.

THE RETREAT

After the legions were forced to retreat from Gamala. Vespasian stood in great perplexity looking at his troops.

"Forgive us, General," one of the rescued called out. "You put yourself in great danger by coming to save us."

The General's eyes were moist when seeing his men beaten, forlorn, and weary. They were covered in ash and looked like an army of ghosts. The morale of the men fell when hearing the celebrations in the city over the Roman's defeat. Vespasian had to speak to his men.

"Take courage, my comrades. Our loss was due to the difficult slopes you were forced to fight from."

"But the enemy has taken the weapons from our dead comrades and they'll use them against us!" one soldier cried out.

Vespasian shuddered. "Take heart!" He mounted his horse so all could hear his speech. "We will not, I repeat, we will not be defeated!" he paused. "Since our comrades have given their lives for us, we, as Romans, must not allow their deaths to be in vain." He raised his hand to continue his speech. The men grew quiet and waited for his encouraging words.

"We've had a harsh lesson. One which we'll not allow to happen again. We'll avenge the deaths of our comrades!" The legions were stirred and in one accord with him.

Vespasian knew the men who escaped death, suffered from guilt as well as grief. He had to encourage their spirit.

"Legions of Rome!" he shouted. "I am here now only because of your courage when escaping the city. If it were not for your courage, I would be among the dead." This touched the men deeply and some broke down and wept in front of their fellow comrades.

"Bear manfully what war presents!" He went on to

Zoheleth

elaborate. "We can't conquer without bloodshed and death. A good warrior is one of a sober mind under misfortunes. One who will take courage with zeal and come against those who provoked this battle!"

The legions began cheering. He waited and went on. "We perform by skill and good order. Those in Gamala are barbarians! We'll avenge the deaths of our comrades!" They took heart in his speech. "I, personally, will lead you against the enemy." He raised his sword. "I will be the first to enter Gamala, and I will be the last to retire from the enemy. I swear by all the gods of Rome!"

The soldiers were striking their shields which made such a racket it drifted into the enemy's ground. Those in Gamala ceased their celebrating. Vespasian knew when the enemy heard such a racket that it would frighten them. He'd seen it before. Many times it made the enemy surrender willingly. The reputation of the Roman Legions had the power to put fear in the hearts of the bravest men. The Tenth Legion, under his command, was the biggest threat to any country in its wake. He ordered the legions to rest. Tomorrow they would enter Gamala once more.

Before dawn, Vespasian was awakened by his body guard.

"What is it?" he asked roughly.

"A courier has brought news from Galilee," said the guard.

"Give it here, man!" He grabbed the note, and the guard lit a lamp. Vespasian held the letter close to the light.

Greetings Father from Titus.

We set up our camps three miles from the shore of Lake Genneasar. Those who escaped from Joppa saw us on the march. They fled to their boats to escape us. We had no transportation for water, so I ordered the men to cut trees and build rafts. We pursued the fugitives and they met with unsympathetic hands when we reached their small skiffs. They panicked as we toppled them one by one. Those who tried to climb on our rafts, lost their hands, and some their

Zoheleth

heads. There was no second chance for them to surrender. They had that chance in Joppa.
This will finish the pirates who wished to invade the shores. Some of my men are injured, but no deaths. Praise the gods of Rome for another victory!
We're on our way to join you at Gamala. I hope fortune favored you in your venture. We'll make our sacrifices to the gods together as we become victorious over the nations.

Vespasian smiled. Titus' arrival was bound to bolster the morale of the legions since he would come with more warriors to join in the destruction of Gamala.

Vespasian felt refreshed after a hearty breakfast. He smiled when Agrippa entered his tent.

"Good morning, General," said Agrippa. "The news from my spy is not what you would like to hear. He tells me the men of Gamala worked all night repairing the wall we broke through."

Vespasian struck his chest and released a belch. "Well then, we'll see to it they can't complete their work. What else have you learned from your informant?"

"The leader of the rebels, an elderly man named Chares, has concern about their food supply."

"Now that's what I like to hear."

"If you're thinking they'll surrender soon, I wouldn't get your hopes up."

Vespasian sensed something. "Is there other news you care to tell me?"

"I hate to tell you this, but my spy has informed me the rebels killed our wounded soldiers."

"What!" Vespasian paced the ground and cursed loudly. "What kind of people are we dealing with?" he ranted. "Such a policy is repulsive to humanity."

"Perhaps you would like to know their leader, Chares, is in poor health. It may be the turning point of the battle should he expire."

"Perhaps we can hasten his exit from life." Vespasian grinned. "When Chares sees Titus arriving with

Zoheleth

more troops, he'll become faint of heart." He peered at Agrippa and asked. "Tell me, where does Gamala's water supply come from?"

"There's a spring outside the walls of the city," Agrippa informed.

"Interesting," said Vespasian. "We'll hold off attacking until Titus arrives. If things are bad in the city, we shall give it enough time to worsen."

"A war of nerves?"

"Yes. Our men can use the rest."

"One other piece of news," said Agrippa as he smiled slightly. "Some people have deserted the city though the night."

"Then things are looking up for us." Vespasian was interrupted by his guard beckoning them to come outside.

Agrippa and the general saw what the guard had spotted. Outside the walls of Gamala a group of men had gathered at the water supply.

Vespasian ordered his men to offer the rebels the hand of Rome. The cavalry rode to the spring and offered peace to the people. Suddenly, without provocation they attacked fiercely and showed no sign of surrendering.

Agrippa and Vespasian watched the Romans retreating, but before the rebels could get back inside the walls, the cavalry turned and galloped into the group without warning and killed every rebel on the spot.

The general smiled with pride. A group from inside Gamala fled on horseback. It was easy to see they were heading to Jerusalem. Vespasian signaled not to pursue them.

"We'll meet them in Jerusalem!" he bellowed. There was nothing like a victory to lift the spirits of his men. Nothing like the taste of wine to celebrate and make the men forget their previous losses. The Roman camp was once again alive!

The following day, Titus arrived.

Vespasian embraced his son. "We've been waiting your return. I thank the gods for protecting you."

Zoheleth

"How's the battle with Gamala, father?"

"Nothing I care to talk about," Vespasian answered. "The only thing in our favor is the rebels are running low on food. We've secured the passage to their water spring outside the wall."

"Tata," said Titus softly. "You look weary."

Vespasian smiled when he heard him address him as Tata, an endearing name by which children addressed their father, but never in public.

"My son, we've taken a sad loss. Sit and I'll tell you all after you've eaten and had some wine."

Agrippa sensing their need for privacy, excused himself.

Titus entered his father's tent, which was quartered into several rooms. One section was divided off as a bedroom. Another room he used for entertaining. The floor had rugs and in the center were folding chairs and tables. The walls displayed paintings his father had obtained from the lands he conquered. They talked for several hours and shared their accomplishments and their disappointments.

"Father, we'll invade Gamala. Allow me to call several of my trusted men and we'll design its destruction." Vespasian was in favor.

Titus called upon men from the Fifteenth Legion. He carefully instructed them in his plans to put Gamala under their feet.

"We're sending you on a dangerous mission," Titus informed. "You're to sneak under the high tower inside the city while the people sleep."

His men studied the map and memorized the area inside the city. They planned to use a passwords in the dark to give the signal when their task was completed.

"Agippa tells me he has a man inside who will give you entrance into the city when it's dark," he went on. "The rebels are losing strength due to lack of food." He went on to explain how they were to operate once inside.

"You will undermine their Tower by removing the largest stones holding its foundation. Then, you must escape

Zoheleth

the city before the tower collapses!" The men accepted the challenge.

"My father will have two hundred horsemen ready, along with foot soldiers, who will enter quietly while you work on the stones," he added. "Our general has informed me he's lost two of his noblest officers and too many of his bravest men!" Titus felt himself choking up. "We must avenge our comrades. My father wants you to know it will be he who will lead the attack once he gets your signal."

The men saluted Titus and Vespasian. They left to establish their own methods of undermining the tower.

That night, the plans proceeded. Around the morning-watch, the soldiers of Titus were successful in removing the stones and escaped before the tower toppled. A great noise awakened the watchmen of Gamala, and the people in the city were greatly confused.

Their leader, Chares, tried to calm them, but in his own fright, he appeared to suffer a stroke or heart failure. His followers wailed when seeing Chares dead. It was a bad omen for Gamala especially when they found Titus inside the city. The people fled in panic, stumbling over their own countrymen.

The soldiers came like swarms of locusts and killed continually. Vespasian led his men to assist Titus. They fought side-by-side. While the battle raged, the rebels fled to the upper part of the city. Vespasian knew they would have the advantage. Remembering the misfortune of his men, he was ready to call the troops back, but a sudden storm blew up. The winds increased in strength and added heavy rains.

The rebels headed to the high cliffs and tried to entice the Romans to follow. Then, as if by divine intervention, the enemy's darts fell short. The Roman's darts took flight with the wind sending them upward to their targets. Thousands of rebels were slain and others took their own life rather than be captured.

When the savage attack was over, Agrippa joined Titus and Vespasian and they rode through the city. The soldiers were permitted to ransack the houses for booty.

Agrippa congratulated Vespasian and Titus. He told Vespasian he would remain in the city and try to regain his rule and get things on an even keel.

"Son," said Vespasian as he faced Titus. "I want you to finish the work I can't finish here."

"What is it, Father?"

"I must return to Caesarea. We may have word from Rome. I'll write to Rome of our conquest." His expression changed. "You must go to Gischala and set things in order. Agrippa has received word of a sedition in that city. Since he must remain in Gamala, you must be the one to restore the peace there."

Titus was not pleased with the orders. Inwardly he hoped Gischala would be more responsive to peace.

He was growing tired of the constant battles with the riotous Jews. He wanted to rush back to Bernice who was waiting for him.

He thought of his victory at Galilee. It was done to honor her. She was all he could think about during the battles. The desire to see her was the driving force that brought him a fast victory. He wanted to be with his Queen. He would hold her in his arms as he did in his dreams, just to have the nights filled with love instead of war.

Zoheleth

A.D. 67 DECEMBER
JOHN OF GISCHALA

All who fled from Gamala did not go in the direction of Jerusalem. Some who fled through the night headed to Gischala.

John, a resident of Gischala, had helped defend Gamala, but when he saw Titus arriving with more Roman troops, he and his men deserted the city. They rode into Gischala to warn the people.

"Gamala has fallen!" he shouted. "The Romans have left it in ruins." The frightened citizens gathered to learn of his news. John raised his voice for the people to hear.

"The Roman legions will demolish Gischala next! We must prepare to defend our city," he impressed.

There were those of Gischala who had no faith in John. It was rumored that he spent his nights hiding in the cliffs after robbing unsuspecting travelers. He was known to band together all sorts of renegades to join him.

Pheroras, a prominent elder of the city, made his way through the crowds. He announced to the people that the city should surrender to the Romans.

John was annoyed. "Why?" he demanded.

"It's better than having bloodshed," Pheroras implored as he gazed suspiciously at John. "We don't want to lose everything we've worked for all our lives."

John pulled the reigns of his horse. "Then," he questioned, "you'll allow Gischala to fall the same way Gamala did?"

"We are farmers," one man spoke out. "What have we to do with war?"

John grew impatient. "You may never farm again if the Romans decide to attack. You will slave for the Romans if they capture the city."

"If we offer no resistance," said Pheroras, "the

Romans won't take us as prisoners or as slaves."

"You haven't seen what happened in Gamala," John challenged.

"John, you and your band of cutthroats and thieves, thrive on fighting. We are husbandmen and will not join you if you so desire to bring destruction on our city," Pheroras stated.

John was increasingly irritated. He needed the majority to support him.

"If you've made up your mind," he said after much thought, "let me inform you that General Vespasian has returned to Caesarea, but his son, Titus, is on the way to attack this city."

Pheroras thought for a moment. "I hear he is more than a fair man. One who doesn't want bloodshed."

John spun his horse around and glared at Pheroras. "It was Titus who finished off Gamala!" he declared.

The people talked among themselves, but John didn't want to give them much time. "Do you know what the Tenth Legion can do?" he shouted as the people turned to Pheroras. A cloud of doom seemed to fall over the crowd.

"Shall we submit?" Pheroras asked the people. They hesitated and John thought them pathetic fools.

"You grieve over Gamala," he added. "Yet you're reluctant to protect your own property. You must make a decision soon!" he demanded.

They debated and finally Pheroras spoke. "We have decided to take a peaceful stand," he announced.

This angered John. He glanced maliciously at the old man. He feared Titus would find him. He was sure by now it was discovered it was he and his men who had attacked the soldiers from Ashkelon. This was why they fled the caves and had gone to Gamala. Now he might be forced to flee Gischala. John hated the son of Vespasian, but could in no way come against the Romans without the support of the people of Gischala. He figured a way to trick them. He would agree to a peaceful strategy.

"If it's peace you want, then we should talk." He saw

Zoheleth

his men looking at him puzzled. "I'll go along with a peaceful settlement," he declared.

"We're willing to listen," said Pheroras, looking with intense scrutiny.

"Allow me to represent the city," John suggested. "Since you're not all of one mind, then I can arrange to send ambassadors ahead to meet with Titus before he enters."

The people considered his offer.

"Do you plan to divert Titus from entering?" questioned Pheroras.

"Not divert him, but to welcome him to enter after he and his men have rested."

The majority were ready to go along with John. He was elated to have fooled them. He didn't want Titus to place a garrison in the city. His group were in desperate need of money and planned to rob the people while they slept. "We'll give you security," he assured the people. "My men will guard the walls tonight and I'll stand guard by the gates," he added. "You can feel safe in your homes this evening."

Pheroras was not happy about leaving the security of the city in John's hands. Still he advised everyone to return to their homes and prepare for the coming Sabbath. He did feel certain that John wouldn't turn against his own countrymen, and by Jewish law, he wouldn't break the Sabbath. He offered John his assistance, but John convinced him the city was in capable hands.

Titus and his legions arrived outside the city shortly before sundown. He scanned the area and saw Gischala could be easily conquered. The city was small and its walls were not great in structure. He learned that the people were farmers and husbandmen. Some of the finest fruits in the nation were cultivated by the people of Gischala. There were no signs of any threat as he rode around the walls. Had Agrippa given him the wrong impression? He remembered that it was mentioned there could be an uprising if the escapees from Gamala reached Gischala.

He was anxious to garrison the city and capture the escapees who fled from Gamala. He didn't want these rebels to stir the people into fighting against the Romans. He soon learned through one of his men, that the city sheltered a notorious band of thieves headed by a man named John, the son of Levi. It was learned they were the same culprits who attacked the soldiers from Ashkelon. He had good reason now to get inside the city.

"We'll camp far enough from the walls for the watchmen to see our strength," Titus suggested. "When we enter," he added, "seek out one named John. I want him and his band of thieves."

The legion displayed their mighty engines for the people to witness what they would be facing. He allowed his men to do mock battles to put a scare into those watching. He hoped Gischala would forfeit the battle willingly and he could be on his way to Bernice.

Inside Gischala, John put his plans into action. "I'll send two men as ambassadors to greet Titus." He grinned through his thin lips, and rubbed his pockmarked face.

His phony ambassadors met with Titus and when they returned, they had a message for the people of the city.

"Titus offers the right hand of Rome," said one man who was appointed as an ambassador, "if the residents of the city will allow him to enter unprovoked."

John smiled. "Isn't that convenient. Take this message back to him. Explain to Titus it's the coming of the Sabbath and he ought to have regard for the Jewish law. It's unlawful for the Jews to make a treaty on the Sabbath."

His men returned with an answer. "Titus wishes you to know he's not ignorant of the fact that the Jews cease from all labor on the Sabbath. He has agreed with the terms."

"Good!" John laughed. "He doesn't suspect a thing."

"Titus will comply with the conditions," said the

Zoheleth

acting ambassador. "He said he and his men could use the rest."

"Ah! That's more than I hoped for." said John.

He and his men made it appear they were settled for the night. He noted the Romans hadn't placed guards around the city. This gave his men the opportunity to do what they planned. A group of his thieves quietly broke into the homes of the rich and robbed them. Another group stole the horses and walked them to the gates of the city.

"John," called one man softly. "I can't leave my family behind to face the Romans."

"Families will hold us back!" John said angrily. "We've only enough horses for ourselves."

"I won't go without them!" said the man. Suddenly John found more of his men feeling the same way.

"You're all fools!" he said through the dark. "How can we be burdened with your families?" He found them reluctant to go and finally agreed to their insistent request.

"You can bring them, but they must follow on foot," he ordered. The men grumbled, but settled for John's terms.

The journey was slow after leaving Gischala. The moon gave no light and the night was darker than usual, which helped John's men not to be seen by the Romans.

When the passing clouds broke, the moon gave its light, they were able to speed along on the horses. Their destination-Jerusalem. John was sure the zealots and the sacarii would allow him to join them to come against Rome.

Hours had passed, but the women with children could not walk fast and began to fall behind. Their husbands heard their cries and grew alarmed. The men stopped their horses to turn back for their families.

"My family is lost out there! I must rescue them," cried one man.

John rode up to him and grabbed the reigns of the horse. "You can search for your family but not with a horse."

"I'll never find them!" he cried desperately.

"You whimpering swine!" John spat on the ground.

"Can't you get it through your thick skull that we're wanted men. When it's daybreak, the Romans will be hot on our trail!"

"What will happen to my children?" one man wept.

"Your family knows where we're heading. The Romans will ride past the women and children. It's us they will hunt down!"

John impressed the urgency for a speedy pace before dawn. The husbands relented. Some wept openly while turning away from their families.

"Look, men!" John shouted. "There's the lights of Jerusalem up ahead."

The men forced the horses into a gallop toward the city, no longer showing concern about the women and children left behind, lost, hungry and thirsty.

At sunrise back at Gischala, Titus gave the orders to march into the city. He expected to be met by the ambassadors as agreed, but instead he was met by the peaceful citizens who eagerly opened the gates to him.

"Where are the men who made the terms which I honored?" he demanded as he rode forward. "Why are they not here to present themselves?"

Pheroras spoke. "They were the men of John."

"Are you telling me that you sent his men to present an agreement with me?" Titus was angered.

"I regret to inform you, noble Titus," said Pheroras as he bowed. "We had no idea what John did. He and his men robbed our homes through the night, and have taken our horses from the city."

Titus was furious at being tricked. "I should have killed them on the spot, these false ambassadors."

"Please," Pheroras pleaded. "We offer Rome no resistance."

"Are they armed?" Titus asked.

Pheroras hung his head in shame. "All the arms in the city are missing. I beg of you, do not retaliate against the innocent."

"By the gods," Titus cried out. "I'll hunt them down if it takes me the rest of my life!"

"Spare us, Titus," begged the citizens. He knew they had been victimized and replied, "You will not suffer punishment for John's trickery. You have my oath."

His men were sent to pursue John. After several hours, the Romans returned with hundreds of deserted women and children who were left to die on the plains.

"One more offensive act by a defiant scum!" Titus declared as he trembled in rage.

He shouted at the helpless people for following John. The children were brought to tears as they clung to their mothers.

"Titus, what shall we do with the people?" asked an officer.

"They should have their homes burned to the ground for what they have done," Titus answered. "Instead, have half the wall of the city pulled down."

The men of Gischala were bitter at this decision. It was a disgrace to them, because it would show they had been conquered. But they could do little to prevent it.

Before Titus left the city, he placed a garrison within. He didn't have the heart to punish the people any further.

He sent a messenger to the palace where Bernice resided. He requested her to come to Caeseara where he would be joining his father. His message read how he would like to take up from where they left off. Titus never forgot the touch of her lips against his face. He was madly in love with her, and had the feeling Queen Bernice was well aware of his passions.

Zoheleth

THEOPHILUS

The watchmen opened Jerusalem's gates to John and his men. They entered boldly and were met by crowds of anxious people wanting to hear what news they brought.

John dismounted and smiled through broken teeth. His smile faded as he raised his arms to silence the crowd.

"Let me catch my breath," he coughed. "For those who don't know me, I'm John of Gischala, the son of Levi. I've come to report the events at Gamala."

The city of Jerusalem was noted as a fountain of news and the people rallied around John. They were curious about his hurried entrance. They never suspected he was a fugitive on the run.

John saw a high priest coming through the crowd. He stood in front of John and looked with a fixed gaze.

"You and your men appear to be under great distress," said the high priest, Theophilus. "Tell us, are you fleeing from the Romans?"

"Never!" John lied. "But I come to warn you that the Romans are on their way here. You must make ready your defense of the capital."

"I have heard no rumors," Theophilus replied. "Your announcement comes as a surprise." The priest paused and glanced around at the crowd gathering. "What is this threat you speak about?"

"We have escaped from Gamala," John began. "The Romans struck the city with such force that we had to warn the people of Gischala how Gamala had fallen."

The people of Jerusalem were shocked by this news.

"What happened in Gamala?" asked the priest. "And what about Gischala. Why did you leave there?"

"To warn this city of what has occurred," he implied as he mounted his horse to allow the multitude to hear.

"People of Jerusalem," he announced loudly. "We

Zoheleth

have no idea what has happened in Gischala since we left, but Titus was camped there and preparing to seize the city." He held back the truth as he continued his propaganda. "We find it urgent to warn you should the Romans head this way. We are willing to join you in protecting Jerusalem."

Some people thanked him and praised him for his courage to warn them. The young men of the city gathered when they heard the Romans might come into the city. John saw their youthful eagerness to be ready to fight.

"Young men!" he shouted. "You are the strength of this city. Don't fear the Romans!" he persuaded. "They have a love-sick Titus as their leader. One who wishes his life to be spared for the sake of King Agrippa's sister."

Some citizens laughed, but John had to find a way to incite those who were outraged with Rome and the tax collectors.

One elder of the city spoke. "We might look upon Titus' love for Agrippa's sister as favorable," he smiled and continued. "If Bernice has any influence over the son of Vespasian, we could be spared. Remember how Bernice came to our defense when Florus was here."

John glared at him. "That's an assumption, sir," he disputed. "It's the orders from Rome which Titus will obey, not a Jewess." A silence fell over the crowd. "You know Rome has had three emperors in the past eighteen months," John stated. "Rome has civil disruptions, along with the riots created by the zealots in the provinces of Rome."

"It makes sense!" shouted one youth. "We should make this our time for readiness to defend our city." The young man turned to his companions and asked. "Are we willing to fight?" They began cheering in agreement.

"I like your spirit, young man," said John. "Look around, do you think the Romans will grow wings to fly over these great walls shielding Jerusalem?"

He stirred the youths and they began raising their fists in the air and yelling, "We'll forge weapons!" The hot-blooded young men followed suit. At last John had the youth of Jerusalem on his side.

Zoheleth

Theophilus stepped in front of the young men and demanded their silence. "Hold your eagerness to start a war!" he commanded. "We don't know if what John says is true. Ask yourself where this man will lead us?"

His words angered John, but he began smiling when he heard the young men mocking the old priest. Theophilus frowned and seemed caught in the middle.

The people were divided: the enthusiastic young men eager for war, and the old citizens wanting peace.

Theophilus gave some thought to the situation. "When do you think the Romans will march on Jerusalem?" he asked rather timidly. "I hold much contempt for encouraging war, but I have a duty as a priest. This duty calls for defending the city if it deems necessary."

"We believe Titus will join forces with his father in Caesarea and head to Jerusalem." John went on to elaborate. "Remember it was the Jews of Jerusalem who captured the rear division of the Roman Twelfth Legion," he paused. "Governor Gallus was disgraced and Rome will call for retaliation." He paused again. "Of course, the procurator, Florus, added problems by fabricating the workings of the Jews in this city. Rome has no idea who reports the truth."

"You may be right," said the priest. "While the Romans are stationed at Caesarea, it gives us time to prepare ourselves before they decide to move against us."

"They will come!" John affirmed. "Rome will want retaliation, since the Roman garrisons have been slain by the zealots."

"I must agree with you," said Theophilus. He turned to face his people. "We may choose not to listen to John, or be foolish and find ourselves defenseless when an attack occurs. We should carefully consider what has already occurred in Gamala, and possibly in Gischala."

Some of the citizens challenged the priest and John. One man came forth. "I've heard of you, John, son of Levi," he pointed an accusing finger. "You are known as a liar and a thief!" He turned to the priest and continued his accusations.

Zoheleth

"You, Theophilus, as high priest," he stated, "would allow a band of thieves to lead us into a war with Rome?"

John pulled back on the reigns of his horse to be ready for an escape should the people turn against him. He grew impatient with the citizens expressing their disapproval of Theophilus, since they saw he was being swayed by John.

"Hold on!" Theophilus said in a strong resolute tone of command. "How is it you dare to insult a man who has risked his life to warn us? He and his men have offered to join in protecting the city."

The man stood defiantly before the priest. "I've heard of John's tactics," he insisted. "I've no personal dealings with the man, but I know of those who have been at his mercy." The mood of the crowd was changing, but the priest demanded respect from his people.

"We have never refused our fellow countrymen entrance to this city," he reminded them. "You are acting in a hostile fashion to John and his followers."

One elder spoke out contemplatively. "Forgive me, Theophilus, I mean no insult, but it is my impression that John and his men are seeking refuge behind our walls."

"So be it!" declared the priest. "John and his men are welcome to a refuge."

John spoke loudly to interrupt the elder.

"Men of Jerusalem!" he announced, and the crowd grew quiet. "I recall when only a handfull of dedicated men were able to reduce Gallus to shame. These same men, without swords, sent Florus running for his life!"

The youths were encouraged as they recalled the defeat of Gallus. They began laughing about the episodes with Governor Gallus and Florus. The temperament of the crowd had now changed from doubts to courage.

John caught a glimmer in the eye of the priest and wondered if there wasn't a touch of evil behind his religious mask. John put forth an effort to hold back his malice as the people continued to complain among themselves.

"Listen to your priest," John said diabolically. "Your high priest thinks the city should be defended. He wants you to make the choice to defend your homes and your families." Murmurs kept rolling through the crowd.

"People of God!" Theophilus called out. "Have we not come against greater perils?" he reminded them. "We are not strangers to tribulation. Let us use wisdom and spare our families by defending our holy city."

"What about John?" yelled one who challenged the priest. "Are you going to permit him to remain when you don't know if he tells the truth?"

"I see no reason not to believe John," said the priest. "He could have fled to other parts of the nation and not warned us of the impending dangers."

John saw his own men smiling with satisfaction. His band dismounted and joined the priest to discuss the possibilities of war with Rome.

From the back of the crowd an elder called. "Theophilus!" he cried out in a trembling voice. "I heard your decision. Beware priest!" he warned with a wagging finger. "Bring to mind the prophecy spread among the Christians. They said Jesus warned the people when they see the armies surrounding Jerusalem, know that her desolation would be at hand" (Luke 21:20).

The high priest turned to face him. "It's all pure superstitious gossip!" he replied. "We have God on our side and we'll not lose the battle, even if it's with Rome!"

The young men quickly headed to the workshops to forge weapons. Word spread through the city of a possible attack by the Romans. Some people panicked while others looked forward to defeat the Roman rule forever.

In the market place of Jerusalem, Metilius, the spy sent by Vespasian, was disguised as a traveler. He maintained a low profile while learning the plans of John. He witnessed the forging of weapons, and saw the young men testing their skills for battle. It was time to leave the city and alert Vespasian of the preparations being made by the Jews for a war against Rome.

When the merchants closed for the night, he gathered his belongings and left by one of the tunnels beneath the city.

Zoheleth

He made haste to the stable and paid for his horse and headed toward Caesarea.

The moon was hidden by a dark cloud and his escape was easy. If he rode all night, he would need only one change of horses and a short rest before he reached the Roman camps.

Zoheleth

THE RETURN

Marcus Severus was using a long hollow reed to blow air under the skin of the dead goats to separate their skin from the carcass. He laughed when an officer's slave asked if he knew how to tie the open ends of the skins. He informed the man that his brother, Nicator, taught him the skill.

While walking back to camp with the skins over his shoulders, he thought about Nicator. He recalled how his brother would put a goat skin on his head and chase him around the stable. Marcus laughed when he remembered how it scared him and he would run crying to his mother.

Joseph looked up when Marcus entered the tent and dropped the skins to the floor.

"Some of our wine skins have dried and cracked," he said.

"Good of you to replace them," Joseph replied. "In your travels did you hear of Vespasian returning?"

"I did hear the soldiers talking," said Marcus. "Will we go to meet them?"

"I think we can be present when they arrive," Joseph answered. He watched Marcus wash his hands in vinegar and water to remove the odor.

"I'm finished my reports," said Joseph. "We can join the soldiers when they meet the general."

Marcus freshened his appearance by brushing his black curly hair and tucking it under a clean turban. He changed his robe and oiled his sandals.

Outside, they saw the legions standing in line. When the general arrived they began chanting in a rhythm. "Ves-pa-si-an! Ves-pa-si-an!"

The general waved and greeted the legions. Later he dismissed them.

Marcus was impressed by the display of admiration

the legions had shown to their leader. On the way back to the tent he questioned Joseph. "Do you know Vespasian personally?"

"Somewhat," said Joseph as they strolled between the soldiers. "Why do you ask?"

"I wondered about his family background."

"I recall his grandfather fought alongside of the great General Pompey. He was a centurion who secured an honorable army discharge. He later became a tax-collector."

"What was his name?"

"If my memory serves me, it was Titus Flavius Petro. He had a son named Sabinus, like your father."

"What happened to Sabinus?"

"He was in command of a cohort but due to poor health he resigned." They pushed their way though the soldiers to reach their tent. Joseph continued. "I understand he took up tax-collecting as his father before him. He was known as an honest tax-gather."

"I see that Vespasian has followed his father and grandfather in the service of their country," said Marcus.

Joseph smiled and added, "I recall that Sabinus turned to banking before he died. He left a wife with two sons to raise on her own. Sabinus and his younger brother Vespasian.

"Is Vespasian's brother a soldier?"

"No, he's in Rome. He holds the rank of city prefect." The physician noticed a group of injured soldiers being taken to the infirmary. "Let's hurry, Marcus, we have much work ahead of us."

When they arrived they found the wounded lined up outside the entrance. The infirmary was filled to capacity. Joseph looked in despair and had to send the less seriously wounded to another camp infirmary. He kept the severely injured in his infirmary.

Vespasian entered while Joseph was attending a man in need of surgery.

"It appears his leg has been crushed," said Joseph. "He may never march again." He examined him closely.

Zoheleth

"Do what you can for him," said Vespasian as his eyes moistened. "I'll see that he gets a medical discharge with honors." He looked at the solder and rested his hand on his shoulder. "Young man," he said, "I'll arrange a pension coverage for you." Vespasian sat down wearily.

Joseph sedated the soldier and worked on him. Marcus aided through the surgery and when it was finished, Marcus made a splint and wrapped the leg in linen soaked in vinegar. When it dried, the linen would shrink and stiffen to hold the leg in place with the splint.

Joseph washed his hands and noticed that the general had remained. "There's a chance the soldier might hobble around in a few months. I didn't have to amputate."

"Your skill has impressed me, doctor," said Vespasian as he grinned widely.

"Get the general some wine," Joseph motioned Marcus. "General, tell me, how did the injury occur. Did his horse fall on him?"

Vespasian drank the wine and wiped his mouth. "A house fell on him!"

"A house?"

"My men took to the roofs of the houses in Gamala. The homes couldn't hold them and came crashing down."

"I've seen the houses in Gamala," Joseph confirmed.

"Then you can imagine how they came down like an avalanche. So many men died needlessly." Tears streamed down his wide face. Marcus refilled the general's cup. Vespasian remained silent for a time and after much thought, said. "War is not cheap. Enemies are expensive. They rob you of peace as well as sleep, not to mention your life!"

Marcus saw a tenderness in this man of war. A guard entered the infirmary and saluted Vespasian.

"General," he said. "We have received news about Jerusalem."

Vespasian leaped from the chair. "Speak out, man!" he shouted. "Stop niggling and get on with it."

"Your son brings one named Metilius."

Vespasian smiled and bellowed out. "Bring them in!

Zoheleth

Or are they waiting for a royal invitation?"

When Titus entered, he was still smiling at his father's wit. Metilius followed. Vespasian greeted Titus with open arms.

"General," Metilius saluted. "I've seen first hand the young men of Jerusalem forging weapons to come against the Romans."

Vespasian groaned. "Why doesn't that surprise me?" He frowned and asked. "What's the state of the people in the city?"

"The city is divided. There are those who want to avoid war at any cost."

"But?" Vespasian urged.

"Well, there's John from Gischala, who encourages a sedition. The youths are willing to follow his ideas."

Titus glared at Metilius. "Are you saying that John is in Jerusalem with his band of thieves?"

"Yes, sir!" said Metilius. "He rode into the city to report the news of Gamala. He put fear into the people by insisting Jerusalem would be the next target after the Romans finished with Gischala."

Titus threw his hands in the air. His father was puzzled by his son's actions.

"Who is this John?" Vespasian asked.

"He betrayed me while I remained outside Gischala. He sent two of his thieves to act as ambassadors. They lied and led me to believe they could do nothing about a treaty during their Sabbath." Titus removed his helment and wiped the sweat from his head. "I trusted them and we settled down to rest for the night. My men were tired and I thought it would be best to be refreshed in case there was an uprising the following day."

"What happened?" Vespasian asked.

"The next day, we marched to the gates and were welcomed into the city by the inhabitants."

Titus shook his head. "It was then I noticed that the ambassadors I dealt with were not among the people." He paused. "I learned that the residents of the city had been robbed of their possessions through the night. Their horses where taken for a get-away by this John and his gang."

"This is unpleasant news," Vespasian replied.

"We couldn't pursue them because the group of soldiers I sent had to rescue the families John left to die on the plains."

Vespasian shook his head. "I must report this to Rome. I fear they will not take kindly the news about Jerusalem." He motioned his son. "Follow me to my quarters." He turned to Metilius who was still awaiting orders.

"Metilius!" he groaned and rolled his eyes upward. "Will you get shaved. And get out of that outfit!"

CHAPTER SIXTEEN

IN ROME

The new emperor of Rome, Aulus Vitellius, was enjoying a banquet in the palace. His closest friends and their associates were invited to witness just how an emperor could entertain.

The tables were overflowing with fruits, rolls, tarts, and various nuts. Exotic foods were imported from different countries at an enormous cost.

The guests were served pike-livers, and lamprey milt, peacock brains, and flamingo tongues. Jugs of sweet Jordan wine was served in gold goblets

Vitellius had his favorite men seated near him. They flattered the emperor with words of praise, and toasted him with boring speeches. He enjoyed their lies, as he reclined on the palace cushions in the dining hall.

His huge body with its pouch, met his plump chest which gave the appearance of women's breasts. His round chin rested on layers of fatty flesh. He gazed through glassy eyes and dribbled as he toasted his guests.

"Drink up, my friends," he laughed, which made him cough heavily. "This is how the rich enjoy life," he added, and raised his cup to the vulgarity of the hired female dancers.

He allowed his guests to be rowdy, because his own lusts were never satisfied, nor was his sexual appetite. He looked at his son who was wide eyed and staring at the naked entertainers.

"I drink to my son, Lucius," he chuckled, and when attempting to raise himself he lost his balance and rolled to the floor. He felt pain in his thigh, and remembered how he received the injury in a chariot race with the awful Emperor Caligula, who didn't take losing a chariot race lightly.

Vitelius felt the blade of the wheel cut into his thigh

when he was thrown to the ground after his chariot was sliced. Sweat rolled down his face as he lay on the floor remembering the terrible event of the past.

"Fa-fa-a-ther," Lucius stammered, as he ran to help him, but accidentally tripped over his father's robe.

Vitellius struck out at his son, but when hearing the laughter in the room he joined in to cover his anger.

Two guests lifted him back on his cushions and handed him a another cup of wine. He diverted his guests' attention by pointing to his servants entering. They came in carrying large silver trays bearing elaborate foods.

The guests were astounded by the parade of special dishes being placed before them. Stuffed birds with their feathers tacked on and their heads neatly pressed into place, and garnished with greens. Other trays were filled with dumplings the size of a man's fist, and sausages still simmering in their own fat. Fresh eels surrounded in cloves of garlic and shallots. Oysters on their shells were packed in mounds of snow. The snow had been brought down from the mountains in carts. Bowls of fish sauce were served for dipping breads and using over meats. The servants set out trays of cheese surrounded with huge olives. Another tray displayed fresh cucumbers which were neatly cut into shapes of animals.

Fresh vegetables of broccoli, squash, and cauliflower. Then arrived the delicate succulent meat of baby deer, covered with juices from the drippings. Fancy dates and figs trimmed the meat platters.

No Roman banquet was without a variety of eggs which were piled high on platters. Hard boiled swan eggs, goose eggs, and sea-bird eggs. A Roman meal was never without licker-fish. Some guests would never touch a fish which lived in the dirty Tiber River and fed on slop.

The guests ate and drank until they were sickened. They excused themselves to go outside and empty their stomachs, then return to gluttony again.

Vitellius was dipping into a platter of stuffed udders from nursing sows. A delicacy fit for a king. He sat licking his greasy fingers one at a time, when a guest stood to make a toast to their new emperor.

"Hail Vitellius!" he shouted, and the men chanted his name. "Hail Vitellius!"

From the rear of the room someone shouted. "Hail Spintria!" A dead silence came over the people, except for the sound of Vitellius' cup hitting the floor. He glared at his guests through bulging blood-shot eyes.

"Who dared to call out in such a manner?" he fumed. "Who?" His face burned red with anger as he scanned the room. His body swayed from drunkenness, but no one dared to answer.

"If I find the one," he warned as he pounded his fist on the table, "I'll have his head served on one of these platters!" He cursed, spat, and swore vengeance.

"Emperor!" called Gnaeus, as he stood up. "We are not guilty of such profanity," he said, trying to hold back his smile.

Gnaeus and others knew Vitellius had earned the pet name Spintria, meaning sexual invert. They knew him to be a prostitute as a lad who served the sexually depraved Emperor Tiberius.

"We have fought by your side through the German wars," Gnaeus reminded him. "Never has anyone been disrespectful to you."

Vitellius nodded his head and agreed. Gnaeus suggested that it might have come from the slave quarters.

"I believe you, Gnaeus," said the emperor. "I don't think it came from one of you." A sigh of relief was heard through the room and the eating and drinking resumed.

Gnaeus was pleased with his own wit. He looked at Vitellius and sugested. "With your permission, my Emperor, allow me to search the slave quarters. But please permit your son to join me that he may lead the way."

The emperor gazed at him and was somewhat confused from too much wine.

"You may be escorted by Lucius," he said. "When you find the guilty one, bring him to me. I can use him to

Zoheleth

entertain my guests." He clapped his hands and addressed his company, "And now my friends, let's have some music and lurid entertainment."

The dancers came running into the middle of the room. Some were draped in veils and others naked. Their dancing was an art form displaying immoral acts.

Gnaeus motioned Lucius to lead the way. The young man seemed reluctant to go when seeing the dancers.

"We must question the slaves first," suggested Gnaeus. "You take the section to your left," he pointed. "I'll make inquires in the other section."

"B—b—but...," the lad stammered pitifully.

"Don't hesitate, lad. Just ask each slave what was said when we were about to toast your father."

He was laughing inside as he watched Lucius making an effort to refuse, but he was too ashamed to put forth his objection.

Gnaeus returned to the party. He gathered a handful of sweet tarts from a tray and stuffed them in his garment. He drank some wine and joined his companions to tell them what he had just done to Lucius.

The story became the private joke of the night as it passed among his friends. Sudden outbursts of laughter in the room delighted him. He told how it would take Lucius the rest of the night to question one servant.

His friends kept his secret when they learned it was Gnaeus who called out the name Spintria.

The following day the emperor was sleeping late when he was awakened by his personal guard.

"What kind of a fool are you?" he burst out shouting, "to wake me at this hour?"

"My Emperor, its urgent," said the guard. "A messenger who claims to have come from Caesarea is waiting to speak with you."

Vitellius jumped to his feet. His head was pounding from the heavy drinking. He limped across the room and grabbed a garment to cover his flabby nakedness. "By the

Zoheleth

gods!" he yelled. "Bring the man in!"

He felt his heart quicken its beat. He wondered if his plan succeeded. He ran his trembling fingers through his thinning hair.

The hired spy entered and the guard was dismissed. The spy looked around and admired the comforts the palace offered.

"Greetings, my Emperor," he said as he bowed. "I come with some unfortunate news."

"What is it?" Vitellius asked. He waited to hear if his plan to murder Vespasian had taken place.

"There was a failed attempt to assassinate General Vespasian," the spy informed.

Vitellius stood in fear. His lower lip quivered.

"Who would attempt such a thing?" he pretended ignorance. "Did they capture the culprits?"

"They were caught, Emperor," the spy went on. "It seems that someone informed the guards of Vespasian, and they were waiting inside the general's tent when the would-be-assassins entered."

Vitellius paced the floor, limping more with each step. He clasped his hands together and felt the sweat rolling down his back. He thought his legs would give out at any moment. His heart pounded and his breathing grew rapid. He glared and shouted at the messenger. "Get out!"

He felt himself sinking into despair. The news meant that the assassins were caught and tortured to reveal who sent them with orders to murder Vespasian.

He limped back to his bed and fretted over what effects this would have on him as emperor? If the Senate learned about his plot to kill Vespasian, he would suffer the consequences and could be claimed as an enemy of Rome. He remembered the foiled attempt by Nero to assassinate Galba. He sat down and sulked.

Who betrayed him? Surely he did all this in secrecy. How did Vespasian's guards know ahead of time?

He summoned his barber, and while being shaved, a series of ideas ran through his mind. He remembered the brother of Vespasian held an office in Rome. He heard that Vespasian's youngest son, Domitian, was in Rome visiting his uncle. He rested back in his chair and asked his barber,

"What's the name of Vespasian's brother?"

"It's Flavius Sabinus, my Emperor," said the barber. "I understand that his nephew is visiting him"

Vitellius was now secure with this news. Surely Vespasian would never jeopardize his brother's office in Rome, nor would he endanger his youngest son.

"If I may speak, my Emperor?" asked the barber.

"Feel free,"

"There's word in the city that someone was sent from Rome to assassinate General Vespasian."

"All lies!" said Vitellius. "I would be the first to know if such a thing was true. I must talk with Vespasian's brother and assure him that no such order came from Rome." Vitellius worried. What if the brother didn't believe him? What then? Could the brother come against him? Nonsense, he convinced himself. He was the one in control and there was one thing he could do and it was hold Vespasian's son as hostage.

He feared that Vespasian may have sent word to his brother about the attempt on his life and reported that the orders came from Vitellius. If this was the case, then, he, Vitellius, must be prepared. He would take his army and go to the Forum to meet with Flavius Sabinus. He would be ready should Vespasian's brother come against him.

Outside the bedroom, Asiaticus, an ex-slave boy of Vitellius, heard all the orders given by the emperor. This beautiful young man with milk colored skin was known as the emperor's love-boy. As a slave, he had run away more than once from his master. But he would be found and returned. Vitellius loved the lad so dearly that he couldn't bear to strike his fair white skin and see it damaged.

Asiaticus hated his master, but used wisdom. He was angry ever since his master sold him to a gladiator trainer. It happened because Vitellius caught him stealing gold. His master missed him so much that he paid a large sum to buy him back from the trainer.

This time his master granted him what he wanted. He gave him his freedom and with this freedom he could wander anywhere and not be subject to questioning. It was he who heard the plot to kill Vespasian. It was he who sent word to Caesarea. It would be he who would go to Flavious Sabinus and warn him of the trap to kill him, or kidnap Vespasian's son.

He careful slipped out of the palace and sent word to the Forum. All he had to do was await the outcome. What pleasure it would be to see Vitellius' fat head on a pole in front of the Forum!

Zoheleth

THE TURNING POINT

Across the Mediterranean Sea from Rome, the Roman camps were stationed at Caesarea. The troops gathered for a conference.

The plot to assassinate General Vespasian had its repercussions. The men of the legions were outraged.

The commanders and tribunes, along with their officers gathered before Vespasian. The scene was like a sleeping giant who awakened inflamed with a desire for revenge.

"Kill Vitellius!" the legions chanted. "Give us a worthy emperor!" they demanded.

Vespasian stood amidst the men and trying to keep their anger at bay.

Mucianus, the legate of Syria, pointed to Vespasian.

"We call upon you, Vespasian. Take the position of our emperor." The officers demanded silence from the legions in order to hear the legate.

"I speak for all the commanders," Mucianus stated firmly. "Save Rome! We beg of you."

The soldiers began cheering and chanting. "IM-PER-A-TOR. IM-PER-A-TOR!" Vespasian stood shocked. His troops were formally hailing him with power and the title of "Emperor!" He knew his men's morale was sinking after the attempt was made on his life, and from the constant upheavals in Rome. His men longed for stability.

Their shouts were deafening. They were making the claim that he, along with his sons, would be the ones to bring stability to Rome.

"Men!" he shouted. "This could be taken as an act of revolt against our Caesar!" An angry protest arose.

"No!" Mucianus shouted. "Any passivity on your part, after seeing Rome suffer defilement under the discreditable rulers, is a disgrace!"

Vespasian was dumbfounded. A thousand thoughts

ran through his mind. Rome was divided, true, and there was no military loyalty. But make him the emperor of Rome?

Mucianus spoke out again. "You can no longer be indifferent to the power we place in your hands," he stressed. "You, Vespasian, are our only refuge."

The general stepped back stunned. "Are you suggesting I overthrow the emperor of Rome?" His face took a grim frown. With over thirty years committed to battles, he thought of himself as a man of war, not one to pursue an empire to rule. The thought frightened him. But he saw his men were not about to accept his excuses.

"We declare you Emperor..or..accept death!" Mucianus threatened. "We will march on Rome with you, or without you!"

Vespasian was in disbelief by the threat, but nodded his approval. He remembered the prophecies of the Jewish general, Josephus, who was captured at Jotapata.

"Remember the words from the little man we captured?" Mucianus asked. "You are destined to rule," he convinced him. "You can draw upon Judea, Egypt, and Syria to serve you. You will hold nine legions who will give their allegiance to you!"

He nodded humbly. "I will do as you wish," he said as his heart beat wildly with excitement and with fear. He turned to Titus, who was smiling with joy.

"Where's the Jewish general?" he asked his son.

"He's in prison, father," said Titus. "You want him released?"

"Yes! Set him free! Present him with honors as a way of expressing my apologies. Give him everything he needs and allow him any request he desires."

Vespasian and his sons would one day rule the world like Josephus predicted.

Mucianus' men were joyful with Vespasian's acceptance for rulership.

"Your son, Titus, is ready to hold the position of supreme commander in your absence!" Mucianus proclaimed. "I'll remain and stand with him. Entrust to me the fighting."

A roar of applause came from the legions. The general, their new emperor, shook his head and grinned slightly. "As you will have it," he said. "May the gods give us wisdom. And may my trip to Rome be without bloodshed."

"Father," said Titus, "in the morning, we'll make sacrifices to the gods, but tonight we'll celebrate your new role in the world of Rome."

Meantime in Rome, the Roman Senate received word that Vespasian's men were entering the city to declare their general as emperor of Rome. The Senate was unanimous in the legions choice in declaring a man of iron to rule the failing empire.

Vitellius soon learned the disturbing news of a vanguard coming to dethrone him. At first he panicked, but then reasoned with himself to meet the vanguard head on.

"Prepare my army!" he ordered his commanders, who were now used to an easy life of drinking and carousing. His men were dissipated and unruly and liked having women and wine. They never had to answer to any indecent act.

Vitellius gathered his most trusted men and informed them of a secret mission. "Search out the brother of Vespasian," he ordered. "When you find him, inform me where he stays." The men returned saying Sabinus was located near the Forum.

Emperor Vitellius rode with his army to the Forum, but to his surprise he saw Sabinus meeting him with his own army. How did Sabinus know to prepare for a battle? He fumed when seeing many of his own men now marched with Flavius Sabinus. Vitellius faltered and had some misgivings about his plans. He urged his trusted men to move forward. He would attempt to speak with Sabinus openly.

"Your brother has dared to declare himself emperor of Rome!" he announced brazenly as he rode closer. "What makes him think I'm willing to advocate?"

Zoheleth

Sabinus stared at him with contempt. "Why not spare your life? Step down as emperor and my brother will avoid a battle. Vespasian is not a cruel man. He will accept your surrender peacefully."

"Better spare your own life, brother of Vespasian!" The people gathered around and began to curse the emperor. His feelings were lacerated and he was no longer willing to hide his treacherous designs to kill Sabinus.

"Listen to me!" he bellowed. "Sabinus, prefect of the city. It is I who offer you your life. I order you and your men to put down your weapons and save yourself and your family."

Flavius Sabinus refused to move. His men held to their swords and when Vitellius gave the order to attack, both sides rode forward with all their might.

The battle was fierce and Vitellius drove Flavius Sabinus and his family into the Capital. The men who helped Sabinus to secure his family, found themselves surrounded by Vitellius' men and trapped inside. Every exit had been covered by Vitellius' men. Sabinus tried to force a way open to do battle outside the Forum, but it was useless. Vitellius had ordered his men to set fire to the temple of Jupiter where Sabinus' family were in hiding. Flavius Sabinus tried reaching them but all inside were at the mercy of the flames.

Vitellius rode around the Forum shouting orders. "Kill anyone who tries to escape!" He headed back to the palace allowing his men to finish his dirty work.

The citizens witnessed the horror and were in disarray. Some men made an effort to enter the Forum to rescue Sabinus' family but they were unable to break through the lines of soldiers. Citizens wept aloud in the streets. Some took a daring attempt to dismount the soldiers. A few of Vitellius' men were stoned to death when the citizens succeeded in throwing them to the ground.

The following day, Vitellius sat in his sedan-chair and was carried through the city to survey the damage at the Capital.

"Were they all killed?" he asked one of his soldiers.

Zoheleth

"They perished in the blaze, my Emperor."

"Was Vespasian's son with those who died?"

"We didn't find Domitian with his uncle," the soldier reported.

Vitellius was outraged by the possibility the lad had escaped. "You fools!" he screamed. "Seek out the son of Vespasian! Find him and hold him as a hostage." He waited while his men searched the city. They returned saying they couldn't find Domitian. This worried Vitellius. He ordered his men to take him back to the palace.

When he arrived, not one of his friends came to greet him as they had in the past. Was there a traitor among his men? Who could it be? He knew someone warned Flavius Sabinus to be ready to defend his life.

He entered the palace and ordered a slave to bring wine. He hobbled through the rooms in search of his love-boy, Asiaticus, but he was not to be found. He inquired of his guards to the whereabouts of the lad. No one had seen him.

Vitellius limped to his bedroom and his old dog came running, wagging his tail fiercely.

"Hello, old friend," he said and took time to pet the animal. "At least you haven't deserted me." The dog followed him around the room while barking playfully and nipping at Vitellius' heels. The emperor was not in the mood for him. He reached for his money-belt and strapped it around his waist after filling it with gold. He had no bargaining power without the son of Vespasian.

He was ready to make his escape unseen when the vanguard entered the palace. He changed into old garments belonging to the janitor. Wild thoughts ran through his mind. Thoughts about the people he killed without provocation. Thoughts of how he robbed the rich and secretly had them killed to keep them from protesting to the Senate.

"Lucius!" he shouted pathetically. "Where are you, my son?" he groaned and shook his head in disgust. "What good would he be?" he moaned. "A stammering fool who could never rule Rome," he cursed. "How could Lucius give orders to an army when he can't even order breakfast for himself. Let him perish!"

Despair came. "What's that?" he asked softly when he noticed his dog listening to the sounds. "Great gods of Rome. They're here! I'm going to be found!" Sweat ran down his face and his heart beat heavy under his fat chest. He heard the sounds of looting in the palace.

His dog began barking. Vitellius grabbed the dog's collar and tied him outside the bedroom door and piled mattresses against the door. He hid in the janitor's closet and waited. His dog kept barking and Vitellius regretted he hadn't slit the animal's throat.

Suddenly he heard men pushing through the door and footsteps coming closer. He held his breath and was paralyzed with fear. His dog came sniffing at the closet door and began whining and scratching the door.

Under his breath he cursed the mutt. He trembled and closed his eyes while curled up in the dark closet. The odor from the clothes sickened him and the lack of air was making him dizzy.

The soldiers threw open the door and found him cowardly shaking in the corner like a trapped bird. The dog licked his master's face and jumped in circles with delight.

Vespasian's men hauled him out and laughed loudly when seeing he wet himself. They tied his hands behind him and dragged him across the floor leaving a wet stain trailing. The dog barked continuously behind his master and put his nose to the emperor's tear streaked face.

The men took Vitellius to the Forum, the same place where he so willingly killed the brother of Vespasian.

A noose was placed around his neck and he received great insults from the people. They threw garbage and dung in his face and cheered as he was tortured severely.

The Roman citizens and the men of the Senate were satisfied when seeing Vitellius dead.

The old emperor's bloated body was tossed in the Tiber River to float with the garbage and the dirty licker-fish!

Zoheleth

DESTINATION JERUSALEM

The Roman legions received their orders to leave Caesarea and march to the city of Jerusalem.

Emperor Vespasian gave Titus permission to make the decisions necessary to bring order to the city.

The soldiers along with the caravans, traveled fifteen miles the first day and set up camp for the night.

Inside Joseph's tent, Marcus was writing the reports of the day. He didn't extinguish his lamp after Joseph knelt to pray before retiring.

"I must send news to my brother and my mother. I'll be writing for a time," he said to Joseph.

"It won't keep me awake," Joseph laughed. "I'll be asleep as soon as my head hits the bed."

Marcus worked his ink-block with water and began his letter home. It would take time before his letters arrived in Antioch, since the legion's couriers were sailing to Rome daily and returning with news from the emperor.

Marcus found it costly to pay a private courier, so he would wait for a caravan heading in the direction of Antioch. His letter would be dropped off at a mail stop.

The Roman army would march again tomorrow, perhaps when they settled outside of Jerusalem, he would find couriers.

His letter began.

Dear Mother and Nicator; Greetings from Marcus.
First and foremost, I pray the gods have kept you well. We have traveled fifteen miles today and our destination is Jerusalem.
Father is on night watch but he promises to write later. He's in good health and wishes to be remembered.
The news I share with you might be old news by the time you read it. It is rumored that the Emperor Vitellius sent

Zoheleth

assassins to kill General Vespasian. The assassins were caught before they could execute their plan. They were interrogated and are now prisoners.

The legions have voted General Vespasian as the new emperor. He has sailed to Rome to claim his position. Vespasian's brother, Sabinus, along with his family, were killed by the men of Vitellius. Titus had tears in his eyes after reading his father's letter. Titus is deeply concerned about his younger brother, Domitian. There's been no reports about him. His brother was in Rome visiting his uncle.

Titus is in command of the Tenth Legion and the Twelfth. (The Twelfth Legion was under the command of Governor Gallus.) These soldiers have sworn to regain their Roman ensign which they worship before going into battle. It's a disgrace to have it siezed by an enemy.

Titus has troop contingents and auxiliaries joining him. Allied kings throughout the nations offer their support. Many nations desire to fight the Jewish rebel uprisings in every domain.

Tiberius Alexander, the ex-governor of Egypt is arriving to act as military advisor to Titus, our young Caesar.

Nicator, please ask Martha to write to me. Ask her to give the letter to you and you can send it without her parents knowing. I wish you would write to me about her. Perhaps you don't see her often, but try to get word to her that I'm well and I think of her every day. I know you are busy from dawn till early evening with the horses. I don't mean to give you more work. When you write tell me how things are with your racing horses. Did we have good crops this season? Has mother been busy baking? I can smell the sweet fresh aroma of her breads. It makes me homesick.

Zoheleth

SPRING OF A.D. 69

Marcus took his early morning run before breakfast. He rested on a hilltop overlooking the Roman camps. His breathing was rapid, and his garments damp from perspiration after his one mile jaunt.

Below him lay a panoramic view of the regimental exercises the soldiers performed daily. On one side of the camp was the division of legionnaire cavalry along with the junior officers. The other side of the view were the road-builders.

Marcus stood counting the artillery engines, including the catapults. He gave up after one hundred and sixty. The stone-projectors were enormous and were able to hurl a fifty pound stone up to seven hundred yards.

The Roman camps were stationed three miles outside the city of Jerusalem. The sight of the mobile towers stood like giants rising high above the city walls. The towers were on wooden platforms with wheels. Each floor of the tower was screened with iron plates to protect the soldiers from the enemies darts. The towers were moved to given positions by soldiers and oxen. Once placed against the wall, a plank was dropped down to act as a bridge for the soldiers.

Among the Roman machinery were the battering rams and the wall borers.

Marcus climbed higher to view the rear-guard infantry. The horsemen paraded with long swords and shields at their sides. He saw the light-armored auxiliaries which his father commanded. Not far from them was the heavy infantry and then came the cavalry.

When the sun rose, it was his signal to return to his tent. The aroma of hot chickory filled his nostrils and he heard the sound of eggs sizzling when they hit the metal plates. Joseph had fresh bread and chunks of cheese.

"You look like you worked up an appetite," said

Joseph.

"You bet!" Marcus quickly seated himself and gorged on the food in front of him.

"Where's Titus?" he asked with his mouth full.

"I believe he's viewing the grounds surrounding Jerusalem."

"Why are some horses wearing sandals?" asked Marcus as he reached for more bread to dip in his hot drink of chickory.

"It's done to protect their hooves should the ground be rocky."

"They look funny dressed in sandals," he smiled and rose from his seat. Wiping his mouth with his hand he said, "I'll be with the cadets should you need me."

"And what will the cadets learn from you today?"

"I'll show them some fancy maneuvers Antonius taught me. Watch this!" He jumped around the tent in a mock battle looking much like a puppet. "I'll fight like Antonius!" he laughed as he swung an invisible sword and tripped over garments on the floor. Landing on his rump, they both burst out laughing.

"So much for that battle," Joseph chided. "Your dirty laundry has defeated you."

Marcus threw them on his cot and headed out.

"Don't forget, you'll be needed in the infirmary, gallant warrior." Joseph kept smiling as his assistant ran hastily from the tent.

Titus rode with six hundred men behind him. He kept a distance ahead of his men. He dreamed of Bernice and the letter she had sent to him. She would be staying in a nearby village where they could meet. He lost track of all time, and how far from his men he had ridden.

He approached a section of the wall referred to as the "Women's Tower" when suddenly from the gates of the city a group of Jewish rebels intercepted him.

They fell upon him with such fierceness that his horse reared from the sudden attack. Titus lunged forward, but found it impossible to advance due to the trenches around part of the wall. The trenches had gardens which grew sturdy hedges high enough to foil any attempt to break through. He raised his sword above his head and shouted to his men, "AMBUSH!" He turned his horse and swung his sword wildly and the rebels had to flee.

His men saw him in mortal danger and headed toward him. Titus with a burst of courage ran his horse with a violent charge, directly into the midst of the rebels. He realized he wasn't wearing his helmet and breast plate. He cursed himself for doing what he had warned others never to do.

The Jews on the wall began sending darts, but none touched him. He shuttered when they whisked past his bare head. He thrashed the air on all sides, slicing the arms and skulls of the rebels in his path. Any who made an effort to dismount him, sadly found themselves without fingers and hands.

His horse reared and came down on the enemy as though the animal wanted to protect its rider. The Jews turned and fled, shouting that Titus was a devil.

It seemed to take forever for his men to cover him and get him safely back to camp. When they did, he was urged to visit the infirmary. He thought how fortunate he was to be alive. He pictured his father's sorrow should he be killed at the hands of a small group of enemy. The thought of never seeing Bernice again, brought anguished tears to his eyes. While fighting he found strength by thinking of her. She became his reason for living.

Word got to him that his valor had the watchers on the wall cheering. It was unbelievable how Jews were being killed, yet the enemy admired the bravery of Titus.

He was sorry about losing two men and a horse. One rider was thrown directly in the path of the enemy and was killed. Another took a dart through the scales of his armor. It hit his lung. Titus tried to rescue him but seeing the blood spurting from his mouth, he knew the soldier would die. The enemy managed to steal the horse.

Zoheleth

At the infirmary, there were fifteen men who needed to be treated. Titus insisted they be first when he entered.

"Any badly wounded?" he asked.

"Nothing serious," said Joseph. "Please Caesar, allow me to check you."

Titus looked at him through dark brown eyes. He nodded to young Marcus standing beside the doctor.

"Why were you in enemy territory without a helmet or a breast-plate?" Joseph asked as he listened to the heart beat of Titus.

"I never saw them," he sighed. "I can't believe I fell into their trap."

"God was with you, young Caesar," said the doctor. "You could have been killed, but the Lord has a future mapped out for you."

Titus smiled through quivering lips.

"I believe you for some reason," he said. "I regret that I lost two brave men who gave their life for me."

"I heard of their bravery," Marcus spoke out while cleaning the instruments. "The gods favored you today," he added.

"You're the son of Sabinus, the Syrian," Titus smiled. "I remember your father telling us about you. I want you to know your father is safe."

Marcus thanked him.

"Have you heard from your father, Vespasian?" asked Joseph.

"Yes!" answered Titus. "We learned he arrived safely in Rome. But the good news is my brother, Domitian, has been found alive."

"I'm glad to hear some good news!" Joseph said, as he motioned Marcus to bring wine.

"A toast to you, Caesar," said Marcus as he poured wine in two cups. Joseph and Titus drank.

"Where was your brother?" asked the doctor.

"A woman rescued him and dressed him as a priest. She hid him until the soldiers of Vitellius were killed by my father." Titus' cup was refilled. "When the opportunity came the woman sent my brother forth to claim himself as the son of Caesar!"

"Thank God!" Joseph sighed as he watched Titus stand to leave.

"It's been a troublesome day," Titus said. "I must return to my quarters." He walked toward the doorway and turned back to Joseph.

"I just remembered. You'll have a visitor shortly. Perhaps you can put him up for a time?"

Joseph was puzzled. "Who might it be?" he asked.

"You recall the Jewish general we captured at Jotapata?"

"Ah!" said Joseph. "Josephus, the priest and general."

"Correct," said Titus. "My father remembered the man's predictions."

"It was my father who captured the general," Marcus said proudly. Titus nodded.

"Josephus has been released from prison and given full honors as a Roman citizen," Titus informed.

"Why is he coming here?" asked Joseph.

"He's offered himself to act as a mediator for peace," Titus went on. "I guess you know the people in Jerusalem have lost respect for him. They think he should have chosen death rather than being captured."

When Titus departed, he left Joseph somewhat dazed by what was said.

"Is there something bothering you?" asked Marcus while he collected the cups to wash them.

"I'm not sure," he replied while staring into space. "If Josephus has joined the Romans, the Jews definitely will classify him as a traitor. I wonder if Titus is aware of it?"

"I see your point," Marcus said. "But it could be in favor for the Romans to have him as a mediator. Isn't that so?"

Joseph had a doubtful expression. "If the Jews allow him into the city," he reasoned, "and mind you, they may not. The Romans will never know which side his loyalty leans."

Marcus understood. "If they let him in the city he may never come out!" Marcus reaffirmed Joseph's doubts.

"Titus will need someone to translate the conversations spoken in our tongue."

Marcus' eyes lit up. "Are you thinking Titus doesn't completely trust the Jewish general?"

Joseph shrugged his shoulders. "Whatever. We'll learn more when we have our visitor."

SIMON SON OF GIORA

The citizens of Jerusalem were uneasy with the Romans camped within three miles from their city.

Theophilus, the priest, reminded the people how John from Gischala warned this would happen. The priest made little impression on the zealots at the temple. The zealots were having serious problems arising from John.

Eleazar, a young governor of the temple and high priest, called the citizens to make an announcement.

"Religious Jews of our city!" he shouted. "As you know, before Emperor Nero's death, it was I who refused to make sacrifices to Nero who called himself a god." He went on. "I refuse from this day on, to make sacrifices to any emperor of Rome, or any foreigner or pagan."

The peace loving people were shocked. Theophilus, the priest, challenged him. "I can't agree with you, Eleazar. It will be further insults to Rome. We have never refused to offer sacrifices for Rome. It is our purpose to make an effort to pray for all pagans to come to the God of the Jews. You have no right to put yourself above Rome or above God. You declare yourself God to deny the pagans the blessing from the God of the Jews." He paused and added. "You complain about John's violence, but you have defiled the temple by permitting the sicarii inside. They have blood on their hands and it's the blood of our own people!"

Theophilus frowned under his gray brows. "We don't need your political assassins here. Where will this all lead to?"

Eleazar rubbed his tanned face. His dark eyes stared at the old priest. "You're quick to forget how we came to join you to fight against Florus!" he reminded. "You needed us then."

Theophilus wet his lips as he stood thinking.

"I understand you," he said. "But consider what has

Zoheleth

happened since then. Our people have become divided. John has encouraged the young men to forge weapons of war."

Eleazar glared at him. "I was one to protest John's arrival here. You allowed him to remain and you see how we've been at odds with John since his arrival."

Theophilus shook his head negatively. "Look around you, Eleazar." He glided his arm through the air. "You can see John's army outnumbers your men. Why not join with him and be more equipped to face the Romans?"

"He wants to rob the temple! He's not interested in aiding us." Eleazar insisted. "You should have turned him away from our city!"

"Even if John were not here," said the priest, "Rome would retaliate for the killing of the garrison at the Tower of Antonia." Theophilus looked at his followers. "The Romans will blame us for the uprisings and the murder of the soldiers. John told the truth and I thought it unwise to force him out. We may need him."

"You've allowed a devil to enter this city," Eleazar responded. "You see how John torments us, because we refuse to join him. He has forced us to take refuge inside the temple." Theophilus disagreed with Eleazar.

From the crowd, a holy man made his way toward the temple and stood beside Theophilus and spoke out.

"You, Eleazar, dare to call someone a devil when it is you who allow unclean men inside our most sacred court of the priests." The holy man tore his garments to display his disapproval. "You have polluted all that is holy to us!"

Eleazar hesitated a moment. "We take the temple to preserve its provisions," he announced. "Until John leaves, we stay here." He stood defiantly before the holy man and disputed. "Do you think John wants to help you? Behind your back he tries to rob the temple of its treasures. You must make a choice."

The people held a lengthy discussion with the priest and the holy man. Theophilus came back to Eleazar.

"We are at a loss to determine what to do," he

admitted. "While you're in the temple we do agree you'll keep John from ravishing the treasures. We have one condition we expect from you."

"Speak out," said Eleazar.

"Allow us into the temple to conduct the sacrifices for the people!" Eleazar agreed to the terms and said they could enter without incident.

In another section of Israel, a man named Simon, the son of Giora, was in the business of thievery as well as murder. Simon and his men fought at Masada with the zealots who killed the Roman garrison stationed there. Later, the zealots and the sicarii fled to Jerusalem and joined the young priest, Eleazar.

Simon didn't follow them because he had other plans. He and his men raided Idumea but lost the battle. The Idumeans put up a strong resistance and forced him to leave. His raiders were determined to return.

Simon, was a man of strength, but not cunning like John of Gischala who was in Jerusalem. He was a stone-faced man with a square chin which jutted forward. His dark hair lay tangled on his shoulders and a wiry beard outlined his face. He peered through dark brown eyes set deep in their sockets. His skin was rough and weather beaten. A scar over one eye gave him a sinister expression. The old injury caused the brow to separate, leaving a deep gouge above the eye. Simon gathered the most wicked men to join him. Men of questionable background, such as escaped murders and thieves. By joining Simon they found safety in numbers.

After his raids on the cities, he offered the homeless slaves freedom and riches. No slave could resist his offer. He was known to be incorrigibly brutal and his men held the same contempt as he for justice.

Twenty thousand men rode with him to the borders of Idumea. They would strike again. This time Simon was determined to crush the city. The element of surprise was in their favor. The Idumeans never expected Simon to attack after his last defeat.

In the dark, he and his men moved quietly toward the sleeping city of Idumea. The people were unprepared and hundreds fled as Simon left a wake of destruction in Idumea.

After he won the battle he stood surveying his conquest. His men, like animals, began fighting over their findings. Some were striking down their own comrades over a piece of gold. Others fought over the women they wanted to rape.

Simon watched and turned to his close comrades and said. "Look at them! What can you expect from a bunch of wild dogs?" He laughed at their violence, and joked about their rapes on the women. He sneered at the Iduman heads placed on poles, their eyes still open and their blood dripping to the ground. He spat at the foot of the poles.

The following day, he and his men celebrated and distributed the spoils. He was drinking heavily and was unable to control the private fights breaking out among his undisciplined band of violators. He raised his goblet over flowing with wine and shouted. "Drink and get rich!" he urged. "Soon we'll go to Jerusalem and become the richest band of criminals in the world!"

His men drunk with wine and power, cheered and shouted obscenities to the holy city of Jerusalem.

The people who escaped Idumea made their way to the hills for safety. One of the leading men, Ezron, decided to ride to Jerusalem to seek help for the displaced people.

The gates of Jerusalem opened and Ezron rode into the midst of the people.

"I must speak to the men from Masada," he pleaded to a guard near the temple. He was breathless and badly shaken. His horse was lathered in sweat and its nostrils were flaring.

The guard returned with an emissary from Eleazar.

Zoheleth

The man faced Ezron.

"How can we help you?" he asked.

"Please. It's important. Tell Eleazar that Simon has pillaged the entire city of Idumea!"

"What!" gasped the emissary. "Come with me." He took Ezron into the temple to speak with Eleazar.

"Hear this man out, Eleazar," said the emissary. "Simon has forced him from his home in Idumea."

"That scoundrel," Eleazar ranted. "It can only mean one thing. Simon will make his next move on this city."

The zealots were concerned and one spoke out. "If Simon gets into Jerusalem, we'll have two factions fighting us for the treasures in the temple."

Eleazar agreed. "He outnumbers John's men." He paused a moment. "We must figure a way to keep him from entering and destroying Jerusalem." He looked around while deep in thought. "He's sure to join forces with John," he added. "I think I have an idea," said Eleazar. "While Simon is in Idumea, he's not with his wife."

His men were confused, but waited to hear him out.

"I'll need volunteers to go outside the city," he requested. Several men volunteered and he gave them instructions. "You're to capture Simon's wife and bring her here. It will give us a bargaining power if we hold her hostage."

Simon celebrated for several days with his men. He selected five hundred of his chosen to go with him to Jerusalem. Little did he know that his wife was being held hostage in the temple of Jerusalem where no woman should be. His small band would present no threat to the people of Jerusalem. He was about to make his men rich. He planned to enter the city with only a few, and pay a watchman to allow the rest of his men to enter.

Simon marched onward, completely unaware of his wife being held prisoner. On approaching Jerusalem, he separated his men into smaller groups. He rode forward slowly, but heard someone riding and calling franticly.

"Simon!" shouted the man. "Wait!" He recognized

Zoheleth

the rider to be his neighbor.

"What's your problem?" he asked as the man rode up to him.

"I fear it's your problem, Simon," the man said breathlessly. "I must warn you, the zealots have taken your wife hostage. She's in Jerusalem at this moment."

Simon was infuriated. His lips quivered and his heart beat wildly. The news set him into a frenzy. He raised his sword and commanded his men to speed to the walls. His stomach churned when he thought his wife might be harmed. He loved her dearly and would give his life to save her.

"How dare those devils take my woman hostage," he screamed while forging forward. "Men of Jerusalem!" he shouted brazenly. "Release my wife, now!"

He looked up to the wall and saw a zealot pulling up his skirt and showing his bottom to Simon. The insult outraged him. He noticed six elderly men gathering vegetables from a garden outside the wall.

"Capture those men!" he ordered his band. "Bring them to me!" Simon remained on his horse and held his sword in the air as he called out to the men on the wall.

"ZEALOTS!" he shouted. "WATCH THIS!" His sword came down on the hand of one man and the fingers of another man. The old men screamed in agony as they were carried back to the wall. The remaining men were in unbelief when seeing what happened.

The watchmen opened the gates to the mutilated men. The zealots sent darts down on the band of thieves. Simon moved out of range and shouted louder. "SEE HERE, ZEALOTS! I hold your men. I'll send them back without hands, without feet, without arms! Are they your fathers? Are they your brothers?" The darts ceased and there was silence from inside.

"Send out my wife!" he demanded. "And she better not be harmed." The gate opened slowly and a frail figure came out. Her hooded cape covered her head as she stood alone, trembling in the shadows of the wall.

Simon rode to her and embraced her after lifting her

to his horse. He rode off with his wife after giving a warning. "Zealots! You'll pay for this!"

Right now his only desire was to take his wife home and stay with her for a time. Jerusalem could wait!

Zoheleth

HIGH PRIEST ANANUS

When the priest Theophilus learned about the zealots unlawful act of holding a woman as hostage in the temple, it brought serious arguments between the zealots and the holy men.

As a result, Eleazar forced all the priests out of the temple and secured it. He broke his agreement and refused to allow the sacrifices to be made.

The people's most trusted chief priest, Ananus, was called upon for advice. Ananus was outraged when hearing about Simon's wife. The incident cost the lives of several old men who died after being severely mutilated.

Another piece of information to his dismay, was that a few unscrupulous zealots in the temple, late at night, were secretly robbing the wealthy people in the city. He wept when he heard how innocent people were killed in their homes when putting up a defense against the burglary. Some had put up quite a struggle against the intruders.

The old priest, Ananus, made his way to the temple to address Eleazar. Many citizens followed.

"Eleazar!" he called. "What sins are you committing against your own people?"

Eleazar came out from the temple and faced the elderly priest. "What do you want old man?" he asked disrespectfully.

"Remove your men from the holy house!" Ananus ordered. The people raised their voices against Eleazar.

"Who will make me?" he mocked. "You? Let me inform you, this is the time predicted when we bring in the messianic rule!"

Ananus frowned and his tired eyes strained in the sunlight. His aged skin was wrinkled and cracked and white strands of hair showed under his blue headdress. His beard reached down over his blue fringed robe, a robe with gold bells attached to the bottom. On his chest he wore a gold purse with twelve different gemstones mounted, representing the twelve tribes of Israel. He took his time before making a reply to Eleazar's comment.

"And do you think it is you who will bring in the messianic rule?" he challenged. "You who have become a liar and a scoundrel! Your men have turned thieves and murderers!" he added. "As a priest, you must abide by our priestly laws!"

"You, Ananus," shouted Eleazar, "are not the law anymore!" Eleazar sent several men to remove Ananus from the temple area.

"I am your chief high priest!" Ananus raised his fist and reminded the zealots of his position.

"My men will appoint our own chief high priest. One who will obey our orders!" Eleazar threatened.

Ananus was shocked when the zealots physically dragged him away. He turned and cried out. "It's not too late to come to your senses. Let us cleanse the temple for the people to worship as before."

Eleazar ignored his plea. He hated Ananus and was envious of how the people greatly admired the old priest. There was a time when he feared Ananus, but now he feared no one.

"Let me remind you, Ananus," he said, "our purpose is to bring the Jews out of bondage. We are to put down foreign rulers. You old ones have no fight left in you."

"This is inappropriate behavior for a priest," Ananus declared. "If we are to be free from Roman rule, then we must let God open the way."

"You've lost touch with reality," said Eleazar. "The ancient predictions say that one will be raised to establish a new kingdom."

Ananus tried pushing his way back to the temple, but the zealots restrained him. The chief priest saw his followers forming a human shield around him. He raised his hands in a warning not to instigate an incident. He had more to say to Eleazar.

Zoheleth

"Is it you who desires to be the Messiah and establish the new kingdom?" he asked with animosity.

Eleazar replied loudly. "The God of Abraham will bring forth one of His chosen."

"And I suppose God has chosen you as the one?" Ananus ridiculed.

"You fool!" shouted Eleazar. "Your time is finished in the temple! Before you go home you will witness the ordination of a new chief priest. One who will replace you."

"You wouldn't dare!" Ananus stared insolently.

"Oh! Just watch." He told his men to hold Ananus where he could see the event taking place. The zealots forced Ananus to remain and watch Eleazar as he brought forth a group of men to elect a new chief priest. Ananus wept over their wickedness.

He struggled with his offenders as they held him secure. "You know the priest must be chosen in succession by their heritage," he entreated.

The zealots were laughing while casting lots and it fell upon one named Phanni, a man completely ignorant of the priesthood. Phanni was a man so frail that a wind could topple him.

"I know why you're doing this," Ananus revealed. "You want access to the money in the temple. I warn you it will cost you dearly for this sacrilege." He pulled away from the hold of the zealots and fell to his knees calling out to God for condemnation on the zealots.

"Eleazar! Son of Destruction!" he cried out. "Have you set yourself up as God?" (2 Thes. 2: 3)

"Get him out of here!" Eleazar demanded. The zealots forced him to the ground and the people became enraged by the act. They threatened the zealots as they lifted Ananus to his feet. The zealots grew alarmed and backed away from the multitude.

"You dare defile the holy altar!" shouted Ananus, his face streaked with tears. He continued to pursue the treacherous designs of Eleazar. "The holy altar has never been touched by a metal tool. Your sword, stained in the blood of your brothers, is now on the altar. You have defiled what is sacred!"

Eleazar smiled. "My sword was used to keep this city from being sacrificed to the Roman armies," he boasted while staring insolently at his opponent. "You, Ananus, deserve death, since you would turn the city over to the Romans and make slaves of us."

Ananus was not about to retreat. "The sacredness of this place has never been defiled. Even the ravens of the air don't come near it." He spoke out bravely and went on to say what was in his heart. "Now a different bird of prey defiles it. It's you, Eleazar!"

The newly elected priest, Phanni, ran out to Ananus and challenged him.

"I'm chief priest now! You have no authority here, and you have no authority over me."

Ananus squinted his eyes and grinned as he emphasized his words. "You are a nothing, Phanni. You're not a Zadokite. The last Zadokite was Onias IV. Do you know where he went after a situation like this occurred?" He watched Phanni standing speechless. Ananus fixed his gaze. "Let me educate you. Onias fled to Egypt and built a temple. Even the Hasmonean rulers were not of the Zadokite line. You stand wondering who is Zadok? He was the high priest to King Solomon!"

"You chose to think me a fool?" Phanni accused. "How is it when Herod the Great ruled, he allowed Rome to appoint our high priest?"

"Don't mock me," said Ananus. "I've enough influential people with considerable political power, who can have you out at a moment's notice. In fact I could have your throat cut in an instant!" Phanni stood stunned.

"Are you threatening us?" Eleazar interrupted. "I can have your people dead with one signal."

The crowd turned mean and they forced Eleazar to retreat back into the temple. The zealots followed.

"Ananus!" the people shouted. "Lead us against the zealots! Just say the word and we'll fight them."

Zoheleth

The zealots were fearing the followers of Ananus. They saw the possibilities of them forcing their way into the temple. Eleazar needed to control the conditions and ordered Ananus to be killed. The zealots boldly came out and fought the followers of Ananus. Their efforts to reach the chief priest failed. Blood splattered over the streets and once again the zealots were forced back into the temple. This time Eleazar bolted the gates to keep the angry crowds from entering.

Ananus ordered his people to go no further. It was sinful to attack the sacred gates with unpurified crowds. Ananus continued to exercise his restraining influence over the lawless priest, Eleazar (2Thes.2:7-12).

The people shouted. "Eleazar defiles everything! We can call on thousands to come to our aid. Ananus, give us the order and we'll send for more men."

"God sends Eleazar a misleading influence, and his followers believe his lies." Anunus collected his thoughts and suggested, "Since Eleazar locks us out, we'll lock the gates from the outside and let them be their own prisoners."

After the gates were locked, Ananus stationed guards at the porticoes all night. "We'll see how long they like being locked in." He felt secure in his decision and permitted some of his followers to return home.

The following morning, John of Gischala learned of the disturbance at the temple site. He and his men rode there to determine what had happened. When he arrived, he found Ananus and many guards around the temple.

"Chief priest," he called as he steered his horse directly in front of him. "Is it true the zealots are locked in the temple?" he asked as he dismounted. "I can offer you my assistance if you need it." He contrived, knowing the priest didn't trust him.

Ananus shaded his eyes. "You come here to join us?" he asked directly. "What is it you offer?"

"I offer you my oath," John lied. "You can make me to do so with the people as my witness."

"Are you bound by your oath, John?" Ananus asked.

John bowed down slightly. "Yes," he said.

"But will you also give your oath to the zealots for a price?"

John straightened and glared at the priest. "Are you calling me a liar?"

"I want the people to hear from your lips how you are willing to aid us."

"You have my word." He made a sincere effort to impress the priest and the people.

"I'll rely on your oath," said Ananus. "If you will go and negotiate with the zealots, you will then be above suspicion to us. They refuse to deal with me."

"What would you have me say to them?" John asked.

"Tell them we'll release them under one condition. We must be permitted to cleanse the temple and resume our worshiping there."

"That sounds reasonable," John said. He walked slowly to the temple gates and called out to Eleazar. The guards opened the gates outside and Eleazar opened to John. The people waited and soon they began to complain.

"John will return as a traitor!" shouted one man.

"It's possible," said Ananus. "But right now we need control of the temple. How else can we purge it?"

Inside the temple, Eleazar talked with John.

"Why has Ananus sent you to negotiate with us?" Eleazar asked.

"Forget about negotiations," said John. "I've news which will shock you."

"On with it, man!"

"I want you to know the priest Ananus has secretly sent an embassy to the Roman legions."

"Why would he do such a thing?" Eleazar questioned. He was doubtful of what John was telling him.

"Ananus wants a purification service tomorrow. His followers will force their way in and attack you and your men. This is why he's sent for the Romans." John saw how angry Eleazar became with his propaganda.

"Tell Ananus we won't come out."

"But they have enough forces to overpower you," John brought to his attention. "You must devise a way to get out before the Romans enter."

Eleazar was disheartened, but also ready to come up with some way to solve his dilemma. "We need outside help," he said. "But who?"

"You can't get a man out. The guards surround the temple," John informed.

"My men can't, but one of your men could," he suggested to John.

"What plans can you design?"

"I'm thinking of the Idumeans who are hiding in the mountains," said Eleazar. "Their leader, Ezron, came to us for help. We'll help them if they come and free us from here." He told John to get word to the Idumeans on how they were being held prisoners by Ananus. Tell them we'll help them regain their land."

"Sounds good," said John. "Do you think the Idumeans will go for it?"

"I'm sure they will. See that your man supplies them with horses and the weapons they need. We have gold to offer you." Eleazar handed him a bag of coins.

The word "gold" delighted John. He had plans of his own. He tucked the bag of gold away and walked out of the temple to report back to Ananus.

"They refuse to leave the temple," he lied. "Eleazar refuses any terms you offer. But I think if you give him time he will come around."

Ananus had no idea what went on beyond the temple gates. But he considered what John told him.

John sought out a man to send to the Idumeans. Once the battle started, he would find his way into the temple while his men were doing the fighting.

Inside the temple, Eleazar laughed. "John thinks he's come to save us, but that sneaky fox is in for a surprise." His men were about to learn of his true intentions. "When the Idumeans come to free us, we'll wipe out John and his band.

And, we'll get rid of Ananus and his followers!"

The zealots drank the sacred wine until they were drunk. Before they were imprisoned, they had secretly set up their own court in the temple. They became judges, jury, and executioners. They did this sinful act to take possession of the citizen's properties who wouldn't join them. Wealthy citizens were put on trial and judged as traitors, then killed. Those who had money outside of Jerusalem were now being held in the temple for a ransome from their families.

Zoheleth

CHAPTER SEVENTEEN

THE IDUMEANS

John's messenger found hundreds of Idumeans who escaped Simon's attack. They hid themselves in the mountain caves.

The Idumeans received Eleazor's plea for help and mustered their forces to march to Jerusalem. They had one single aim in mind and that was to regain their homeland, Idumea, located outside of Masada. With their hopes of regaining their city, they were more than willing to fight for the zealots.

Evenus, somewhat of a zealot himself, would lead the horsemen. His ancestors were known descendants of Esau (Gen. 36:9). Although the land of Idumea was once known as Edom, the Maccabeans had successfully campaigned against the residents and placed the Hasmonean, John Hyrcanus, as both king and high priest of Edom. It was known that Hyrcanus made all the males to be circumcised and follow Judaism to prove their loyalty. King Hyrcanus appointed Antipater, the father of Herod the Great, as governor of the city. In due time, Edom became known as Idumea.

Evenus led his men to the walls of Jerusalem and waited for the men on foot who were led by Ezron. Together they would enter the city.

While Eleazar and the zealots were held prisoners in the holy temple, Ananus was soon to learn that an army of Idumeans were approaching the gates of Jerusalem. He immediately ordered the gates closed against the invaders. He was quick to realize how John of Gischala had betrayed them. He regretted ever giving John the chance to honor his oath to the people. Ananus called on a few young priests from his people.

"Joshua," he said. "Go to the top of the tower and address the Idumeans from there." Young Joshua did so and called down to Ananus.

"Hundreds of Idumeans are aligned outside Jerusalem and they're fully armed." The priest waved his arms to the Idumeans. "Men of Idumea!" Joshua shouted. "Listen to me. We have locked the gates. We must talk first before allowing you to enter."

Evenus was angered when he heard this. His men cursed and shouted, claiming they were weary from their journey. Joshua ignored their pleas and they complained louder. It began to rain and they had no shelter outside the city walls. There was no response from the priest and the Idumeans grew hostile the longer they were forced to stay outside the gates.

Evenus threaten the priest, Joshua. "We don't take kindly to being locked out of the city!" he shouted. "We've traveled miles to offer our service, and now we're not welcome?"

"Why have you come?" Joshua finally replied.

"We've been asked to save the city from being turned over to the Romans!" He rode closer to the wall. "I've been informed that Ananus desires to welcome the Romans. Why else would you refuse us entry?"

"You have been told lies!" Joshua defended. "There have been no negotiations with the Romans by our chief high priest, Ananus."

The men with Evanus were turning mean and making threatening gestures to Joshua. The young priest turned to Ananus and asked. "What shall we do?"

"Tell them they may enter under the condition that they enter unarmed."

"Let us in!" demanded Evenus. "Can't you see there's a storm raging?" Joshua gave them the conditions.

"What!" roared Evanus. "You exclude us from the city and now you ask us to come in without weapons. Why? So you can attack us while we're defenseless?"

His men were responding like hungry lions, growling

Zoheleth

blustering sounds of jeering and hissing.

Joshua failed to convince them of the terms and the Idumeans began throwing stones and firing arrows at him. He fled the tower.

The Idumeans insisted on talking with Eleazar. Evenus swore they would remain outside until his request was honored. Inside, the men questioned Ananus' decision. "Perhaps we have been too hasty in barring out the Idumeans," said one man.

"We can't allow them entrance," Ananus insisted. "I'm aware of the storm, but their plans are to help the zealots. They won't even agree to talk with us. Why?"

His followers realized that Ananus was suspicious of the Idumeans bearing arms.

The rain came down heavily and the citizens in the city scattered for shelter. Thunder rolled in the distance and the darkened sky lit up with lightening.

Ananus ordered the guards to keep alert that no Idumean would slip into the city unnoticed. He made his rounds to check his guards at the temple. He found them shivering and drenched to the skin. His own priestly garments were soaked as he went about the stations.

The night grew wicked as the rain mixed with extraordinary thunder, giving reason for Ananus' guards to hide themselves from its drenching chill. The bolts of lightening with the heavy rain made visibility impossible.

Inside the temple, Eleazar learned that the Idumeans were refused entrance. He searched for saws and they began sawing the bars which locked them in, while the storm covered the sounds. When they cut through they were able to open the gates for the Idumeans.

The soaked Idumeans were hot for revenge, since they were exposed to the violent storm without shelter. Once inside the city they went wild and killed the guards placed by Ananus.

When other guards heard the clamor and came running to fight, they were shocked to see both zealots and Idumeans together in an orgy of slaughter. They lost heart and dropped their weapons in an effort to escape, but soon met their death.

Evenus rode through the streets in search of the priests who closed them out. "I want the arrogant upstarts to feel my sword!" he declared to the zealots. Together they searched for Ananus, the most holy man in the city.

Evenus found Ananus and slew him instantly. The zealots cheered when the old priest met his death.

Young Joshua came with his sword to defend Ananus, but met his death in the same manner.

The followers of Ananus looked upon his death as the last hope for Jerusalem. Many mourners cried out claiming how the murder of their chief high priest was a bad omen for the holy city.

So many senseless deaths occurred that one man, Jesse, who was among the zealots, could no longer go along with the bloody violence. He hid in a dark alley and waited for Evenus to ride in his direction.

In time he saw Evenus who was still seeking to kill. Jesse stepped out from the darkness and called him.

"Who is it that calls?" Evenus asked, as his sword was tightly grasped to plunge.

"I am Jesse. I'm with Eleazar." He showed himself.

"What kind of a man am I meeting who hides in the dark to set a snare for me?"

"Please, Evenus," said Jesse. "Take my sword if you don't trust me. I'm here to tell you how you're being used."

"And by whom?" Evenus questioned.

"You must stop this killing!" Jesse pleaded.

"Have you not dipped your sword into the belly of one of these rebels?" Evenus challenged.

Jesse stepped back for a moment fearing he might be seen by one of the zealots.

"You were given the wrong information about Ananus, the priest," said Jesse. "He never sent word to the Romans. He only wanted to cleanse the temple so he could continue the worship service."

Evenus wiped the rain from his beard and looked at

Zoheleth

his wet hand under the torch light. It wasn't rain on it, it was blood, and not his own.

"My dagger will not know the difference in your blood, Jesse, if you lie." Jesse felt the dagger pushed against his chest.

"I swear by my God that I haven't lied," he pleaded. "The zealots have tricked you into doing what they couldn't do."

"Explain this so I might understand," Evenus frowned and tilted his head downward to listen.

"Eleazar needs you to come against John of Gischala, who tries to rob the temple."

Evenus released his dagger. He pulled at his kinky beard and wasn't sure if he trusted Jesse.

"Why do you tell me this?" he questioned him suspiciously.

"Look, I could be killed by my comrades if they find out I've revealed this to you," Jesse confessed. "Something has changed Eleazar. I can't explain it, but he believes he will lead our people to victory over the Romans."

"That's a mighty task," Evenus replied. "I don't want to be around when the Romans decide to move on Jerusalem. They'll annihilate everyone here."

"I'm not turning against what we're fighting for," said Jesse. "But I'm against warring with our own people. And especially our chief high priest, Ananus."

Evenus shook his head. "How could I have been deceived into thinking that Ananus was our enemy?"

"Eleazor is not finished with you," Jesse announced. "He'll ask you to join him in destroying John and his men." Evenus began to have doubts about Eleazar.

"What you're telling me is that Eleazar has no intentions of helping us regain our homeland."

"I'm afraid that's right," said Jesse.

Evenus was angry. "He's tricked me into killing a holy man of God. And now wants me to do more killing for him. Let him face John alone!" He was dreadfully sorry about the priest he had killed.

Zoheleth

"I should have given Ananus time to explain his side of the story," he said regretfully.

"It's too late to do anything now," said Jesse.

"But it's not too late to leave these zealot devils to their own private hell with John!"

"All has not been a loss," said Jesse.

"What are you telling me?"

"You freed the wealthy citizens held captive in the temple by Eleazar. They were to go on trial."

"What! You mean they held citizens captive?"

"Yes. Ananus learned how those who resisted were killed by the zealots. Ananus didn't know that the men who had money outside of Jerusalem, were being held for a high ransom from their families."

"This is incredible. I'm glad we set them free, at least some good has come from this." Evenus decided to retreat from the city. He summoned his men and they rode out of Jerusalem, without Eleazar learning his reason.

The wealthy prisoners freed by this incident, banded together. They found horses and rode a great distance from Jerusalem. They needed to make plans to overthrow Eleazar. They complained how there was little they could do as a small group, but they did want retaliation against the zealots who inflicted much pain upon them.

"We can't do much alone," said one man. "But I understand that Simon seeks revenge against the zealots for holding his wife hostage. There's a chance for us to join him in his efforts."

They were edgy about joining a band of thieves, but the idea began to look most promising the more thought they gave to it. They decided to seek out Simon.

They searched the hills and were accosted by several of Simon's men. They explained their situation and were taken to Simon.

"You have come to the right person," said Simon as he poured wine and ordered food to be served for the hungry travelers. "I'm always delighted to add numbers to my band, and especially men with horses."

Simon knew by their dress that they were men of wealth. He learned all that happened in the city and he

Zoheleth

pictured how he could use the circumstances to his advantage.

"Together we'll plan our way into Jerusalem," he promised the new arrivals, "after we're certain the Idumeans have left the city. But now, let's celebrate our new partnership."

CHAPTER EIGHTEEN

DEMONS OF THE CITY

Jerusalem was left in a dreadful condition after the Idumeans rode out. In the morning, the alleys and streets were lined with the slaughtered.

People were seeking their dead to give them a proper burial, but were met with the grueling reality of what Eleazar had done. His men already disposed of hundreds of bodies by throwing them outside the walls.

Those who hid themselves during the outbreak of violence were stunned to find their chief priest, Ananus, was among those disgracefully deposited like garbage. The evil was like a serpent laying its eggs inside the minds of the zealots, and when hatched, drove these men to insane acts.

Word went out by the religious people about a man named Jesus of Nazareth. The small groups were repeating what Jesus revealed in a parable about an unclean spirit seeking a place to rest (Luke 11:24). When the unclean spirit found the house neat and clean it went out and got seven other spirits more evil and deadlier than itself and returned to the house. It appeared to the people witnessing the atrocities, that unclean spirits and demons had taken possession of the city.

Lamenting widows wailed (Luke 23:28) and their cries were heard in the camps of the Romans.

The zealots suffered the people to be silent. They didn't want the rebels to lose heart by the women's wailing nor did they want the Romans to hear the cries.

Frightened children clung to the garments of their mothers. In their innocence they trembled when seeing the bloody streets on which they walked.

The zealots became more vile and demonic after the Idumeans deserted. They were left to face John's men. John was keeping a low profile, but Eleazar lived in fear that he

Zoheleth

might attack when least expected.

Phanni, the newly elected chief priest, joined the zealots in getting drunk on the holy wine. When night came their drunkenness drove some zealots to sin in a most disgraceful manner. Their own people who refused to join them against Rome were killed. So vile were they that the noble people began nailing their doors shut against the zealot's invasion. The people became prisoners in their homes.

The Roman legions heard reports of the fighting but they remained at a distance. They had orders not to interfere with the disturbance. Even when they saw an army of Idumeans outside the city of Jerusalem, the Romans remained stationed.

Titus was joined by Tiberius Alexander who had arrived from Egypt to act as his military advisor. Tiberius was a man with much experience in war. He listened to the reports from the officers receiving news from their spies near the city. One commanding officer questioned Tiberius.

"Why not attack Jerusalem while the Jews are at war with each other?"

Tiberius smiled and shook his head. His dark eyes stayed on the officer as he pushed back his thick gray hair and replied. "It would not be wise. They would put aside their personal differences to come against us."

"Shall we do nothing?" asked the officer.

"We shall wait them out," Tiberius announced. "Allow them enough war against themselves and they'll weaken within." He saw Titus walking toward him.

"Caesar!" said Tiberius. "You heard about the fighting inside the city?"

"I've heard," said Titus as he and Tiberius walked out of ear shot of the officer. "I've been thinking," said Titus. "We should station our Tenth Legion northeast of the temple wall." He pointed toward the city and added. "They can set up camp at the Mount of Olives facing the Golden Gate leading to the temple." (Zech. 14:4-5)

"Let's go over your plans," said Tiberius. "Show me

on your map how you intend to surround the city."

The two entered Titus' quarters and spent the next few hours going over the best locations for the legions of Rome. Titus was in agreement with Tiberius to wait before they ventured any display of aggressiveness.

"We must offer them the right hand of Rome," Titus said. "If they accept, we will end the revolts without blood shed."

"I've a piece of news for you," said Tiberius. "I got word that a band of outlaws are heading to Jerusalem. They may be out for revenge against the zealots."

Titus raised his brows and smiled. "Are you thinking what I'm thinking? If this band is coming against the zealots, then our battle will be fought for us." The two laughed. "This calls for our finest wine," said Titus. "Let's toast on how to win a war without moving an inch," he jested. They drank and continued to design what moves should be made in the near future.

The people of Jerusalem saw the legions moving to different locations around the walls. Some worried that this was an omen of the wrath of God which was to come.

In the meantime, Simon was headed to Jerusalem, and John renewed his efforts to gain control of the temple.

The watchmen on the wall reported Simon and his horde of outlaws camped near the Romans. Eleazar was deeply concerned that Simon would join forces with John and combined they would siege the temple. He knew he would be killed for holding Simon's wife hostage. He and his men began drinking heavily.

"Simon is camped outside," groaned one man.

"And so is Rome," replied Eleazar, half laughing and half trembling. "Why don't the Romans come against them? Surely they reconize them as bandits."

"The Romans seem to be ignoring Simon," one man noted. "Both parties seems to be playing a waiting game."

"We can play the same game," said Eleazar. "We shall wait and see if the people really want a band of outlaws to come inside the city."

"Do you think John will join Simon?" asked a zealot. Eleazar thought for a moment. "If the people allow Simon to enter, then perhaps the Romans will take the opportunity to come in behind them. Who knows what will happen then?" Eleazar was troubled by the turbulence of his own thoughts. It would appear that a greater hand was coming against him and the people of Jerusalem.

Simon was amused how the Romans allowed them to pass without interception. He assumed Rome had no intentions of attacking Jerusalem now that Vespasian was Emperor. His guess was that Rome would not make a move until she settled her own civil unrest.

He sent a spy ahead while they set up their camps and waited. When the spy returned he had good news for Simon. The chief priest, Ananus, was dead. Simon for the first time in days broke out in laughter.

"That's the best news I've heard out of Jerusalem," he said. "I bet the old priest ran like a kicked cur until they caught him." His hatred for Ananus went back to a time when Ananus learned it was he, Simon, who robbed the people by night. The priest forced him out of Jerusalem with orders not to return until he paid back all he had taken.

Simon remembered threatening how one day he would return when the priest was dead. Often he lay awake wondering who informed Ananus that it was he who was stealing? He longed to know who delivered him up to the priest. Perhaps it was one of his own men who received a nice sum of gold from Ananas for the betrayal? But now, Ananas could no longer point an accusing finger at him.

Simon looked toward Jerusalem and wondered if anyone would open the gates to him? Tomorrow, he and his army would make an effort to talk their way into the city. He would use the wealthy men if he had to. In good faith, he could send them back to their homes and they could find a way to open the gates. He would use them only if he was refused entrance. He didn't know how much he could trust the men who came to him for help. Once inside the gates they might not aid him. He had to make some reasonable plans if he expected to be allowed inside.

THE TENTH LEGION

From a lookout point called Scopus, Titus found it easy to view Jerusalem. He had moved within one mile of the city to study the surrounding areas. He and Tiberius had mapped out favorable fields where to station the troops.

The Twelfth and the Fifteenth Legions would be camped two miles from the city. The Fifth Legion would be placed a quarter of a mile in the rear of the Twelfth Legion. The mighty Tenth Legion was ordered to the east of the city at the Mount of Olives, which was separated from the city by a deep ravine called Kedron.

As Titus surmised, the two factions inside the city began to unite when they saw the Roman legions surrounding the walls.

Within the city, the zealots put aside their differences and joined John's men. They seized the opportunity to make sally on the Tenth Legion. The surprise attack on the Romans came while they were setting up camp and their weapons lay on the ground. Before they could reach their arms, they were suddenly cut down by the Jewish extremists. The soldiers were thrown into disarray.

"Attack!" yelled Ebutius, one of the commanders of the Tenth Legion. "Follow me!" he shouted with his sword in hand. "We'll show those devils what the mighty Tenth is made of!" He struck the insurgents with such fierceness it caused them to flee in fear. His men designed the "tortoise" with their shields and surrounded him, but when he turned to strike another enemy, he took a blow to the back of his leg and fell to the ground.

Titus seeing the Tenth in trouble, mounted his charger and summoned his soldiers to the rescue.

When the rebels saw Titus, they ran for cover and disappeared underground.

"Ebutius!" he shouted when he saw his commander

Zoheleth

on the ground. "Are you able to rise?"

Two soldiers ran to help Ebutius as he struggled, but his leg was bleeding profusely and unable to hold his weight.

"Give me a hand," he beseeched. "They struck me in the back of the leg." His men carried him to the infirmary.

Most of the men of the Tenth sustained minor injuries, but sadly a few were killed.

Joseph and Marcus busied themselves with the incoming wounded. A few slaves trained as field medics helped the wounded into the infirmary. Ebutius was placed on a table face down. His wound was on the back of the calf of his leg.

"We never saw them," Ebutius declared. "They came from underground passages and struck from all sides."

Joseph mopped the blood flowing from the wound and tied a cloth around the upper part of the leg. He ordered Marcus to have the rod hot for searing.

Marcus was impressed by Ebutius' bravery. He heard how gallantly he fought. In the eyes of Marcus, this soldier was a hero. He saw the deep wound and wondered if he would walk again. Marcus judged him to be the same age as Antonius. Ebutius' brown hair fell into ringlets as the sweat rolled down his forehead. The soldier tried to give a weak smile, dimples appeared in his cheeks and vanished when his smile did.

"How bad is it, physician?" he groaned when the Joseph touched the area.

"I think you may be out of commission for a few weeks, but the wound can be mended," said Joseph.

Ebutius lay his head down and his face turned pale.

"I have a lot of sewing to do," said Joseph. "How would you like the cross stitching?" he kidded as he mixed a potion to give him. "First take a good sip of this opium. You can visit another world for a time."

When the surgery was over, Marcus covered Ebutius with a heavy blanket. Two soldiers carried their commander on a stretcher to a cot before they returned to duty.

Marcus examined others who were injured and administered the medications prescribed. He wrapped the wounds after Joseph had treated them.

Titus came to the infirmary and asked to be directed to Ebutius. He found the commander glassy eyed, but awake.

"You were very brave out there," Titus revealed. "But I must reprimand you and your men for their carelessness. There should always be guards about while you set up camp."

"Forgive me, Caesar, we were wrong," Ebutius slurred his words. "I should have known not to allow my men to be lax, but to be aware of the possibilities of an attack. My thanks to you for saving us."

Titus patted him on the shoulder. "Don't worry, my friend," he smiled. "You just regain your strength and heal quickly."

"H-ail... Caesar!" said Ebutius in an effort to salute. Titus returned the salute and grinned.

"I hear your wife has followed you."

"Yes, sir," Ebutius grunted. "She's camped with her...own guards not f..ar from ...us."

"I'll send word and have her escorted by our soldiers so she may visit with you." Titus saw his commander had fallen asleep. He left the infirmary.

Later that afternoon, Antonius of Ashkelon came to the infirmary to visit Marcus in the hopes of wetting his thirst with some straight wine.

"Ebony," he laughed, "I heard you have a friend of mine, Ebutius, as a patient."

Marcus greeted him, but kept wrapping the arm of a wounded soldier.

"See for yourself," Marcus replied. "I can't take you to him right now. He's in the back of the infirmary. I'll be there later to check on him."

"Joseph isn't around?" asked Antonius. "Where's the wine?"

"Not now! Antonius." Marcus replied, and went on working.

Antonius slapped him on the back and headed to the rear of the infirmary to find his friend.

"Ebutius!" he laughed loudly when he saw him with his leg elevated in the air. Cat-tail ropes hung from the ceiling with a papyrus sling to hold the leg.

"Aren't you a sight." he said as he stood next to the cot.

"Well, if it isn't my old wine-guzzling buddy," said Ebutius as he struggled to raise himself. "When did the devil turn you loose?" Ebutius made an effort to laugh. "You're a long way from Ashkelon. The last I heard you were met with a small war of your own out there."

"And I heard you had a private war with the zealots," said Antonius. "Did you think you were the son of Mars?"

"Just a son of Fortune," Ebutius replied, and lay back.

"The Jewish extremists are a force to be reckoned with," said Antonius as he looked around the tent. He hesitated a moment before he asked. "Is your wife with you?" He tried not to show any anxiousness.

"She's on her way," Ebutius informed. "Titus sent for her. If I know her, she will try her best to have her woman doctor check me over."

Antonius laughed nervously. "And I know you well enough to never allow it."

Ebutius glanced past Antonius. "Here she comes with Marcus."

Marcus approached and asked. "How's the pain?" He motioned Antonius to move so he could examine the bandages. "No signs of seepage," he said. "You'll heal quickly, now that your wife is with you."

Doris walked over and kissed her husband. They embraced tenderly.

"You met our young medic, Marcus?" asked Ebutius. His speech getting stronger.

"Yes," she smiled. "When I arrived, my private

Zoheleth

physician needed a few rare herbs, and Marcus gave her a supply."

Ebutius smiled. "Look who has come to visit. You remember Antonius."

She raised her blue eyes and looked directly at him.

"Antonius," she said softly. "How nice to see you again." She turned back to her husband.

"It's a pleasure to see you again, Doris," Antonius said in a low voice. "It's been a few years." He stood longingly staring at her while she stroked her husband's face.

He was spellbound by her beauty. Never had he longed for any woman the way he longed for her. His thoughts took him to the past, and now seeing her again only rekindled his desires.

Marcus noticed Antonius staring at Doris and he nudged him. "How about that wine you asked for?" he whispered. "Let's give them some privacy."

Antonius' face saddened as he turned and said his farewell. Marcus sensed something about the moment.

"Are you coming to our tent tonight?" Marcus asked.

Antonius shook his head as though he'd awakened from a dream.

"Oh," he said. "You bet. As long as you have wine to offer, I'll be your guest every night." He forced a laugh and gave Marcus a brotherly hug.

"You like the wine too much," Marcus warned gently. "But you look like you could use some right now. I'll account for it somehow."

"Never mind," said Antonius. "I'll see you later."
He headed outside and passed his comrades who asked him to join them in gambling. He barely glanced at them while he kept walking as though in a trance. He heard their laughter and for some reason he was no longer happy. His comrades were puzzled when he declined their offer to join them.

Later that night, he needed a drink. He visited Marcus where the wine was. Since he had lost his wages the night before in gambling, he had no cash to buy enough wine

Zoheleth

to get drunk.

Making friends with Marcus was the best thing he had done. He knew Joseph frowned on his habit but he also knew how the physician taught Marcus never to be inhospitable to a guest.

He entered the tent. Joseph glanced up, and went back to his writing. Marcus looked at his friend intently. "What's bothering you, Antonius?" he asked. "You're not your joyful self."

He wasn't aware his sadness was so obvious. He tried to joke around but it was forced. How could he tell anyone what tormented him. Did Doris suspect how he felt, he wondered. How could she know he was secretly in love with her from the first moment they met? But it was Ebutius who won her.

He slumped down in the chair and looked past Joseph while Marcus filled a goblet and placed the skin on the table in front of him.

"What do you think of Ebutius' wife?" he dared to ask. "Isn't she a beauty."

The question cut him to the heart. He gave a sigh and glanced at the floor saying, "Ebutius is a fortunate man."

Joseph looked up from his writing. "I hear she carries another child," he said while watching Antonius' reaction. "Her personal physician came to us for the herbs she might be needing."

Antonius glared at Joseph. Did he say that for a reason? It didn't matter that she was carrying a child. It didn't take away her beauty nor did it take away his longing.

"How long have you and Ebutius been friends?" asked Marcus. Antonius stared dreamily into his cup.

"We've been friends since childhood. I lost contact with him after he married, but I did visit them when their first son was born."

Marcus had never seen Antonius so solemn.

"It looks like it goes deeper," Marcus said shyly. "I bet the two of you were in love with her."

Antonius was shocked. He felt his face getting hot.

"You could say that," he admitted.

"Did you fight over her?" Marcus asked, pushing his inquiry further.

"Never!" Antonius shot back. He leaned himself forward and held the cup for a refill. He would have fought for her if there was any chance of winning her. His envy for Ebutius had turned to jealousy, and he wished his friend had been killed.

"You must have many girls in love with you," Marcus said in an effort to get him to smile. "You, who looks like a god!"

Antonius burst out laughing and Marcus' eyes lit up. He continued in his teasing. "I bet you have many single maidens who desire you. And, perhaps a few married ones also. Why haven't you married?"

"None of them had money," Antonius grinned, as he hit Marcus on the top of the head. "I need to find me a very rich young widow." He teased and drank more wine until his eyes grew heavy and his speech slurred. He became loud and Joseph walked over and removed the wine skin.

"I think you've had enough wine for the night," said Joseph. Antonius groaned and cursed Joseph under his breath as he left the tent.

When the lamps were out, Marcus lay on his cot.

"Joseph," he asked softly. "Do you think Ebutius' wife comes from money?"

"I would think so," came the answer from the other side of the tent. "She travels with the army and has her own private physician, as well as private guards and slaves," he added. "I'm certain she doesn't do that on the salary of a soldier."

Marcus listened and said rather discreetly. "My girl, Martha, doesn't come from money."

"What is Martha like?" Joseph asked through the dark. "You don't speak of her very often."

"I think she's beautiful. We have loved each other since we were twelve years old."

Zoheleth

"My, such a tender age." Joseph smiled in the dark.

"I send letters to my brother to give to her. Her parents don't know that we pledged ourselves to each other. I hope they'll allow us to marry."

"So," whispered Joseph, "you want to marry this young girl, Martha?"

"Yes, if she'll wait for me," he replied. "Tomorrow, I will show you a golden lock of her hair which I carry in my travel bag. It seals our pledge."

"That's very romantic," Joseph whispered as he yawned. "Now let's get some sleep."

Marcus stared into the darkness as he lay thinking. He envisioned his sweetheart as they ran through the fields of barley. Martha was fascinated by his dark skin and long black curly hair. He was just as fascinated by her pale face surrounded by long straight golden hair which glistened in the sunlight. He remembered her eyes, the color of the heavens and recalled the first time they kissed. It was near the rocks of the river-bed where they hid their notes to each other.

He also remembered her father who was never cordial to him. His thoughts changed to Antonius. He wondered if Antonius were secretly in love with Doris.

A WALL OF TOWERS

Whatever was going on inside Jerusalem was of no concern to Marcus and Joseph as they searched the wayside for wild herbs.

Marcus paused and scanned the area of the walled city. "I see three outstanding towers from here," he said as he pointed to the western end of the city.

"Herod the Great built those towers," said Joseph as he placed a few roots into the sack on his belt. "One is called Phasael. It was named for his brother. The tower to the right is called Mariamne, who was his favorite wife. The tower next to it is Hippicus which is named for one of Herod's friends."

"They look huge," Marcus commented.

"You haven't seen the towers inside the city's third wall," said Joseph as he stretched his back and shoulders.

"How many towers are in the city?"

"About ninety in number. You would be amazed by the beauty of some. They have rooms furnished in gold and silver. Some rooms are large enough to accommodate one hundred people."

"I'm impressed," Marcus replied.

"You would be more impressed if you saw the temple gates with their majestic doors covered in gold."

"Gates of gold?" Marcus repeated dreamily.

"The tower on the east side, connecting to the Holy Temple is the Tower of Antonia. It was constructed in honor of Mark Anthony."

Joseph walked a few steps and tried to get Marcus interested in digging for roots, but the lad was staring out over the land.

"I got a letter from my brother," Marcus informed. He reached inside his garment and withdrew a small scroll. "Would you like to read it?"

Zoheleth

"Why don't you read it aloud while I dig."
Marcus opened the scroll and began to read.

Dear Marcus and Father:

May the gods be with you and keep you safe. Mother sends her love. She feels better since she heard from father.
My friend Virgil is home from Rome. He tells me that the people of Rome are pleased with Vespasian as emperor. They like the fact that he gives Rome heirs to inherit the empire. His sons will follow in his footsteps.
Neither Galba, Otho, nor Vitellius proved to meet the expectations of the Senate or the Roman citizens.
Virgil said how Otho was a close friend to Nero. They grew up together, but as young men they were evil. They would drink and rob people who were out late at night. Their friendship soured over a woman named Poppaes Sabinus.
It is said how Otho fell in love with her and became the rival of Nero. While Nero was emperor, he married the woman, even though he was already married to another. Poppaes was married also to someone else. Virgil said Poppaes was kicked to death by Nero while she carried his unborn child.

Mother likes it that you are in training as a medic. I like it when you tell me stories about your good friend, Antonius.
She does worry about father. I told her that he has only three years left in the service of Rome. After that we'll be given Roman citizenship.
All is well here. Crops are good. Goats are healthy and the horses are cared for as usual.
May fortune be with you and father. Please write and let me know when you are camped at Jerusalem.

Marcus rolled the scroll and tucked it away in his belt.
"Your brother seems to get the news long before we do. He's lucky to have a friend who gives him the events," said Joseph. "Thank you for sharing your letter."
"Do you think I read well?"

"I think you do just fine. Who taught you?"

"My father's brother. I learned how to read and write and do mathematics." Marcus walked alongside of Joseph as they started back to their tent.

"Joseph, where did you go to school?"

"I was very young when my father taught me the Torah at home. By the age of five I was sent to an elementary school called the House of the Book." Joseph walked slowly as he examined the ground beneath their feet. He spotted a plant off to the side of the path. "Would you pull that out for me?" he asked.

Marcus gently pulled the plant and handed it to Joseph.

"How long were you in the School of the Book?"

"I spent five years there. We had to attend six days out of seven, and I was well fattened with the Torah."

"I can't picture you as five years old," Marcus laughed.

"At that age I had to get up at day break and walk to school. One of our servants went with me. He carried a torch to light the way. At noon, my mother would pick me up." He smiled as he reminisced. "Boys had to memorize the Torah every day. You see it is not proper to copy the Torah, which is our most sacred religious writings handed down by Moses, our prophet."

"I was about to ask you what the Torah was," Marcus smiled. "My Uncle Grates made us memorize mathematics until we could do it without thinking. We used sticks to write our problems on the ground."

"Yes," Joseph smiled. "We used waxed covered tablets with a stylus to scratch out our numbers."

"Where did you go after elementary school?"

"By the time I was ten, I entered the House of Learning. That's where we studied oral law."

"When did you become a doctor?"

"My father was a healer, as well as a surgeon. My family moved to Alexandria and there I was able to study music, and the arts, also philosophy. I learned the art of surgery in Alexandria's School of Medicine. I was encouraged to be a doctor like my father."

"Are your parents dead?" asked Marcus.

"Yes," Joseph sighed. "I still remember working along side of my father when I was your age." He lowered his head and went on. "He taught me about herbs, the same way I teach you."

"Do you have brothers?"

"No, but I had a sister," Joseph informed. "She died before she was given in marriage. I liked watching her as she weaved at a loom. Our girls are taught the practical side of the law, as well as how to be a good wife."

"You said she died. What was wrong with her?"

"I don't remember the details clearly, but I do remember there was a plague. My mother would take my sister with her and go to the mothers who were ready to deliver their babies." Joseph picked another plant and checked it carefully before putting it with the others. "My father had developed a drug that reduced the pain while in labor. My mother was in demand as a mid-wife because she used the drug on the women."

"Your father discovered a drug?" Marcus raised his brows. He heard his voice cracking in the middle of a sentence. At times he could speak deeper.

"My father was a broken man when my mother, and then my sister, both died." Joseph shook his head sadly. "From what I learned, my mother and sister may have been in contact with a woman infected with the plague." He wiped his eyes.

"That's too bad," said Marcus.

"My father never spoke of them again."

"Joseph, did you ever get married?"

"I was wondering when you would ask," he laughed.

"After my medical studies were completed, I married and settled in Alexandria and we lived with my father. My wife died giving birth to our son. She aborted unexpectedly. Unfortunately my infant son died shortly after. I never remarried." Joseph fell silent.

In the tent they separated the herbs for drying. Marcus was at a loss for words.

"You look sad, doctor."

"I'm all right. I was thinking of the songs my sister would sing. I had forgotten how pleasant the times were when we were together."

"I didn't mean to get you upset," Marcus apologized.

"I'm glad you stirred up memories," Joseph smiled kindly.

They worked under the lamp light until all the herbs were tied with a vine and hung to dry.

Marcus felt closer to Joseph, since they shared their personal experiences. He wished to know how Joseph kept such faith in a god whom he never sees.

CHAPTER NINETEEN

A THIRD FACTION

The Jews came by the thousands to make their yearly pilgrimage to Jerusalem. They were completely unaware of the terrorism that had taken place inside the city by the zealots.

Simon, son of Giora, was camped outside the walls of Jerusalem in view of the Roman armies. He kept his vigil for a time when he could enter the city. He desired revenge for the kidnapping of his wife by the zealots. He knew his presence was a threat to them.

People from all nations entered the city with no resistance as they came to worship. This gave Simon the incentive to devise a plan which might get them inside the gates. He called several of his men.

"I want a few men to go to the gates," he ordered. "Tell them you have come peacefully as ambassadors, and assure them that we desire only to be allowed to worship."

"Shouldn't we storm the gates while the people are entering?" asked one.

Simon disagreed. "The more people in the city the more pickings for us," he laughed. He advised the ex-prisoners of Eleazar to stay at the rear of his division, because the zealots might recognize them and expect trouble. He didn't want to expose his cover too soon. His plan was to convince the people how he could help free them from the zealots' rule over the temple. He would tell how the ex-prisoners informed him of what was happening between John and Eleazar.

One thing in his favor was his strength in number. It would be no problem to send for the other half of his band stationed in Idumea. His promise to help the escaped prisoners regain their losses was a lie. His mind was on making their losses his gain.

Zoheleth

Hours had passed, and the gates were shut after the visitors filed into the city. Simon sent his men to negotiate. He watched while his men spoke with the guard. The guard entered the city and presented the plea from Simon to the priest, Theophilus.

The priest was greatly distraught over the number of additional people entering the city. It was now overflowing with travelers from many nations.

Theophilus gave serious thought to Simon's request, and summoned a council of priests before deciding how to deal with Simon.

"How are we to conduct the ceremonies of worship while the temple is under control of the zealots?" asked Theophilus to the council of priests. "And now we're faced with a plea from Simon who sits outside our gates. He has made an offer for us to consider."

The small group of priests grumbled. They were uneasy over the request sent by Simon.

One priest spoke out. "The greater question is," he said, "how can we stop this infernal turmoil between Eleazar and John?" The priests looked at each other with concern.

"We have been made powerless," cried one priest. "Whatever we decide will bring John's men down on us."

They were troubled until a priest named James, attempted to make a suggestion.

"I don't know if I'm saying the right thing," he commenced, "but if Simon has offered to expel Eleazar from the temple, then he could be our answer."

"Have you gone mad?" an elder priest argued. "Simon is as bad, if not worse, than what's inside the temple!"

"Exactly!" said James. "The zealots are in fear of Simon! You know they held Simon's wife hostage." He paused to allow his words to sink in. "Simon and his men could forge their way into the holy temple and help us take control. I'm sure he could overthrow John if we offered to pay him a tidy sum. We need a man vile in temperament."

Theophilus and the council sat in silence while they

listened to James.

"We can offer Simon sanctuary in the upper section of our city and cooperate with him to overthrow John first. Then with our combined efforts, we can draw Eleazar out of the sacred precincts."

James watched their expressions while they seriously contemplated his idea. He went on to say, "Once we get Simon fighting Eleazar, we'll seize control of the temple," he added.

James sat back and waited for the council to make a decision. They believed it was a good strategy to put into operation.

"We agree," said Theophilus, "we will open the gates to Simon under the conditions you offered." He glanced at the others and asked. "Are we all in accord?" They voted to allow Simon entrance to the city.

Simon entered with his men and was given control of the upper part of the city. He followed the terms the priests presented and attacked John's men first. His onslaught shocked the priests. They witnessed Simon's men stealing all the loot gained by John and his men. After much bloodshed, John's men retreated.

To the dismay of the priests, Simon took control of the lower half of the city as well. He was now in a position to wipe out the zealots and take the temple with all its gold.

The city became a war zone, and the citizens of Jerusalem were fleeing for their lives. Many left all their belongings, except their gold.

The tribulation became too great. Three factions were at war with one another. John and his men, Eleazar and the zealots, and now Simon and his cutthroats. The priests saw these factions being more deadly than an army of scorpions.

Many people made an effort to escape with their possessions and found themselves facing John's guards posted at the exits of the city. These people, some who were cititzens of Jerusalem, paid dearly by relinquishing all their gold. They were given the choice, their gold or their life.

Zoheleth

They paid their way for a safe exit, hoping the Romans wouldn't capture them when they got outside the gates.

The city was a battlefield and innocent visitors found themselves in the midst of it. They were robbed and slaughtered if they resisted Simon's men.

Theophilus hid himself when it was revealed that he introduced Simon into the city. He feared for his life, since he was already in deep trouble for allowing John's men inside.

Many of the innocent priests were killed when they tried to talk with Simon's men.

The Romans were informed that after Simon entered, all hell broke out in the holy city of Jerusalem.

NEWS FROM ROME

Titus waited to hear from Bernice. In his message he requested that she stay close to where he was stationed with the legions.

The day arrived when her servant delivered her answer. His hands trembled as he opened the sealed scroll in the privacy of his quarters. It read:

Titus, beloved prince and son of Caesar:

My heart was shaken when I learned how your life was in peril. The frightening news reached me after your request for my visit. Why, dear prince, did you not wear your helmet or a breast plate on that dreadful day?
The knowledge that my own people caused you to be so close to death, troubles me.
My servant has arranged for my living quarters a few miles from your camp. A village close to Bethel had a small house to rent. I understand it has a lovely garden where we may spend time together. Hurry to me, I shall be lonely until your arrival. May God speed you to me. Lovingly Bernice.

After Titus read her letter he sent for his personal servant to fill the portable tub with water. He was bathed, oiled, and had his skin scrapped. He then added perfume and had his hair cut.

Tiberius Alexander entered his quarters and wrinkled his nose to the sweetened air.

"Greetings, Caesar," he smiled. "Do I assume you are expecting guests?"

Titus' face shone as he smiled widely. "No," he answered. "I'm to be someone's guest."

"Well, I hope the news from your father won't change your plans."

"You have word from my father?" Titus looked at his reflection in a shiny disk on the wall. In his heart, he prayed it would not be news that would detain him from Bernice.

"Do me the favor and read it. My barber needs to shave the back of my neck."

"As you say, Caesar." Tiberius opened the scroll and stationed his foot on a chair. His tanned legs displayed thick muscles under sandals laced high on his calves. His gray hair held signs of a mixture of brown. He was not a tall man, but stocky. He threw his cape back over his shoulders and read.

"Your father says he's repairing the buildings of Rome which were destroyed by fire," he looked at Titus. "I believe he's referring to the buildings that Vitellius put ablaze."

"Any orders about Jerusalem?" asked Titus.

"Definitely!"

Titus felt his heart sink. "What does he want us to do?"

"He wants you not to incite an attack on Jerusalem. He wants to settle Rome first."

Titus sighed in relief. "This will give us time to get our plans established, while my father takes care of things in Rome."

"There's a special note for you. Do you wish me to read it?"

"Go ahead," Titus replied. Tiberius opened the second scroll.

My son, Titus:
Greetings from your father. I pray the gods have protected you in my absence. I did hear of your foolishness at the walls of Jerusalem. Never allow yourself to be a target for those belligerent rebels again.
Now for the news about Rome, which I know you want to hear: By the time my vanguard reached Rome, many of Vitellius' men had fallen ill. They came down with dysentery from using the water of the Tiber River. Some suffered from malaria according to our medics.

Zoheleth

Our troops had no problems in defeating Vitellius' army since they were physically weakened. I warned our soldiers not to drink or use the water from the Tiber River.

I'm rebuilding the Forum near the Temple of Jupiter. The Rostrum needs repair, except the side of the Forum used by the Senate. You know the place, the Curia. It seems in good shape. The place referred to as the Basilica, or the Court of Justice, is in dire need of repair. The shops and the school rooms facing the Forum were not damaged.

Some of the would-be-advisors suggested that I use machines to remove the debris. I quickly insisted how it is honorable for men to work with their hands to feed themselves and their families.

One thing, my son, which I have learned in my years, idleness breeds mischief.

Need I mention how I mourn the loss of my brother? We both chose different paths in life. I was proud that he had a more distinguishing career, although I'm sure he would be proud to see me as the emperor of Rome.

Rome is easing up on civil disruptions. The Senate has been more than cooperative with me and my men. Your brother is taking a short leave from his service to help me until you have put an end to the trouble in Judea. When you return to us in Rome, I will name you Proconsul Imperium, and you will be a partner in my Tribunician power.

I've expelled all the men who held office by the power of Vitellius. I need you here since you are familiar with how this royal stuff is handled.

It's fortunate that I became the owner of several copper mines which paid for my sons' education in Rome. You were fortunate to become a favorite to Britannicus, Emperor Claudius' son. Your living in the palace will prove to be a piece of good fortune.

There's much to learn if I'm to rule the world of Rome. You are the one familiar with its workings. I need you!

How I wish your mother was alive to see this day! My men and I have made sacrifices to the gods. May Jupiter favor Rome!

Zoheleth

Tiberius rolled the scroll and placed it on the table.

"Well," he said, "what do you say now? It looks like you'll rule Rome with your father."

"We shall see," he said. He admired his reflection and thanked his barber who brushed away a few hairs. He felt like a new man, more handsome than he looked in a long time. He ran his fingers through the dark ringlets formed around his face. His hair was sprinkled with a touch of gold dust. Roman men used this when they wanted to impress a lady and Titus wanted to impress Bernice. He turned to Tiberius and said.

"I want you to take command while I'm away."

"Yes, Caesar. That will be no problem," Tiberius said as he removed his foot from the chair. "Should I ask where the noble Titus will be, and for how long?"

"You may," said Titus, still smiling. He walked closer to Tiberius and whispered. "I'll be five miles outside the camp. One of my servants will return to let you know where I'm staying."

He patted Tiberius on the shoulder and reached for the wine skin. His servant set out cups and Titus motioned the servant to leave. He and Tiberius seated themselves.

"I don't want the word out that I'm with Agrippa's sister. Do you understand?"

"Ah-hah!" Tiberius burst forth with laughter. "Now I understand!"

"You know what soldiers are like when they get a piece of gossip."

"You have my word, Caesar," he said, "but how certain are you of your own guards?"

"I trust them in battle and nothing else," confessed Titus. They laughed and Tiberius lifted his cup and toasted.

"Good fortune in all ways, noble Titus," he gave a sly grin and added, "especially with the lady." Titus felt his face flush. He smiled and drank another cup of wine. He instructed Tiberius on how he wanted the camp run, telling him not to allow the soldiers to be without work each day.

Zoheleth

The sun had gone down and twilight appeared across the land. Titus made his departure from the camp and led the way. He and his escort of guards traveled the main road, but his men knew nothing as to where they were going.

The clouds turned purple and then a dark gray. The mountains stood draped in shadows, and the breeze was cool and soft.

As he rode, he thought about his father's letter. It brought to mind a man in the royal family named Narcissus. It was he who brought Vespasian to the attention of the emperor after winning many courageous battles. Narcissus encouraged Emperor Claudius to allow Titus to study in Rome with Britannicus, the son of the emperor. Titus became close friends to Britannicus. They were the same age and he and Britannicus were inseparable. Titus liked how royalty lived.

"Caesar!" called one of his guards. "My horse has grown lame. I need to check his hoof."

"Take care of your horse. If he's unable to continue, then walk him. We're near our destination," said Titus.

With the help of a torchlight, the guard was able to dig out a stone that lodged in the horse's hoof.

Titus saw the house set back off the road. He wanted to race his horse, but hesitated. It would be a childish move to show his anxiousness in front of his men. He would be there soon enough.

His thoughts drifted back to Britannicus. He pictured the night when they were at a banquet with the very young Nero, the adopted son of Emperor Claudius. Britannicus was legally the next in line to rule after the death of his father, Claudius.

Nero's mother, Agrippina, who was also a cousin to Emperor Claudius and his latest wife, had ambitions for her son, Nero. She was determined that he would be the next ruler of Rome and not Britannicus.

Titus recalled he was seated next to Britannicus when his friend drank from a cup, and suddenly fell to the floor in agony. Titus recalled the fear when he himself had tasted his own drink and became extremely sick. He remembered seeing Britannicus dead.

If it weren't for Narcissus, one of his teachers who hid him away until he was strong enough to travel, he would be numbered among the dead.

He pulled his horse to a stop before the small house. The moon had risen and was bright enough to see the outlines of the surrounding trees and a wooden fence wrapped around the front and back garden.

His heart raced and he felt the blood rush to his face and pump through his veins like a raging river. He wanted to be calm, but love was something not in his control. He ordered his men not to stray from the area until he was ready to return to camp.

When he left his escort, they joked among themselves. They recognized Agrippa's guards coming to meet them. They knew there would be plenty of food along with fine wines coming from the house of the king's sister. They were in a very good mood!

Zoheleth

THE GARDEN

His legs were shaking when he knocked at the door. He was greeted by a Greek house servant.

"Welcome, honorable Titus," he said as he reached to accept the cape and helmet from Caesar. "My mistress is expecting you," he added.

Titus looked around nervously at the interior of the house. It was small but sufficient. The servant led him into a room with elaborate paintings on the walls. The tile floor had a luxurious Persian rug covering it. His sandals sunk into its thickness.

He wanted to remember every portion of this house. His thirsty eyes drank in the scene. The chairs were of swirling colors of silk and their wooden legs intricately designed with flowers. Each leg of the chair was carved with vines wrapping around from the top to the foot.

He was amused by thinking how Bernice chose to bring some of her finest treasures to decorate a small village house.

"How good to see you again," Bernice said as she stepped from an adjoining room.

Titus spun around and caught his breath. Her beauty stunned him. She stood like a goddess in a pale blue garment with sheer veils drapping over it. Gold braided straps outlined her breasts and wrapped around her slender waist. The garment clung to the curves of her body and reached down to the tip of her golden slippers. He smiled and bowed.

"The son of Caesar has come to pay tribute to a Queen." He felt his lips trembling. His emotions were pleasurable as he watched her moving toward him.

"And how does the son of Caesar intend to pay tribute?" she asked teasingly.

He felt his face flush.

"However you desire," he replied. "I'm at your mercy." He broke into a wide smile.

"My first desire," she said as she took his arm, "is to feed you after your journey." She led him to a corner table, where many delightful dishes had been prepared for his visit.

"I trust you're hungry," she said smoothly. He followed her like a child. His heart beating wildly.

They seated themselves and were served by her servants. Titus handled one of the gold goblets and admired the inlaid gems sparkling in the lamplight.

They lifted the goblets of wine and she toasted.

"To Caesar, long may he live," she said wistfully. "My servants will see that your men are provided for," she assured him.

"Just don't spoil them," he chided.

"May I spoil you?" she asked.

"You have my permission." He wished there were no one else in the room. He wasn't hungry but in no way would he offend his hostess who went to the extremes to please him. He ate slowly and drank slowly while his soul grew hungry for her.

Through the meal, Bernice asked about his battles. He was at ease discussing matters of war. They talked in idle chatter until they finished eating. She studied him while the servants cleared the table. They drank sweet Jordean wine while engaging in conversation.

"Come with me," she whispered. "Let's visit the garden."

They stepped outside and into the light of a full moon. The path was lit by torches, and the aroma of roses scented the gentle breeze.

"Wait until you see the waterfall," she said with laughter in her voice. "It's the most romantic spot in the garden."

They watched the water cascade over the rocks, bubbling down into an oval pond. The water captured the reflection of the stars and shattered them with every ripple.

He turned his gaze on her. "At last," he whispered in

her ear, "we're alone." He touched her shoulder, and she turned her head toward him. He felt her tremble for a moment as he kissed the side of her face. She closed her eyes and sighed softly.

"Looking at you in the moonlight is like living a thousand years in a moment of time. If I never live another day, I will have lived a lifetime in this one evening."

She turned and faced him.

"You're such a romantic," she smiled. "Is it the moonlight?" She smiled and glanced back at the waterfall.

He wondered what she was thinking at that moment.

"The garden is enchanting and so are you," he whispered. He put his arms around her, then, lowered his head and kissed her lips fully. She pulled away but he drew her closer to him and kissed her again.

"I've dreamed of this moment ever since our first meeting," he confessed. She stared at him strangely.

"What are you thinking?" he asked tenderly.

"I'm thinking of what it feels like to be in the arms of the prince of Rome. One who will rule the world one day."

"You overestimate me," he laughed lightly.

"One night, not too long ago," she began, "I had a feeling that something wonderful was going to happen. I wonder if this is it?"

"I hope this is the moment you were waiting for."

"Beloved Titus," she whispered. "Let's go in."

They held hands and walked back to the house. Once inside, she dismissed her servants.

Titus couldn't stop admiring her.

"And what are you thinking about?" she asked.

"You!" he answer. "My thoughts are filled with you. There's no room for anything else." He saw the kindness in her eyes as she gave into his loneliness.

The morning rose with a pink and golden sky. Titus stood in the garden where they stood the night before. He stretched as though he could touch the clouds. The aroma of flowers fresh with dew filled his nostrils. He caught the sound of crowing roosters in the distance and waking birds singing their private song. The new day was like the Goddess of Love. His mind was dreamy and he was happier than he'd been in years. He was in love and wanted the world to know. His Hasmonian beauty of royal blood, he envisioned as his wife. She had all the credentials to be the wife of a Caesar, he thought.

Bernice walked out to the garden. She yawned and hugged him. He kissed her forehead and put his arm around her shoulders.

"My prince of Rome," she teased. "I hear you write poetry and play the harp. I also learned that you sing."

He stroked her hair hanging loosly over her shoulders. "You've been checking around about me?" he smiled. "Well, I do write poetry, but don't ask me to sing."

"Darling, recite one of your poems for me."

"Never!" he chuckled.

"Don't tease me," she pleaded.

"What I will do," he said, "is write one to you. One that I hold in my heart."

"You're so sweet," she hugged him.

"Did you know that love makes your eyes shine?"

"Is this the beginning of your poem?"

His fingers outlined her face and rested on her mouth. She kissed them. He looked out over the garden and thoughtfully said to her. "When the poem is born, you shall be the only one to read it."

"Darling," she whispered.

"Bernice, I love you," he said softly. "Will you be my wife?" She pulled out of his arms.

"Your wife?" Her words were almost harsh.

"Please, beloved. Say you'll marry me," he begged.

"How can I hold all this joy?" she cried. "But you know I can't marry you."

He stepped back in disbelief. "You can't! Or you won't? What is there to stop you?"

"Titus, beloved. It's my religion. I believe in one God. I couldn't marry a man who worships pagan gods."

Zoheleth

He grabbed her arms and shook her gently.

"I promise to put away all the pagan gods!" he declared. "They can't do anything! I'll accept your God. How's that?"

"Do you really mean it? You will accept the God of the Jews?"

"I mean every word! I love you! I want you and need you by my side. Together we'll rule Rome!" he announced.

"I do believe you mean it," she marveled.

"I won't be the first Roman to denounce the gods and worship one God. For you I will worship your God."

"You would be willing to?"

"Under one condition," he replied, "that you allow me to worship you."

"Beloved, Titus." She threw her arms around him and he lifted her off her feet.

"I take that as a yes!" he laughed. "My life will never be the same. I'm so much in love!"

Titus felt new and alive. He didn't care if she were older, he told himself. He loved her with all his heart. When he became emperor, no one will dare to speak of their age differences.

THE FAREWELL

On the third sunrise, Bernice and Titus stood in the garden. It was a lovely sight seeing the night sky being swallowed by the dawn. The dew shone on the flowers while birds awakened and chirped.

Titus kept his arm around her. She was shivering from the dampness.

"I wish you didn't have to leave," she sighed softly.

"And I the same," he answered as he hugged her lightly. "But I must get back to the camp."

She rested her head on his shoulder while he stroked her hair.

"I love you, and I'll return quickly," he promised.

"Tell me you'll not be foolish in your bravery while trying to impress those you fight."

"You amuse me," he laughed. "How shall I treat the enemy?" He searched her eyes when she lowered her head.

"Yes," she whispered. "The enemy. It's my people who are your enemy."

"Don't talk that way. I didn't mean how it sounded." He grew tense when he saw a tear on her cheek. "You are not my enemy," he said, and wiped her tears. "You know I'll do all in my power to prevent a war against your people."

"Oh Titus," she wept. "I know you will. I believe you, my darling."

"You're to be my wife," he reminded her. "I want us to be happy together."

"Marriage," she sighed as she regained her composure. "I've never known it to be good!"

He looked sternly into her eyes.

"What are you saying?"

She turned away from him. "You know so little about me." She walked toward the pond, touching the flowers as she passed. "I was made to marry my uncle,

Herod of Chalcis, when I was thirteen."

He followed her. "That's the past," he said.

"When my husband died I went to live with my family." She rested her head against his shoulder. "I never wanted to marry again, but I did what was best for my people. It was planned that I accept the proposal from the King of Cilicia. That's how I obtained the title of Queen."

"Shh!" he whispered. "I said it was the past."

"Here stands a queen without a king," she forced herself to smile.

"You won't be for long," he assured her. "I will be your king!" They kissed.

He was troubled over leaving her. But he had commitments to Rome and to the legions waiting.

His last kiss was filled with bitter sweetness as he pulled himself from her outstretched arms.

He wept as he walked to his men and mounted his horse. He looked back and saw his goddess waving farewell.

She watched him ride away until she could only see his outline in the distance. It was when she entered the house that she found herself hating the loneliness.

She drew the drapes across the bedroom doorway and refused to look at the un-made bed.

On the table, she caught sight of a small scroll and knew that Titus had left it for her. Her heart beat wildly as she ran to the garden to read it. A thrilling sensation filled her when she found he had composed a poem for her.

To my beloved. As I held you in my arms last night, I created a poem while gazing at your beauty. Words will never tell you how I feel inside my heart.

Our Last Night Together

Lie here beside me.
Love makes your eyes shine.
Rest your head close to me.
I feel your heart beating with mine.
Hold back the dawn, for tomorrow

I'll be gone.
But this will always be
a precious memory.
Hold me, my love.
And don't say a word.
Let your kisses tell me all
the things I haven't heard.
Oh, I don't know if we are
wrong or right.
Just lie here beside me tonight.

She kissed the words written on the papyrus.

    Titus rode ahead of his men. He was deep in thought. His personal guards smiled amongst themselves at their Caesar, but didn't mention his stay with King Agrippa's sister.
    Along the roadside there were men offering sacrifices to the gods at the altars built for travelers. Titus pulled his horse to a stop and dismounted.
    "Wait here!" he ordered and he joined others praying to the gods. When he returned to his men, he was in good spirits.
    "Race you to the camp!" he shouted. His men let the horses loose into a full gallop. Their hooves digging into the earth and kicking up clouds of dust behind them. Boisterous shouts were heard as the men competed against each other. Titus laughed as he sped ahead in full splendor on his great steed.
    When they arrived at camp, the horses were lathered in sweat and snorting heavily. The young cadets came to walk the horses until they cooled down.
    Titus made his way to the camp's worship chapel. He greeted the Roman priest, and fell to his knees and prayed to the gods. He thanked them for all his good fortune. But only the gods knew that his joy was to be short lived.

CHAPTER TWENTY

THE RETURN OF TITUS

The field hospital in the Roman camps received the injured escapees from Jerusalem after the onslaught between John and Simon. Many citizens fled the city and took their chances and surrendered to the Romans.

Joseph checked the conditions of the people, and Marcus set up additional cots for those wounded.

In Titus' absence, Tiberius had offered the innocent citizens of the city the right hand of Rome.

Joseph noticed a figure standing in the doorway of the infirmary. "If you are injured, please take a seat. I'll attend to you shortly," Joseph instructed.

The man called out. "Are you Joseph?" he asked.

"You have me at a disadvantage, sir."

"I'm Josephus. I was the general of the Jewish army," he introduced himself.

Joseph welcomed him. "When did you arrive in camp?" he questioned.

"I came the day after Titus left," said the general.

"Please," said Joseph, "come in. Let me introduce my assistant."

Marcus shook hands with the general. "I remember seeing you at Jotapata."

"Not a very pleasant event," the general answered.

"You're also a priest?" Marcus questioned.

"That I am, young man."

"Will you excuse me, General?" Marcus requested. "There's a civilian who needs my attention."

"May I be of assistance?" asked the general.

"Come along," Marcus said, as he motioned him to follow. "I've soaked the linen cloths in vinegar to wrap this man's leg. He has a fracture. The linen, when it dries, will shrink and act as a cast to support the leg."

Marcus did the wrapping while the general held the man's leg upright. When the wet cast was finished, Marcus suggested the man keep off it for a time.

"Do you have many citizens of the city in the infirmary?" asked the general.

"We're overcrowded," said Marcus. "Our physician fears that we'll not have enough drugs on hand to help these unfortunate people." Joseph joined Marcus and at that moment a military guard entered to announce that Caesar was approaching. When Titus entered the infirmary, his face drained of color when he saw the number of wounded.

"Physician!" he called. "Explain all these civilians among our wounded soldiers?"

"In your absence, Caesar," said Joseph, "the rebels dared another sally on the Roman camps."

"But why are these Jews in here?"

"They are refugees, Caesar," Joseph explained. "They accepted the hand of Rome, but were wounded for doing so."

"Who harmed them?" Titus raised his voice.

The general stepped forward. "Their own people," he said. "Caesar, if I may inform you that I was sent to the walls of the city in an effort to ask the rebels to surrender peacefully."

Titus turned to the general with a look of surprise. "Forgive me, General, for not being here to welcome you. I'm pleased you are with us."

The general nodded and smile. "I understand."

"I'll set up a refugee camp for your people," Titus assured the general.

"May the Lord God of Israel keep you," said Josephus.

"Come with me, General," said Titus. "I need your help in determining how we can negotiate with the usurpers in the city."

Before he left the infirmary, Titus took the physician aside to talk privately.

"Get all the information you can from the civilians.

Zoheleth

Keep me informed if you learn anything of value."

Titus took the Jewish general to his quarters. Wine was served and he and the general sat at the table.

"I return to find too many of my men injured due to the sneak attacks from the rebels." Titus stared at the general, then questioned. "Why, when we have offered no hostile signs, they bring on this outrage?" He tried to hold back his anger. He was being forced to put Bernice from his mind.

"I'm sorry this has happened," said the general. "I had no idea of the inner workings of the zealots and the three factions. You must remember I've been in prison all these months."

"I regret that, General." Titus apologized. Titus saw in front of him a small man with dark brown eyes and a nose too large for his thin face. He found the general spoke as a well educated man, but would he help Rome? he wondered.

"Your stay in prison was necessary," said Titus. "After the resistance at Jotapata, there was not a worthy reason to spare your life. You were spared by your prophecy, if you recall."

"I do recall," said the general.

"How can we learn of the workings in the city?" asked Titus to change the subject.

The general thought for a moment and replied. "I know of a man in the infirmary by the name of Mattahias. He's an elder of the city and has just escaped. He would know the latest happenings inside," he informed.

"Go on," Titus encouraged.

"If this man had to flee the city, things must have gotten out of hand."

"Will he talk with me?" asked Titus.

"He may not speak Greek or Latin well enough," said the general. "He uses Aramaic or at times Hebrew. I'm sure your physician will be able to communicate with him."

"Why not you?" asked Titus.

"My people don't trust me since I'm here with the Romans," the general confessed and shook his head sadly.

"I understand," said Titus, as he got up from the table. He paced the floor restlessly, with his head lowered while thinking.

"It will be a help if you speak with your people and offer the terms I present to them." He hoped the general would fully cooperate.

"General," said Titus, "when you go to the wall, I'll see that there's an escort for your safety. And, I want you to do me the honor of acting as my historian."

The Jewish general was somewhat taken aback. He looked at Titus and nodded in an affirmative manner.

"We have our Roman historians," Titus continued. "But I would like you to record what you witness." He watched the general nodding. "And some day, through your eyes, tell the world the events as you have seen them. Write how Rome was unwillingly brought into the uprisings against this city. Would you do this?" He wanted the loyalty of Josephus, but didn't want any harm to come to him by his people.

"I will, young Caesar," the general answered. "And please, accept my gratitude for the fine clothes and the shelter you have provided for me."

"You deserve it."

The general smiled and said. "I remember how you pleaded with your father to spare my life. I'm indebted to you."

Titus felt satisfied there would be some trust between them.

WALLS OF TIMBER

Titus was in his quarters reading the reports on the events which happened during his absence. He sent word for Tiberius to join him.

"Caesar!" Tiberius saluted when entering. "You sent for me?" Watered wine was served while Titus mulled over the reports.

"I'm informed that our men were attacked at several sections."

"For two days we fought off their sally," Tiberius said defensively.

"Didn't anyone see them coming?"

"Not until they were on top of us. We can't find their tunnels from whence they come or where they escaped us." Tiberius kept his manner polite.

"By the gods!" Titus threatened. "We'll put an end to this!" He pounded his fist on the table and looked at the map which Joseph drew. "The physician has underlined a few tunnels," he said, pointing out on the map. "But there must be more."

"They strike so fast," Tiberius complained. "And without any order," he continued. "Our men are confused when they attack. You've seen the infirmary, and now we have refugees from the city begging for help."

"I'm having a camp set up for the refugees," Titus said. "They can remain here, but under no circumstances are they to return to the city," he impressed upon Tiberius. "We don't know who is faking injury or who could be a spy."

"As you command, Caesar," said Tiberius.

"Call the officers and the legions' commanders together. I think we can design a way to trap the arrogant reprobates."

"May the gods give you wisdom," said Tiberius.

"I need more than that. If the revolutionaries

continue, I can promise you, I'll attack Jerusalem without orders from Rome!" He looked at Tiberius and added, "These militants engineer their own misfortunes and if it isn't stopped, I will bring Jerusalem to her knees bleeding!"

Tiberius rose and saluted. "Hail Caesar!" He left to follow the orders to assemble the legions' commanders along with the officers.

Titus stood outside his quarters while the officers and commanders were brought in front of him. "Men of Roman command!" he said as he glanced around. "I have summoned you here to draw up a plan to outwit the Jews who choose to draw Rome into a war with them."

The officers began complaining and grumbling. Antonius of Ashkelon stepped forward. "Caesar," he addressed Titus. "How do we stop their madness?"

Another commander joined in and said, "Let's make war on them now! Does Rome desire to see more of us dead before declaring war?"

Titus raised his hand to silence them and chose not to reprimand them for their outburst.

"Hold your tongues," he ordered. "Since we can't find their tunnels, I have a suggestion." He watched the men stirring restlessly. "The insurrectionists are avaricious and cunning," he confessed. "They take us for fools! We will show them we're not fools!"

Antonius had more to complain about. "They're rancorous, Caesar. Give us the order to scale the walls of the city!"

"Without the emperor's consent, I can't give you the order," Titus warned. "Believe me, I don't want to deprive you of your pleasures."

"Caesar, they spit on us and call us Roman swine," Antonius announced. "I speak for my men. We want action!"

"Antonius!" Titus raised his voice. "You command a legion. You earned the command by obeying orders your commander gave. You must serve to know how to rule!"

"Forgive me, Caesar." Antonius stepped back in line.

Zoheleth

Titus brushed aside his rashness.

"This is what we'll do," he began. "We'll close the city in with walls of timber. I want every tree cut down and when there are no more trees, then go to the next village and get more! We'll close ourselves in and close the enemy out!"

The commanders and officer were jubilant. They hailed Caesar for giving them a way to protect themselves from sudden attacks.

"You have fired their hopes, Caesar," said Tiberius.

"Tiberius, I want the walls completed by this time tomorrow!" He looked at the men and shouted, "Did you men hear me?"

They cheered Titus and spurred each other on.

"Let the walls begin!" Titus shouted. The men ran to their legions.

"Great stratagem!" Tiberius said. "We'll have some peace until Rome decides our move."

"Take charge, Tiberius," said Titus. "I must get over to the physician. There's an injured Jew in the infirmary who may be able to give us some insight." He paused and added. "Tell the men I want the walls at least six feet high."

"As ordered!" Tiberius returned to his quarters to draw the plans for the timber walls. He designed openings at each section to secure guards who would be hidden from the enemy. He would set up a prison camp for those captured when attempting to make sally on the Romans.

Titus had other plans for the evening. He sent word to Joseph to have the Jewish refugee present when he arrived. His personal guards followed him to Joseph's tent.

"I'll be with the physician for the evening. You are free to do as you like," he told the guards.

"We will stay with you, Caesar," said one.

"You make me laugh. I'm not a child. I don't need to be chaperoned."

"The son of Vespasian forgets his life is in danger at

Zoheleth

all times," one guard warned. "After all, he is the son of the emperor of Rome!"

"Oh, have it your way," he waved in disgust. One guard rode ahead to announced the arrival of Caesar.

"Welcome, honorable Titus," said Joseph.

Marcus hurriedly arranged the seats at the table and placed out cups for wine.

"I've invited the refugee as you instructed," Joseph added. "This is Mattahias." He introduced the elderly man.

Titus noticed the old man didn't seem to suffer from lack of money or food.

"Does he speak Latin or Greek?" asked Titus.

"He prefers the old tongue," answered the physician. Joseph motioned Titus to sit. "Please, son of Caesar, taste our Jordean wine."

Titus was stunned for a moment when he heard the words "Jordean wine". It took him back to the nights he drank it with Bernice.

"Has Mattahias told you anything?" he asked as he seated himself next to the physician.

"I've recorded his statements," said Joseph. "He begs the Romans to enter Jerusalem and save the innocent people from more slaughter."

"I can appreciate his request," said Titus. "If he wants such a thing, can he tell where the weakest point of the outer wall may be." Joseph spoke to Mattahias and turned back to Titus.

"He claims there is a breach at one section," Joseph pointed to the map. "He said the men inside grow weary from guarding it."

Marcus listened to the discussion and poured wine.

"Can we trust the old man's instructions?"

Joseph smiled. "He's an honest man. I've known him from years back. He wants to help the citizens of the city."

"Ask who has the strongest party in the city since there are three factions at odds?"

Joseph talked to Mattahias then turned to Titus. "He

Zoheleth

said Simon has many men, but the one called John is more treacherous."

"John?" Titus scratched his chin. "I remember him. He left women and children to die on the plains while he and his men escaped to Jerusalem."

"Mattahias informs me how John has incited the young men to forge weapons. He also said how Eleazar and John are mortal enemies."

"Yes, until they see us Romans. Then, they join forces to come against us," Titus revealed. "John lied to me when I offered terms of peace at Gischala." Titus studied Mattahias and thought he seemed troubled. "What happened when Simon entered the city?"

Mattahias lowered his head and sighed. He spoke with Joseph.

"Mattahias says Simon robbed John and his men. He says everything John stole is now in the possession of Simon. Mattahias informs me how Simon took control of both the Upper City and the Lower City."

"I presume John is still alive?"

"He's alive from what Mattahias tells me."

"Tell your friend I thank him for his help. I'm sure it's painful to him."

Joseph stood and shook hands with Titus. "The Lord is the leader of your army!" Joseph said. "It is written how Christ will come with His army and Jerusalem will be destroyed to the last stone of the temple" (Matt. 24:2).

Titus was taken by surprise. "I'll keep that in mind," he said gratefully as he left the table. Marcus walked Titus to the door and when he returned, he found Mattahias speaking to Joseph in Greek.

"He speaks Greek?" Marcus questioned somewhat puzzled. "How is this?"

Joseph raised his hand and smiled slightly. "He had no way of knowing how much he could reveal to the Romans. He doesn't want to be called a traitor. He trusted me to decide what parts of his report to tell Titus."

"So he understood every word," Marcus said.

"He understands much. Now, Marcus, get your pen and scroll so we can finish our reports."

Zoheleth

The next morning, Marcus saw Mattahias had slept in their tent. "I didn't know we had an overnight guest," he said to Joseph who was already up and dressed.

"I thought it best to keep him with us," Joseph said. "I feared the other refugees would learn of our talk with Titus."

Marcus nodded as he dressed. "I'm on my way to check the patients," he said. "When I'm finished, I would like to visit with my father, if it meets with your approval."

"You may," said Joseph.

By early afternoon on the completion of his duties, Marcus searched for his father. He walked a quarter of a mile before he found a man from the auxiliary. "Where are the others from the auxiliary?" he asked the soldier who was weeding a vegetable garden.

"They're building a wall around Jerusalem," he answered and went back to digging.

"Why?"

"It will keep the Jews from making sally on our camps."

Marcus ran again until he could see the soldiers at work. He was astonished with the amount of trees erected as walls. The legions had hundreds of trees rolled into camp on wagons. From where he watched, he saw Jewish rebels attempting to stop the soldiers from enclosing them inside the city.

The Jews began raining fire darts at sections of the wooden walls. The fire darts failed to ignite the walls because the trees were fresh. Marcus decided to return to the infirmary after seeing it was dangerous to get closer to search for his father. Something caught his eye. He saw a fire dart hit the wheels of a ramming machine and set it ablaze.

The soldiers worked desperately to extinguish the flames but the wooden cart carrying the machine was old and dry and burned out of control. When the soldiers attempted

Zoheleth

to dampen the blaze, they received a barrage of stones coming from the Jerusalem wall. Other soldiers ran with metal shields to cover their comrades while buckets of water were passed down a long line of men. Marcus saw a second machine catch fire which must have been discouraging to the Romans.

Titus came riding speedily in the direction of the soldiers. He signaled the men to pull back the ramming machines. By doing so, the machines were taken out of range of the fire darts. Marcus gave a sigh of relief. He had to return to the infirmary because he knew there would be many needing medical help. When he arrived, he told Joseph all that happened.

Titus rode back to his quarters. He paced the ground in fury. "They loath us," he shouted to Tiberius. "They curse our gods and call us unclean!"

"Our men were brave," Tiberius reminded him. "You saw how they exposed themselves to the dangers."

"The zealots are a bunch of blood crazy monsters!" Titus raged. "How many of our men did they wound?" he asked.

Tiberius shook his head and couldn't answer. Titus went on complaining. "How long can we stand this?" He looked at Tiberius and asked. "What do you suggest we do?"

"I suggest we return the insults," he answered. "Allow me to have our regiments take battle formation, using only archers. We'll keep firing until the men finish completing the walls."

Titus smiled and nodded in agreement. "Position your archers!" he ordered. "Good thinking, Tiberius. Be sure you have plenty of fire for the arrows. I'll enjoy watching them trying to figure out how to escape a barrage of our darts. We offered the right hand of Rome, they refused. Now we offer the hands of the archers of Rome!"

MATTAHIAS

The Roman legions completed building the timber walls. They placed guards at various sections. The soldiers were no longer in fear of sudden raids on their camps.

By evening, both Joseph and Marcus were weary after working with those receiving burns from fire darts.

Ebutius, the injured commander of the Tenth Legion, limped around the infirmary on a tree-limb crutch. He helped Marcus by writing letters for the wounded, and feeding those who suffered burns on both hands.

"Joseph is a remarkable man," said Ebutius.

"He's a genius!" Marcus replied, as he hung linens to dry. Ebutius smiled and shook his head.

"How he convinced me of his God amazes me."

Marcus was somewhat amused by what he said.

"You believe in his God?"

"For some reason I do. I believe in the Christ he speaks about."

"What makes you believe?" Marcus questioned.

"I don't know, but the fact that I'm limping around is a miracle. I've seen soldiers injured the way I am and they never returned to duty."

"Some of the soldiers say he has magic in his prayers. Do you think he has?"

"I can see why," said Ebutius. "Don't you believe?"

"I respect his God," said Marcus. "As long as he allows me to worship the gods of my father."

"Marcus," said Ebutius, as he put his hand on the lad's shoulder. "I've seen men in this infirmary brought to peace by this man's prayers. I wanted that kind of peace. Can you understand what I'm saying?"

Marcus walked away. His feelings about the physician were mixed. He thought perhaps he was too young to understand what Ebutius meant because he never had the same desires. He looked upon Joseph as a holy man, like the priest of Rome. These Jews served an invisible God, but he liked the gods he was taught to worship. He wasn't ready to believe that Jesus had walked on water. He heard Joseph tell how Jesus of Nazareth healed the sick, and gave sight to the blind. It all had to be some sort of magic!

That night, while the moon was high and the black sky dazzled with stars. Marcus lay on the ground not far from the tent. He liked the cool breeze after a tiring day. He looked to the vast heavens over him and wondered how the moon got there. He wondered if the stars were the eyes of the gods. It never concerned him before, but what if Joseph was right? He heard Joseph call.

"Where are you Marcus?" He got up and walked over to meet the physician.

"I was enjoying the night sky."

"You had me worried," said Joseph, showing concern. "Don't wander too far from camp," he warned. "We can't be too trusting because there's a fence around us."

"I was listening to a shepherd's flute," said Marcus.

"We have several musicians in the camps." They walked back to the tent where they found Mattahias reading a scroll. Joseph served tea as they sat together.

"Marcus, please record what Mattahias tells us."

Mattahias sat stroking his beard as he commenced to tell his story. "The zealots allowed the priests to enter the temple." He rocked his round body back and forth. "John of Gischala, sneaked into the holy temple while the priest were sacrificing and his men struck them down. The priests' blood mixed with the animals' blood on the altar. John took control of the temple and forced Eleazar into the vault. He stole the gold items from the temple and his men acted disrespectfully while drinking the temple wine. They robbed the people and dressed as women to seduce men."

"God have mercy!" Joseph said in anger.

"Later," Mattahias continued, "the zealots fought John and forced him out of the temple. Eleazar was freed from the vault."

Mattahias composed himself and continued.

"Not long after that horrendous act, the men of Simon and John began fighting over food. Then, some crazy fool set fire to the grain storehouse."

"What!" Joseph could hardly contain his shock. "Who would commit such a fool-hearted deed?"

"When the people saw the storehouse ablaze, they panicked," Mattahias went on. "They frantically fought to put out the flames, but failed. Then, one faction poisoned the water supply."

"How did they do that?" Joseph asked.

"We don't know how they did it, but when so many fell ill and died after drinking at one of the wells, it was obvious it had been poisoned."

Joseph began pacing the floor.

"I believe Jesus told the truth," he said without thinking. "He predicted a tribulation like we have never seen. He said men would pray for the mountains to fall on them" (Luke 23:30).

Mattahias looked up curiously, like someone just struck him. He just realized what Joseph had said.

"Did I hear you right?" he asked firmly.

"About what?" Joseph turned to face him.

"You named Jesus. I recall you telling Titus about predictions of the destruction of Jerusalem."

"That I did!" Joseph declared.

"You!" Mattahias stammered. "You are not one of them?"

"If you mean a believer in Jesus? Yes."

Mattahias was stunned. He shook his head and spit the tea to the floor.

"I must leave this tent!" he said scornfully. "I'd rather be with the refugees who may think me a traitor, than with one who thinks I condemned this Jesus to be crucified!" He knocked over the chair in his hasty departure.

"I'm sorry you feel so strongly," said Joseph in a gentle manner.

Mattahias wobbled to the doorway and turned with

Zoheleth

hatred in his eyes. "You are not safe, my man. No refugee will trust you as I have. I'll see to it!"

His words wounded Joseph as he watched him leave the tent.

Marcus saw Joseph's sadness. He walked over and put his arm around his shoulder. "Why did he get so upset?"

"It's a long story. Let's put out the lamps and get some sleep.

In the dark, Marcus tried to make sense of what just happened.

"Your friend, Mattahias," he said softly. "He doesn't believe in your Jesus?" He heard Joseph turning on his cot.

"He doesn't believe Jesus of Nazareth to be the Messiah."

"What is this Messiah going to do?"

"He's to return to consummate His kingdom, and fulfill all Biblical prophecies."

"How will He return if He's dead?" Marcus raised himself on one elbow. "You said He was crucified."

"Yes, He died but the miracle is that God raised Him from the dead! He ascended into heaven in a cloud (Acts 1:9-11). He will come back with clouds and all shall see Him, even those who pierced Him" (Rev.1:7).

"What do you mean He'll come in clouds?"

"In old Scriptures, clouds symbolize the power of God (Isa.19:1). He'll return in the power of God and bring God's wrath on those who hated Him and killed the prophets" (Matt.23:35-36).

"I find that hard to believe," said Marcus. "I can see why Mattahias is annoyed with you."

"Mattahias is one who is still waiting for a Messiah. He is one who rejected Jesus as the son of God."

"How can a dead man set up a kingdom if he is not here to rule it?"

"I'm impressed how you're thinking. You see, the kingdom is not an earthly kingdom. It's a spiritual kingdom" (John 18:36). Joseph went on. "The kingdom of God is from the foundations of the world of Judiasm. Christianity's roots are from Judiasm. The Jews are fighting for an earthly kingdom which they will rule with a Messiah."

"Why don't they believe it's a spiritual kingdom?" Marcus asked.

"They're thinking of a material kingdom. But Jesus explained how flesh and blood couldn't enter the kingdom of God" (John 3:5-6).

"Then, they didn't understand Jesus."

"I think the Lord is touching you, Marcus." Joseph gave a little laugh. "We have been given physical demonstrations by God throughout time. Such as the ark of the covenant, and the holy temple, and the blood of animals as a sacrifice for sin." Joseph paused. "When the time was right, God sent into the world His son in the flesh. Jesus came with a new covenant from God, the creator of all things."

"Well, why did your Jesus have to die?"

"It was to be as the old prophets had written in Scripture. Jesus is the lamb of God who takes away the sins of the world (John 1:29). He gave himself as the final sacrifice for sin. He died in the flesh, just as the animals died. But now we don't need to slay animals since Jesus has become the final sacrifice for sins."

"But your people still sacrifice animals."

"Not for long, Marcus. We're seeing an end of an age which is near and a world which is ending."

"Are you saying the world is ending?"

"Not the world as you know it, Marcus. I'm speaking of the end of the Jewish world. A covenantal world. The ending of the old covenant God made with the Jews."

Marcus gave a deep sigh and turned to his side. "I'm sleepy, Joseph. Good night."

"God bless you, Marcus. May tomorrow give you new wisdom."

THE DEBATE

Many grief-stricken citizens escaped from Jerusalem and surrendered to the Romans.

Joseph checked their general health before transferring them to the refugee camps.

Marcus recorded the names of every refugee as Joseph spelled them. A well dressed man stood in front of the physician. When asked his name he announced.

"I am Nathan ben Seir, a Horite."

The physician smiled. "You're from the northwest region of Edom, am I right?"

"That's right. My ancestors migrated there. But I'm from Galilee."

"How did you get here?" asked Joseph.

Nathan shook his head sadly. "I came to Jerusalem for the feast days, only to find myself in the midst of a civil uprising." He lowered his eyes and continued. "I could hardly believe what I was seeing. The priests were being killed in the holy temple."

"We've heard about it," said Joseph. "Can you tell me what has happened to Eleazar and the zealots?"

Nathan shook his head. "Eleazar and the zealots had to take refuge in the temple vaults to get away from John."

"Don't they see the Romans outside?" asked Joseph.

"They're not worried about the Romans. There's too much going on inside to be concerned about who's outside. John's men set fire to the Phasael Tower."

"How sad," said Joseph. "Do you know the number of John and Simon's men?" he asked.

"I would say Simon has around ten thousand. John has lost many men. I can't give you a count." Nathan paused a moment. "For what it's worth the rebels are trying to learn how to operate the Roman stone slingers. I don't know how they got them."

Zoheleth

Joseph regarded him with interest. "They obtained them from the Twelfth Legion when Gallus retreated," he sighed. "It means they will use them against the Romans." Joseph guided the conversation in a different direction. "Tell me how you got through the guards inside the city?"

Nathan smiled and drew out a pouch, shaking it in front of the physician. "How else?" he smiled. "Gold was my safe passage by the guards."

"You bought your way out?"

"Yes! Most of us did. Simon's men are annoyed because they're forced to guard the gates. They complain how they're not getting to steal from the homes left vacant."

"So, they're fattening their purses by collecting passage from the city."

"I had to slip several men some gold. They were frantic about getting away from the warring factors in the city. Poor devils."

Joseph checked him and replied, "You seem to be in good health. You're free to go to the refugee camp."

"No thanks, doctor. I'm heading back to Galilee.

Joseph frowned. "I understand all roads leading out of Jerusalem are blocked by the Romans."

Nathan patted his belt with the pouch of gold. "I'm sure the Roman guards are just as hungry for gold. I'll take my chances."

The rebels inside the city were not impressed by the walls of timber the Romans had erected surrounding the city. They labored to operate the stone slingers and sent huge stones over the timber walls. Some stones landed too close for comfort.

The commanding officers complained to Titus about the bombarding. He sent for General Josephus to negotiate with the Jews. The guards had horses ready for Titus and the general.

"I need you to try to talk some sense into your people," said Titus as they rode toward the Jerusalem walls

Zoheleth

with a number of soldiers following.

"I'll try, Caesar," said the general. "They're not on friendly terms with me since they learned I'm speaking for you."

"You speak their language, and as one of their priests they may listen," Titus said sharply. "You must try!"

He allowed eight soldiers to escort the general to the wall. Josephus shouted to the watchman.

"Fellowmen! Rome wishes no bloodshed. Open the gates and consider peaceful terms."

The watchmen refused to answer. Suddenly a group of men came out crouching near the wall. One called out.

"Rome! Give us your right hand as a sign of peace." It appeared that they wanted to accept the terms and Titus rode closer. "We offer the right hand of Rome to you."

Josephus translated, but he noticed the group were acting suspiciously. He was sure he saw men hiding in the shadows near a wide bush.

"We'll open the gates to you, mighty Titus!" one man promised. Josephus suddenly shouted a warning.

"It's a trick! Don't trust them!" It was too late. A few unsuspecting Romans were willing to believe them and went forth on their own. Another group of rebels encompassed and struck them with heavy stones. The soldiers on foot were killed.

Titus saw the rebels flying out from their hiding places. They headed toward him and he turned his horse and sped away. He cursed them as he rode toward his escort.

"Rome will hear of this!" he swore. "I'll force my father to give the orders to strike Jerusalem!"

Josephus had been struck on the head by a stone while escaping and was taken to the infirmary.

The physician wrapped the head wound which bled profusely. Joseph checked on the other soldiers and made a suggestion to Josephus.

"General, I think you should stay with us for the night. A head injury can be tricky."

"I accept your offer," said the general.

Zoheleth

That evening, Joseph, Marcus and the general settled in the tent. Marcus filled out his reports and was suddenly interrupted by his friend.

"Antonius!" Marcus leaped to his feet. "Where in the name of the gods have you been?"

Antonius' face was beaming with a smile. "Ebony," he teased, as he hugged the lad. "I've been fighting the Jews!" he said loudly. "How's my good friend, and how's the flow of wine?"

Joseph glared, and the general was shocked by the boldness of the Roman soldier. He looked at Joseph and asked. "Who's he ?"

"He's a commander from Ashkelon. His name is Antonius Salo."

Marcus hurried with a cup for wine. "Antonius," Marcus laughed, "I think you like the wine better than us."

Antonius raised his cup and drank quickly. He walked Marcus to a corner of the tent and whispered. "Why does the physician glare at me?"

"He thinks you drink too much," Marcus revealed.

Antonius grinned. "Perhaps I can prove him right!" He took the wine skin and poured. His dark blue eyes sparkled in the lamp light.

Marcus shook his head. "And I think you drink too much!" he dared to say. Antonius burst out laughing and pushed his fist on Marcus' cheek. They wrestled around in horseplay and Marcus laughed heartily.

Antonius finished the wine. "Ah!" he sighed. "As sweet as the lips of Doris." He shot a glance at the doctor.

"Antonius," Marcus said softly. "I hope you're not referring to your friend's wife." Marcus noticed his manner had changed. Antonius stopped visiting Ebutius, his friend. He learned from other soldiers how Antonius was drinking heavily. Some said he was suffering from a displaced love. Marcus hoped it was all rumors.

"Ebutius asked me why you don't visit with him. What shall I tell him?" Marcus asked slyly.

Antonius spit and walked away from Marcus. He

Zoheleth

glanced at the physician.

"Physician," he said. "You haven't wished me a good evening."

Joseph nodded. "It appears you've had a good evening already." Joseph looked at Marcus and went on to say. "Marcus, save the wine, please. We need it for the infirmary."

"The infirmary?" Antonius mocked.

"We use the wine to wash our hands before an operation," said Marcus. "Also, to clean the instruments."

Antonius was barely seeing with clear vision as he leaned against a post supporting the tent.

"What a waste," he belched. He turned and hurriedly left the tent without saying good night.

Marcus was saddened by his departure. He sat on his cot and sulked.

"You should curb Antonius from devouring our wine," Joseph scolded. "Antonius abuses your friendship."

Marcus lowered his head. Just then they heard another voice calling. Marcus opened the tent door.

"Joseph! It is I, Mattahias!"

"Welcome, friend." Joseph stood to greet him. "Join us and have some wine. Have you met General Josephus?"

"I've heard of him," Mattahias said as they exchanged greetings. "May I talk with you, Joseph?"

"You don't mind if Marcus and Josephus remain?"

"Well, why not." Mattahias said as he eased himself into a chair. "They might find what I have to say interesting." Marcus listened as the men engaged in earnest conversation.

"First, I apologize for my behavior," Mattahias began. "When you were kind to me, I returned your hospitality with rudeness. We are of the Jewish blood," he added.

"No need to apologize. What's on your mind?" Joseph inquired.

Mattahias sat staring at the flame of the oil lamp. He seemed to be searching for words.

Zoheleth

"I was thinking about you," he measured his words. "We had many Jews who left Judaism to follow Christianity."

Joseph nodded.

"Judaism has been active for fifteen hundred years."

"I'm aware of that," said Joseph.

"We have Abraham as our father." He seemed to labor for more words. "We have the laws which God gave to Moses."

Joseph agreed. "True, we have the laws God gave to Moses, but the priests and Pharisees have added their own laws to keep the people in bondage."

Mattahias sat back quickly as though Joseph had hit him. "Our holy priest thought it necessary," he defended.

"They were anything but holy," Joseph accused. "Their piety never included forgiveness."

Mattahias wiped his mouth. "Joseph," he said. "I know you have not been bred in rudeness. But why do attack me in this manner?"

"I don't mean to be unkind," said Joseph. "We were of the same mind from the beginning. And as you know, Judaism is the root of Christianity."

Mattahias stroked his beard and rocked his body.

"You are younger than I," he went on. "Young men have a tendency to stray from the truth." He hesitated while his feelings intensified.

"I haven't strayed from the truth," Joseph defended. "I have found the truth in Jesus as the Messiah!"

Mattahias broke out in a sweat. He looked at the Jewish general and directed his words to him. "Did you hear that?" The general raised his hand and shook his head in a refusal to get involved in the debate.

"This man believes Jesus was the long awaited Messiah!" Mattahias still directed his words to the general in an effort to draw him in. Joseph interrupted.

"Mattahias, you're missing the point," he said.

"Now don't get upset," said Mattahias. "Let me tell you there were many who left the Christian faith to return to

Zoheleth

Judaism after Jesus was killed" (Heb. 6:4-6).

"Those who returned to Judaism," said Joseph. "They were with us, but not of us (1John 2: 19). Why else would they not remain true to the living God?"

Mattahias drew a quick breath and stared blankly. The silence was thick. He grinned and merely said. "I know this Jesus produced miracles, so I've heard. But why give up a religion which has been in practice for so long?"

"Have you forgotten the ancient prophesies?" asked Joseph. "Didn't God promise to bring in a new and better covenant?" (Jeremiah 31: 32-33)

"It's you, Joseph, who has forgotten that we are the children of Abraham," he challenged.

"Mattahias, our writings in Genesis say in the house of Abraham dwelt two sons. The son of the bondwoman and the son of the free woman, who was the son of promise. Allegorically speaking, these women represented two covenants." Joseph added, "Hagar, a slave, and the bearer of Ishmael, a child of the flesh. Hagar's offspring corresponds to the present Jerusalem, which is in slavery with her children. They're in bondage to the law which produces nothing but sin and death" (Gal. 4:21-25).

"What kind of madness is this?" Mattahias said in anguish. "You have strayed from the Torah. Have you put aside the Mosaic laws?"

"The Son of God has freed His followers from the law" (Rom. 6:14-15) Joseph replied with confidence.

"I'm trying to be patient with you," said Mattahias. "What has led you to believe that Jesus is God?"

"Jesus claimed His kingship," Joseph declared. "You put him on trial with trumped-up charges against Him."

"Trumped-up charges? We heard the blasphemous utterance from his lips," Mattahias accused. "His impious declaration that he was the Son of God! What more did the priests need to condemn Him? He condemned himself!"

"Did you think He was a mad man?"

"Of course," Mattahias admitted.

"Then why didn't you excuse Him if you thought His

mind was deranged?"

Mattahias eyes searched the tent as though he could pull answers from the air. He hesitated before speaking. "You don't understand," he groaned. "This Jesus was deceiving many people every day."

"Do you call His miracles of healing, deceptive?" Joseph shot back. "How do you explain it?"

"We thought Him governed by Satan or some demons" (Mark 3:22).

"No!" shouted Joseph, he could no longer listen to Mattahias. "Your concern was in losing too many people away from Judaism. You feared the loss of control over the people, plus the support of the temple would dwindle. You feared Rome would hear about the division and remove the priests from their duty."

"How dare you!" Mattahias flared. "To accuse us of this! You, who go around believing an impostor."

Joseph stood over the old man and glared. "Your own children are believing in false prophets. There's imposters who preach in Jerusalem! They lie and lead the people astray at this very moment" (Acts 5:36-37).

Mattahias rose. "I see we can no longer talk," he declared with an indignant tone. "Yes, we have those who assure the people that God will deliver us from the Romans. And God will deliver us!"

"You forget you condemned yourself and your children," Joseph replied abruptly.

"More foolishness," Mattahias mocked.

"Not foolishness," Joseph snapped. "Remember when Governor Pilate was forced to condemn Jesus? You were among those who cried out to let His blood be on you and your children! You brought damnation on yourselves" (Matt. 27:25).

Mattahias groaned like he was mortally wounded. "You've turned your back on our people," he accused. "You and this one who sits in silence. This general who has turned traitor to our people." He pointed to the Jewish general and addressed him. "You help the Roman pagans. May you die in disgrace. I curse you both! You wretched fools!" He made his departure in haste.

Zoheleth

Marcus was confused by what had just occurred. He walked over to Joseph who was still reflecting on what was said. He glanced at the two men then asked, "Does this mean your friendship with Mattahias is broken?"

Joseph looked at him and then to the general. They both laughed.

"I think it's been badly fractured," said the physician.

Marcus joined in laughing.

CHAPTER TWENTY ONE

THE CITY OF FAMINE

John of Gischala and his men were infuriated when they found that Simon had taken all their treasures. This occurred while John and his men were killing the priests in the temple. The zealots, after a bitter struggle, forced them out of the temple. On their way to their hide-out they were attacked by Simon's men. John's men suffered a severe defeat. Hundreds of dead lay in the streets after the fighting ceased. John ordered the remaining men to remove the corpses.

"Where are we going to put them?" questioned one. "We can't throw them over the wall while Simon's men guard the city gates." In exasperation, John looked around and gave the order to find empty houses and pile the dead inside. "We must clear a way of escape in case Simon decides to attack us again," he said.

The men piled the dead on wooden carts and searched for empty houses to deposit them. They nailed the doors and windows shut to contain the stench from the decaying bodies.

John selected a few to ride with him to the Upper City in search of food. Many of his men were growing weak from lack of nourishment. They cursed the conditions when they found the grain storehouse burned to the ground. They cursed the water-well that was poisoned, and they had to seek out other wells from which to drink. No one wanted to be the first to taste the water. His men began complaining and asked what they could eat.

"Whatever you find!" John answered carelessly.

"But we have searched for three days," one complained miserably. "We are forced to scrounge. Some of us are reduced to chewing leather strips to keep from starving."

Zoheleth

John felt contempt for their whining. "Break into the houses and take the food you find. If any resist, kill them!" One man grabbed the reigns of John's horse.

"You and your favorite men ride horses, while we're made to walk," he criticized. "We have no strength to search for food."

"Don't expect me to nurse you," John was hostile. "You need food, then you find food. You need horses, then steal them back from Simon!" He rode off with three of his men while leaving the others confused and deserted.

John came across several women lamenting loudly over the loss of their men. He demanded they cease their wailing. He feared the Romans would hear them and know there was trouble inside the city. When they kept wailing, he killed one of them. The other women looked on in horror. He promised them the same ending if they wept aloud. His threat worked.

While riding to the northern section of the Upper City, John caught sight of Fabius, one of his men. He saw him carrying bread and cheese. Fabius was followed by another man carrying two skins of wine. They ran rejoicing when they saw John.

"We've found food!" Fabius shouted. His dirty face and grimy hands didn't make the food less desirable to John.

"Where did you get it?" he asked as he dismounted. "Are you sure it's not poisoned?"

"The only person in the house is a woman with her small child," Fabius informed. "She has wealth and much food stored in her house."

The man holding the wine skins laughed. "She tried to stop us, but what can one woman do against two scoundrels like us?"

John grabbed the bread and bit into it wildly. He reached for the wine and gulped it down without taking a breath, letting it run down his beard and onto his clothes. His men shared the second skin.

"I'm sure the woman was only concerned for her child," John replied. "You're a pair of maggots. But let's find a safe place to eat."

They squatted in a darkened alley and made haste with the food before their comrades could find them.

"We'll station ourselves in an empty house near the woman's home," said John. "We can have our own private supply of food to survive on."

"Her name is Mary," Fabius grinned. "She tried to threaten us by saying she would inform the new Caesar!"

"Just let her try,"John laughed.

They broke into a deserted home and hid from Simon's men. Each night they sent Fabius to steal whatever Mary cooked. John's men were in a good mood with their appetites satisfied. They were regaining strength.

"This Mary will not put up a fight if she wants her child to stay alive," said John. "We'll remain here and get fed. The people of the city are dying in the streets from hunger. When we're strong enough we'll ambush Simon. This time we kill him!" His men agreed with him.

"Simon's men must be finding it hard to find food also," said Fabius. "Everywhere I look there are children with swollen stomachs and too weak to cry. I've seen mother's refuse to allow their babies to suck at the breast."

"To hell with them!" shouted John. "We didn't burn the wheat! We didn't poison the wells! I say let the people rot!"

After three nights of hiding, Fabius and his friend went out once more to rob Mary. John and his small group waited for his return. Fabius was longer than usual and John became nervous. He peered through the opening in a boarded window. The street was as dark as the room, but they couldn't take a chance of lighting a lamp. They could hear Simon's men roaming the alleys. The night dragged on and Fabius hadn't returned.

John was enraged. He claimed Fabius took the food for himself and left him and the others to starve. He looked out again and his mood changed when he saw Fabius, but this time he was alone and his arms empty.

Fabius entered the house breathless and trembling.

Zoheleth

"Where's the food?" John demanded in a loud whisper.

"May the gods forgive me," Fabius cried. John grew impatient and grabbed him and tore his garments in search of food. When he found none he asked where the other man was?

"You won't believe what I'm going to tell you," said Fabius.

"You ran into Simon's men?"

"Yes, his men found the house of Mary."

"Well, what happened?"

"It was awful. We waited all night for them to leave. I saw them carrying out food and joking about raping her."

"So, she got raped," John mocked. "Is she alive and does she have any food?"

"We couldn't leave where we were hiding because Simon's men might catch us. I was afraid to return here in case we were followed. We waited until dark to venture near her house." He paused to catch his breath. "We had no idea if she were dead or alive until we smelled meat roasting. We laughed how she outwitted Simon's men." He wiped the sweat from his forehead.

"What happened to the meat?" asked John.

"She was eating it when we entered."

"Why didn't you take it from her?"

"Both of us ran out of the house."

"You what!"

The men began to gang up on Fabius. John held them back. "Go back and get the meat!" John ordered.

"I can't do it," he whimpered. "She killed her own child and cooked him!"

John threw his hands in the air. "My god what is this I'm hearing?"

John's men began gagging and groaning.

"Where's the man who was with you?"

"He took off," said Fabius. "We knew the woman had gone mad. She handed me a leg from the child." He shivered as he spoke. "Her eyes were wild when she said

247

she saved the leg for us."

"Shut up!" John snapped. "Don't tell us anymore."

"Maybe the witch has deceived you," suggested one of the men.

"Oh, no! I saw the foot still attached to the leg. She said she was braver than any man and if she could eat her own child, then why couldn't we?"

"Disgusting!" John complained. "We must move out of here. The city is dying."

Fabius dropped to the floor and buried his face in his hands and wept.

John was losing hope. He wished the Romans would enter and end the grotesque conditions. He was not only losing his men to Simon, but he would lose them to the wide spread famine. The few who were with him might desert and try to escape the city on their own. If he could only find a way to trap Simon. Dawn was coming and the men would remain another day without food or water. He worried if he and his small group would have enough strength to fight off another attack.

Zoheleth

ATTACK ON JERUSALEM

The sun rose high over the Mount of Olives and streamed down into the Valley of Kedron. The bright blue sky held small white clouds which appeared to touch the tips of the mountains. The heavens looked peaceful over the troubled city of Jerusalem.

The trumpets in the city announced the first sacrifice of the day. Although the holy temple was never purified, the remaining priests continued to worship but only by burning incense and saying prayers. No longer could they have animal sacrifices since there were no animals left in the city, only packs of hungry dogs.

The Roman camp moved close to the northwest wall of the Citadel to the Upper City. The legions positioned the ramming machines at the weakest section of the Jerusalem wall. Once breached, it would allow them to enter what was called the Assyrian Camp.

Titus received word from his father after he sent reports on what was happening in Jerusalem. Vespasian had approached the Senate of Rome with the request for Titus to commence with an attack on Jerusalem. His request was granted.

Titus and Josephus, along with Alexander Tiberius, surveyed the on-going work of the legions.

"I hope we're not too late to save the majority of the citizens," the general sighed. "Last night I heard women weeping in the city."

"We all heard it, General," said Titus. "Perhaps we can bring it to an end soon."

"May God be with you," said the general. "I regret to say this but I think our God has changed sides."

Titus gave him a quick glance, but said nothing.

The legions moved the six story portable towers to the walls. The soldiers ran up the inside ladders to position themselves. A line of archers moved forward firing their projectiles ahead to keep the enemy from stoning them.

The ladders led to the floors above. The tower roof was perfect for firing arrows and giving an excellent view of the enemy's position. The ramming machines were in place and the soldiers awaited orders.

Titus mounted his horse and raised his sword, then shouted. "Let the rams begin!"

"Hail Caesar!" The soldiers returned the salutes to honor Titus.

The Jews seeing what was about to happen, sent huge fire darts directly to the ramming machines. In turn, the archers in the towers sent thousands of arrows. The enemy never realized how the portable buildings shielded the Romans from anything sent in their direction. Then, the bridge platforms of the towers were lowered, and the soldiers mounted the walls. They were now in hand-to-hand combat with the insurgents.

Inside the towers, the archers and the swordsmen were ready to exit and take Jerusalem's wall.

The rebels were forced to hide themselves from the onslaught of projectiles. Several brave Jews slipped out to set fire to the wooden carts carrying the towers and the ramming machines.

"Capture those men!" shouted Titus. "It's time we made an example of them." Twenty young Jews were caught and brought before Titus. They showed no sign of fear or remorse.

"What shall we do with them, Caesar?" asked the soldier.

"I don't want them as prisoners," Titus declared. "Let the city witness their crucifixion!"

The captives broke down and pleaded for their lives. They begged to be held as prisoners.

"Our refugee camps and prisons are filled," said Titus. "You had your chance to surrender, but you chose to meet your death in Roman style."

Many Roman soldiers were wounded by fire darts. Some men lay on the ground unable to make it to the infirmary. Joseph and Marcus ran to reach them. Marcus felt the excitement when he saw all the action. He still wished to be a soldier. The noise of war shouts and rams pounding was tremendous. Marcus suddenly grabbed Joseph.

"What's wrong?" he asked when looking where Marcus pointed to the men being nailed to crosses. "Don't look, Marcus," he suggested, but the lad was transfixed by the size of the spikes used to nail the men's feet and arms.

"I've never seen a man crucified," he uttered as he tried to hold down his meal. Joseph led him away.

"How can the Romans do that?" he cried. "Blood was squirting in their faces when they struck the nails. How do they stand the screams?" He trembled and his color faded.

"It's what war is about," said Joseph. "Titus hopes the people will decide to surrender when seeing it."

They walked a little further and found a wounded man. "Help me here," Joseph requested. They turned the soldier over and found an arrow through his shoulder.

"Let me remove this arrow," said Joseph. Marcus held the wound open while the doctor inserted an instrument deep beneath the point of the arrow head. He was able to guide the arrow out without tearing more tissue.

Marcus ran to get an ox-cart to transport the wounded to the camp hospital.

Inside the city the three fighting factions ceased their personal grievances and joined forces to come against their common enemy, the Romans.

Simon's men were fleeing from the gates and were warning how hopeless things were getting.

"Shut up, you fools!" Simon cursed. "Get back to the gates! Can't you see the people running to open them to the Romans?" Simon rode fiercely and stopped them by slaying every one near the gates. Men, women and children were brought down in screaming tangles by Simon.

Zoheleth

After five days of the rams' pounding the Romans broke through the wall. Titus stationed men inside the Assyrian camp. Later they celebrated their victory.

The news of the Romans inside the walls spread throughout the nations. A command from Euphrates, which was a long time enemy of the Jews, joined the Romans, and the Fifth Legion from Emmaus became part of the great warhead of Rome. Kings from foreign lands offered their assistance. Their armies came from the four corners of the earth (Rev. 7:1).

Late one evening, Marcus heard his father calling and he ran to meet him. They embraced.

"Father, you're a regular visitor lately."

"I desire to spend time with my son before the battle begins." Marcus poured him wine. Joseph joined him and they talked,

"What news do you bring tonight?" Joseph asked.

"Titus is in an awkward position since he has gained entrance through the first wall," Sabinus sighed. "The rebels are posted close to the second wall and are using stones the size of my head to strike our men."

"That's discouraging," said Joseph. "What about inside the city?"

"There's a famine and people are dying. There are no animals left to use for food or as sacrifices by the priests. We heard that someone was selling wheat and barley for a denarious a measure" (Rev. 6:6).

"That's a day's wages," Joseph revealed.

"Word has it that some buyers don't live long enough to use what they bought."

Marcus joined in by saying how many Jews were hanging on crosses.

"Every day Caesar offers peaceful terms to them," Sabinus informed, "but they listen to some prophet who shouts how God will deliver them from the Romans!" Sabinus wagged his head. "Tomorrow the men will try to

Zoheleth

break through another wall. It's a dangerous situation."

Sabinus stared into space and finished his wine. "Physician, may I speak with you alone?"

"Will you excuse us, Marcus?" Joseph asked as he and Sabinus stepped into the night air.

"Is there something troubling you?" Joseph asked. "Or are you in need of prayer?"

"Both," Sabinus smiled. "I know my son wonders why we're talking."

"Have you told him of your conversion?"

"Not yet. I want to ask you about a dream I had. I understand God gives you wisdom in these matters."

"Sometimes," Joseph grinned. "Go on."

"In my dream I was alone and holding my sword high. Suddenly a brilliant light came from the sword, and I saw dead men around me, but I was alive."

Joseph was stirred. "The sword stands for the word of God and the word of God is a light to the world!"

"Why were there dead men around?" Sabinus asked.

"They could be the dead in spirit. Men who won't accept the word of God are called spiritually dead." Joseph felt there was more to the dream than he could determine.

"If I die, where will I go?" Sabinus asked with deep concern. "Do I go to the place you call Sheol?"

"Since you're a Christian, you will go directly to the heavenlies to await the consumation of the end of the age."

"I don't understand Sheol."

"Sheol is referred to as Abraham's bosom. It remains occupied by the dead until the harvest which comes with the consummation of God's kingdom. The old Jewish covenantal system must first be removed, such as the temple and the animal sacrifices for sin. These things are no longer needed since Jesus became the final sacrifice for sin."

"You once mentioned hell, what goes on there?"

"Hell was created for the devil and his angels. Our Lord bound Satan's activity when He came to earth. It is written that He will bruise Satan's head" (Gen. 3:15).

"What happens to the righteous dead in Sheol?"

"They, along with the unrighteous, will come forth to be judged by God. Sheol will be emptied and the righteous will be in heaven with Jesus. Hell will be emptied and cast into the lake of fire, or what is referred to as the Abyss. Those who rejected Jesus will be in torment forever, and forever be separated from God."

"When will all this take place?" asked Sabinus.

"Jesus said at His second coming there would be not one stone left upon another of the temple (Matt. 24:3). The destruction of the temple will signify the end of the old covenant. The physical Jerusalem will be replaced by the Jerusalem which is from above. Paul writes that the way into the holy place has not yet been disclosed, while the outer tabernacle is still standing" (Heb. 9: 8).

"Then, when I die I don't go to Sheol."

"That's correct. All believers who die after Jesus' resurrection, go to heaven where the saints await the consummation of God's kingdom (2nd Cor. 5:8). Your dream seems to have you preoccupied with death."

"Yes. I have a favor to ask of you," Sabinus said as he reached into a leather pouch. "If anything happens to me, will you see that Marcus gets this scroll?"

"I'll take care of it," said Joseph as he put his hand on the shoulder of Sabinus. "And if anything happens to you, I'll take care of your son."

The two hugged strongly. "Let's kneel and pray," said Joseph. "We'll pray for your welfare. Remember the Lord is ALL there is!"

The following morning, Titus ordered his men to break through the second wall inside the Assyrian camp. This wall connected to the Tower of Antonia on the east side. The soldiers worked under shields for protection. When they made an opening large enough to enter, they were discouraged to find a third wall.

Titus climbed the Roman tower to survey what was behind that wall.

"Don't attempt to break through the third wall," he warned. "They're waiting for the first man to enter."

The opening in the second wall was not large enough to allow the machines access. The only way to get to the other side was to scale the wall. Titus asked for volunteers but his men fell silent. They knew this would be a suicide mission.

The auxiliary of Antioch crawled through the opening of the second wall. Sabinus led them forward. Once inside, Sabinus heard the Roman soldiers complaining about the dangers of scaling the third wall. Titus pleaded for volunteers. No man would step forward.

"Must I do it myself!" he shouted with his fist in the air. He moved forward to make the jump when Sabinus ran in front of him.

"No! Caesar." Sabinus stopped him. "There is no reason for you to go. I offer myself." He stood straight with his fist clenched against his chest to salute Titus. "I will honor Rome and be the first man to scale the wall. If I die, know that I gave my life to help end this madness and to serve my Lord and Savior."

Titus felt a surge of admiration for this soldier's offer and dedication to Rome and to his God. "Such courage," he said as he returned the salute to the black Syrian soldier. It was then that eleven others raised their swords and offered to go with Sabinus.

"Hail Caesar!" they shouted.

Sabinus lifted his shield over his head. Holding his sword upright he advanced toward the wall as the eleven followed.

From overhead a shower of arrows hit their shields, but Sabinus reached the summit and scattered the rebels who fired on them. His boldness frightened them and they fled as though they were facing a possessed mad man.

Sabinus forged his way forward, striking any who dared to come near. He heard the legions cheering him on, when suddenly his fortune failed. He stumbled over a rock and fell from the wall headlong.

When the Jews heard the crash of his shield they turned back and attacked him on the ground.

Zoheleth

"Vengeance!" cried Sabinus as he thought about the villages in Antioch. He rose to one knee and killed two of his attackers. "Hail to my Lord, and my God!" he shouted for the enemy to hear. He fought from a kneeling position until the missiles buried him.

Three of his followers were crushed to death by stones. The remaining men tried to retrieve the body of Sabinus, but were forced back by the enemy. They found themselves pinned against the third wall.

The Romans were ashamed when seeing one man's courage. They began to yell out. "Hail Caesar! We'll scale the wall for the hero, Sabinus!"

Titus was moved by what he witnessed next. His men paid tribute to Sabinus by offering their own lives. Titus heard them shouting to follow the spirited Sabinus. They chanted so loudly on the third wall that the rebels were thrown into confusion.

Titus joined them on the wall and saluted his men. When they saw their Caesar, they cheered wildly.

"Bring back the body of Sabinus!" Titus called out, and the men cleared the way to bring back the dead Syrian warrior.

Titus hung his head when seeing the amount of darts that pierced Sabinus' body. He was compelled to weep. He stood over the corpse and slowly gave Sabinus an honorable salute.

Many soldiers were brought to tears.

MIXED EMOTIONS

Antonius of Ashkelon came bearing sad news. He entered the infirmary seeking Joseph to inform him of the death of Sabinus. Antonius stood by while Joseph presented the news to Marcus. The lad broke down weeping in the arms of Joseph.

"Where's my father?" he asked.

"I'll take you to him," said Antonius.

Joseph followed them. Marcus dropped to his knees when he saw the body of his father. He cradled his head in his arms and sobbed. Sabinus' head was the only section of his body without a dart.

"Father," Marcus cried out. "I love you. Please don't die."

Antonius and Joseph stood helplessly looking on.

"Let him go, son," whispered Joseph.

"I can't," Marcus wailed. "He's my father!"

"He's dead, Marcus," said Antonius. "You've got to accept that."

Marcus lowered his father's body gently and his tears fell on his father's face.

"Why?" Marcus cried in anguish.

"Your father did a very heroic deed," Antonius replied as he put his arm around Marcus. "I asked to bring the body to you. I wanted to give you the chance to pay your last respects."

Marcus looked at Antonius through swollen eyes.

"My father's pain must have been awful," he said while trying to control his weeping.

"Marcus, we're all deeply sorry," said Antonius. "I removed as many darts as I could before bringing him here." Antonius lowered his head.

"Why would he allow himself to be killed?" Marcus questioned in trembling anger.

Zoheleth

Joseph shook his head in sadness and ordered Antonius to take the body away.

Several soldiers put Sabinus on a cart with those who were to be cremated. Antonius had the sword and shield belonging to Sabinus. When they entered the tent, Antonius handed them to Marcus.

"These belonged to your father. Honor them with pride. We retrieved them before the enemy did."

Marcus examined the dents and holes in his father's shield, which showed the fury of the attack.

"I wish my father had lived long enough to know I was with him." Marcus wept openly. "I'll never see him again. What's going to happen to my mother and brother?" He thought about home and longed to be in his mother's arms. He wanted to see the face of his brother again. He condemned himself for not being by his father's side during the battle. He regretted he was made to stay with the physician. He hated everything, including all of Rome.

Inside the tent, Joseph prepared a mild sedative. "Take this, Marcus," he offered.

"I don't want it!" Marcus replied sharply.

"Would you like to return to your home and be with your family?" Joseph asked.

"No!" he shouted. "I want to fight! I have my father's sword and I want to avenge my father's death!"

"Maybe I better leave you two alone," Antonius said. He was about to leave when Titus enter the tent. He saluted and stood at attention.

"At ease, soldier," said Titus. "I've come to see the son of Sabinus."

"Welcome Caesar!" Joseph said.

Marcus wiped his eyes. "Caesar," he saluted like soldier. "I'm old enough to be in your service as a soldier," he stated firmly. "I request Caesar to allow me to avenge my father's death!"

"That's very commendable," said Titus. "But you are needed here." Titus moved closer to him. "You're a skilled medical assistant and your father wanted you here."

Marcus fought back his tears.

"I want to honor my family," he insisted.

"I know how you feel," Titus replied kindly. "I would want to do the same thing if it were my father." Titus addressed him as a man. "You won't honor your family if you are killed! You would only cause them more sorrow?"

Marcus was stunned. "But Caesar," he stammered, "it's the noble thing to do."

"The noble thing to do, Marcus, is to obey your Caesar's commands, as your father would have done!"

Marcus stood motionless while Titus went on. "You are to work with the physician. That's an order!" he commanded. "I see before me the makings of a fine physician."

"Yes, Caesar," Marcus' lips quivered. He tried not to allow Titus to see his disappointment.

"If you desire to leave the service of Rome, I grant you that decision. If you wish to return home you may. If you do, then, you will be permitted to return to finish your training with the physician." Titus stated.

Marcus' emotions were mixed, but suddenly he remembered something. "Caesar," he spoke out. "I gave my father a promise to serve Rome. I will honor him by keeping my promise. I choose to remain in the service of Rome!"

Titus was impressed. He saluted Marcus.

"You're a true soldier," he said. "And now, Marcus, I must return to the walls of Jerusalem. I give you my word as the son of Caesar, Rome will avenge the death of your father and every good man who has been killed by these insurgents."

Titus returned to the wall and stationed a fresh garrison inside the third wall where Sabinus lost his life. He posted guards at the opening of the second wall as well.

He was saddened when seeing his dead soldiers being carried past him. His emotions overwhelmed him and he turned his face to the heaven, saying loudly.

"God of the Jews! Don't blame me for all this suffering!"

His men were stunned by his words. They never saw Titus so filled with indignation. He displayed the greatness of his character which did not lack pity as well as clemency.

Titus wrung his hands and looked fiercely in the direction of the third wall. He cracked his knuckles and took long strides over the ground. He worried how they could get over the wall without losing more valuable men?

Alexander Tiberius met him and the two exchanged words. They worked all night to design their plans to make the next move on the wall. Their guards stood watch until dawn.

Antonius was hot and tired. His body yearned for straight wine. He wanted to dull his mind since he couldn't restrain himself from thinking about Doris. Antonius was not in the habit of accepting rejection from a woman. He wondered if she would reveal his visit to her husband. Deep down he wished his friend evil. Why couldn't Ebutius be the dead hero?

While on his walk to visit Marcus, he relived what happened to him three nights ago. He had made his way to the court of Doris while Ebutius was still in the infirmary. The painful memory haunted him. Doris had wounded him deeply.

He could still see her beauty and longed to entice her into his arms. He hoped she needed comforting, or even a love affair, since her husband remained in the infirmary for over a month.

"Why did I go?" he asked himself while walking. "Why did she turn so cruel?" He was sure she knew how he felt about her. Did she enjoy taunting him? Why couldn't she have said something kind and he would have left. He could still see her eyes glaring as she spoke harshly.

"How dare you enter my court while my husband is not present."

Zoheleth

He heaved a deep sigh and remembered how he desired her. She asked why he came. He assured her he came only to check on her welfare. What was it she said? Oh, he remembered, "Say what you came to say and leave before I call my guards!"

He felt his face flush and heard himself mumble weakly, "I just came to offer my help." He knew she read him. Her answer didn't surprise him.

"I need nothing from you, Antonius!" she replied in anger. "You've been drinking!" she added as she turned from him.

By the time he arrived at Marcus' tent he was trembling with anger. He wasn't sorry he had gone to Doris, but he felt he had lost the last chance to ever mean anything to her. He lifted the flap of the tent door.

"Ebony," he called softly, "it's Antonius. Can I come in?" There was no answer. He entered and found Marcus at the table with his hands covering his face.

"Ebony," he called louder. "Where's your friend the doctor?"

Marcus raised his head and looked past Antonius.

"He's in the infirmary." He didn't greet Antonius, nor did he smile. He pointed to the wine skin hanging on the wall. "That's what you came for," he said.

Antonius felt a pang. "I've come to be with you, lad," he assured him as he reached for the skin. He picked up two metal cups and bounced them on the table. He poured the wine until it overflowed.

"Drink," he said to Marcus. "You're a man now!"

Marcus refused. He had never desired wine. But then he changed his mind. Being called a man impressed him. He swallowed the wine down so he couldn't taste it.

"Slow down, Ebony," Antonius laughed. "Tell me, my friend, what's bothering you, beside the death of your father?"

"It's Titus," Marcus complained. "He won't allow me to avenge my father's death."

Antonius slapped him on the back. "You leave the

Zoheleth

avenging to me," he said confidently.

Marcus looked with pleading eyes. "Promise me, Antonius?"

"You have my solemn word, Ebony. I will avenge your father for you."

Joseph stepped into the tent and heard what was said. He caught Antonius pouring wine for Marcus, and saw the lad drink it with much distaste.

"Stop it!" Joseph ordered. "Both of you, stop it!" He stared critically at Antonius and stood over them in an authoritative pose. Antonius jumped from the chair and faced him.

"Shut up, old man!" he snapped. "It's your people who have left Marcus fatherless!"

"It's not up to you, Antonius, to avenge the death of Sabinus," Joseph shot back. "Titus will do the avenging as he promise Marcus!"

Antonius laughed out loud. "Titus" he said as he gulped down the wine. "That love-sick pup? He prolongs the torture for all of us!"

"You dare speak against the Caesar?" Joseph said in a threatening tone. He removed the wine from the table "How did you come up with that piece of theorizing?"

Antonius was disturbed. He knew what it meant to speak against the Caesar, and feared the physician at that moment. He tried to justify his words.

"All the soldiers know Titus is trying to impress the whore he's infatuated with." He physically took the wine skin away from the physician and refilled the cups.

Marcus gulped down the wine in spite of the doctor, and held his cup for a refill.

"Antonius is right!" Marcus agreed, as he tried to lift himself up from the chair only to flop down again. "Your people are to blame for my father's murder," he accused.

Joseph fell silent. He knew Marcus was striking out. Joseph fixed his gaze on Antonius and commanded, "Leave this tent, Antonius!"

"And you're going to make me?" Antonius jutted his

jaw forward and put his face close to the physician. "I don't trust you, doctor."

Joseph stepped back from his offensive breath.

"Leave now!" he ordered, but Antonius stood before him defiantly.

"Let me tell you, Jew. Some of the soldiers think you and the Jewish general are informing the Jews in the city of our moves."

"If you don't leave this tent, I'll report you're drinking while on duty. Do you understand what that can mean?" Joseph stood his ground.

"I hate your Jewish guts!" Antonius spat and took hold of the doctor.

Marcus saw an impending danger to Joseph and became frightened. "Antonius!" he cried out. "Don't harm him!"

Antonius released his hold. "Harm him?" he sneered. "Marcus, we won't harm him. Let's kill him!"

He reached for Sabinus' sword resting next to the table. He placed it in the right hand of Marcus.

"Here! Kill your first Jew with the same sword your father would have used."

Joseph stepped back, and Marcus stumbled as he rose from the chair. He pulled his hand from Antonius' grip, and began to feel sick to his stomach. He dropped the sword and ran past Joseph and out of the tent.

Antonius glared at the doctor. "You've made him a whimpering coward." He wiped his mouth and threw the cup to the ground.

"You want a boy to do what you can't do!" Joseph accused. "You figure Titus won't punish the boy for my death. You're a deceiver to this lad who loves you!"

Antonius would hear no more and sped out.

Joseph went in search of Marcus and found him retching and emptying his stomach.

"Everything is spinning," Marcus coughed. His mouth tasted sour and he was ashamed of his actions. He did hate the Jews, and resented Joseph who was old and still alive. His father was young and strong and it was he who was dead.

Joseph lifted him from the ground. "Come with me," he said softly. "I'll give you a potion to settle your stomach. But I'm afraid you will have to suffer a headache in the morning." He led him to his cot. After he drank the potion, Joseph covered him with a blanket.

"I'm sorry," Marcus whispered.

"Put away your anger, Marcus. Trust in God as your avenger."

"I don't want to hear that," Marcus groaned as his head began throbbing.

"Your father wanted an end to this fighting. He knew he would volunteer himself to help bring about an end. His hopes were to return to Antioch with his family," Joseph revealed.

"I know," said Marcus as he tried to sit up. He kept licking his dried lips.

Joseph reached into a cubical on the wall and withdrew a pouch.

"Your father asked me to give this to you."

"What is it?"

"I believe it's a letter. Open it, son."

Marcus opened the small scroll neatly rolled inside the pouch. Joseph lit the lamp by the cot and allowed Marcus to read a father's last letter to his son.

Joseph had reports to finish.

The tent was quiet.

CHAPTER TWENTY TWO

CHANGING GODS

Nicator brushed down a racing horse in his care. The owner, Demetrius, stood watching.

"He's a beauty," said Nicator when he finished grooming the animal.

"He's one of my favorites," said Demitrius. "I've always favored the Idumean stallions. They're great racers."

"You have reason to be proud," said Nicator as he limped to the rear of the horse to examine the hooves. "He's clean. I took him out this morning, and I thought I was riding the wind."

"Let's hope he's that fast tomorrow," said Demetrius as he rubbed the nose of the stallion.

"Will you be using the track in Antioch City?"

"Yes."

"He's sure to be a winner."

"You've done a good job with him, Nicator. Your courage amazes me."

"Courage?" Nicator questioned.

"Your father told me about your tragic encounter with a horse when you were a boy."

"That Seluce. He was a great runner," Nicator replied. "My father had to kill him."

"What a pity. I hate to see any of these beauties put to death."

"It was a foolish thing my brother did that spooked the beast."

"Things like that happen, but I heard that you saved your brother's life."

"Yes," Nicator groaned, "but not my leg."

Demetrius noticed a rider in the distance. "Looks like you've got company."

"He's riding fast," said Nicator.

Zoheleth

"Is this the Severus' farm?" called the rider.

"You're at the right place," said Nicator. He saw the rider pull out several scrolls from a pouch on the saddle.

"Two of these are yours," said the rider. Nicator reached with trembling hands.

"Can I offer you a cool drink?"

"I can't linger," said the rider. "I was asked by the army to deliver these. The one with Rome's seal I'm told to handled with urgency." He turned to leave.

"What's happening in Jerusalem?" Nicator called out.

"The Romans are inside the walls of the city," the rider shouted. "The rebels fight against them with all their combined strength."

"Have you been paid?" The man gave a negative nod. Nicator in his generosity, tossed him a denarius.

Nicator held tightly to the letter and spoke to Demetrius. "If you'll excuse me, I must take this letter and read it to my mother. She waits for news from my father."

"Go ahead," said Demetrius. "I'll pick up my stallion early tomorrow."

Nicator felt fear in his heart. The scroll with the Roman seal had to be bad news. He entered the house.

Adana, his mother, was in the pantry kneading dough for bread.

"Mother, there's news from Jerusalem."

She wiped her hands on a cloth around her waist. "When did you get it?" she asked.

"It was just delivered." Nicator noticed how his mother look worried lately. She had complained of sleepless nights, and told him when she did fall asleep she had frightening dreams.

"Nicator," she said. "You're reading it to yourself. Why?" She saw him crying. "What is it, son?" She had no way of knowing what the letter revealed. She wished she had learned to read.

"Is it Marcus?"

"No, mother. It's father."

"Tell me what the letter says before I die."

Zoheleth

"Father has been killed!"

"Oh!" she gasped. She swayed and grabbed the back of a chair. Nicator made her sit down.

"Please, mother," he said, "this has always been like a sword hanging over our heads." He opened the other scroll and it confirmed that his father was killed in the line of duty. He crumbled it and dropped it to the floor.

"Not my Sabinus," Adana cried. "Not your father."

"Mother, let me read the letter to you."

"I can't bear it. Don't read it to me!" Nicator stood confused.

"You must face it."

Adana calmed herself. Tears streaked her face and were smeared by the flour on her hands.

"Marcus has copied a letter which father left."

His mother caressed the chair arms. A chair which her husband had made as a wedding gift to her. She shook her head from side to side and stared at the floor in silence. Nicator began to read.

Dear Mother and Nicator,
It has taken me several days to be able to write this. Father has been killed while inside the walls of Jerusalem. It is painful to inform you of his death. Titus has sent you a notice also. Father gave a note to Joseph. This is a copy.

Dear sons and loving wife.
If you are reading this letter, it means I am dead. I know the daring steps I'm about to take. It will most likely kill me. I've made many visits to Joseph, the physician, and Marcus. During my visits I became familiar with the beliefs of Joseph. He taught me about the Son of God, one called Jesus. I accepted the God of the Jews. I don't expect you to understand. I don't understand it fully myself.
One night I had a dream and related it to Joseph. He can fill you in on the dream. I knew I would go forth as an instrument of God. I have no fear. There's a promise of <u>everlasting life</u> in the kingdom of God with His son, Jesus.

Zoheleth

Beloved Adana,
Dear wife and mother of my children. I thank you for the years you have been devoted to me. It has not been easy for you while I served the army, but it was my choice in life.
Please don't grieve too long, but try to learn about the God of the Jews! My prayers are for you, and I trust we will all be together one day in heaven. I love you, my faithful wife.

To Nicator, my dear son.
You were left with all the responsibility of a man. I'm grateful you're not a warrior, although you're a soldier in many ways. My deepest thanks to you for caring for your mother in my absence. Be there for your mother and keep in touch with your brother. I want to add how proud I am of your skill with horses. Keep with it! I love you.

To Marcus, my dear son.
Don't attempt to avenge my death! I make this last request of you. Try to learn about Jesus from your physician. Jesus will make you a new person. I have entrusted you to the care of Joseph. It is my desire for you not to become a warrior. My lineage must carry forth. Learn other ways to live beside fighting. Write to your mother and brother to keep them from worrying about you. I love you.
I pray God will keep you from harm and one day you will bring honor to your mother and brother.
With all my heart I have loved my family.

Adana broke down and cried, her hands trembling as she covered her face with the cloth around her waist. Nicator knelt beside her. When she looked at him her face was dusted in flour from her hair to her chin.

"There's more to the letter, shall I go on?"

"Let me get myself together," she sobbed. "I can barely believe what Marcus has written."

Nicator held back his tears, as he read on.

Zoheleth

Mother and Nicator,
I'm sorry to send such sad news. I wish I were there, but I gave father my promise to serve Rome. Titus won't allow me to fight, because father wished it so. I must honor his request.
Nicator, please inform Martha of our father's death.

Nicator rolled the scroll. "Mother, what was father referring to when he spoke about the God of the Jews?"

Adana wiped her face and felt angry as she replied. "Your father changed gods! And now he's paid with his life!"

"It would appear this physician had an influence on father." Nicator noted.

"I do hope he hasn't influenced Marcus to turn to that detested Christian group," she wailed.

Nicator thought about what she said. He knew his father was not a man of faith, but this new God he spoke so kindly about, puzzled him.

He walked outside to get away from his mother's crying. He felt a strange peacefulness. Was this what they called grief, he wondered. He thought about all living things. How there is life in people and suddenly there is death. He wondered what the gods did with his father. Did the gods punish him for deserting them? Why did his father choose to change gods? He remembered hearing how some followers of Jesus gave up all that was dear to them, including their lives. He questioned if this God cared about the families left to grieve? His father underlined the words "everlasting life". Why did his father believe in this? Could this new God bring his father back to life? He hung his head and returned to the house. He had no answers, only sorrow. Perhaps tomorrow he would think on it, but for today there was much mourning to share with his mother.

Zoheleth

THREE DOOMED MEN

While the Romans were posted at the third wall in Jerusalem, another sedition broke out inside the city.

Simon's men and John's men fought over food and water. They saw the Romans were not pushing forward after the second wall was broken through and they resumed their personal battles.

Titus tried again to give the rebels time to reconsider surrendering. He sent the Jewish general to convey a message to the insurrectionists. The message was to lay down their arms and allow the Romans to enter peacefully.

The general, Josephus, was escorted with additional soldiers for his protection. He still suffered from the head injury he received by his brother Jews. When he reached the walls of the city he spoke in their language.

"Countrymen and fellow citizens!" he called out, "once again Rome offers a peace agreement. Lay down your weapons and surrender the city! We are aware of the famine. Allow your people to be saved from starvation."

There was a long silence and the general was concerned. He was soon to learn their answer to his request.

"Look traitor!" a voice from atop the wall called out. "We have your father!"

The general was shocked and trembled with anger as he shook his fist threatening the watchman. Seeing his father being held as a prisoner brought him to tears.

His father looked down from the wall and spoke to his son. "Don't fear for me," he yelled. "Do what you can to get your mother out of here!"

The general was filled with pity when he learned his mother was also a hostage.

"How dare you use my parents in such a way!"

The watchman laughed. "Do you want to see your mother?" he taunted. "We can demonstrate to her how we feel about traitors and their family!"

Zoheleth

"Stop this madness!" Josephus commanded. "Release my parents, you scum! Take me in their place."

They showered him with stones and forced him to flee for his life.

"My God," he said to his escort, "how did they find my parents?"

The Roman talked among themselves. They were uneasy over the event, and wondered if the Jewish general would turn against the Romans to save his parents.

More Jews gathered on the wall and made obscene gestures to the general. Josephus' father tried to warn him to ignore what was happening, but the watchman removed him.

Josephus was in despair while heading back to Titus. Suddenly he saw three Jews escaping from the city.

"Capture those men!" he ordered the escort. The soldiers ran them down quickly and brought them to the general.

"Tie them to each other," ordered the general. "I'll take them to Titus." The prisoners fought to be free.

Josephus was angry. "You'll pay with your lives or you'll tell what's going on inside the city," he threatened. "Let those on the wall know that I have methods with prisoners, also."

The men pleaded in their language, and promised to give him information if he would spare them and allow them to flee to the woods.

Titus was unimpressed by the prisoners.

"Caesar! These men will give us the information."

Titus glared at the three prisoners. "Ask them what preparations the rebels are making for their next attack?"

The general talked with them.

"They say the men fight among themselves while woman and children are dying from starvation. They tell me many people are dead from the famine."

Titus wagged his head. The general questioned further.

"They say some rebels are in such pain from infections brought on by injuries, they have amputated their own limbs. There's no physicians in the city." The general paused to wipe his eyes. "Some men do this because their limbs are rotting away and they know they'll die soon."

Titus turned his gaze from the men. He shuddered and paced the tent. He saw the condition of the prisoners and how they were skin and bones.

"God, it's awful," cried the general as he spoke in Greek. He continued to question the prisoners.

"I'm informed the corn and wheat has been burned and there's nothing the people have to eat."

"And still they wish to continue against the Romans?" questioned Titus.

"They inform me that all the sacrifices have ceased in the temple."

"What does that prove?" Titus questioned.

"Caesar, it's not a good sign for the Jews. It proves they have no live animals in the city." The Jewish general pleaded to spare the life of the three. "They only want to flee to the wooded area to get away from Jerusalem, if Caesar will permit?"

Titus searched the faces of the three men, who looked like skeletons.

"Are they citizens of the city?" he asked the general.

"Yes, Caesar. They have not thrown one stone at a Roman. They were stopping to gather food from a garden when I had them captured.

Titus motioned the two guards by the doorway. "Escort these men to the edge of the woods." He turned to the general and said. "But warn them they will be killed instantly if they attempt to return."

The general related the message and they gave their thanks to Caesar.

The guards waited while the general talked with the the prisoners.

"How did you manage to get past the guards inside Jerusalem?"

One of the three smiled slyly. "We paid much gold to the guards. They wanted more, but when they searched

Zoheleth

our garments they found none. They allowed us to leave to show others that they could buy their way out."

The general frowned and shook his head. "How will you men survive without gold to buy food?"

"Ah, we are not so foolish as to be seen with bags of gold. We have swallowed much of our gold," he laughed softly. "We will pass it later."

The general was shocked and forgot himself and spoke in Greek.

"You swallowed your gold?"

The two guards overheard and looked at each other. The general turned the men over to the guards.

"Titus has allowed you to go free," said the general. "Just stay with the soldiers so you will not be harmed."

They thanked him for pleading for clemency.

The guards escorted them until they reached the woods. They had other plans about the fate of the three who were now free. They whispered and plotted with each other since the Jews were not in earshot. They questioned how much difference would three Jews make if they killed them?

The freed men had to pass the crucifixions in the area. They turned their eyes away from the horror. The sight was too distressing when seeing their fellowmen hanging upside down. Others were twisted in degrading positions to bring shame on all who looked. The men wondered how the Romans found pleasure in doing this. They thanked God that they were not so fated to be among those on the crosses. Little did they know their own fate.

They reached the wooded area where two Syrian guards were posted at the entrance. The Syrians stepped aside to allow the Romans with their prisoners to pass. Moments later they heard horrifying screams. The Syrians remained at their post assuming the three prisoners had been sentenced for execution. The Romans returned with smiles on their faces. They wiped the blood from the gold coins and placed them in their pouches. One soldier walked over to the Syrians and pushed several coins in their hands.

"You say nothing!" he demanded, and left them

Zoheleth

counting the blood money.

The Syrians waited until the soldiers were out of sight. They ran into the woods and were sickened by what they saw. Three men lay in their blood, their stomachs ripped open and their intestines pulled out.

"One of them is still alive," said a Syrian guard.

"Finish the poor devil off," the other replied.

"Perhaps the prison camps are overcrowded?"

"I don't think so," said the other. "It looks like their escort found a private sport."

"We can do the same to get gold," one suggested.

They laughed as they deliberately searched each corpse for more coins.

Zoheleth

THE BATTLE

Since there could be no negotiations of peace, Titus commenced to attack with full force.

While the Romans were on the Jerusalem walls doing battle the auxiliary brought in the ramming machines and placed them at strategic points. The Romans constructed timber siege walls inside the city to enclose the market place and areas leading to the Tower of Antonia.

Titus was ready to enter the Second Quarter of the city. He selected a group of Romans to sneak into that quarter by night and loosen the foundation stones of the tower. He needed control of the Tower of Antonia. After the stones were loose enough to bring down the foundation, the men were to give a signal with the blast of a trumpet.

The auxiliary was to enter at the signal and distract the rebels. Titus depended on the fact it would be night and the enemy would not expect an attack.

The Tower of Antonia was directly connected to the temple where the zealots were held up. Titus would send a continuous flow of fresh troops to attack Simon and John's men. Later, he would try to flush out Eleazar and the zealots.

The auxiliary worked the opening in the second wall and made it large enough for the ramming machines. The Jews constantly harassed them. One fiery Jew tried to incite an incident by shouting insults and making obscene gestures.

"Roman women!" he taunted. "Is there one who will meet me in single combat?" The auxiliary ignored him.

"Come!" he tormented. "Lift your skirts, let's see if you are men!" He cursed them continually until one man could no longer tolerate the abuse.

"Jew!" he shouted. "I am Pudens. I'm a man and a soldier of Rome! If it's single combat you request, then let's see if you are man enough to meet your God?"

Zoheleth

Pudens eyed the puny fellow as he stepped out.

"I accept your challenge!" said the Jewish instigator. The two fought fiercely.

Pudens was whipping him severely until the metal nails of his sandals caused him to slip. His challenger saw his opportunity when Pudens fell. He ran him through with a sword. When he killed Pudens, he danced around his dead body and made obscene gestures to the Romans.

One centurion watched in anger and decided to put an end to the heckler's miserable life with an arrow. The arrogant challenger writhed in pain and collapsed on the body of Pudens.

The Romans were gaining ground and the Jews had to cease their efforts in trying to prevent more Roman machines from entering the city.

Many citizens, unwilling to fight, were slipping through the gates and escaping at night. In the meantime, other rebels secretly planned ways to trap the Romans. They had raised a portico inside the city and deliberately left it unguarded.

A group of Roman soldiers, without orders from Titus, decided to cross the porch to gain entrance to another section of the city. Titus heard a great commotion and ran to see what had occurred. To his shock he saw his men stranded on the structure. The Jews set fire to each end of the portico which was built from dry timbers. The enemy had covered it with pitch and the flames burst into the air setting the soldiers on fire.

Titus was furious.

"My men!" he screamed when seeing the agony they endured. He watched them jump from the portico and be killed by the enemy waiting below. His men dropped like torches. But one lone Roman, named Longus, remained unharmed and stood atop the unburned portion.

Titus watched in horror as the enemy held him at bay. They advised him to desert the Roman army if he wanted to spare his life. The young Roman stood frozen as the flames danced around him. He looked down to jump, but decided against it.

"Come down!" shouted one Jew. "We'll spare your life if you jump."

Titus was helpless. Suddenly Longus' brother came running to the scene and stood beside Titus.

"My brother!" he yelled as he held his sword upward. The Jews became quiet as they waited for the soldier's decision.

"Use your sword, my brother!" Don't tarnish your good name as a Roman."

Longus heard his plea and withdrew his sword. He saluted Caesar and killed himself in front of the enemy and his brother. Tears ran down the face of the remaining brother. Titus' emotions were inflamed when he saw how his soldiers disobeyed and fell into the trap the enemy had masterminded. He swore to himself that the Jews would soon face the rage from the son of Caesar!

"Tonight!" he said through clenched teeth. "Tonight will be your final ending, city of Jerusalem!"

Late that night the soldiers worked out the plan devised by Titus. When the Tower of Antonia's foundation was weakened, they sounded the trumpet for the auxiliary to enter.

The rebels in the city were awakened by the loud sounds and fled in panic. But John saw that his men outnumbered the Romans and he ordered them not to flee but to fight.

The night was so black that John's men were killing each other by mistake. The Romans, however, had used a signal word to prevent from killing their own. It wasn't long before John's men were so confused they had to retreat.

At dawn, the Roman soldiers had the holy temple surrounded. The Tower of Antonia was now in the possession of Caesar Titus. The rebels when seeing the ramming machines around the temple, set them ablaze. Many soldiers were being killed in their effort to rescue the machines. Titus had to divert the enemy and give the order to set fire to the outer court of the temple gates. When the Jews heard his command they deserted the machines and ran to protect the temple.

Cheers came from the Romans while setting afire the gates leading to the temple. The flames spread wildly as the Jews desperately tried to prevent it but in their panic they found themselves encircled by the flames.

"Keep the fires going!" Titus ordered. "Let these rebels stew in their own arrogance!"

After many hours, Titus ordered the fires to be extinguished. He didn't want to destroy the temple of worship. Romans always showed respect for the people's temples. They were never sure whose god was more powerful, and they didn't want to offend the God of the Jews. However, Tiberius was of a different mind.

"Caesar," he said. "What will you do about the temple?"

"I haven't decided what should be done."

"If it's not destroyed," said Tiberius, " it will always be a focus for rebellion. Too many of the Jews suffer from messianic madness."

Titus was forced to agree. "Perhaps we can find a way to spare their temple. It's a splendid piece of architecture," he defended.

Tiberius was not in complete favor of Titus' decision. "They will continue to use it as a fortress," he pointed out. "It should be burned, since it's no longer a place of worship!"

Titus nodded, but wouldn't give his approval. "Let's wait until tomorrow," he said as he walked away deep in thought. He had hoped to settle things by setting fire to the gates. Perhaps it would give the radicals a chance to change their minds.

The following morning, the rebels struck again.

Tiberius saw the useless slaughter of soldiers and sent for Titus for an immediate council. He impressed upon Caesar that to hold back on destroying the temple would be a mistake. Titus was enraged when Tiberius informed him about the attacks. He was now vindictive.

"Tiberius," he said while looking directly at him, "Make a note of today's date."

"Yes, Caesar! It's thirty days into the month of August, the year Seventy."

"These insurrectionist have brought upon themselves their own destruction! I want that noted."

He scanned the area and pointed to the temple courts. Against his personal desires, he was forced to give the order to destroy the inner court.

"Tiberius, have the men set fire to the inner court of the temple!" Many Jews heard the orders and shuddered.

"Hear this!" Titus yelled to those within hearing. "You've seen your outer court burned down. Now see the inner court burned down."

Tiberius smiled with satisfaction. "Hail Caesar!" he saluted. "I speak for our legions. You have no other choice but to ruin the temple."

The legions were hot for action and sped to the order. They set ablaze the inner court while the Jews ran to block them from entering the sanctuary. Titus watched and was sure the fire would force the Jews to surrender. If they did, he would spare their temple. But to his dismay he saw an angry soldier grab a burning brand and throw it inside the door of the temple.

The Jews stood helpless and let out fearful cries. Some tried to retrieve the fire brand, not caring about their own life, but were forced back by the intense heat.

"Curse the men!" shouted Titus. "I gave no order to burn the temple!" He ran toward the temple waving his arms in gestures to the men.

"Not the temple! Put out the flames!" he ordered. "Do you hear me?"

His shouts were not heard over the riotous cries from both sides.

One soldier in earshot carried Titus' message. He ran to the soldiers who continued to fire the temple.

"Our Caesar demands the fires to be put out!" He

shouted and signaled, but the men ignored him. They rushed on with more torches and hurled them into the sanctuary. The rebels trapped inside, burned to death along with their holy place. Titus couldn't restrain the fury of his men.

"Romans!" he shouted. "Cease your madness!" His pleas died in the flames.

"Caesar wants the fires out," laughed one soldier. "That's an insane risk. Look at the gold covering everything in sight!" he added. "We'll be wealthy men, once we get inside the temple." By now the soldiers had gold-fever and ignored all orders from Titus.

Caesar covered his mouth and nose with his cape and moved through the smoke to get to the temple. He was forced back by the intense heat. His heart was heavy when he returned to the Tower of Antonia, coughing and spitting all the way. Thick black smoke clouded the streets and alleyways. He heaved a deep sigh when he saw the entire city engulfed in flames.

The war cries of the legions were deafening and so were the shrieks from the people trapped in the flames. He heard shouting that the zealots were escaping through underground passages. He was indifferent to the news. He considered the zealots were no longer a threat to Rome.

Tiberius found him in a grievous mood. "Caesar," he said as he looked at him in pity. "You see how the fires have spread to the buildings throughout the entire city?"

Titus stood like a dead man. He couldn't reply. His thoughts were on what had happened. He complained to Tiberius how he felt betrayed by his men who fired the temple out of greed. He informed Tiberius he never gave the order to burn down the holy temple. "Why didn't they wait for my orders?" he asked.

"Caesar?" Tiberius said softly. "You know how soldiers are when they have tolerated much torment from the enemy. You witnessed how they kept their control while their comrades were being killed."

Titus shook his head. "They're greedy for gold!"

"They wanted revenge," said Tiberius.

Titus seemed not to hear.

"Now, if Caesar will, we are taking thousands of refugees, mostly women and children. What are your orders?" Titus stared into space.

"Are you discouraged?" Tiberius asked. "You have warned these people and made many offers of peace. They left you no other choice."

Titus didn't respond. "Caesar," he continued. "You should hear some of the stories we are hearing from the women we have rescued. Weird stories."

Titus turned and asked. "What do you mean?"

"The women say that a gate fastened with iron bars flew open on its own the night before our attack." He looked at Titus who went back to staring. "Another woman told us that the priests entering the inner court of the temple became fearful when they heard voices coming from nowhere, saying. "We're leaving this place" I told you it was weird." He saw the weariness in Titus. "What are your orders, Caesar?"

Titus snapped out of his trance and glared at Tiberius for a moment.

"Bring me the leaders, John of Gischala and Simon, as well as Eleazar. I want them alive!"

"We will capture them, Caesar. No person can escape the city. We have complete control." Tiberius struck his chest. "Hail Caesar!"

Titus was alone in the Tower of Antonia. He felt something had died within him. He surveyed the smoky area and felt like he had lost the battle, not won it.

The smoke burned his eyes as it drifted upward, but it would give reason for the tears rolling down his face.

His thoughts turned to Bernice. What would she think of him when she learned Jerusalem was totally destroyed? Would she understand he didn't want this to happen? He must get word to her before she receives dreadful lies from conspirators of the rebels. He must inform her of his efforts to keep peace and to save the beautiful temple of Jerusalem.

Five days after the fire there was not one stone left upon another of the holy temple.

The Romans pitched their standards on the temple grounds and offered sacrifices to Rome and to the Emperor of Rome, Vespasian. Their spirits were high when knowing the booty they would gain. They continued to hail Titus as their Caesar.

Titus stood amidst them as they cheered and hit swords against their shields.

"Your men salute you, Caesar!" said Tiberius as he walked up to him.

Titus nodded and thought the soldiers were only set on getting the booty.

"Caesar, you must not allow the men to think you are angry with them," Tiberius reminded. "Many have given their lives for you."

Titus realized his duty as their Caesar and commander. Tiberius was right, there were those who gave their life to save him.

"Thank you, Tiberius," he said respectfully. "I will join the men in celebrating."

Zoheleth

CITY OF ASHES

Titus and the soldiers celebrated with the wine retrieved from the Jerusalem temple. They filled the sacred golden cups. Some soldiers drank from their helmets and sang victory songs.

Titus rode through the city and ordered an inventory of every item of value found. He could visualize the glorious display in his triumphal march through Rome. The items from the temple would be carried on the shoulders of the Jews who were now to be slaves. Much was saved from the flames, such as holy items and vaults filled with gold coins.

Though he celebrated, his heart was not it in. His thoughts drifted to Bernice and how she would receive his letter of the events. He had requested her to join him on his voyage to Rome. He said in the letter how he hoped she was still in love with him. He suggested marriage after his triumphal march.

He didn't want Bernice to witness the victory march over her people. He had mixed feeling about her seeing the Jews captured and sold into slavery. He never mentioned how badly the city of Jerusalem was damaged. Nor did he mention the total destruction of the temple or the amount of treasures rescued.

Next, he sent for Josephus, the Jewish general. He needed him to translate to the prisoners.

Tiberius came riding with a group of prisoners.

"Hail Caesar!" He addressed Titus. "You'll be pleased to know I've captured John of Gischala and Simon, the son of Giora. I regret to say there was no sign of Eleazar."

John and Simon were roped together with other prisoners as they stood in front of Titus.

"May I present the slime of the city," Tiberius

announced as he tugged the ropes. "This burned city is the result of these who call themselves men."

The soldiers began jeering and cursing John and Simon. Titus raised his hand and turned his horse so he could face the prisoners. Josephus stood near and translated Titus' words to the prisoners.

"John, and your enemy friend, Simon," he said with a contemptuous sneer, "tell me, has your God turned his back on you?"

John glanced away, but Simon acted indifferently.

"You call us scum?" Simon dared. "Look at your pagans worshipping their Roman ensigns on the ashes of our holy temple. It's an abomination!"

"The false prophets in the city have led the people astray," said Titus. "And you two have led the people into total destruction. You speak of what we do with our ensigns? What about you killing the priests at the altar? I call that an abomination!"

Simon spat and cursed Titus. John placed himself in front of Simon to stop him from using rude remarks which could lead to their death.

"Caesar," John called out. "Give us a place to go! We'll never come against you again. Send us to the desert if you desire."

"Shut up, you fool!" Simon warned, but John ignored him. "Please!" He begged as his eyes pleaded with the Jewish general in hopes he would convince Titus.

"Give you a place to go?" Titus mocked. "You who were offered terms many times? You refused to surrender and killed those who wanted to accept the hand of Rome."

John's face turned red, but Simon shook his fist in a threatening gesture. "Better to be us that killed them, than let your soldiers rip them open for the gold they had swallowed!"

Titus was horrified by the accusation. He glared at the men in disbelief. "If I learn that one of my men have done such an act, I personally shall slit their throat! But coming from you, I'm not willing to think this is truth."

In the background, two guards stood in fear. Each knew what they had done. Fortunately for them that Titus

Zoheleth

didn't believe Simon.

"So now you want to make the terms?" Titus laughed.

"Have mercy on our families, Caesar," Simon spoke out. "I have a wife and children."

Titus shook his head. "I find it insulting that you make such a request. What mercy did you show when you trampled over innocent children? Then you added insult to injury by trampling over their dead bodies in your riots?"

Simon lowered his head.

"I have a message for you and all standing here. If you don't understand me, Josephus will translate."

"To all the Jews standing before me today," Titus announced. "I want you to think about what I'm saying." He waited for Josephus. "Rome gave you this land for your people to possess. You were permitted to gather tribute to pay your God. We Romans, paid offerings to you and to the God of the Jews. You made war with Rome and used our money to do so."

John looked at the numerous prisoners and pleaded one more time. "Allow the people to restore the city," he begged. "We'll leave here and never return. Let the people rebuild the temple."

"How dare you to keep presenting me with conditions!" Titus grew impatient. "The captives demanding their terms. Ha!" He pointed to the city of Jerusalem. "Behold the death of your city!"

He rode off and ordered his men to burn down all the houses holding the dead.

Josephus listened to the prisoners pleading for him to intercede with Titus. He shook his head in a disapproving gesture.

Titus went to seek out one of his officers.

"Cerealis," he called. "Take the cavalry into the city and search out every man who still fights against Rome! Take anything of value and burn down the houses."

Cerealis was a soldier not much younger than Titus. He saluted his Caesar and broke into a smile when given the order. He knew the rewards and promotions he'd receive by finding the enemy. "We'll burn the houses and find every man hidden. And we'll get the treasures from Agrippa's palace. I'm sure Agrippa won't be coming back."

Titus frowned and commanded. "What you find belonging to King Agrippa you will bring directly to me. It's not to be used as booty. King Agrippa has helped the Roman armies in many of our battles. Is that understood?"

Cerealis looked puzzled. "Whatever my Caesar commands."

"Agrippa is a personal friend. Many of you soldiers were fed by Agrippa when my father was in command."

"I understand, Caesar." Cerealis saluted. "You have my word that all the findings in the palace will be labeled and spared from the booty. I'll bring them to you."

"I trust you, Cerealis. You will be well rewarded."

Cerealis and his men rode through the smoky city. Their horses were attacked by hungry dogs snapping at their hooves. At times, a dog gave pitiful yelps when struck by the horse's hooves. His men searched the corners of the upper city for any insurrectionists in hiding. What they saw sickened them.

The wild dogs were attacking each other to lick the blood off the ground. The animals were starving due to the famine in the city.

Cerealis found rebels trying to escape and struck them down fiercely. One man lost his arm.

The dogs went mad over the smell of raw meat and turned vicious to gain control of the severed limb. They were like a pack of wolves. The taste of human flesh had set them into a frenzy. The soldiers watched in disgust as the dogs tore the limb to shreds. The amputated rebel lay on the ground bleeding to death, and the dogs headed toward him. Out of pity, the soldiers killed him.

From the alleys came other herds of dogs gone wild from the scent of meat. They tried attacking the soldiers who rode them down and slew them.

Cerealis' men searched the underground tunnels. They were ordered to light a fire to fill the tunnels with smoke and seal the openings. Those hiding inside would die.

When the alley was cleared of dogs, Cerealis rode

back to make one more check. He noticed the body of a Roman half buried under some debris.

"Help me here!" Cerealis ordered. His men dug for the soldier and pulled out the limp body.

"I think he's still alive," said one soldier.

Cerealis saw the yellow hair stained with blood. "It looks like Antonius of Ashkelon," he said. "Get him to the nearest camp infirmary."

The Jewish general took notes while riding along side of Titus.

"Look at the strength of the towers," Titus pointed. "No one could have broken through these fortifications. Their God has turned from them."

The general nodded sadly in agreement. "Your victory was by divine providence, Caesar," the general admitted.

Titus glanced at him. "I'll leave the towers as a monument of our victory. They'll be reminders for all to see." He noticed the general's sadness.

"I'm sorry, Josephus," he tried to apologize. "But as you know, Fate has destined Rome to win this war and to rule the world."

They were forced to leave their horses because of the difficulty in maintaining their footing over the areas drenched in blood. The horses were stained in blood up to their breast.

"I will reward my men as soon as they return from the upper city," said Titus. "Many brave men have risked their lives in offering peace to your people."

They walked in silence. Titus suddenly remembered something.

"General, I want the son of Sabinus."

"You mean Marcus? I'll bring him to you." The general walked back to his horse and rode to the infirmary. He was relieved to get away from the dreadful sights in the city. He thought about his parents and wondered if he would find them alive. If they were among the prisoners, he was confident that Titus would set them free. But were they alive?

CHAPTER TWENTY THREE

THE AWARDS

The Jewish general located Marcus who was working in the infirmary.

"Why does Titus want me?" he questioned the general.

"I'm sure you will learn when you arrive," said Josephus.

Marcus was reluctant to leave the infirmary. Work was what helped him not to think about the death of his father.

The physician noticed the general talking with Marcus and asked why he had come.

"Caesar wants the lad," said Josephus. "But Marcus is not willing to leave."

"I think I know why Titus wants him," said the physician. He turned to Marcus and said. "I'm certain Titus will honor your father today. You must attend the ceremonies in your father's place, Marcus."

"Can't he do it without me?" he asked.

"It would be an insult to Caesar, if you refused to attend."

Marcus' eyes were tearing. He looked at the doctor and asked, "Will you come with me?"

Joseph smiled. "I wouldn't miss this for the world!"

"Father would have liked you to be at my side," Marcus remarked.

"You get freshened and I'll send for the mules."

The general rode his horse as the two mule riders trudged behind.

"Look at the city," said the general, "it looks like a furnace of burning embers."

"It will smolder for days," Joseph replied.

The three reached a clearing in the city and saw the

soldiers erecting a tribunal for Titus. Caesar mounted it and raised his hands. His military cape hung limply from his shoulders as he placed his plumed helmet on his head.

"Soldiers of Rome!" he bellowed. "For your courage and gallantry, I thank you!" There was much cheering and clamoring of shields. He waited for the noise to dim.

"You fought magnificently," he added. "You're an honor to Rome and to my father, the Emperor Vespasian!"

The message was carried to the men far back in the lines. The cheering continued. He raised his hand for silence.

"You fought with admirable spirit! All who performed noble feats in action I will call forward."

He was handed a scroll and he called out the names. The soldiers came forward to receive gold crowns. The legions applauded their fellowmen. Some were awarded gold neck chains, others received metals, and some were awarded special pins.

"Those who stand in front of me will be promoted to higher ranks for their obedience and fearlessness during battle!" Titus announced.

Marcus stood in awe. He scanned the area for his good friend, Antonius. He was sure there would be a reward for him, and the promotion he so desperately desired. He could find no yellow haired man with fair skin.

Titus spoke again. "For those who died in the line of duty," he paused and wiped his eyes and continued, "their families will be compensated with the pay due the warrior, along with a bonus and living expenses for the survivors."

Many soldiers became emotional. Titus coughed from the drifting smoke. Tears streaming down his face.

"To a brave man, Sabinus," said Titus. "I now present to his son, the Corona Maralis."

Some soldiers gasped. This was the most envied award given to the first man over the enemy's wall.

Marcus was shocked. Joseph nudged him to move forward to receive the reward. He stood in front of Titus and was given his father's gold crown, and a silver spear for his father's hand -to- hand combat to death. Titus then placed a gold chain on the neck of Marcus.

"Wear this in memory of your brave father."

Marcus was in tears. Very few men had dry eyes at that moment.

"Also," Titus empathized. "From my father, the emperor of Rome, comes the honor of full Roman citizenship to the family of Sabinus, one who served Rome for over twenty three years!"

A thunderous applause filled the area. Marcus was dazed. He stepped away and walked over to Joseph.

"This should have been my father's day!" he cried. Joseph put his arm around him.

"Marcus, you're standing in for your father."

He lowered his head and felt unworthy, but he knew his father would want him to accept his rewards.

The general patted him on the back and congratulated him on having a brave father. He shook hands with Marcus, and then remembered he had something to tell him.

"Marcus, on my way to get you, I noticed your friend, Antonius. He was being carried out of the city."

His words startled Marcus.

"Where is he?"

"I would think he was taken to an infirmary."

"He's not dead?" Marcus' heart was beating rapidly. This was the reason his friend wasn't here to see him get the rewards, or to receive one for himself.

"I think he's alive," said the general

"What infirmary are you talking about?"

"There's an infirmary for every legion. You'll have to search which one he has been placed in."

Joseph overheard the conversation.

"I take it your friend is all right," he said. "If he has been taken to an infirmary, it means he's alive."

Marcus was relieved by Joseph's words. He then said, "Antonius must be wounded. I hope it's not serious."

"I hope not, also, for your sake," said the physician.

"Please, Joseph. Can't we bring him to our

infirmary?"

"Certainly, Marcus," Joseph assured. He turned to the general and asked. "Where could they have taken him?"

"I don't know," the general admitted.

Joseph looked at Marcus. "We'll find him, son."

"Can't we go now?"

Joseph saw men on stretchers being placed on carts heading to the infirmary.

"We have an influx of wounded," he told Marcus.

"But you have medics on duty to handle the injured," Marcus reminded him.

"I don't like leaving the Roman slave medics in control too long. There may be some wounded who need surgery."

Marcus relented, he said good bye to the general and they returned to the infirmary.

While on their way they saw thousands of travelers passing them. They came in caravans, on camels and mules.

"Why are these people flocking to Jerusalem now?"

"They have come to see for themselves the destruction," said Joseph, as he sighed lowly. "I heard that many come from different nations. The word has spread about the fall of Jerusalem."

"You predicted the city would be destroyed," Marcus remembered.

"Correction," said Joseph. "The Lord predicted the destruction. Jerusalem was cursed because they rejected Jesus as their Messiah" (Matt. 23:37-39).

"I don't understand it." Marcus said as he looked at the gold chain around his neck. "But I believe you even if I don't understand."

They saw the travelers staring in disbelief at the smoldering remains of the holy city.

"What will the Romans do now after they have won the war?" Marcus asked.

"They'll spend a few more days celebrating while the staff officers index the spoils."

"Will we join them?"

"I think not," said Joseph, "unless you like seeing oxen and bulls slaughtered?"

"Is that what they do?"

"Their ceremony brings in their Roman priest and a slaughterman. They feed the bull drugged fodder, then hit it on the head with a mallet. Once the bull's knees buckle they slit its throat and the blood is poured out as an offering to their gods."

Marcus fell silent.

"Still want to see it?" Joseph asked.

"I think I've seen enough blood spilled."

They reached the infirmary and saw it would be a long night ahead of them with the number of wounded.

Zoheleth

SAMUEL

The physician asked each soldier he dismissed from the infirmary if they had seen Antonius. He didn't like Antonius, but Marcus had turned to this scoundrel since the loss of his father. The doctor wished to hear Marcus laugh again and it would be Antonius who could accomplish this.

One morning while Joseph and Marcus searched for plants, Joseph heard someone calling. He stood up and looked in the direction of the caller.

"Samuel!" He recognized his friend and the two embraced like long lost brothers.

"Joseph of Alexandria! It is really you. My old class mate." Samuel broke out with a belly laugh. They exchanged greetings and Joseph introduced Marcus.

Samuel shook his hand. "How are you, young man?"

"I'm fine, sir," said Marcus. Samuel looked at Joseph and added, "Thank God this war is finally ended."

"Samuel, I thought after you finished medical school you were going to live in Spain."

"Ah!" Samuel declared, "that was a long time ago. I've been trying to get to Rome for over a year."

"Rome?" questioned Joseph.

"Right. But I got caught up in this disaster. Titus' father asked that I take over an infirmary. How do you say "No" to the emperor?"

"I didn't know you were here."

"Well, he's offered me the position to be his private physician in Rome."

"You are going to settle in Rome?" Joseph was surprised. "Are you telling me you will be at the palace to serve the emperor?"

"You guessed it," said Samuel. "I'm going to buy property in Rome and stay close to Emperor Vespasian."

"So," Joseph said contemplatively, "you've stepped

into royalty. Tell me, where are you now?"

"Come with me to my quarters and taste some fine wines. Where did you get this lad?"

"Marcus is my assistant. It's my hope that I can encourage him to become a doctor," he said softly.

They followed Samuel and entered his luxurious tent. It was beautifully decorated. One wall had coverings of skins from wild animals. Another wall displayed great paintings. The tables tops were of marble and on each stood a gold lamp stand. In the corners of the living quarters stood large jugs holding live miniature fruit trees and exotic plants. The floor was covered by richly colored Oriental rugs. A comfortable bed was in one section which was divided by a hanging drape woven with intricate designs. On ropes hanging from the ceiling were metal masks of strange faces, some with horrible expressions. Marcus thought they might have been ritual masks from foreign cultures.

Samuel's wine bearer set out golden goblets for them.

"Tell me about yourself," Joseph broke the silence. "By the looks of things you have collected many treasures through your travels."

"You're right," said Samuel as he grinned widely. Marcus noticed he was rather a handsome man with a neatly trimmed mustache and a narrow protruding nose. He was tall and muscular but slender. His beard was cut short and covered only his chin. The three sat and began talking.

"My friend," Samuel began, "I've practiced medicine in every nation as far as France and Britain." He wiped his mouth. "I liked France and remained there for many years."

"What was so interesting in France?" asked Joseph.

"The Druids!" Samuel revealed. "I tried stopping their bloody sacrifices of humans."

Joseph was shocked.

"Why would you want to be connected with the ancient Druids?" he asked. "Did you witness their "Wicker" Man"?"

"I know about that," Samuel shrugged.

"What's a Wicker Man?" asked Marcus.

Zoheleth

Samuel gave out a laugh. "They put criminals inside a huge wicker monster shaped like a man. They build it from dried limbs tied together. They bind the criminals inside and set it ablaze."

Marcus shook his head when he was handed wine.

"Would you like tea, lad?" Samuel asked. He motioned his servant to bring tea.

"What else was so interesting?" asked Joseph.

"Secrets, my friend, secrets!" Samuel laughed loudly. "These Druids have cures with herbs that we'll never learn about."

"I can't believe that."

"Joseph, my old friend, I tell you the truth!" He pounded his hand on the table. "They worship the mighty oak tree, and make use of the mistletoe which grows around it. They have potions for almost every illness. Their potions are used to ward off spells." He pointed to one wall. "Look over there. It's a relic from the Druids."

"What is it?" asked Marcus.

"It's a drinking horn. Notice the fine gold trimming at each end. And before you is a flagon which the Druids serve wine from. Look at the brightly painted designs." He lifted it to be admired. "This was presented to me by an arch druid priest."

"Did you ever learn the concoction to cure all ills?" Joseph eyed him with skepticism.

"No, my dear man. Those Druids guard their secrets with their lives. They got wise to me when I tried to enroll in their college."

"How could you? You know it's against the Jewish beliefs we stand for."

Samuel tilted his head and began laughing. "Listen to you. I heard from your friend, Mattahias, that you turned Christian. Isn't that against the Jewish beliefs we stand for?"

Joseph and Marcus looked at each other.

"I've become a Christian, but I never turned to cultic practices."

Samuel motioned his wine-bearer to refill the cups.

"I wasn't serious about their religion," he went on, but not convincingly. "I was looking into their history. They claim to be the descendants of Dispater, the lord of the earth!" He reached for a piece of fruit. "What really turned me off was when I learned how the priest behead a man every year and bring out another man who looks like the dead one. They convince the people that the beheaded man was brought back to life by them. One thing it does is keep the people under their control!"

Joseph shook his head. "Disgusting. How could you stay with them?"

"I liked their prophets," Samuel answered. "They always hit the mark. Although I could never get inside their Sacred Woods, where they hold their ceremonies beneath the oak tree. I did learn the priest cut the mistletoe with a knife of gold and let the plant fall onto a white cloth. After they gather the berries they sacrifice bulls.

Marcus roamed about the tent. He saw Samuel's surgical instruments left unwrapped. He wondered how Samuel could be so careless. Joseph would never allowed such uncleanliness.

Samuel went on. "I managed to get on good terms with the arch druid," he boasted. "They call themselves the "Oak Men". During their ceremonies they wear masks and huge head dresses. It's all quite impressive and scary."

Joseph bit into a ripe papaya. "What else did you learn?"

"You'll be amazed by this. Their young men study in college for twenty years." he laughed, "and we thought ten years was rough."

"I've never seen a Druid," Joseph admitted.

"They impressed me," said Samuel. "They're tall with skin as pure as milk. Most of them have yellow hair and they keep it light by washing it in lime water."

"If I remember correctly,"said Joseph. "Emperor Claudius forbade any Roman to join the Druids. Why do you suppose he did that?"

Samuel pulled his chair closer to Joseph. "Perhaps

Zoheleth

because they cut open the sacrificed body to examine the entrails and learn how the human body operates."

"You watched them open the dead?"

"Joseph, where else could I study a cadaver? I've gained much knowledge of the human anatomy that I couldn't learn elsewhere."

Joseph pulled back. "You shock me. Did you learn how they put their young men through extremely torturous test?"

"It's all to train them to use their mind over their body," Samuel declared. His eyes narrowed as he continued. "I witnessed these youths standing in ice water for hours. I've seen them standing on the ledge of a cliff all night long, sometimes on one leg. They wait for the spirits to torment them in an effort to make them fall." He leaned back and drank his wine. "Some of these lads fall to their death," he added. Samuel looked at Marcus who seemed rather distant.

"Is Marcus always so quiet?"

"The lad has lost his father in this war."

"I'm sorry to hear that," said Samuel. He made himself comfortable and continued his story.

"I'll tell you about the students who make it through the night's venture."

"Must you?" Joseph interrupted him. "I don't think Marcus wants to hear more horror stories, and I don't care to either."

Marcus came over to the table. "I'm interested!" he broke in. "Please, Joseph, allow your friend to finish."

"That's what I call the making of a man," Samuel laughed and went on. "Well, these young men are made to drink a cup of poison."

"What!" Marcus eyes widened.

"After they drink it, they fall into a death trance. It's called Life-In-Death. Those who live through it, come out with powers like I've never seen."

"They've sold their souls to the devil!" Joseph snapped. He stood up and was ready to excuse himself when a slave entered.

"Master, you're needed in the infirmary."

Samuel slammed his cup down. "This be-damned duty," he groaned. "Joseph, why don't you and the lad give me a hand?"

Joseph paused a moment. He glanced at Marcus who nodded his approval.

"We would be glad to, but only for a short time," he paused. "I'm sure our own infirmary will be in need of us. Marcus and I have to search for more herbs."

"Don't bother," said Samuel. He motioned his slave to fill a bag of different herbs. Joseph took them willingly and thanked him.

Samuel led the way. His fine linen garment had no signs of being soiled by wounded men.

They arrived at Samuel's infirmary. The stench of death permeated the tent. The wounded lay on the ground without blankets. Only a few cots were inside the infirmary. Marcus saw how Samuel with all his wealth, spent nothing on the welfare of the wounded. He thought how Joseph used his own money to buy cots, blankets, and wine for his men.

Soldiers lay in dried blood. Dying men had insects crawling over them adding to their discomfort.

Samuel said to Joseph. "I'll be glad when they take these half dead soldiers to Caesarea's hospital. When this infirmary is cleared out, I'm sailing for Rome." He lit two torches for them. "You and Marcus take that section," he pointed to the far end of the tent. "Not much hope for the poor devils. Just see if any need amputations and inform my slave medics to do the job."

Joseph felt pity as he walked down the infirmary. One soldier at the far end of the tent, cried out and thrashed about, cursing his gods and his fellowmen.

Joseph found a soldier who had no signs of injury.

"Why are you here?" he asked. "I see no wounds." The soldier groaned in pain. His face was discolored like a dead man. The soldier next to him spoke out.

"He swallowed a leech. We were drinking from a water container and it was too late when he realized one went down his throat. I tried to get him to cough it up, but he said it was probably a dead one."

Joseph stiffened. "Even a dead one is dangerous."

"What does it mean?" asked Marcus.

Joseph took him aside. "There's no hope for him." He saw sadness in Marcus' eyes. "Will he die?"

"The leech poisons the entire system."

"But we use leeches to suck blood," Marcus replied. "How come they can kill someone?"

"They're harmless for drawing blood, but their body is extremely toxic if swallowed. We have no antidote."

Joseph asked the soldier. "Are you a Christian?"

The soldier nodded. Joseph prayed over the lad, but was forced to stop due to the disruptive foul language coming from another soldier.

"See what you can do for the one doing all the cursing. Keep your torch in front of you, and use caution when you're close to him. He may have gone mad," Joseph warned.

Marcus approached in fear. When he got close to the cot, he dropped his torch and was stunned when seeing the face of the wounded soldier.

"Antonius!" he cried out. "Antonius! I've found you!"

A TRUE FRIEND

Marcus drove the torch into the ground and knelt beside his friend.

"Antonius, please don't die," he pleaded despairingly.

Antonius' face twisted and he shook violently while begging for help.

"I'm here, Antonius. It's me, Marcus. Please hear me." He broke into tears.

Antonius groaned in agony and cursed continually. Saliva ran from the corners of his mouth. Marcus lifted his friend's head the same way he had done with his father. He painfully looked on the pale face and saw how his friend's eyes were bloodshot and swollen.

"Antonius." He tried once more to get him to respond by saying, " It's your friend. It's Ebony."

"Ebony," he murmured. "You're here?"

"Yes, it's your ebony friend," Marcus was joyful that he heard him. He touched the bloodstained face and the yellow hair now brown with dried blood.

"Joseph!" Marcus shouted frantically. "Come quickly! I've found Antonius!"

Joseph came to his call and began checking Antonius thoroughly.

"Get me the pail of water over there," he requested as he looked at the sad condition in which Samuel's infirmary was kept. "How does this doctor expect a soldier to get water when it's not within his reach?"

He bathed Antonius' face gently, then washed the blood out of his hair until the gold shone through. He turned the wounded soldier's head and was shocked.

"This side of his face is badly bruised," he observed. "His lips are cracked and bleeding. Marcus, moisten them with oil."

Zoheleth

"How is he?" Marcus asked as he reached for the oil.

Joseph shook his head. "Bring the torch over here." He examined the wound. "Just as I thought."

"What's wrong?"

"Look for yourself, Marcus."

"There's a trickle of blood coming from the ear."

"What does it mean?"

"There's nothing we can do."

"Is he going to die?" Marcus looked woefully into the eyes of the physician. He sensed his seriousness. "Make him live!" he demanded as he glared at Joseph. "You know how to save him!"

"He's dying," Joseph said softly.

"Don't let him die!" Marcus insisted.

Antonius heard. "I don't want to die," he cried out. "Can't you see them waiting for me?"

Marcus looked around. "Has he gone mad?"

"He's delirious from the infection," said Joseph.

Marcus watched his friend thrashing around.

"How do you know he will die?" he cried.

"His head injury is severe and I'm sure there's internal bleeding."

"Give him opium for his pain," Marcus insisted.

"We can't force anything into his mouth, son. He might choke to death. I'm sorry."

Joseph was ready to leave. He picked up his medical box. Suddenly Antonius' eyes flew open and his expression frightened Marcus.

"What does he see?"

"Don't let then take me!" Antonius cried out as his gaze became fixed on a corner in the infirmary.

"Look at him!" Marcus grew agitated. "Antonius was so brave. Why is he whimpering like a pup?"

"Come lad, let's return to our infirmary. Men die every day. You must learn to accept it."

"Is this from your God?" he asked sarcastically and stared defiantly at Joseph.

"Marcus, every man must meet death on his own

Zoheleth

terms. Antonius is no different. Let him go."

Marcus refused to leave. He remained near his friend even though Antonius' cursing grew more vile.

"I'm losing him," he sighed. He took the hand of his friend and clung to him. "I hate it here," Marcus groaned. "There's death everywhere I look."

When Marcus saw Joseph was gone, he walked slowly out of the gloomy infirmary, his heart grieving. He missed Antonius. If they would have found him first he would live. He wondered about Antonius' private phantoms. He had no answers.

When he entered their infirmary Joseph had a wounded soldier strapped to the table.

"Thank God you're here," Joseph said. "I need you!"

Marcus saw the torn leg and felt sick.

"Come lad. I must amputate to save this man's life!"

Marcus stood frozen and backed away.

"Where are you going?" Joseph called out.

"I won't help you cut off his leg!" he declared.

Joseph looked despairingly. "You can't leave me now."

"I'm not under your orders. The war is over! And I'm going home!"

"Would you desert this man if he were your father?" Joseph snapped.

Marcus cringed. The words stung like a scorpion. He thought of his father and knew he couldn't leave.

"I'm sorry." He sniffed and trudged over to the table reluctantly. Angry tears blurred his vision.

They worked several hours, but it was futile. They lost the soldier.

"Was he one of your Christians?" asked Marcus, while washing up,

"Yes. Why do you ask?"

"He was different. He wasn't afraid to die."

"He knew he would be with the Lord." Joseph released the straps from the soldier's body.

"Why is Antonius so frightened of death? he asked,

Zoheleth

as he stared at the dead man on the table.

"Your friend has no one to trust in. Not even his own gods help him."

"How can he trust in your God? One he can't see."

"It would be better for Antonius to trust an invisible God, than to fear his demons, which are invisible to us!"

Marcus hung his head. Nothing made sense to him.

"Do Christians think they're going to live forever, like my father wrote in his letter?"

"Your father was referring to resurrection. Which means a Christian will be in God's presence after their death. This everlasting life gives us a hope for a future. We are not afraid to die."

"Do you want to die?"

"We all want to live, but the thought of death doesn't frighten me."

"I think it's all foolishness," Marcus stated.

"Marcus, you have witnessed Antonius who curses the darkness. His deeds give him no rest, because his soul is in torment."

Marcus clinched his fist and frowned strongly. "You're unkind," he accused. "You tricked my father into Christianity, but you won't trick me. You keep your God. He showed no mercy to my father!"

"Your father made the choice himself. He believed in Jesus as his Savior."

Marcus grew angry. "Antonius called you a fool, and I call you one!"

Joseph lowered his head. He motioned two solders to remove the body from the table. He washed his hands and turned to face Marcus.

"Better to believe Antonius." He replied and walked past him. "I hope you find meaning to life and not turn your back on all which is good."

CHAPTER TWENTY FOUR

A VISIT TO PELLA

The news of Jerusalem's fall circulated, but in Pella things were peaceful. King Agrippa read his sister's letter several times. Bernice was on her way to visit with him. Agrippa called on his servants to make ready his sister's quarters. He informed them she would be arriving tomorrow.

He walked out on his veranda and took a deep breath of the morning air. He wondered what exciting news his sister decided to keep until she arrived. She was not one to hold back anything of great importance from him.

His day was spent in ordering special foods to be served at the banquet for her. He barely slept that night.

Early the next morning he bathed and had himself oiled, and his barber trimmed his hair and beard. He dressed in his finest attire to greet his sister. Agrippa had two sisters; Drusilla, who was married to Felix, the procurator of Judea, and Bernice, who had been married twice.

Breakfast was served on the veranda. When he finished eating, he heard his neighbor calling.

"Greetings! King Agrippa," said Thomas.

Agrippa looked over the railing and called down.

"Thomas! Come join me." He waited for him to be escorted by his servants.

"I saw you from my roof," Thomas smiled as he shook hands with Agrippa. "For a king to rise this early it must mean an important event is about to happen."

"How did you guess?" asked Agrippa.

"I noticed your servants receiving all the fineries from the merchants. Let's say I have a nose for a party."

"Ah! Thomas, and also the eyes of an eagle." They laughed. "Bernice will be arriving today."

Thomas felt his heart leap. Her name brought back

memories. He admired Bernice for years, but his attempts to court her between marriages had failed.

"This is good news," he managed to say. "You need refreshing news after hearing how Jerusalem fell." He noticed Agrippa expression saddened. "It's on everyone's lips," he added.

"Don't remind me," Agrippa responded. "Thousands of our people are being sold into slavery, and Rome is shipping them to Egypt like cattle." He stared into space and sighed deeply. "Isn't it ironic," he continued, "our ancestors were once brought out of slavery from Egypt by Moses. Now Rome reverses the scrolls of our history!"

Thomas nodded. "We knew it would happen," said Thomas. "The zealots brought this on." He reached over and took a piece of fruit. "I hear there are people from different nations going to see what's left of Jerusalem."

Agrippa looked past him. "I must go and see for myself, but it will have to wait."

"Will your sister be staying?" Thomas inquired in an effort to change the mood of the moment.

"I don't know," Agrippa replied. "She's up to something. It's all hush-hush."

"If I know Bernice," said Thomas. "It won't be a secret for long. She does like to talk," he grinned widely.

"You mean her secret will be everyone's?" They broke out laughing.

"Please give her my regards," said Thomas.

"Give them to her yourself," said Agrippa. "You're invited to join us tonight for the banquet."

Thomas was overjoyed. "Is there anything I can bring?"

"No, dear man. Just bring yourself. I'm sure my sister will be pleased to see you."

Thomas could hardly contain himself. He hoped Bernice might have a change of heart toward him. He knew Agrippa approved of him, even though he wasn't a wealthy man. But one day he would be the owner of his father's leather business. His wealth would increase and it might be more attractive to Bernice. He knew many men fell in love with her at first glance, and he was one of them. Although he was younger than she, he never could forget her.

When he was an adolescent he met Bernice in Jerusalem during the feast days. He remembered how he wished he were old enough to approach her. She had just become a widow. Even then he noticed how she attracted men to flock around her. He didn't see her after that time but learned she was married off to some king.

Agrippa watched him leave.

A servant entered, excusing himself, and asked if Agrippa was finished with his meal.

"You may take the tray," said Agrippa.

"Your guest has left?" he asked.

Agrippa turned to faced him with a smile. "You mean that mournful would-be-lover?" The two chuckled. His servant removed the tray and emphasized.

"Thomas has been in love with your sister since he was a lad."

"Your mind serves you well, my friend."

"Too bad Bernice never liked him."

"My sister found him handsome, but to be interested in a tanner?" Agrippa shook his head in disgust.

"He's a good man and a religious one," said the servant. Agrippa broke out with side splitting laughter.

"Try telling that to my sister!"

Bernice had entered the Palace without her brother's knowledge. She told the servants not to announce her arrival until she was bathed and dressed.

Her woman servant went directly to her mistress' quarters and drew the bath.

Bernice undressed and slipped into the warm water. "Let me soak for an hour," she said to her servant. "The trip was too long, and I'll never get the dust out of my hair." She loosened her hair and let it fall over her bare shoulders.

"Mistress," said her servant, "a letter has arrived for you. Shall I open it?"

Zoheleth

"No!" she answered. "Hand it here!" She reached out for the letter and opened it.

Her thoughts were joyous when she learned that God had spared the life of Titus. She slid deeper into the water and dreamed of what she would say in response to his letter. She relaxed and hummed softly. Yes, she still loved him, and yes, she would sail to Rome with him.

She read the letter again. He promised to have Tiberius escort her to Caeserea, where he would be waiting. He begged forgiveness for not being the one to escort her, but his duties wouldn't permit him to leave.

What more could any woman desire in life? She was to become the wife of young Caesar for all the world to see. Her thoughts were interrupted by her brother's voice.

"Where's my beautiful sister?" he called out, as he dashed into her bathing room.

She wasn't alarmed, but welcomed him.

"Agrippa," she yelled out. "You pick the most inopportune times."

"Quiet!" he said, as he knelt down and kissed her forehead. "I've missed you."

He kissed her again and she threw a handful of water in his face. He laughed and tried ducking her. She screamed in protest. "Hurry and finish," he ordered. "I must learn the news which you find delightful to hold back."

"It will keep!" she laughed.

"Don't take too long. Thomas knows you're here and he's dying to see you."

"Oh, no!" She ducked her head under water.

"Dear sister what's wrong with our good friend, Thomas?"

"You know I can't stand the smell of leather. It permeates his skin." She looked up at him and knew he was goading her. "I would never marry a tanner."

"His mother married a tanner," Agrippa joked.

"Agrippa!" she shouted. "His mother was granted a divorce, because she couldn't stand her husband's odor, or have you forgotten?"

"Ah!" he laughed again. "I guess that's why no tanner can keep a wife."

Bernice heard his laughter through the hall as he left. She shook her head and smiled to herself.

The guests arrived at the palace of Pella. Agrippa was surrounded by women who craved his attention. Bernice noticed how they made fools of themselves whenever her brother was in their presence.

The guests were enjoying the wine and food. Bernice found herself with several men kissing her hand and having a longing in their eyes. She was accustomed to being admired and was never impressed by the attention. She felt a hand on her shoulder and turned.

"Good evening, Bernice," said Thomas, as he bowed. "You look lovely tonight. And, may I add I'm delighted to hear you'll be here for a time."

Bernice greeted him formally. "You're looking well, Thomas." She became aware that he was following her around the room while she greeted others and she was growing uncomfortable.

Agrippa broke away from the ladies when he saw his sister's pitiful expression as Thomas tailed her. He hurried to her rescue.

"Thomas," said Agrippa softly. "Would you excuse us for a moment?" He took his sister by the arm and led her to the garden, leaving Thomas shaken by their departure.

"You're a beast, Agrippa," she thrashed out. "What took you so long to get him away from me?"

Agrippa chuckled as they walked in the garden. "You better tell me the news, or I'll invite Thomas to join us."

"Stop it!" she laughed. "You win. I'll talk."

They were unaware that Thomas had followed them secretly. He kept his distance and watched as they sat on a garden bench. When they began talking he moved in the shadows and hid in the bushes to learn why they needed privacy.

Zoheleth

"Now tell me, dear sister," Agrippa began. "I can't stand it any longer. What is your secret?"

Bernice smiled and took his hand. "Agrippa, I'm in love."

"Well, this is news. No wonder you're all aglow tonight. Even I couldn't take my eyes off you."

"Stop teasing," she demanded. "Does it really show that much?"

"I've never seen you more beautiful, my lovely sister." He leaned over and kissed her forehead. "Now tell me who is this man who is taking you from me?"

Thomas trembled while straining to hear the name of her lover. His heart was heavy.

Agrippa spoke. "Don't tell me it's Vespasian? I heard rumors how he was quite taken with you."

"No, silly," she answered. "It's the son of Vespasian!" She looked up at him playfully.

"You monkey!" he laughed and squeezed her. "How did you pull this off. You really mean it's Titus?"

"Yes. He's asked me to marry him."

"What!" Agrippa stood up and looked at her with a stern expression. "Are you serious?"

"I'm serious," she replied as she put her head on his chest. He held her for a moment. "Do you approve," she asked softly, "or is there something you're not telling me?"

He gently pushed her away and looked into her eyes. "You know he's been married twice?"

"Yes. He's told me that his first wife died, and he divorced his second wife. He has a daughter from the second marriage."

"How do you think our people will react to this?" he asked. "Do you think this is a wise choice?"

"Do I think him a wise choice?" she repeated. "Agrippa are you forgetting I'm older than he? You should be asking if I'm a wise choice for him."

"You know he worships the Roman gods!" he reminded her.

"He has promised to convert to Judaism."

Zoheleth

"Did he?" Agrippa was surprised. He put his arm around her. "I hope this is true. Will he honor our religious traditions?"

"I know he will," she answered. "I love him."

"Are you certain he feels the same?"

"Why not?" she pulled away. "He's asked me to marry him. He wants me to go to Rome. Tell me, how does he prove himself to you, my brother?"

Agrippa turned away. "It might not be such a bad union," he said while contemplating. He paced back and forth a few times and turned to her. "This could give our people some say in the Roman rule," he suggested. "Perhaps we will be permitted to rebuild Jerusalem." Neither had seen the total destruction of Jerusalem.

"Agrippa!" she snapped back. "You're always thinking of politics. Your ideas are for your own future. Your concern is with how many nations you'll gain control over once I'm his wife."

"My sister," he pleaded, "your engagement to him is good news. We must do something to get the Romans out of Jerusalem. I would like to return to my palace, if it's still standing."

She stepped away from him. "Are you thinking of using me to accomplish your plans for Jerusalem?"

He turned to her. "I'm not the one marrying you off for political reasons," he reminded her.

"I know that," she admitted. "I've been married off since I was thirteen, and it's always been to better the alliances for our people. Titus is marrying me for love!"

Agrippa took her in his arms to calm her. He smiled secretly. He was Agrippa the Second, and was known to love power. Why not? he thought. This marriage with Titus could move him to greater heights than his father, Herod Agrippa the First, had obtained. His father became close friends to Emperor Caligula, better known as the mad emperor. Caligula made his father king of the Judea. When Claudius became emperor, he also favored his father. It was when he, Agrippa the Second, came of age that he received

Zoheleth

his father's kingdom under the rule of Emperor Nero.

The Herodians were favored by Rome. Herod the Great, became king of Judea, and the builder of the temple in Jerusalem.

Herod the Great married a second wife who was of royal blood. She was Mariamne, a Hasmonean beauty, and the granddaughter of John Hyrcanus the Second, who was king and high priest of Idumea at the time.

Agrippa thought about the children from Mariamne who were of nobility and of royal lineage. That royal blood was in him. He wanted to keep the bonds close between Rome and himself, and now he would be the brother-in-law to the future emperor of Rome. It was perfect!

"Agrippa," Bernice interrupted his thoughts, "tell me what you're thinking?"

"I'm in full agreement. I'm sure Titus loves you. Forgive me if I gave you cause to think differently. I'm sure your marriage will be accepted by our people after Titus has converted to Judiasm."

"Oh, Agrippa," she cried. "I knew you would approve. You will make the wedding plans so my Titus can show the world that he loves me!"

He kissed her. "Let's return to our guests."

"Dear, brother," she said slyly. "Don't start thinking of ways for me to influence Titus to raise you to a higher position of power."

Agrippa raised both hands in the air and smiled. "My sister, would I do such a thing?"

Thomas was shocked. His feelings were deeply hurt. He would soon let it be circulated among the guests about the engagement, and impress on all that Titus is a pagan!

Zoheleth

BROTHER NICATOR

Joseph finished packing his herbs into wooden boxes when Marcus came running into the tent.

"I've got a letter," he announced cheerfully.

"Well then, why don't you catch your breath before you read it?"

"It's from Nicator, my brother." He reached for a water skin and drank. "I'll read it to you." He opened the letter and tugged at his short beard sprouting from his chin.

Brother Marcus. This is Nicator.
We thank our gods for the ending of the war in Jerusalem. I trust you are in good health.
Mother has taken father's death badly. She's gravely ill.
If it were not for the two boys helping us, I would be giving up my work with the race horses. These young men lost their parents in one of the raids in Jerusalem. They managed to escape along with others and joined a caravan. One morning I found them hiding in the stable in one of the stalls. I don't know who was frightened more, them or me. When I learned they were not dangerous, I was relieved. They explained what had happened with their parents and asked if I would allow them to work in exchange for food. How could I turn them away.
The gods favored us. The boys offered to work our fields. We gave them a place to sleep. I hope they stay for a time, but they intend to travel to their relatives in Egypt.

Now. brother. Do you think your physician would accept our hospitality? I wish to invite him to spend time with us. We have no physicians to look in on mother. Most of them have gone to serve the Roman armies.
The good news about you coming home has helped mother, and may I add she is learning to read. I teach her every day.

Zoheleth

It keeps her from thinking about father. Her goal is to read father's last letter.
The village people inform us that people from other countries are traveling in caravans to see the ruins of Jerusalem. You have no idea how strongly I desired to make the journey. I would have, if mother were not ill.

Virgil writes that the Emperor Vespasian has done great work in Rome. He's restored the burnt buildings to their original beauty. He writes how the Capital has been refurbished, and many temples refinished. He said it's well known that Vespasian has a mistress who has been with him since the death of his wife. They say he won't marry because when he dies it would divide his wealth and leave less for his two sons. He's a loving father, but a shrewd military man. As an emperor, they say he's like a fish out of water.
Virgil heard that some men have little respect for Vespasian as their emperor. They address him as the "Mule Driver".
It seems that at one time Vespasian had to sell his estate to his brother, Sabinus, who held office in Rome. He did this to keep out of the "Debtors Prison". He took work selling mules throughout the countryside for a living. That's how he got the name "Mule Driver".
The gods have favored Vespasian when he entered the army of Rome. He has won over thirty battles and proved himself by his continuous triumphs. And now he rules the empire of Rome! Virgil said how Vespasian laughs at those who resent him, and reminds them it's a Mule Driver who now drives the world of Rome!
This might interest you. Vespasian has designs to open schools for those who wish to become physicians.
I'm sorry to hear about Antonius being injured. How is he? Write to us before you leave the city. I heard the mail routes are opened again from where you are.
Mother will grow stronger knowing you're returning.
May the gods keep you safe for us, my beloved brother.

A smile came to Marcus lips. He read the letter

again. Joseph sat listening.

"Joseph, will you honor my family by spending time with us in Antioch?"

"I think I can arrange it," he said politely. "I had plans to visit a few churches in Antioch before sailing to Alexandria. I could visit and check on your ailing mother."

"That's great! How soon can we leave here?"

"It depends on how soon we can make provisions for the wounded."

Marcus was curious about the Roman army. "What will Titus do now that the fighting has ended?"

"It's my impression he will return to Rome after the Romans separate the Jewish prisoners. Many are to be sold as slaves, and others will be paraded through the streets of Rome. God help those who will be chosen for sport in the arenas."

"I guess they'll be killed." Marcus sighed.

"Most definitely!" said Joseph. "From what I observe, the slave markets will overflow. No profits can be made if the cost of slaves drops steeply."

"I'm sorry about your people," Marcus said softly.

Joseph shook his head and changed the subject by suggesting they see what's going on outside.

The land around them looked forlorn and the city a shell of what it once was. Joseph thought about the homeless who were once happy residents in the beautiful city of Jerusalem. No longer would they hear the early morning trumpets sound for the first sacrifice of the day. No longer would the nations come and pay tribute to the God of the Jews!

Fallen is Babylon the great! A dwelling place for every unclean spirits and demons (Rev. 18:2).

THE SERPENT'S STONE

Titus walked with Tiberius over the smoldering ruins of Jerusalem, their clothes dusty with ashes and their sandals thick with soot.

"The city has offered you much booty, Caesar," said Tiberius. "Your father will be proud when he gets the news."

Titus smiled. He touched a portion of the veil which once covered the holy of holies in the temple of Jerusalem. "Tiberius, feast your eyes on this," he said as he handled the material. "Look at the rich colors of blues and purples and take notice of the crimson designs. Have you ever seen such artistry?"

"It's beautiful," said Tiberius as he admired the veil. "Who would ever believe the riches contained in their temple."

"Tell me, have you counted the dead?"

"We took count, Caesar. There's one million of Jewish blood."

Titus shook his head. "I want you to instruct the Tenth Legion to remain in the city. Give them orders that no Jew is to attempt to enter the city. It is my belief there will be those who will never give up trying to get back and rebuild what has been destroyed."

Tiberius made a note. "Anything else?" he asked.

"Yes! Ebutius, the commander of the Tenth Legion, he's still having problems with his leg. Give him a few months leave."

"I'm sure he will appreciate it since his wife is expecting. Caesar is most generous."

"Have they burned every house in Jerusalem?"

"Your orders have been followed." said Tiberius. "I saw to it personally. I know you're concerned about an epidemic. Our men share the same fear, Caesar."

Zoheleth

Titus glanced away. "Plagues follow wars like the gods of death," he said with emotion. "I'm heading back to my quarters. Dismiss all the generals and the officers first. Just leave some staff officers to remain with me."

"Right!" said Tiberius. "When will you leave for Caesarea?"

"Shortly, I hope. I do have a personal request to make of you, my friend."

"Just ask," Tiberius offered.

"I've written to Queen Bernice saying you will escort her to Caesarea." Titus paused and looked at him. "I guess you know she'll be my bride. But I would appreciate it if you were to hold off on this news until we arrive in Rome."

"You have my word," he said. "Caesar will have pleasant company on the voyage." He smiled.

"One other thing," said Titus. "I need two couriers sent to my quarters. I must apply to the Roman Senate for permission to hold a triumphal march to show our booty."

In his quarters, Titus thought about Bernice. They would sail to Rome when the waters were calm. After the triumphal parade they would marry. He knew little about her religion and he wondered if they would be made to wait. He finished his note to Bernice and a messenger was now headed to Pella.

Titus would have her wait at her brother's palace in Pella until Tiberius arrived. He ordered the messenger to take the fastest horse and go straight to Pella from Jerusalem. He warned the messenger not to mention the conditions in Jerusalem. He would relate what happened when he and Bernice were aboard ship.

The last of the wounded were safely on mule carts. Their destination was to the hospital at Caesarea.

Marcus shook hands with the patients as they were discharged from the infirmary.

"Good fortune to you, lad," said one soldier. "Here, catch this!" He tossed a small bag of coins to Marcus.

"Hey! I can't take these," Marcus asserted.

"Lad, I insist! We soldiers have chipped in to show our appreciation for all you've done. We know you get no pay!"

"I wish you wouldn't," Marcus contested.

"Lad, you earned it. You'll need something to get you home. If you refuse, I promise to dump them out and watch you pick them up one by one."

Marcus laughed. "Thanks," he said as the cart rode away. He waved to the last of them and felt an emptiness.

The infirmary cots had to been scrubbed and Marcus gathered the linens to wash.

"Slow down, Marcus!" Joseph said. "You keep this up and we'll send you home in a cart."

"I want to finish laundering these," he said.

"Don't wash the linens or the blankets. We must burn them. Also burn the woven sleeping mats, they can be infected."

"But there's no reason to," Marcus complained.

"Yes, Marcus. The war is over, but the disease is just beginning."

"Disease?"

"It's best to burn everything. A plague often occurs after so many deaths. Dead bodies are a breeding ground for an epidemic. We must not carry anything which could have fluids from an infection."

Bond fires were burning throughout the camps. He and Joseph used their head-cloths to wrap around their nose and mouth while they burned the items.

Anguish cries came from the Jewish refugees leaving the camp. As they walked, they looked back upon the remains of the city. They were left destitute and their homes and families wiped out. Another section of the camps had long lines of Jewish prisoners marching behind the soldiers on horseback.

"Where are the Romans taking the prisoners?" asked Marcus.

"They're being shipped to Egypt to be sold as slaves." Joseph looked despairingly at them. "They look like a parade of ghosts." Marcus saw his despair and tried to change the subject.

"When we get to Antioch you will meet my mother and brother," Marcus intruded on Joseph's thoughts. "You will also meet Martha. I'm old enough now to ask her father for her hand in marriage." He noticed Joseph hadn't heard a word he was saying. The physician looked through watery eyes as he watched the people tied with ropes and being led away.

"Joseph," Marcus raised his voice. "Did you hear the story one solder told about a woman in the city?"

"Which story are you referring to?" Joseph turned from the sad sight. "I've heard several stories."

"A woman went mad and ate her own child. Can you believe it?"

The physician lowered his head. "It's not the first time this has happened. Our sacred writings warn of such atrocities."

"You mean you have it recorded?"

"Yes, it's in our Scriptures. The Lord warned how He would bring the people back to Egypt in ships and be sold to their enemies as slaves" (Deut. 28.). He paused a moment and then continued. "The omens predicted what would happen to God's people if they sinned against Him."

"Did your people know of this?"

"Oh, yes. They knew the writings which speak of siege and distress. It even predicted they would eat the offspring of their own body" (Deut. 28:53).

Marcus coughed from the smoke when his wrapping dropped from his face. He looked in the direction of the prisoners and asked.

"Now what are they doing?"

"They're covering themselves with the ashes of the city. It's a sign of sorry and repentance. The ashes are all they have left of their land. See how they mourn. Who will comfort them where they are going?"

"It makes me feel sick at my stomach," Marcus turned away.

Zoheleth

A Roman soldier called to Joseph. "Physician! You're needed at the refugee camp. Doctor Simon is leaving the camp."

"Is something wrong?" asked Joseph.

"We're checking to see if any of the refugees have signs of a disease."

"We'll be right there."

When he and Marcus arrived, there were only a handful of refugees left.

"What are we looking for?" asked Marcus.

"Check the throat, and note if there is any rise in their skin heat. Most of them suffer from lack of food and exhaustion, not a disease." One more man entered for a check up, and Joseph was surprised to see him.

"Mattahias," he said, "how are you?"

The old man looked worried. "I'm hoping I'm not sick," he groaned. "I know when they're trying to stay ahead of a plague. That doctor, Simon, wanted to check me but I insisted that you be my physician."

Joseph examined him. "Your chest is clear and your heart sturdy. Your skin is cool and you've no symptoms. Let me see the back of your throat."

Marcus watched. He could see the throat was clear. Joseph lifted the eyelids of his patient and studied the coloring.

"You're fine, Mattahias." The old man gave a deep sigh of relief.

"You have a visitor," Mattahias motioned. Joseph saw it was Samuel who entered the tent.

"Go home, Mattahias," Simon said cruelly. "Where ever that may be." The old man hung his head in shame.

Simon whispered to Joseph. "We've just removed seven men from my infirmary. The prognosis is not good. They have definite signs of the plague."

"God help us all," Joseph twinged. He glared at Samuel and remembered the filth of his infirmary.

"What have you done with the men?" he questioned.

"I had to ship them to the desert to die. I didn't want

a panic among the remaining soldiers."

"You should have seen it in time!" Joseph accused.

"You saw the patients I had. They were all ready for the funeral march," he replied nonchalantly. "Say, you and Mattahias come join me in a farewell drink at my tent. Bring the lad along." Joseph wanted to refuse but saw how Marcus brightened with the offer. They went with Samuel.

Marcus hoped to see Antonius.

Samuel's tent was bare. The paintings and skins were packed away by his servants.

"Sorry, no gold cups. Most of my things are ready for shipping. The wine will be fine in these metal cups."

Marcus watered his wine. He never had a taste for straight wine since he got drunk with Antonius. Joseph had finally encouraged him to drink wine in his water in case the water was contaminated.

"Everything I have is being shipped to Rome," said Samuel. "I'll store them until I can get settled in my own house. Then, it's off to the palace." His mood was light but no one but himself was enjoying his expectations.

Mattahias sat groaning and trembling while drinking his wine. "What tribulations our people have gone through," he cried. "Never before in our history have we lost so much and suffered such humiliation."

Joseph looked up from his cup. "Put it behind you. You still have a life to live."

"I feel like the city," Mattahias sighed, "completely burned out."

"We all stink from the city!" Samuel jested.

Mattahias looked displeased but he continued talking to Joseph. "Do you realize all our records were burned in the Archives, including our genealogy records? Our books and money have now gone to the Romans. Our holy temple is smoldering in ashes," he lamented.

"The city was possessed by demons," Joseph added. "She has lost her place of exalted rule among the nations."

Samuel agreed and poured more wine. He looked at his guest and asked, "Mattahias, why are you so dismal?

Zoheleth

Have you forgotten how the Jews of Jerusalem turned against the Christians? They even aided Nero in hunting them down. Nero was delighted to use the Christians in his arena for the lions. These people were of your blood and you betrayed them!" Samuel was heartless in his accusations. He didn't hide his contempt toward Mattahias. "The city of Jerusalem became a scorpion," he added. "A varmint who inflicted torture on her own people, then stinging herself to death."

Mattahias' eyes widened in shock. Joseph held back a smile because this time he had to agree with Simon.

Marcus saw the tension rising and decided to speak up. "Samuel, did you know that Joseph will be going to Antioch with me?"

Samuel was puzzled. "Why Antioch?"

"I want to stop in to see Marcus' ailing mother," he confirmed. "Then I'll visit the church in Antioch." Joseph tried to persuade Mattahias to go with him.

"If I go with you," Mattahias replied, "you'll expect me to believe in what you believe!"

"Haven't you seen enough evidence?" asked Joseph. "What's left here for you? Come with me."

"I'm too old," he moaned. "I'm too set in my traditions. I can't go with you."

"You mean you won't go! What do you fear?"

Mattahias turned away. He watched the servants rolling up the rugs.

"What will my fellow countrymen think?" he finally admitted. "They'll shun me. I would be dead to them. As dead as our city. I would be ignored, like you."

"It won't matter," said Joseph.

"You don't understand," said Mattahias as he stood up and looked down at the doctor. "You see, there will be one who will deliver us, and restore our people to their rightful place. The Messiah will come!"

"The Messiah has come!" Joseph announced. "This event shows He has returned in the full power of God. Jesus said this generation would not pass away until they saw Him coming on the clouds!" (Matthew 24:30-34)

"There you go!" Mattahias whined. "Always referring to Jesus as the Messiah."

"Yes!" Joseph insisted. "And this event is His second coming! You know the word "clouds" means the power of God! It is commonly used in our Scriptures," he saw a frown on his friend's face. Joseph went on. "God used the Roman armies as His instrument of destruction. Christ has returned with God's wrath to destroy those who would not accept Him as the Son of God."

"He was not our Messiah. Our Messiah will come!" Mattahias flared.

"You will never be able to prove what line the Messiah comes from since all the genealogies have been burned. How will you prove he's from the right line to be the Messiah?"

"I'll not listen to this rubbish!" he shot back. "You tell your story to others, not me!" He walked out of the tent.

Joseph fell silent and Samuel was grinning.

"Poor devil," he said. "I guess he'll always hope that Jerusalem will rise again with a new and better temple. As for myself, I could care less."

Joseph nodded. "Mattahias will never see the true meaning of the fall of Jerusalem, as the ending of the old covenant world!"

Samuel looked around his empty tent. "It looks like my walls will be coming down next," he joked as he shook hands with Joseph. He held a firm grip on the hand of Marcus. "Stick with Joseph," he said. "You'll have a business all your own someday."

Marcus didn't agree, but nodded. He then took the opportunity to ask about Antonius.

"Where have they sent my friend, Antonius?"

Samuel appeared somewhat puzzled. He pulled his hand away and looked at Marcus. "I'm sorry, lad," he said. "I thought you knew that he died shortly after you left my infirmary."

Marcus felt sick. He looked at Joseph pitifully. "I

Zoheleth

should have stayed with him." He condemned himself.

"Marcus, you knew he was not going to live." Joseph reminded him.

"I guess I didn't want it to be true," Marcus sighed. He had to think about home and forget all that had happened. He and Joseph left Samuel's tent and headed back to pack their personals. On their way, Marcus noticed men making sacrifices at a stone altar.

"What's going on over there?" he asked.

"They're sacrificing at the stone of Zoheleth," he said. "Some call it the serpent's stone" (I Kings I: 9).

"Zoheleth? Why is it called that?"

"The site had cultic associations during the reign of King David," said Joseph. "King David was on his death bed when his son Adonijah claimed himself heir to his father's kingdom. He thought the kingdom should be his since he was the eldest." Joseph paused. "He had a younger half brother named Solomon, who King David favored."

"I don't follow," said Marcus.

"Let me give an example," said Joseph. "The Pharisees and Saducees and the high priests, thought they were the only heirs to God's kingdom, because Judaism was here the longest. They believed they would bring in the kingdom of God and rule the world, but Jesus told them differently."

"How are you comparing the story of David's son to what happened in Jerusalem?" Marcus asked. "Are you saying the eldest isn't always the one granted all the rights from his father?"

"God has often passed over the eldest many times in our Scriptures," Joseph informed. "The eldest son of David thought he should be the one to rule."

"What happened?" Marcus asked.

"Adonijah went ahead without informing the high priest, Zadok, of his plans to take rule of the kingdom. He gathered his friends and they sacrificed oxen and sheep on the altar of the stone of Zoheleth. Not at the holy altar of God!"

Zoheleth

"Did his father, David, learn of this conspiracy?"

"Ah, yes. David's wife, Bathsheba, informed him. Bathsheba is the mother of Solomon. King David promised Bathsheba that Solomon would be heir to his kingdom."

"So Adonijah thought he could rob the kingdom from his brother. Then what happened?"

"King David immediately made Solomon the king over Israel."

"It must have surprised Adonijah. But how does it fit into the Jerusalem story?"

"It's symbolism," said Joseph. "God the Father sent His son, Jesus, as the true heir of His kingdom. A kingdom not seen by the eye. The priests in the city didn't want Jesus. And to stay in favor with Rome, the priests began making sacrifices to a false god by making sacrifices for Emperor Nero who claimed himself a god."

"I thought you had only one God and were not permitted to have another god."

"You're right. But the priests knew that Judaism was here the longest. Judaism held its power for fifteen hundred years, but when Jesus came, things changed. The true heirs to the kingdom of God were those who believed in the Son of God. Do you see the parallels?"

"You're saying the Christians are not the oldest, but they are the heirs to your God's kingdom."

"You're beginning to understand," said Joseph.

"I don't think I'll ever understand this kingdom that nobody can see."

"Jesus said the kingdom of God is within. It's not a city or a country. We, as believers in Jesus, become a living temple where God dwells."

"What you were saying to Mattahias about the wrath of God, how did you mean that?"

"The Scriptures promises a Savior of the world. John the Baptist, claimed Jesus is the Lamb of God who takes away the sins of the world (John 1:29). The Judaizers trampled underfoot the Son of God, Jesus, they demanded that He be crucified." Joseph paused a moment. "God's wrath fell on those who condemned Jesus. It is written "Vengeance is Mine, (says the Lord) I will repay" (Hebrews 10:30).

"So you feel that the destruction of the city and the people, is the wrath of your God?"

"What else would you call it, Marcus?"

"Bad fortune?"

Joseph smiled. "Let's go pack our belongings. Tomorrow we move out of Jerusalem. I know you'll be happy to leave. I also know how you feel about losing your friend, Antonius. I'm sorry, Marcus."

Marcus sighed and glanced over the area. He was leaving Jerusalem, but also leaving the ghost of his father, Sabinus, and his close and dearest friend, Antonius, to rest in the ashes of a forsaken city.

CHAPTER TWENTY FIVE

CARAVANS HOME

A stream of caravans rolled across the roads leading away from the smoldering city of Jerusalem. Among the travelers were Marcus and Joseph.

When the sun began to sink, the caravans moved slowly to a halt. Campfires were lit and the aroma of roasting birds and fish permeated the air.

The people talked and sang while their children danced to music. Many of these people were on their way home after seeing the ruins of the holy city.

Marcus listened to the laughter which was refreshing. He and Joseph laid their sleeping mats on the ground. The night sky was peaceful and the air not too cool.

Joseph lay looking at the trees which stood like guards in the dark. It was good to see trees, since the Romans had cut down all they could find for crosses, as well as the wooden walls they erected around Jerusalem both inside and outside. He found it hard to forget the past events.

Marcus looked at Joseph who seemed to be dreaming with his eyes open.

"I like hearing the singing," he said. "But I'm waking up many times through the night."

"You're not sleeping well?" asked Joseph.

"I have nightmares," Marcus replied.

Joseph sat up and tilted his head. "Tell me about these bad dreams."

"I see men hanging on crosses. I can't get it out of my mind."

"I know how you feel," said Joseph. "Our Lord died in the same manner." Joseph rose to his knees and said. "Marcus, let's have prayer together."

"How will prayer help?" Marcus asked. He felt like turning his back on Joseph.

"Perhaps it will help you to sleep peacefully. It has helped many soldiers if you recall?"

He decided to give in to Joseph praying. Marcus didn't mind when two children came and knelt beside Joseph. Then, their parents joined the circle. Others followed and prayed aloud after Joseph ceased. Each gave praise to God. Marcus knew they were poor peasants but they were cheerful. They began singing hymns and he found himself humming along. They sang about Jesus, and some broke down and cried. What was it to bring them to tears and still fill them with joy? he wondered.

Marcus did sleep until the dawn. Joseph awaken him because he was sobbing in his sleep.

"Wake up, lad," Joseph shook him gently. "You're having a bad dream." Marcus sat up somewhat dazed. Tears ran down his face.

"What is it, son?" Joseph took him in his arms and held him.

"It's my father." he managed to say between sobs. "I saw him. He talked with me!"

"Tell me about it," Joseph pleaded. He waited until Marcus held back his crying.

"It wasn't a bad dream," he began. "My father came to me looking alive and happy."

"I'm glad you had a pleasant dream."

"There was more," said Marcus. "My father stood before me and said; "The Lord is all there is!" I still hear his words. I think my father was giving me a message."

Joseph was shocked. "Marcus, those are the last words I spoke to your father. How could you have known?"

"I don't know," Marcus continued. "My father said I brought him honors. I don't understand. I'm no hero. I'm not even a soldier."

"God has allowed your father to reach you."

"But how could I bring him honors?" Marcus questioned. "It's scary."

"All heaven rejoices when one person accepts Jesus Christ as their saviour."

"Why is that?"

"When we accept the Son of God, we are resurrected unto new life. Christians are now in the kingdom of God and no longer spiritually dead or separated from God. We are not bound for hell!"

"I don't know about hell, but if it's anything like the war we just experienced I want no part of it!"

"Hell is reserved for those who chose to be separated from God."

Joseph patted him on the back gently. " I think your father wanted you to know the peace he's obtained by believing in the Lord Jesus."

"I remember his letter." Marcus replied timidly. "I want his prayers to be answered. I do want to bring him honors."

"Would you like to follow in your father's footsteps and accept Jesus as your Savior?" Joseph saw him hesitate before he consented. He led him in prayer and Marcus accepted Jesus as his Savior.

The dawn was bright and the clouds parted revealing a morning sun rising majestically in the sky. The veil of night surrendered to the dawn. A heavy burden had lifted from Marcus' heart. He saw the mountains glowing in the sunlight and heard the birds singing while the earth stretched forth the new day with its sweet scented air.

The caravans moved onward after breakfast.

"Joseph," Marcus said while walking. "Do you remember when you scolded me and warned: Don't be anxious to see blood, it might be my own blood on a sword one day!"

"You mean when Antonius gave us the battle details of Joppa?"

"Yes. It occurred to me you were right."

"I'm afraid I don't follow."

"My father is my blood and his blood was on the enemy's sword that delivered the final blow."

Zoheleth

"I see how you're interpreted that. I meant no harm when I said it. I do believe you've grown in wisdom overnight." He smiled and asked, "Will you be marrying Martha when you get home?"

"I'll ask her parents if we can marry," he replied. Then with a deep sigh added, "What if she doesn't love me anymore?"

"You'll have to trust in God. He always has a plan for His children. You are now one of His."

"I don't know how my mother and brother will take it when I tell them I've chosen to be a Christian." He worried and was frightened of what they might think. He decided to face it when the time came to reveal his new belief.

After several days on the road, Marcus' heart leaped when he saw the outline of Antioch. He was home at last!

Zoheleth

PRISONERS OF WAR

Titus was now in Caesarea Philippi at the arena where he would celebrate his brother's birthday. Although Domitian was not present, he would dedicate the event to him. His brother was in Rome with their father. Titus got word that Domitian was to be sent to Germany where recent uprisings occurred against the Romans stationed there.

Titus called on one of his men.

"Commander Fronto," he said. "I want you to send a few hundred of the strongest prisoners to be used as sport in the arena."

"It will be my honor to please Caesar," said Fronto as he saluted. Commander Fronto was not a young man, his hair was thinning and his face etched with deep lines. He was a long and faithful servant of Rome, but a deadly foe to the enemy.

Titus trusted him in choosing which prisoners would live and which would serve as reasonable sport in the arena. When the prisoners realized their destiny they became obstinate.

"Caesar," Fronto complained. "Some of the prisoners refuse to eat any food we offer."

Titus was annoyed. "Send them to the arena first! Since they seem to be in a hurry to die."

Those who understood him, glared with hatred, but held their stand and refused food from the Romans.

Titus was not a cruel man, but in front of his men he had to induce stiff penalties on the enemy. He was also aware that keeping too many prisoners would cost them much of their food supply.

Fronto came later to report that his orders had been fulfilled. "I've spared the tallest and most handsome of the young men," he informed. "They'll make a splendid display for the march of triumph in Rome!"

Zoheleth

"Get it over with, Fronto," Titus groaned and turned away. "Send the leftovers to the arena." He heard foul cursing as he rode away. He would never forget this month of September, it was the month which ended the battle. The year seventy would go down in history.

He saw a horseman in the distance. It was Tiberius.

"Caesar Titus!" Tiberius greeted him as he pulled his horse to a halt.

"I'm glad to see you Tiberius. Tell me what I want to hear."

"She's here!" he answered. "Queen Bernice is lodging outside the city."

Titus was delighted. "Thanks for convincing her not to see me now. I don't want her to witness what's happening to her people."

"I understand, Caesar."

"Come ride with me, Tiberius." The two rode together. "I've temporary living quarters next to a saloon. Let's quench our thirst."

They stabled their horses and entered the saloon and ordered barley beer. Titus began asking about Jerusalem.

"The Tenth Legion is not happy about remaining there," Tiberius informed. "But you and I know they will remain at their post like towers."

Titus spit out the beer, it was warm and bitter. He ordered wine instead. They watched while a young peasant girl came with two cups and a jug of wine.

"The tower they call Phasael was the headquarters for Simon and his men. Am I correct?" Titus asked.

"Correct," Tiberius said. "The one called Hippicus still stands, and another called Mariamne."

Titus nodded.

"Does Caesar know about the tower called Mariamne? It was named after the great grandmother of your Queen?"

Titus smiled. "If my history doesn't fail me, Herod the Great, married Mariamne for her beauty and her royal blood."

"Caesar is right." Tiberius poured wine from the jug. "Herod's wife was a Hasmonean beauty who drove him insanely jealous."

"It is said he murdered her." Titus recalled.

"What some men will do for the love of a woman," Tiberius threw his head back and laughed. Titus didn't share the humor. He stared into space.

"Caesar seems far away. Do you desire I don't speak?"

"Go right ahead, Tiberius."

"Where did you send the Twelfth Legion before we left Jerusalem?"

Titus smiled. "I stationed them at the Euphrates River, the farthest limit of Rome's control. They deserved it."

"Ha! You might as well have exiled them as to send them there."

"I can't allow a legion which deserted its commander to join in the triumphal march."

"They cost Gallus his position," said Tiberius.

"They should have died for Gallus, and not lost the Roman ensign," Titus complained. "They left ammunition which the Jews used against us. In my eyes that rear division ran away when the fight was the hottest!"

Tiberius raised his thick brows. "I guess you learned that it was one from the Twelfth Legion which threw the first fire brand into the temple?"

Titus wiped his mouth and poured more wine. "I learned too late. I should have killed them outright for not obeying my orders. They were too hot for revenge, but why weren't they that fierce when Gallus needed them?"

"They found their Roman ensign," Tiberius affirmed. "They retrieved it in Jerusalem!"

"They have disgraced the gods of Rome," Titus scoffed. "They have no right to carry a Roman ensign with them. I call them cowards and deserters!"

"I have yet to find where Nero exiled Gallus," Tiberius replied.

Zoheleth

"Nero was wrong. He should have had the soldiers put to death for their disgrace to Rome!"

"No reason to be bitter," said Tiberius. "It was all in the hands of the gods."

"You're right."

"See how the gods have favored your father. He now rules Rome."

Titus watched the men in the saloon drinking and laughing over trivial things. Tiberius noticed that Titus' thoughts were far off.

"What sport are you planning in honor of your brother's birthday?"

Titus paused a moment before answering. "Wild beasts will be turned loose to kill the prisoners and the strongest prisoners will fight each other unto death."

"Seems like a useless contest," said Tiberius.

"What would you have us do with the enemies of Rome?" Titus rebuked him. "I don't find pleasure in sending thousands to their death."

"I know you must set an example. The enemy must be executed in some fashion. Why not give the citizens the pleasure of seeing justice in action."

They spent another hour drinking and reminiscing. The more wine they devoured the more battles they recalled and the more they boasted. They were mellowing and laughing when they were interrupted by Commander Fronto.

"Caesar! There's a message for you from Antioch."

Titus sighed and swayed. "What is it Fronto? Open it and read it!"

"Yes, Caesar." Fronto opened the scroll and read.

Honorable Caesar Titus.
From the leading citizens of Antioch.
We request that Caesar Titus dismiss all the Jews living in Antioch.
May we remind Caesar that the surrounding cities have done just that. They no longer receive any Jew from Jerusalem. We, of Antioch, wish not to be a haven for the displaced

Jews, and beg our great Caesar to consider our request and permit us to remove these Jews out of the city!

Fronto rolled the scroll and stood at attention.

"Who are they to request such a deal?" Titus faced flushed in anger. "You take this message back to the so-called "Leading Citizens of Antioch". Tell them that Caesar has no intentions of dismissing the Jews from Antioch! And, Caesar forbids any uprising where they will blame the Jews. The first word I get that there is dissension among the people of Antioch over the Jews living there," he paused and added, "warn them it will cause me to enter Antioch and leave it as bear as Jerusalem!"

Fronto wrote out the message.

"Also tell them how the Jews of Antioch have been responsible citizens of that city for many years," he went on. "Remind them that the Jews who fled Jerusalem have no place to go since the surrounding cities have been as heartless as Antioch desires to be. I refuse to allow innocent Jews to be made homeless by a few disgruntled peons!"

Fronto saluted and left.

Tiberius gave out a belly laugh. "You were not delicate with them, Caesar. My compliments."

"Let's get to the arena before I get too drunk to move from this place," he chuckled.

"Just one more," Tiberius laughed and poured the last of the wine. They toasted each other.

ROME'S CAESAR

Emperor Vespasian walked defiantly to the middle of the room, his eyes glaring at the man in front of him. The emperor walked with a slight limp as he paced the marble floor. His square face set firm as he roamed back and forth like a caged animal.

Several Senate members stood in the room waiting to speak with him.

"Catullius," Vespasian growled. "What is this piece of garbage you bring me?" He fixed his gaze on the thin Roman who stood draped in a toga. He had an instant dislike for the puny fellow and wasted no words with him.

Catullius pulled at his garment nervously. "Caesar," he whimpered. "I said that your son, Titus, brings the Jewess Bernice with him to be his bride!"

Vespasian bit his lip and turned from the toad-like face before him. "I hope your eyes will have sight when your head is severed." The runt of a man tremble and it made Vespasian burst out laughing. "Is it your wish to be exiled from Rome?" he jested. "Or perhaps you would like to be served as a tid-bit for the lions."

"By all the gods, Caesar!" Catullius gasped. "I tell you what all Rome knows."

"I better not find that you're the creator of lies!" Vespasian clenched his fist, but he didn't get a chance to finish his threat.

"Forgive me, Caesar, if I've offended you."

"Catullius, I find you like a sponge," he taunted. "You sneak around the city to soak up all the gossip. Then you sell it! But you wouldn't dare tempt me. Would you?"

"My Emperor. The thought never occurred to me."

"Good!" Vespasian faced him. "Do you know what would give me pleasure?"

"What would give my Caesar pleasure?"

"I think it would give the Conscript Fathers from the Senate a treat, by seeing the bottom of my foot making contact with your rear end. Now get out!"

Catullius was shocked by such common talk from an emperor. He backed away and left the room.

The members of the Senate began chuckling as they watched him trip over himself in his hasty departure.

"Damn!" Vespasian swore, "Where did he get that piece of news?"

The men of the Senate were quiet.

"Well," he forced a laugh, "young men will always get involved in love affairs."

One of the Senate spoke out. "If it is true, Caesar," he bowed his head, "I'm sure it will burn itself out in time."

"I hope you're right," Vespasian reasoned. He took a seat and looked into space. "My son may be trying to frustrate me, or he's craving for his father's retribution."

He thought for a few moments. The report had to be a bit of gossip. Then again, he never knew who to believe or who to trust. It was a lonely place to at the top of the world and to have so many depending on you.

He dismissed the men from the Senate saying he needed time to think. He then summoned one of his private guards. "Mucianus!" he called.

"At your service, Caesar," said the guard.

"Forget the formalities, Mucianus. You're here for personal reasons." He got up and paced the floor staring at the designs beneath his feet. "This business of being emperor is not what I planned for my life."

"We need you, Caesar," said his guard.

"Mucianus, I've never thanked you for being a faithful officer. I know you were with the vanguard I sent to de-throne Vitellius. You're a fine soldier and I consider you a friend."

"I'm honored, Caesar," he answered. "How can I serve you?"

"Are you being treated well?" Vespasian asked.

"You've been most generous, Caesar."

Zoheleth

"Good! I need to talk with you." Vespasian asked him to sit. He paced the marble blocks and glanced at his guard. Mucianus was a large man, nearly as large as Vespasian. He was tall and had dark brown hair. His eyelids were droopy which gave him a sleepy expression.

"What concerns my Caesar?" Mucianus asked.

"I've just heard that my son is arriving in Rome with King Agrippa's sister."

"Hmph!" Mucianus moaned. "Then you have heard the rumors how they plan to marry?"

Vespasian began sweating under his toga. He hated wearing it but it was expected of him. He shook his head and looked at Mucianus.

"That twirp Catullius, puked out the news to me."

"Caesar will hear many rumors. Why not wait and ask Titus of his intentions?"

Vespasian stopped pacing. "You're right." he agreed. "Why don't I ask Titus? But it's you I'm asking!"

Mucianus stiffened. "Our soldiers put meaning into things which have no meaning, Caesar."

"Don't try being soft. I asked you, do you think he has plans to marry her?"

"It would appear to be," he answered half heartedly.

Vespasian frowned. "Has my son lost his wits?"

"Caesar will have time for personal problems after the triumphal parade," said Mucianus. "You're the emperor now! Your personal concerns must wait. Caesar must know that Rome comes first!"

Vespasian softened. He patted Mucianus on the back. "Thanks, friend," he sighed deeply. "You have no idea what it's like to be an emperor. I hunger for companionship, but who can I trust? I've only the men who have fought together with me over the years."

"You can depend on our faithful service, Caesar."

"I can tell you this," said Vespasian. "There are some snobs in the Senate who will never let me forget my lowly background." He motioned his wine bearer to bring two mugs and he and Mucianus drank.

"Behind my back they call me the "Mule Driver". They think I don't hear," he laughed loudly. "Let them refer to me as such. But I'm their emperor! And it's this Mule Driver they bow their noble rumps to!"

"Caesar, we'll drink to that!" They broke out laughing.

Zoheleth

TRIUMPHAL PARADE

With a favorable voyage the two lovers reached the shores of Rome. Bernice would be escorted to the apartment Titus had rented before hand. He thought it best for her to wait there until he returned from the triumphal parade.

They walked together to the litter which would transport her. They kissed long.

"Hurry back to me, my beloved," she whispered. "I'll be longing for you."

He kissed her again and watched as she departed. Already he found himself missing her even though he was filled with pleasurable memories from their voyage.

It was difficult for him to face the overwhelming crowds running to welcome the son of Caesar. He liked hearing the cheers from the men and women, and the young ladies swooning as they threw flower petals at his feet. Some ladies clung to his hand. The Roman ladies considered him an eligible bachelor who one day would rule the world. To every Roman father, he would be the finest choice as a husband for their daughter. Some of the wealthiest men would be very generous to the prince in order to gain his favor and pave the way for their daughters to become empress of Rome.

Many ladies addressed him as the darling of Rome! Even married women spoke openly of how they dreamed to entice him to their bed. The rumors that he had a mistress didn't dampen their enthusiasm.

Titus, with his first triumphal in Rome, was about to learn that his father was designing an Arch in honor of him. He hated to think about the months ahead with their endless celebrations and ceremonies. These events would keep him away from Bernice too long. Through all the shouting and cheering, he only thought of her. He hoped that she would like the apartment. He advised the messenger to search out the finest living quarters. He threatened the messenger with banishment should he fail not to rent a suitable residence for his bride-to-be.

Bernice opened the curtains in the litter for one last glance of her beloved. She thought he looked so lonely, but suddenly he was surrounded by people. She sat back and rested. She was relieved that Titus didn't expect her to go through the crowds which welcomed him. She was feeling tired from the journey, but mostly, she had little knowledge of Roman traditions, and was satisfied not to be exposed to the public at this time. Especially with her hair damp from the sea mist and her clothes clinging from the damp sea air. She hoped there would be a fine bath in the apartment. She thought how she would have to share Titus with Rome, but he would be hers after Rome filled its thirst for him.

Rome received him with great enthusiasm. He was delighted to be with his father and his brother. The cheering was deafening when the citizens saw Titus, their prince of Rome.

"Father!" he cried as they hugged.

"Welcome to Rome!" said Vespasian. His eyes scanned to see if Bernice was with him.

"Domitian!" Titus embraced his brother.

"Welcome, brother," Domitian said. "I trust your voyage was smooth?" he forced a smile. His square face was like his father's with firm lips over a chiseled chin. He was handsome, but didn't have the gentleness of Titus.

"You look like you've grown since I last saw you," said Titus. He pulled his brother to his chest and hugged him. "I thought you would be in Germany."

"You know the Germans," Domitian said as he held his head high. "They think they can defeat the Romans," he laughed.

"Ha!" Titus threw back his head. "That will be when Mars resigns as the god of war!"

"You heard the Senate has decreed the triumph for

Zoheleth

us?" asked Domitian, as he glanced at his father who mingled with the peasants.

"Yes, I've heard. And I'm happy you're in Rome to celebrate with us!"

"Seems that you hear the news before I can present it to you." Domitian frowned.

Vespasian was counting the ships at port. "You've many ships. I can't wait to see all the booty."

"One of the ships holds a friend of yours, father," said Titus.

"And who might that be, if I may ask?"

"It's Trajan. He sailed with us." Titus saw his father was pleased. "He's offered his service in the operation of the spoils. He will have them rolled ashore in preparation for the artist to design the floats."

Vespasian laughed loudly. "By the gods! It's good to have you with me, son." They made their way through the crowds leaving Domitian with his private guards to trail behind. Domitian sulked as he followed Titus, his father's favorite.

"It's always Titus," Domitian complained, as he turned to one of his guards. "Titus gets all the praises. Titus gets all the metals." He hung his head as the people walked past him and reached to touch Titus.

Domitian's guard said in a low voice. "Domitian, of the Flavian Dynasty, you will one day rule the world!"

Domitian grumbled. "How long must I wait? Look at him. Now he brings Trajan. I remember when Trajan fought a battle in Judea and was not permitted to claim the victory."

"Why was that?" questioned the guard.

"My father insisted that Trajan remain until Titus arrived at the defeated city to claim the victory."

"Son of Vespasian, your turn will come!"

Domitian was not to be pacified. "Titus, the favorite, the poet, the singer, and the most learned in the Roman law. What chance have I?"

They hastened their steps, but the crowds pushed

Domitian aside. They craved to be near their hero, Titus.

Domitian's guards forced the people back so the younger son of the emperor had room to walk.

Domitian was sweaty and angered. "Titus," he spat, "the conqueror of Jerusalem? I bet it was Tiberius who did all the planning so Titus would have all the glory." He poked his elbow in the ribs of one man too close to him.

"Father," he whispered under his breath. "I walk behind you today, but one day I will be a ruler."

His guard heard him. "Hail! To the future Caesar," the guard said. "May Domitian live long!"

The days of preparations were completed and the floats made ready for the parade. The entire city was draped in colorful garlands.

The people offered libations to their gods for their emperor. Rome was overflowing with those who came to view the victory pageant, and to feast at the many banquets open to the public on such days of celebration.

"Rome loves her parades," Titus said while smiling for the public.

"Rome loves her heroes," laughed Vespasian. They bowed to the crowds applauding as they passed.

The next morning Vespasian's family met by the Temple of Isis. It was the custom in Rome for the emperor to worship at the temple before sunrise. Vespasian walked with his two sons to the Temple.

In the background the legions marched in their companies. The officers rode in front of their divisions. They dressed in capes and helmets adorned in plumes to honor this victorious occasion.

The early sunlight shone on the divinely dressed Caesar and prince Titus. Their royal robes of purple and their gold laurel crowns were a sight to behold. The troops erupted into loud cheers when seeing them.

Vespasian waited until they were silent before he recited the prayers. He gave a brief speech before dismissing

Zoheleth

the legions, and announced they would be served breakfast which the emperor provided.

By afternoon the crowds had tripled. They were in awe when seeing the procession of articles which included gold and silver furnishings from Jerusalem.

The gigantic floats rolled along carrying gold covered items and ivory carved stands, as well as tapestries from Babylon. A display of colorful rugs were hung on lines which were tied to poles stationed at each end of the float.

Gold goblets were inlaid with jewels and their stems fastened down onto tables of marble. Tables made of ivory carried the finely crafted utensils and gold plates.

Huge carved wooden chests were covered in liquid gold and overflowing with coins retrieved from the vaults in Jerusalem's temple.

It took six men to carry the golden candelabrum of seven branches, which had stood in the temple. All the holy items were open to the public. These objects were considered by the Jews to be too sacred to be handled by unclean hands. They were now in the hands of pagans.

The prisoners were next on display.

"My son, see the prisoners how they weep over the holy objects removed from their temple," said Vespasian. Titus nodded but didn't respond.

"They're a sorrowful looking lot," Vespasian added.

"I gave them every opportunity to surrender," Titus snapped back. "I offered to save their holy temple," he defended. "They refused my every plea."

"Come, son," said Vespasian. "Get into your chariot and follow mine."

They rode in fancy trimmed chariots, but Domitian refused to ride in one. He mounted himself on an enormous steed and followed his father and brother. He dressed in a magnificent garment of gold, to outshine his father. He glared at the crowds, but kept his head high and consoled himself. These people will certainly never forget my fine garments, he thought, even though they don't honor me as a son of Caesar.

Zoheleth

Vespasian rode to the Temple of Jupiter where they awaited the news that Simon, a leader of the uprisings, had been put to death.

Titus stood thinking how Simon, an arrogant rebellious bandit, could never be punished enough for what he had done to innocent people. He felt how death would be too quick. John of Gischala would spend his remaining life imprisoned.

When Simon was killed, Vespasian and his sons offered sacrifices to Jupiter.

From the Temple of Jupiter, the guests withdrew to join the emperor and his sons at the palace for an elaborate banquet.

Rome had great expectations with the Flavian family now in rule.

CHAPTER TWENTY SIX

A CRITICAL DECISION

Thirty days of celebration was over and the triumph parade was a thing of the past. The palace of Rome was now empty of guests and the business of running an empire was in order.

Vespasian sent for Titus in private. He walked the floor until he arrived. How to approach the subject of Bernice still plagued him. Titus entered, somewhat weary and anxious to leave the palace.

"There's something we must discuss," Vespasian stated. He seated himself in an over-sized chair. His huge hands clasped the arms. He wiped the sweat from his forehead and fussed with his toga. He was always uncomfortable and desired to be in uniform.

"Father, can't it wait?"

"No! It can't wait! I know you want to see your Jewess." He glared at his son. Titus was startled by his remark.

"You know about Bernice?" he asked. "I wanted it to be a surprise."

"It's a surprise. So it's true you brought her to Rome. Why, may I ask?"

"I brought her to Rome so we could be married here." he said boldly.

Vespasian held his anger. He motioned for his wine bearer to pour wine, and then dismissed the man. He sat back, his legs sprawled apart, and his body half slouched as he stared at his son.

"Why do you want to marry her?"

"Because I'm in love with her!" Titus declared.

"Tut-tut. In love? Son, a love affair is not worth all the trouble it brings."

"It's not a love-affair!" Titus persisted. "I'm going to

make her my wife."

Vespasian gulped the wine and belched loudly.

"You may love her, but Rome never will!"

"Rome will love her," Titus snapped. "She's strong willed and well versed in politics. She helped you when you needed help!" Titus shot a critical glance at his father. "Her brother supplied you with arms and food for the legions. Can you turn your back on that, now that you're the emperor?"

"Women have no place in politics!" Vespasian insisted. He stumped his feet and sat upright. His strong features were showing signs of stress. "Look son," he spoke frankly, as he tried a different approach. "You don't have to marry her. Keep her as your mistress."

Titus was indignant. "What, and be like you? She will never consent." He stared defiantly at his father. "I can't make her a whore!" he shouted.

"Well now. You've done a good job of it so far," Vespasian smiled.

Titus steamed with resentment. "We've been engaged for months!" he stated. "She has informed her brother of our intentions."

"Engaged?" Vespasian looked like a sly old fox as he sized up his son. He gave a rude laugh and added, "I know what you're engaged in."

"Don't jest with me, father. I'm not in the mood for it! I love her more than I've ever loved anyone." He began pacing the floor like his father. "I'll marry her whether you approve or not!"

His father saw his determination. "She's an ambitious woman," he implied. "There's always someone ready to be the wife of an emperor. She's only one woman," he reminded, and his voice softened. "And she's a woman of the world!"

Titus looked sharply into his father's eyes. He walked over and put his face close to him.

"What is it you're referring to?" he demanded.

Vespasian rose from the chair. "Do you know what

Zoheleth

is said about her and her brother?" His dark eyes pierced Titus. "Even the Jews speak of a scandalous affair between them."

Titus flew into a rage. "You would stoop to anything, wouldn't you?"

"I'm only repeating what I've heard. Think son, this deserves your serious attention."

"Perhaps father, you would have liked adding her to your scandalous affairs?"

Vespasian was shocked. His son had never spoke to him in such a disrespectful manner.

"Are you thinking I'm jealous?" he replied grimly.

"You forget how I hear rumors also. But I love my father and I dismiss such gossip. I've heard that you were infatuated with Queen Bernice. Perhaps your attempts to seduce her were rejected?"

Vespasian's face turned red. "I can't deny she's a beauty," he stammered, "but I had no designs on her!"

"Father, I know you love your mistress. But I've known you to turn to other women when it suited you."

Vespasian broke into laughing. He walked over and patted his son on the back, but Titus remained somber.

"Forgive me," he said. "At times I forget that you're a man now!"

"Father, I would like your blessings," Titus requested. "But if not, we'll return to her homeland and be married there."

It all sounded so final to Vespasian. This was one battle he was losing and he wasn't one to lose a battle. He never suffered defeat on a battlefield, but this battle he was not prepared for.

"Don't do this, son," he warned. "I need you! Rome needs you!"

"Father," Titus replied as he felt his voice getting shaky. "You're the emperor of Rome. It's you who Rome needs!"

Vespasian paced the floor. "You're wrong!" he shot back. "Rome need us!"

Titus spun around. "What are you trying to say?"

"What I'm saying, I'm offering you the kingdom of Rome. You and I, in partnership. Equal in all things. How does that sound?"

Titus was speechless. He lowered his head. "Why not choose my brother?" he asked with suspicion.

"Your brother?" Vespasian groaned. "He's not loved by Rome the way you are. That's why! He's still an angry child because he must wait in line!"

"I'm willing to wait in line," Titus declared. He saw his father's anger rising.

"You know I have the power to banish you at this moment?" he threatened.

"Have you thought how the people will lose faith in you?" Titus played the game. "Or have you forgotten how Herod the Great lost the respect of the Senate when he brought charges against his sons?"

Vespasian gave a disgruntled sound as he poured more wine. He insisted that Titus drink with him. His son accepted the cup reluctantly.

"I'm going to tell you something, son. I tell only you. I'm not cut out for this job!" He stared into his cup. "I never wanted to rule Rome," he confessed. "The citizens of Rome like what I do for them, but I'm over burdened with civil cases and I have no idea how to judge them." He raised his hand to keep his son from interrupting. "Yes, some of the men in the Senate come forth to help in the decisions of the cases brought before me." His expression changed to one of concern as he looked into Titus' eyes. "I'm not certain if they're doing it for me, or as a favor to the one brought before me," he paused and put his cup down on a table and stared into space. "I don't know who to trust. That's why I turn to you. I've spent a fortune for my sons' education," he continued. "You, Titus, have lived in this palace while Emperor Claudius reigned. You were best friends with the emperor's son." He paused. "You have dined with the kings of the world. You have been trained in the law and the etiquette of society. What training do I have?"

Zoheleth

Titus lowered his eyes in shame. His father stood before him pleading his cause. Vespasian continued to talk with him.

"If Claudius' son, Britannicus, had lived, I believe you would have risen in power through him!"

Titus felt his spirit failing him. He was hearing the truth and it tore him apart.

"Please, father," he said softly. "I know my education was paid for by the blood of Roman soldiers on the battlefield," he admitted, and fought back the tears of anger. "I know you risked your life for us to obtain the booty of the rich copper mines. But you must give me a life of my own."

"Yes, I did offer my life's blood to give you and your brother what I never had. You went to the best schools. Even a patrician didn't have it much better. Don't you think you owe me something in return for my investment?"

"I'm sorry, father. I understand where you're coming from, but..."

"Wait!" Vespasian shouted. "Don't marry her behind my back. I will not allow you to enter Rome again!" he warned. "I would rather see Rome have a tyrant, like your brother, before I would allow you to step into the position of emperor while you have a Jewess as a wife!"

"Are you threatening me? Why are you doing this to me?"

"My sympathy is with Rome! That's where your heart should be. Don't force my hand!"

Titus was grievously hurt. "You're asking me to marry Rome!"

"Son, the love of a woman will fade. But Rome will never fade. The Senate favors you and looks to the day when you will serve as emperor. I say give them that day now!"

Titus softened. There was a long silence before he could say anything. "I won't fail you, father. Together we'll rule Rome."

Vespasian saw his son was wounded deeply by his decision. He would try to make it worth his while. "May the gods grant you every desire, my son. This is a new era. The

Zoheleth

Flavian dynasty makes its entrance. Rome has been ruled by the Claudian reign until Nero."

"I know," Titus sighed, still keeping his head down.

"We know Nero was not a Claudian, but history tells us he was of the Domitian family. Claudius adopted Nero. But you and I are one blood! We shall make the Flavian dynasty go down in history!"

"I'll stay with you, father. I'll do all I can to aid in your rule."

Vespasian hurried over and hugged him. "You have made me a proud father!"

"What shall I do about Bernice?" he asked through teary eyes.

Vespasian looked at his son who was now a helpless child standing before him. "You will have to tell her," he said earnestly.

Titus shook his head. His sorrow was too severe to raise his eyes and look at the father who was destroying his love and happiness. His father went on talking.

"She must know that Rome comes first. She will understand our position. Be truthful to her as far as you're able to, my son."

Titus left the palace and walked aimlessly through the streets of Rome. He hated himself for giving into his father's demands. He tried to think things over for himself.

Perhaps he and Bernice could postpone their wedding? After all, he thought, his father was not a young man, and the gods of fortune were known to turn against those they once favored.

He kept walking in a trance while talking to himself. If he worked with his father, he was certain to be next in line as emperor. As emperor, he could have Bernice beside him. Would she be willing to wait?

The sounds of laughter in the streets annoyed him. Children running past and tripping over his feet angered him. He wished he had never seen Rome and all her so called "glory".

He saw Tiberius up ahead with a group of men

outside the inn where he had temporary lodgings. He quickened his steps to join them.

Tiberius greeted him. "Caesar, good to see you again." The men standing saluted Titus. He returned the salute and told them to be at ease.

"Tiberius, if you have time, can we talk?"

"Sure, my friend." Tiberius excused himself from the men. "Let's go in and get some chilled wine. We can have some privacy there."

"Sounds good," said Titus. They sat in a darkened corner of the inn and began drinking. Titus started discussing his situation.

"How will I tell her?" he asked through bleary eyes. "It's been over two months since I've seen her, and now I can't face her."

Tiberius studied him and tried to think of the best advice to offer. "Titus," he began, "what if you write her a letter?"

"I've been writing to her every two days since we came to Rome. She writes back how she's planning the designs for our new home." His grief was visable.

"Will Caesar allow me to help compose the letter? Also allow me to be the one to personally deliver it."

Titus looked dazed. "I can't ask you to do that," he groaned and lowered his head. "May the gods help me in this decision."

"Come on, lad, be a man. If you can't face her, then you must put it in writing." Tiberius watched his Caesar raise his head and stare through glassy eyes.

"Sit here while I get paper and quill," said Tiberius. He returned and seated himself. "It's the wisest thing," he said to Titus. "If Bernice refuses to leave Rome, it could prove very dangerous for her."

Titus suddenly sobered. "Dangerous? In what way?"

"Rome looks forward to heirs," said Tiberius, in an effort to explain. "Your father has two grown sons. This to Rome means a steady rule of command in the future years."

"What has that got to do with Bernice?"

"Titus, wake up!" Tiberius spoke with urgency. He had to impress upon Titus how serious the situation is. "You must understand how the Jews have been a thorn to the Romans. Your father has spared her life, if you see where I'm heading? The hatred for the Jews is still very strong since we lost so many men in Jerusalem. Your father is trying to show you the dangers in marrying a Jewish woman."

"Are you trying to tell me that her life would be in danger?"

"Exactly!" Tiberius put his hand on Titus' shoulder. "It's been done before," he whispered truthfully. "Women have been found murdered under stranger circumstances," he continued. "She's alone in Rome, and there are those who feel that she could present a threat to the security of Rome."

Titus shook his head. He didn't realize what might happen to his beloved. She could be killed.

"Think, Caesar," said Tiberius, as he tried again to make him understand how serious it could turn. "The Jews will always make an effort to influence her. Rome won't stand by and allow it to happen!" He leaned over to Titus. "You know what happened with Mark Antony and Cleopatra. Rome will stop at nothing to keep a foreign woman from having any political influence."

"You could be right," Titus murmured. "If I love her, I must allow her to live!" he groaned. "I can't be the cause of her death. Tiberius, I'll write to her and I'll trust you to deliver the letter."

"Yes. It would be better if it's presented by a friend. Bernice will think more kindly of you."

"Thank you, friend," said Titus.

After composing the letter, Titus handed it to Tiberius. It was a painful for him. He wondered what his decision would do to her.

"Stay with me, friend," he pleaded with Tiberius. "I want to get so drunk that I won't be able to walk. When I pass out, will you carry me upstairs? Then deliver that awful letter."

"You'll get through it, Caesar." They ordered more wine.

Zoheleth

Vespasian received permission from the Senate to go ahead on the plans for an Arch to be built in honor of Titus.

He watched the designs being drawn and approved them down to the last detail.

"I want the Arch to have scenes of the fall of Jerusalem," he told the engineers. "The Arch will be placed at the eastern entrance of the Roman Forum!"

The artist sketched the scenes and made notes for the builders to follow. They squabbled among themselves about the etchings to be imprinted in the stone.

Vespasian shouted his orders. "This Arch of Titus is to be inscribed in Latin, as follows."

THE SENATE AND THE ROMAN PEOPLE TO THE DIVINE TITUS, SON OF THE DIVINE VESPASIAN, AND TO VESPASIAN AUGUSTUS.

He smiled as he thought how proud it would make Titus. All Rome would honor him and fall at his son's feet. There was nothing like the strength of real power to make a man forget the softness of a woman!

Zoheleth

THE MESSENGER

Tiberius hired a litter to go to the apartment where Bernice was staying. He tried to keep from attracting attention to himself by not being in uniform

After announcing himself to her servant, he was ushered into the apartment. A young wine bearer recognize him and made ready the wine cups to serve the friend of Caesar.

He sat in a high-backed chair and regretted that he volunteered to do this. He knew the letter he carried was a request from Titus advising Bernice to leave Rome. He didn't know all that the letter contained.

He gulped the wine and poured another while waiting for Bernice. She entered the room.

"Good afternoon, Tiberius," she greeted him, as she lifted her long garment slightly off the floor and glided toward him. She refused the servants request to light more lamps.

Tiberius stood and bowed. He took her hand to kiss.

"My Lady," he said politely. "You are more radiant than ever."

She smiled and stepped back into the shadows. He talked about the weather and asked if she was well. Finally he handed her the scroll and wished he could hurry out.

"Tiberius," she said. "You've come with news." Her hand shook slightly as she took the letter. She pushed back her long hair hanging loosely, which was unusual for this hour of the day.

"It's a letter which Titus desired that I deliver personally." He noticed how she showed neither enthusiasm, nor surprise, but remained aloft. Did she suspect anything? It made him think of his younger days. He recalled his own wife often said how she knew without being told, when her husband had been injured in a battle.

Zoheleth

Bernice opened the scroll carefully. Tiberius hoped that Titus wasn't unkind in his drunkenness. He watched her walk to the small window and turn away from him to read.

She began weeping softly. He wanted to rush over and take her in his arms, but he knew better. She turned to him, her face not visible against the window light.

"Do you know what's in this letter?" she asked nervously.

"Only Caesar's request for your departure, my Lady," he choked. "And he begs you to wait for him. I'm sorry to bring such disturbing news." He fumbled for more words, but he failed to find them.

"Sorry" she repeated. "Do you know he kills me!" She threw the letter to the floor. Her face twisted in anger, and tears streaming down her cheeks. "How could he?" she cried. "How could he?"

"My Lady. Titus had no other choice."

"No other choice!" she mocked. "I was his choice! I was his oath! You Romans give with your right hand and without cause you strike like a serpent with your other hand."

Tiberius approached her and looked into her tortured eyes.

"I hate him!" she yelled, as she took her fist and pounded his chest.

"Please, my Lady. Just listen to me. This is only temporary."

She looked at him through teary eyes and put both her hands to her abdomen and pulled her gown tightly. Looking down, she asked tearfully. "Is this only temporary?"

Tiberius was shocked when he saw she was with child. "Does Titus know?" he asked.

"No!" she blurted out angrily. "He's never to know. I won't have him crawling away from his father and his Rome. I don't need his pity, nor do I want it! Never!"

"You must allow him to know that he's to be a father," Tiberius pleaded. He saw her stiffen and wipe her eyes. She glared at him.

Zoheleth

"This is my child," she announced. "This is not Rome's child! May Rome and Titus rot with maggots! May his marriage to Rome be a disaster!"

Tiberius admired her boldness. He knew that she could change Titus by announcing she was carrying a future heir to Rome. If he had the courage, he would inform her how she could change the course of history. But he held back. He thought it best to leave the situation run its course. His concern was for his own future. He knew how his military strategies helped Titus trample the uprisings in Jerusalem. All the world knew how the Caesars rewarded their confidants generously. He saw her pick up the letter and place it in a drawer.

"I assume you've given your oath to Titus that you will not reveal what this message holds?" she asked.

"Yes, my Lady. No one knows of its full contents excepting you and Titus. I know only the reason why it was written."

"Good," she replied. "I have grown to respect you while you journeyed with us to Rome. I'm about to ask an honorable thing from you."

Tiberius held his breath. "Whatever I can do," he said hesitantly.

"Tiberius, I want your oath that you will never reveal to Titus that I carry his child!" she requested.

He bowed humbly. He couldn't have asked for anything better, he thought. He was relieved that she was not going to hold Rome hostage while she bargained for one of its Caesars!

"You have my oath as a Roman!" he swore. He saw her give him a cynical smile.

"I free you from your oath when Titus is sole ruler of Rome. Do you swear what you have learned today, will be with you until then?"

He wiped the sweat from his brow. She was a shrewd woman. What she was planning, he couldn't surmise. He was certain a scorned woman as she, would wait a lifetime for revenge, but he gave her his word. He

Zoheleth

thought of the possibility if she had a son, he could one day come against Rome. It's happened before in history. But this was too far into the future for him to be concerned.

"Do you know Titus gave me an oath in his letter?" she asked.

"I was not privileged to read what he wrote."

"He swears to never marry another woman," she revealed. "I believe him," she added. "I know the decision for me to leave Rome was not his own."

He was astonished that Titus would make such an oath. He should have written the letter for him. This could mean the future Caesar would give no heirs from his own loins. But, he thought, oaths have been broken.

"Caesar does urge you to leave Rome as soon as you can," he hated saying it. "He feels that..."

She put her fingers to his lips to silence him.

"Inform your Caesars that I have no intentions of remaining another hour in Rome!"

She summoned her servants and her guards. She ordered them to start packing. She sent a servant to book passage on the next ship out of Rome.

"I refuse to remain in Rome and be a target for some crazy Roman who will think he's doing Rome a favor by killing me, especially should he learn that I carry a future heir to Rome!'

"Where will you go, my Lady?" he asked. "Will you return to your homeland?"

"What?" she gasped. "In this condition? You, Tiberius, should know my people," she spoke harshly. "I would be addressed as a harlot, especially when they learned that who grows inside me is of pagan blood. I would be worthy of being stoned."

"What about your brother?" he asked.

She threw back her head and laughed cruelly. "My brother would take me in, but have you thought of the consequences?"

"You're saying your brother would seek revenge?"
He thought how Agrippa could send assassins to avenge the

disgrace put upon his sister.

"Perhaps," she said softly, "But most likely my people would turn against him."

"Because he took you in?" he asked.

"You don't understand," she stated. "It would look suspicious in the eyes of outsiders."

"I'm confused," he said.

"Agrippa would fall out of favor with our people when some "scum of the earth" swears that my brother is the father of my child."

"Are you serious?" He was stunned.

"Think about it," she suggested. "My brother has no children and I'm living with him and carrying a child. I didn't make it public that I was engaged to Titus."

"You're telling me even if it's not true, your people would dare to accuse King Agrippa?"

"That's what I'm saying. I love my brother too much to lay this shame on his house." She watched the servants carrying the furniture down the stairs.

"If you will excuse me, Tiberius. There's much I must attend to."

"Where will you live?" he asked, truly concerned.

"I'll remain in seclusion until the child is weaned." Tears filled her eyes as she watched her items being emptied from the apartment.

"What will happen then?" he asked.

"Then I shall place the child where he will grow in secure surroundings." Her eyes were red as she concluded. "After that, I'll lose myself perhaps in Pompeii."

"You won't keep the child with you?"

"Have you given thought to the dangers?" she frowned. "If I keep the child with me, especially if its a male, I will put his life in jeopardy."

He looked at her and shook his head. She was a lioness who would protect her cub to the end. "May the gods be with you," he said, and then saluted her honorably.

She smiled sardonically, then with a deep sigh, said. "Whoever thought at my age I would have another child.

Life laughs at me, and so do your gods!"

"If you ever need me, please send for me. I promise I will not reveal where you are."

"I'm leaving Rome the way I came in, unnoticed. If I see you again, it would only bring back this sorrowful moment."

"I understand." He kissed her hand and left.

She watched him leaving and held her hands on her stomach. "Be quiet, my little darling," she whispered to her unborn. "We'll see it through. Our future is in the hands of our God!"

BERNICE'S LETTER

Thomas, the neighbor and friend to Agrippa, waited to hear of the wedding plans in Rome. He was curious why there was a delay. He sent word to Agrippa that he desired to visit with him.

Agrippa was resting on the veranda when Thomas arrived. He greeted him and offered him a cool drink.

"Thomas, how are you?"

"Not well," said Thomas. "I've had bad news. My uncle in Coreae has been taken seriously ill."

"I'm sorry to hear that. Will you visit him?"

"Yes, I must go since my father isn't strong enough to make the trip." Thomas paused to think how to ask what he wanted to know. "Have you heard from your sister?"

"As a matter of fact, I have," said Agrippa. "Bernice is voyaging to foreign lands. She hopes to return within the next year."

Thomas' mouth dropped. "But," he stammered. "I thought she was in Rome."

"She did go to Rome." Agrippa didn't mention her engagement, but felt that Thomas was fishing for information as he saw him hesitate before asking,

"Is it true she's engaged to Titus?" he dared to inquire.

"When did you hear that rumor?"

"It's common gossip," said Thomas as he lowered his eyes.

"Is that right?" Agrippa was puzzled. "I suppose I'll have to add more gossip for the people." He smiled.

"Is she to marry the Caesar?" Thomas pressed on.

"There was a possibility of a marriage with Titus," Agrippa admitted. "But you understand that he's a pagan?"

"I'm aware of it," said Thomas.

"I have her letter. Would you like me to read it to

you?"

"Only if King Agrippa desires to. I wish not to intrude on what is personal."

"I'm sure it won't be personal for long," Agrippa laughed softly. He opened the scroll and read.

Beloved brother, this is Bernice.

By the time you read this I will be aboard ship on my way to Corsica. From there I will visit the Isle of Sardinia. After that I shall sail along the coastline of Africa.
You may wonder why I'm alone on this journey?
Dear brother, I need time to forget the pain I now feel.
I must tell you how disappointed I am. I thought my future husband would become a believer in the God of the Jews. You were right when you warned me, but I believed him.
Please, Agrippa, don't blame him. I understand the pressures placed on him by his family. I must forget and so must you. When I put the past behind me, I will come to you. I'm thinking about finding a house in Pompeii. I can start a new life there. Pompeii has enough excitement to be the antidote for all sorrow.
When I'm settled, perhaps you will visit with me and we can spend time together. I do miss you, my beloved brother.
May our God keep you safe and well.
Don't worry about me, I beg of you!

"Well," said Thomas. "She seems to be sad. Why hadn't she mentioned the name, Titus?"

"I believe to prevent further knowledge of which Caesar she is referring to."

"In other words she still protects Titus."

"That could be. I know she loved him."

Thomas fell silent. "She must be heart broken."

"My sister is a fighter. She'll come back with spirit. I do wish she would have returned here. We could have traveled together."

"I wish the same," said Thomas.

Zoheleth

"I hate it when they do this to our Jewish women!" Agrippa snapped. "I warned her. But she's old enough to know the risk she was taking."

"Our woman are too willing to believe. They think they can bring a Roman to accept the God of the Jews."

"Bernice has ambitions, but also has a weakness." Agrippa rolled the scroll and returned it to his belt.

"Her only weakness," Thomas defended, "Is her delicate beauty. The Roman saw her beauty and took advantage of her!" He stood frowning and his legs shaking. He raised his voice in anger. "If you call her ambitious, I'm sure it was to help our people to regain some ground in Jerusalem!"

"Take it easy, Thomas."

"What are you going to do about this insult?" he demanded from Agrippa. "Isn't it enough how the Romans destroyed everything we hold sacred? Can't you see what's happened?"

"I see what's happened, but what do you expect from me?"

"Agrippa, as king, I expect you to avenge the dignity of your sister!"

Agrippa stood up and looked over the railing. He shook his head and turned back to Thomas.

"You're speaking out of anger."

"Why aren't you angered?"

"I am!"

"Then why not gather an army to come against this betrayer?"

"Do you expect me to make war with Rome?"

"I expect you to honor your sister."

"Thomas, my sister made a choice. She made the wrong choice. You see how she protects him in her letter. There are things I'm sure she's not telling me. I must learn the truth before I go fighting an imaginary injury."

Thomas tried to accept Agrippa's explanation, but it wasn't easy for him.

"Forgive me, Agrippa. I spoke in haste. I know you

can't go against Rome." He paced the floor and turned to Agrippa. "But if and when, you want revenge, I'll be the first to join you in retaliation for what Rome has done to our land and our women!"

Agrippa shook hands with him. "You're a good man, Thomas," he said. "Don't think I'm not in agreement." Agrippa paused and shook his head. "But we must wait for Bernice. Until I hear the full story from her lips, I'm forced to wait."

Thomas' face was red with anger. He wagged his head, and then patted Agrippa on the back.

"I must leave now for Coreae. When I return, I'll stop in to learn if you have more news."

"Have a safe journey. I hope your uncle is well by the time you arrive."

Agrippa stood alone and read the letter again. He knew there was more to this than his sister was willing to reveal. He knew how much she hated sailing and he knew she would never spend time on ocean voyages. Agrippa thought about Thomas who had the same feelings about the Romans. Yes, he could muster up enough men to go against Rome. But at what price, since his people have suffered severely from the Romans. It would never be wise to raise an army of zealots. He could lose all the provinces awarded by Rome.

Whatever happened between Bernice and Titus, he was sure Titus would want to keep the friendship with him going. In fact, Titus might even compensate the brother of the one he claimed to love. After all, it was Titus who changed his mind. He was sure Vespasian would remember it was Agrippa who saved his army from starvation when the Romans were being robbed of food by the pirates at Joppa. Rome never forgets those who remained loyal to her cause.

How he wished things would have turned out differently. His dreams were lost at sea as much as his sister's dreams.

CHAPTER TWENTY SEVEN

YEAR A.D. 72

Virgil watched the clouds breaking to display a clear blue sky. The sea was calm and the sun bright. He stood staring at the wake following the ship, and cursed his luck for missing the ship which should have taken him straight to Rome. This cargo ship would dock at one of the islands to unload and from there he'd board another ship to get him in time to his law classes.

It would have been a relaxing journey, if it weren't for the groaning of slaves in the lower part of the ship. He strolled the outer deck and eyed the crew. They were a hardy bunch which moved to the orders of one dark skinned young man.

Virgil studied the face. He was sure it was familiar. He held to the deck's railing to balance himself and made his way closer to the man recording the ship's inventory. With a surprised shout he called, "Marcus Severus!" The boat tilted and Virgil grabbed the railing to pull himself toward Marcus.

"Virgil, what are you doing here?"

"I was about to ask you the same thing, son of Sabinus." Virgil laughed.

Marcus handed his record book to a ship mate and greeted Virgil.

"I've been working this ship for nearly two years," he answered. "You could say I was kidnapped!"

"What?" Virgil said.

"Where are you heading?" Marcus asked.

"I'm on my way back to Rome. It's my last term. I'll be staying in Rome to practice law."

"Have you seen my brother?" asked Marcus.

"Just three days ago," said Virgil who found it hard to be heard with the wind blowing in his face. "Nicator has been fretting over your disappearance. We gave up hope in ever seeing you again." Virgil looked seriously at Marcus. "Everyone thinks you're dead."

Marcus hung his head. "I guess you could say I was dead!"

"Did you know your mother passed away?"

Marcus was stunned. "I didn't know she died." Tears ran down his face as he turned to Virgil and asked, "How did she die?"

"I think it was her heart."

"How is Nicator?"

"He's married," Virgil reported. "I guess you didn't know you became an uncle! He has a son."

"What! I can't believe it. How did he meet his wife?"

"He met her through your doctor friend. It wasn't long after their meeting when they fell in love and were married."

"I can't believe what I'm hearing."

"Your mother lived long enough to see her first grandchild."

Marcus smiled through his tears. Virgil gave him time to digest the news.

"Are you going to tell me why you disappeared?"

"Hold on a moment," said Marcus. "I must finish the count on the kegs. We can go to my cabin and talk."

"Sounds good," said Virgil. "I hope you have some decent wine available."

"Ah! I've the best money can buy!" Marcus boasted.

When they settled in the private cabin of Marcus, Virgil noticed how lavishly it was furnished. Beautiful paintings hung on the walls and the tables were pure ivory. A cabin boy served them wine in gold cups.

"It looks like you fell into a gold mine," said Virgil. "And the wine is the finest!"

"I agree on both counts," Marcus replied as he drank with Virgil.

"How did you earn this?"

"Well, I guess you could say some men do strange things for the love of a woman."

"You're in love?"

"I was," Marcus admitted. "How much did my brother tell you?"

"Nicator did tell me how the physician healed his leg. Nicator is able to walk without the help of a staff."

"That's great!" said Marcus.

"He calls it a miracle, and so did your mother. Both she and Nicator believe in the one they refer to as Jesus."

Virgil talked of many things and laughed at past memories. Marcus talked about the wars until neither one had anything else to say. They sat listening to the creaking of the cargo ship.

Virgil broke the silence. "I heard about Martha. I guess you were very hurt by her marriage."

Marcus stared past Virgil and was silent. He sipped his wine, and suddenly brightened up and said, "Did Nicator tell you the crazy thing I did after I read her letter?"

Virgil burst out laughing. "You cut off all your hair. Nicator thought you'd lost your mind."

"I know it was a wild thing to do," Marcus admitted. "But her letter told how her parents married her off to a widower with a child. She informed me that she was carrying his child." He sat dreaming. "I guess it doesn't matter any more. She told me not to attempt to see her. She wanted to remain faithful to her husband."

"Wow!" Virgil laughed. "Sounds like she's still in love with you."

Marcus tried to control his emotions. "She wanted a lock of my hair for a keepsake. I was to leave it under a stone near the edge of the river where we met as kids."

"So?"

"So, I cut off all my hair and tucked it under the rock where we hid our love notes."

"Now I understand. You must know how your brother tried to spare you more sorrow. The death of your father, and then your friend, Antonius."

"Nicator did what he thought was best."

"I see you have all your hair again," Virgil laughed.

"Too much!" Marcus tugged at his full beard.

"You've come through a war, the loss of a father, the loss of a friend, and the loss of your girl. Now how did you get here?"

"I think drinking wine gets me into trouble," said Marcus. "As you notice, I water mine. After I cut off my hair, I found an inn and got drunk." He paused and recalled the night. "It didn't take long for me to get sick. I must have passed out."

"So you woke up sick, but what then?"

"I found I had been abducted and held as a slave to work on this cargo ship."

"Go on," Virgil pleaded as he leaned forward.

"I was forced to work long hours rolling kegs aboard, as well as, loading boxes below. I didn't care how hard the captain drove me. I wanted to forget all that had happened. Work made me too tired to think on the past!"

"So how in the name of the gods, did you earn a cabin like this?"

"I never let it be known that I was a Roman citizen," Marcus smiled. "Until the captain thrashed me one time too many. I showed him my papers and let him know I was the son of a hero and a Roman citizen!"

"Were you touched in the head?"

"Not really. I informed him of the penalties for thrashing a Roman citizen." Marcus laughed. "He looked like a dead man. He took me in his cabin and gave me wine. He begged me to forgive him and offered me an easy job."

"What?" Virgil looked surprised.

"The captain learned I could read and write. His profits increased due to my accounting abilities." Marcus smiled as he went on to give more details. "One day he saw me treating the slaves who were sick. He learned I was a medic. He offered me a partnership with a third of the profits."

"You sly dog."

"And now you see before you a young man with a comfortable income and many luxuries."

"The gods have favored you," said Virgil. "Seriously, I wish you would write to your brother. He will be happy to learn you're alive."

"I'll do that," Marcus promised. "Tell me, do you know what happened to Joseph, the physician?"

"Nicator said he waited over seven days for you to return. He left to go to a church in Antioch. He later returned and took Nicator with him to search for you."

"Poor Joseph," Marcus sighed. "I guess he returned to his home in Alexandria."

"Maybe," said Virgil. "Unless he got caught up in the army. You heard that a group who fled from Jerusalem, stationed themselves against the Romans at Masada?"

"You mean they're still fighting?"

"A group escaped through underground tunnels. They headed to Masada."

"Even though they see the destruction of Jerusalem, they still want to fight?" Marcus was puzzled. "Which legion is at Masada?"

"I heard General Silva sent for the Tenth Legion stationed at Jerusalem. He asked them to join him in his effort to take Masada."

Marcus felt his heart racing. Suddenly he had the urge to go to Masada.

"Virgil, would you do me a favor?"

"Sure."

"Write to Nicator and tell him of our meeting. Also tell him I'm on my way to Masada!"

"You're what!" Virgil nearly choked on his drink. "What is it with you? Do you like living dangerously?"

"Masada is where they'll need a medic," he replied.

"Well, they need more than a medic. You better take plenty of water with you. I heard it takes days to get a water supply to the Roman troops stationed there."

"Good Lord!" Marcus cried. "In this heat they must be dropping like flies."

Zoheleth

"What will you do about your captain?"

"My captain will be more than happy to see me leave," Marcus laughed. "He won't have to share his profits. I'll sell my goods at the next port and buy supplies for the journey. I pretty much know what an army needs."

"Good fortune to you," said Virgil. "I'll write to Nicator. I feel I have made a new friend in you."

The following day the ship docked at an island. Virgil set sail to Rome on another ship.

A few days later, Marcus boarded a ship going to Ashkelon where he would buy barrels for water. He would fill them at the wells nearest to Masada. He had many days of sailing ahead of him, but it would give him time to make plans for his new adventure. He knew where he could buy foods wholesale to take to the camps. He needed to find a barber to trim his hair and beard. New clothes had to be purchased since he needed very little while at sea.

Zoheleth

FORTRESS OF MASADA

Flavius Silva was appointed by Emperor Vesapsian as the new governor over Judea. Silva took on the title Flavius in honor of the emperor.

Vespasian's orders were to clean out the nest of zealots who took refuge at the fortress of Masada.

Silva sent for the Tenth Legion and instructed them to bring the Jewish prisoners with them. The Tenth Legion was released from guard duty in Jerusalem which lasted over a year. They prevented the Jews from entering the city to rebuild. The Tenth Legion was eager for their new assignment with Silva, and were more than ready to capture the zealots and the sicarii, along with Eleazar.

The Jewush rebels had set up their headquarters in Masada to carry on their fight for freedom. Unknown to the Romans the group were joined by their families who took up residence in the fortress.

The Tenth Legion reached Masada in late afternoon. The sun was unbearably hot leaving the soldiers tired and thirsty from their march. When they arrived at their destiny, they found the water supply at Silva's camp rationed.
Silva stepped out of his tent to meet their officer.

"Honorable Silva, I'm officer Terentius Rufus. We are ready and eager to wipe out the nest of rebels."

Silva, a tall lanky man, moved slowly toward him and greeted the red haired Rufus. "Glad to have you with us. But you may regret coming here. Our water supply is dangerously low."

"What would you have us to do?" asked Rufus.

"Let your men rest," Silva said in a sociable manner. "You'll find it too wearisome trying to work with such a short supply of water."

"Has Governor Silva sent for a supply?"

"Three days ago," he shook his head. "I don't know

Zoheleth

how we'll spare water for the prisoners you've brought?"

"Perhaps if you allow me to ride out in search of the water train?"

"I can't allow you to endanger yourself or a horse. You and your men have covered a lot of ground. It's fortunate you had your own water supply." Silva wiped his head with a cloth as the sweat poured down the side of his face. "Damn this heat!" he groaned. "If these rebels think Jerusalem was an insult, wait until they see the atrocities I'm planning if they don't surrender soon!"

"Is there any access to the fortress?" Rufus inquired.

"Look at the place," Silva griped, and pointed upward. "I curse Herod the Great for every ounce of work he put into this monster."

"From where we stand I see two paths to the summit," said Rufus.

"Both paths are too narrow and dangerous for our men to climb." Silva paced.

"What's behind the wall of Masada?"

"I don't know. One of my men is searching for a physician who knows Masada well." Just then a guard approached.

"Commander," he addressed Silva. "You sent for the physician. He's here."

"Step forward, physician!" Silva commanded. He stared at Joseph whom he recognized as a Jew.

"I am Joseph Abtolim of Alexandria," he introduced himself. "I served as a physician for the legions of Caesar Titus during the siege of Jerusalem."

"Welcome to my camp, Joseph of Alexandria. Please enter my tent to get out of the hot sun."

Silva motioned Rufus to follow. A slave brought watered wine.

"Excuse the small portion I serve you," Silva apologize. "But the shortage of water, food and wine, has me concerned for my army."

"We share your concern, Commander," said Joseph.

"Physician, what can you tell me about the layout on

Zoheleth

the summit?"

"I hope my memory serves me," said Joseph. "If you will supply me with a quill and paper, I will sketch a diagram."

He sat at a table and began to draw. "There's a fortress at the southern end. It has a well with a great underground cistern." He looked at Silva and wagged his head. "They have plenty of water."

"That doesn't help my men's thirst," Silva groaned.

"The northern portion of the summit, Herod built a three-tiered palace. In front of the palace is a large storehouse." Joseph pointed to his drawing.

"Go on," Silva requested.

"There are royal apartments built near the western wall," Joseph informed.

"So they have all the comforts of a king," said Silva as he cracked his knuckles.

"On the east side there are living quarters. The bad news is the rebels have an abundance of weapons and food. Enough food to last a year and an everlasting flow of fresh water."

"It sounds like a disaster for us!" Silva sighed. "Are you sure their food will last that long?"

"Never overlook the fact how the altitude allows food to remain without spoilage for a long period of time. Plus they have gardens and enough animals to keep them from starving. Masada is a city within itself."

"You're telling me we can't out wait them."

"I'm saying they won't go hungry or thirsty. Your men will faint from lack of water and the intense heat." Joseph handed the drawing to Silva. "I don't think there's anything I've left out."

"Thanks for your help. At least I have an idea of their strength, since we have a head count for them as less than a thousand."

"Is that right?" asked Joseph.

"Yes. Oh, listen. If there is anything you need, please let me know."

Zoheleth

Joseph rose and thanked him. He thought for a moment and the said, "Hopefully Commander Silva will think of the injured in the infirmary when the water supply arrives?"

"Physician," said Silva courteously. "You shall be the first to receive water when it comes in."

Joseph left Silva's tent. He walked slowly back to the infirmary. He was deeply concerned that the water carts might have fallen into an ambush. His herbs were dwindling and in this area nothing of worth was growing.

Silva stood under a shelter outside his tent. He removed his helmet and wiped the sweat. He squinted to look in the direction of a half finished ramp. After seven months his men hadn't completed the embankment. Now it stood like a death trap. The soldiers could no longer work it since they were weakened by lack of water.

"The ramp, have you given up on using it?" Rufus asked.

"Not completely," said Silva. "I ceased the work after my men were bombarded with huge rocks."

"I see you've constructed a wall of timbers surrounding the entire circumference of Masada. The same method Titus used at Jerusalem."

"I say if we can't get in, then we keep them from getting out, and others coming to join forces with Eleazar."

"If I may make a suggestion," said Rufus.

"Be my guest."

"Why not use the prisoners to do the labor and allow our men to save their energy?"

"You read my thoughts. When the water train comes I'll use the prisoners."

"Why wait for the water supply?" said Rufus. "You can start early before the sun rises. The prisoners can work until the sun is directly overhead."

"You might have something there," Silva agreed.

"These prisoners are to be executed anyway, so why not use them first?"

"Since you say they are to be put to death, I'll take

373

your advice. I'd rather see them keel over from the heat than see my soldiers drop. The way things are now, we can't possibly feed all the prisoners to keep them alive."

Silva didn't like his decision but he had no other alternative.

The next morning Silva saw the prisoners lined up and assigned their duties. He allowed the Roman soldiers to use the prisoners as shields from the onslaught of stones fired by the zealots.

The soldiers were now able to get closer to the wall with the Jewish prisoners ahead of them. This enabled the Romans to complete the ramp. With its completion, they were ready to move the ramming machines into place.

Rufus made the prisoners pick up the stones fired on them. Some refused, but changed their mind with the threat of crucifixion. These same stones would be used as ammunition by the Romans to send back over the wall.

Many prisoners were struck dead by the stones. Others cried out to their fellow Jews atop the wall to have mercy on them. The zealots hearing their plea ceased throwing the rocks.

Silva rationed the water so no man was to get any until the sun was high. He ordered the soldiers to lay back on the labor and work the prisoners.

Rufus joined Silva while they surveyed the workmanship on the ramp.

"How are the men holding out?" asked Silva.

"They're progressing, since Masada's insurgents refuse to strike the Jewish prisoners."

"That's the kind of news I like to hear," said Silva. "Now send the young water boys with their buckets. Make certain that our men drink first!"

"As you have ordered!" Rufus saluted his commander and left.

Silva watched in pity as the soldiers drank sparingly from the one cup they were rationed. One man dampened his brow with the precious liquid. While the soldiers were lined up for their supply of water, many prisoners seized the opportunity to escape and hide behind boulders.

Silva ordered his men to run them down on horseback and kill them. The zealots watched in anger from on high.

"They're a strange lot," said Silva, "they long for freedom, yet when they were free to rule their people and worship their own God, they chose to war with us."

He looked upward to Masada and cursed as the Jews mocked them in their distress.

"Look at them," said Rufus. "They're refreshed by the constant breeze from the height where they stay."

"Yes, and see how they taunt my men by hanging dripping wet garments over the wall," Silva groaned. "They add to their pleasure by tossing pails of water over the wall and letting it cascade down the rocks."

"We can thank the gods for the nights," said Rufus.

"Not for long," Silva uttered. "Soon panic will take over. I've seen men kill for one sip of water when the supply is drastically low." He wiped his brow and looked at the men resting on the ground, weary and suffering from heat exhaustion. He wouldn't allow a man to stand to salute him.

Silva knew what it was like to taste the salt from your sweat and feel the chaffing under your armor.

"May the gods have mercy on us," said Rufus. "If the water wagons fail to arrive, we're all dead men."

"There's not a cloud in the sky," Silva noted. "How long can we go on? We're at the mercy of the gods, as well as the Jews."

The ground was covered with Romans. They lay not exerting themselves until the sun went down. The evening brought some relief, but the next day would be the same foreboding disaster they all had to face.

A WATER BLESSING

Marcus hired mules and carts for the merchandise he was buying. Offshore, he met a group of merchants who were willing to travel with him to sell their wares to the Romans. Certain women liked to join the caravans and visit with the soldiers. They traveled several days before reaching within sight of the camps at Masada.

A Roman watchman signaled there was a merchant caravan heading this way. A few of the young boys went running and shouting with excitement. The word spread about a caravan with provisions. No one knew who the strangers were, but the thought of water and food was a blessing.

"What have you brought us?" begged one boy, as he and the others danced around the mules. They skipped to the back and found the merchants. They made faces at the drivers and jumped in front of the mules in playfulness.

The caravans entered the camps. Wagons were loaded with barrels of water, crates of food, skins of wine and many women to bring entertainment for the soldiers. The aroma of smoked meats and fish was delightful to the lads as they ran alongside of the water wagons catching the drippings from the kegs. They cupped their hands and sucked the water eagerly. Soon they were spurting water from their mouths at their buddies. Some of the lads pulled off their turbans and wet them to wrap around their heads. They ran shouting.

"There's water! Tell the soldiers!" They ran with hind's feet.

Within minutes two soldiers on horseback arrived to escort the caravans. They rode slowly and waved Marcus forward after scanning the properties.

"Marcus! Is that you?" called one soldier. "By the gods of Rome, I couldn't believe it when the boys said you had water. Is it true?"

"Yes!" Marcus cried out. "You see before you carts of water. But how do you know me?"

"I'm Thaddeus," said the soldier. "You took care of me in the infirmary back at Jerusalem."

Marcus' mind drew a blank.

"Perhaps you will remember my injury. Look at my arm. I took a fire dart."

"Ah! Now I recall," he answered.

"By the gods, Marcus, who sent you to us?"

"I learned there was trouble at Masada while I was working a cargo ship. Someone advised me to bring water."

Thaddeus rode along side while they talked.

"We've been at a stand still because of no water," he said, "But come, we can talk when we get out of the sun. Did you know Joseph is with us?"

Marcus smiled. "I should have known." He felt a sinking feeling in his stomach. Would the physician even want to speak to him after Antioch?

Thaddeus sent for prisoners to help the merchants set up their camp to sell their wares.

"Our soldiers will remove the kegs of water," Thaddeus announced. "We can't trust the prisoners who may get the idea to sabotage the water supply."

"Are you serious?" asked Marcus.

"Very serious," said Thaddeus. "They're in no fear of dying. It would be easy for them to drop a few kegs and rejoice in their breakage."

Silva rode to the caravans, and saw the soldiers rolling water kegs down a plank and placing them in the shade. He ordered a soldier to stand guard over the kegs.

"Who, besides the gods," said Silva loudly, "do I thank for this blessing of water?"

Thaddeus directed him to Marcus. "Commander, this is Marcus Severus, he was an assistant medic to the physician, Joseph."

"Marcus Severus?" Silva repeated. He eyed the young man before him. A tall slender lad with dark skin and curly hair and a neatly groomed beard.

"At your service, sir."

"Marcus, I'm Flavius Silva, governor of Judea and commander of the legions. I wish to express my gratitude." Silva dismounted and shook hands with him.

"Glad to be a help," Marcus smiled widely.

"I'm happy to hear you're a medic. Our physician will be in need of you when we begin the siege."

"I was his apprentice," Marcus revealed.

"You must come to my tent and have supper with me. There's more I desire to know about you."

"I will be honored, sir." Marcus saluted him.

"Oh," said Silva, "I promised Joseph he would get the first ration of water for the sick."

"Your promise will be honored, Commander," said Marcus. "With your permission, sir, I would like to deliver it personally?"

"You have my permission, young man."

"Also, Commander, I've many casks of wine for your men and one special cask reserved for the Commander at Masada."

"You're a gift from the gods," Silva smiled. "My camp is yours!" He ordered the prisoners to carry water to the guards on duty who could not leave their post.

Silva became outraged when he saw the craftiness of the prisoners who deliberately spilled water while carrying it to the guards.

"Halt!" he shouted and rode directly to them. "Anyone here understand my language?"

"I understand you," said one prisoner. "What's your problem?" he asked arrogantly.

Silva decided to display a bit of his own arrogance. "I want you to explain to these men that if one spills any portion of water they carry to the guards, I've ordered my men to kill the one next to the guilty one!"

The prisoners were shocked when the message was translated.

Silva chuckled when he heard them groaning and

complaining. But not one drop of water was spilled from that moment on.

By late afternoon the men had their thirsts satisfied and their spirits lifted. Thaddeus and Marcus went to the infirmary. They rolled the casks off the cart and placed them in the infirmary. Joseph was not in sight, and Thaddeus left to care for the mules.

Marcus stood looking around the infirmary with the feeling of nostalgia.

"Welcome back from the dead!"

Marcus spun around and saw Joseph with outstretched arms. He threw himself on his friend and the tears flowed freely between them.

"Joseph," he managed to choke out. "I should have guessed you'd be here."

"Marcus, my son. Let me take a look at you! You're a grown man." They hugged again. "Where have you come from?"

"I was on my way to Italy when I got the news about Masada. The cargo ship I was on made a stop at the Isle of Cyprus," Marcus caught his breath. "I gathered a supply of herbs I thought you would need and took the next ship to Gaza. I found merchants willing to join me and sell their supplies to the soldiers. We formed a caravan and along the way I purchased wine and found wells to fill the kegs with fresh water."

"You had to be moved by God," Joseph smiled. "How did you obtain the kegs?"

"I'm well known along the shipping coast," said Marcus. "While working a cargo ship I made many friends. They were willing to help Rome to uproot this nest of vipers at Masada."

Joseph couldn't stop smiling. "Perhaps you would like to walk with me while I give my patients some long awaited water?"

"I'll do more than that," said Marcus. "You take one side of the infirmary and I'll do the other side. Like old times."

By sundown they finished bathing the sick and giving them water. Some were permitted wine.

"Physician, where are your quarters?" Marcus asked.

"I have a cot in the infirmary," said Joseph. "Since I'm alone I don't need much space."

"You'll be my guest and share my tent."

They stepped outside and found Thaddeus unpacking. "Tell me what to do, Marcus," said Thaddeus. "Silva has assigned me to assist you personally until you're settled."

"In that case let's put up our dwelling," said Marcus. "Then we'll share wine together."

"I'm for that!" They erected an elaborate tent and placed two cots with thick pads at opposite sides of the tent. They found folding chairs and tables along with oil lamps and a richly woven rug for the ground. Marcus ordered that the crates with wine to be stacked in one corner. He placed the sacks of herbs and grains beside the crates of dried fruits. When they were finished, Marcus poured wine into silver cups. He saw how astonished Joseph looked.

"Please, Joseph, have a seat." Marcus placed a silver chalice for wine on the table. The lamps were lit and fresh grapes, apples, dates and figs were served.

Joseph bowed his head and offered prayer.

"You have a handsome covering," he said to Marcus. "I'm thinking you have become an heir?"

"Not that easy," laughed Marcus. "I worked hard to pay for my belongings. But it's a long story."

"Perhaps you'll share your story with me at some time?"

Marcus nodded. He saw Joseph looking weary and thin. Perhaps it was the heat, or lack of food which made him look drawn. He poured more wine for his guests and the stories began.

Outside the tent someone called to Thaddeus. "It's Demetrius, are you in there?"

Thaddeus asked if he could invite his friend, and Marcus said he was welcome.

"I saw your lights and thought perhaps you might

need help in setting up your living quarters."

Thaddeus laughed out loud. "You smelled the wine!"

"Well," said Demetrius. "I can help with that."

They toasted, ate and drank while the soldiers outside were laughing and singing. The two soldiers began complaining about the inability to move the ramming machines up the ramp.

"Have you any predictions, physician?" asked Demetrius. "I learned that you have a gift."

"I can only predict that more men will die," said Joseph.

"You're right! I can't wait to get my hands on one of those who taunted us with water." Their boasting was loud, but Marcus liked his new found friends. He rose from the table and wiped his mouth with his hand.

"You men enjoy yourselves. I've been invited to have supper with Silva."

"Well!" Demetrius laughed loudly. "Don't let us keep you from the big man!"

"Joseph, I'll be back soon. Wait up for me."

Joseph walked to the doorway with him. "I'll stay up, son. I want to hear all that's happened with you."

Silva and Marcus ate a light supper and spent several hours talking about the events in Jerusalem.

It was late evening when Marcus returned to his quarters. The lamps were still lit and the two soldiers gone. He was thankful for the peaceful surroundings. When he entered, Joseph was doing his records. Marcus felt at home. More at home than he had in the past two years.

"Marcus, you said you had herbs? May I examine them?"

"Help yourself." Marcus emptied a large sack onto the table. He saw Joseph's eyes light up. They began sorting them.

"Ah!' said Joseph as he held up a stem. "Thank you for this healthy looking weed." They broke out laughing.

"I do slip up now and then," Marcus confessed.

They worked several hours in mixing potions needed for the

infirmary.

"Can I ask you what happened in Antioch?" Joseph whispered.

Marcus looked into the old man's sad eyes. "I apologize for leaving without telling anyone."

"Are you able to talk about it?" He didn't want to pry too much.

"I can now," Marcus admitted. "In fact I think I owe you an explanation."

"You owe me nothing, son."

"Let me start from the beginning. Nicator saved a letter from Martha which he never sent. I learned when we arrived home that Martha was married to someone else."

Joseph hung his head. "Nicator was deeply hurt. He couldn't forgive himself for holding back the letter."

Marcus filled him in on the details.

"So now you're a sailor, as well as a medic."

"You will like hearing how I attended to the sick men aboard ship."

"You were valuable to the captain."

"I kept his records and also shared in his profits!"

"Are you sorry you left the cool waters of the sea to come to this desert?"

"I don't regret anything. When I was a slave on the ship, I turned against the Christian God," he lowered his eyes. "In fact I turned against all gods. My anger was too strong. But one day I was sitting on deck and watching the beautiful sunset. It was overwhelming in its splendor." He paused and looked at the physician. "There came a peace over me. I remembered that peace when I accepted Christ. I longed for it again. I wanted to be reunited with a God of mercy."

"You were touched by the Holy Spirit," said Joseph.

"I guess you're right. I recalled the things you told me, and I remembered my dream about my father." His eyes filled with sadness. "I recalled you reading the writings of John when he wrote his revelation of Christ. I believed we witnessed His return in power, and the ending of the old covenant which God made with the Jews. The Son of God returned with vengeance on all who murdered His saints and refused to accept Him as their savior." Marcus sighed. "I didn't understand His return was as a spiritual force, not as a physical being, but He used the armies of Rome as His instrument of destruction."

Joseph listened to him expressing what the Lord had revealed to him.

"When I saw the tribulation in Jerusalem and heard about the tribulations the apostles went through and so many of the followers of Christ. It saddened me. I knew there was a greater hand at work," Marcus confessed.

"You have come a long way," said Joseph. "Jesus promised that that generation would not pass away until He returned (Matt. 24:34). Christ meant that for the people He was addressing at that time, not people in the future."

"There wasn't a stone left standing in the temple of Jerusalem, just as Christ had predicted. But I didn't see the stars fall from the sky." Marcus teased.

"As Jews, apocalyptic writings are familiar to us. All writings are not to be taken literally. The moon and stars refer to the rulers. It was the elements of the old religious system which melted (2 Peter 3:10). The old covenant had to pass away to make room for the new covenant which was promised in our Scriptures of old. One must decipher what is spiritual and what is physical. This is what is meant by the end of the age or some call the world. The world of old Judaism."

They talked through the night. Marcus told of Nicator's marriage and his new son. He told of his mother's death and all the news Virgil reported.

The two knelt in prayer before sleeping. It was a quiet night in the Roman camp at the Masada site.

A FIRE BLESSING

Commander Silva had ordered the prisoners to haul the ramming machine to the top of the ramp outside the wall of Masada. The zealots refused to throw stones at the Jewish prisoners.

Silva called Rufus' attention to the next procedure of the operation.

"Move our tower to the flat area on the ramp and keep it behind the ramming machine. Inform the men inside the tower to commence firing arrows over the walls when we start using the ramming machine.

As the sun rose the prisoners wheeled the battering ram up the ramp and when it was in place, they fled and hid. This gave the defenders of Masada an opportunity to fire on the Romans. They sent a barrage of stones to obstruct the path to the battering ram.

The soldiers in the tower fired hundreds of arrows to shower the insurgents. The unexpected attack forced the enemy to disappear from the wall.

The Romans cheered, and Silva was pleased that the tower left an impression on the enemy. He returned to his quarters and a soldier called to him.

"Commander Silva, the watchmen see our water trains arriving!"

"Thanks for the news," Silva replied. "I wonder what took them so long. If it weren't for Marcus, we would have many Romans beyond saving."

"Shall I send an escort?"

"It won't be necessary. I'll ride to meet them myself. I must learn the reason we were made to suffer without water. Their explanation better be good!"

When he met the water supply wagons, he found the men weary and some injured. They informed him how they were ambushed on their way to the wells.

Zoheleth

"You're a sorry looking bunch, but I'm glad you made it through. Those who need medical help will report to the infirmary." He turned his horse to the last wagon. "I see you have brought much awaited mail for the soldiers." He was pleased to know his men would now have plenty of water and news from home. "When you unload the wagons, report to me at high noon, after you distribute the mail!"

Silva saw heads pop up over the wall to spy. They looked down from that giant monument which faced the Dead Sea on one side and the mountains of Moab on the other. From the top of Masada, the revolutionaries could see the hills of Judea and the oasis of En-Gedi. They could also see every move the Romans made.

He rode back to the embankment where the ram was ready for action. With the first thundering sound, his horse reared. "Easy boy! That ram should wake them up!" Giving a light kick he steered the animal in the direction beneath the ramp to witness the effects of the battering ram's force. The sounds echoed as the iron head hit the stone. Sparks flew in all directions with each blow. Silva was satisfied.

Rufus rode to him. "Commander, the enemy hasn't put their heads out since the rain of arrows began!"

"Don't be too optimistic, Rufus. I want you to erect a protective canopy over the ramming machine's wooden framework. These devils will take the chance with fire darts to set it ablaze."

"Do you think they'll risk exposing themselves?"

"You can count on it," said Silva. "Right now it's my impression they're preparing themselves with shields to block our missiles. They'll cover their comrades long enough to fire on the wooden structure holding the ram."

"Consider it done!" said Rufus. The sun was high and the heat was intense.

"I'm concerned about the men in the tower," Silva said. "See that you don't keep the same crew on top of the tower or inside too long. It's like an oven in there."

"I'll change the crew every hour of the sand clock,

Zoheleth

sir," Rufus assured him.

"I wonder how the rebels liked the wake-up call?" Silva laughed.

"They'll hear it all day, Commander. They should know the reputation of our Tenth Legion!"

"Ah!" said Silva. "That they should!"

Behind the walls of Masada the earth shook violently with each blow of the ram. The zealots saw the mighty iron ram's head mounted on a gigantic tree trunk. The trunk was suspended by ropes allowing it to swing back and forth on a wooden frame. They watched the Romans pull the ropes back until the ram was in position to strike. The Romans, with all their force gave it extra man-power to drive its weight against the stone wall.

Eleazar witnessed this. He saw pieces of chipped stone spraying the ramp. He took note how the Romans covered the ram. Several times he was forced to duck the arrows. He and his men clung close to the wall.

"Get the women and children back into the apartments!" Eleazar ordered. "Keep them inside."

Husbands ran to lead their families to safety, but several of the men met with misfortune when they were struck in the back by arrows.

Sudden chaos broke out in Masada. One man came running to Eleazar with the terrifying news.

"The wall is weakening!" he cried.

Eleazar felt his insides knot. He used his shield to peer over the wall. He couldn't believe his eyes when he saw the wall bulging with each blow. His face registered shock.

"Get the heaviest timbers you can find in the store house," he ordered. The men returned carrying timbers one at a time, because of their weight it took several men for each timber.

Eleazar stood near the weakened section and instructed his men. "Dig out a section of the earth and start making a double timber gate to withstand the blows!"

Zoheleth

The men forced the timbers into the dug-out and slanted them against the weakened section. After a time the timbers stood side by side and on top of each other. The zealots stepped back and prayed the timbers would withstand the constant beating from the ram outside. When the ram struck again it drove the timbers deeper into the earth. Eleazar's men cheered.

"Praise the God of Israel!" shouted the men. "Let the Romans break the stone wall, but they will never budge these timbers!"

"There's no other way they can get inside but to break through at that spot," said one man. "Brothers, we can rest well. See how the timbers are angled against the wall."

"Well done, men," said Eleazar. "Let the Romans sweat it out while we sit back. Later we can set fire to their machine when they're forced to cease their work. How long can they go without water?" He was unaware they had a supply. His men laughed and began drinking wine to celebrate their inventiveness.

Silva learned that the stone wall was broken through. He rode directly to where he could see. He wondered how soon he could enter the breach.

Rufus came running down the ramp. His face was red and his eyes filled with anger. "Commander," he shouted. "We can go no further."

"What are you saying?"

"The rebels have secured the opening with mighty timbers. The ram can't move them."

"Curse them!" Silva shouted. "Will this ever end?"

"We must cease our work," said Rufus, "The heat is too much for the soldiers."

"Replace the men!" Silva spat. "We'll not cease the activity! The enemy must not think they have us at a disadvantage." Silva had to restrain his horse until he finished addressing Rufus. "We can't allow any portion of our machines to go unguarded. This is what the enemy wants. It would give them time to set fire to the machine."

Zoheleth

"As you say, Commander."

"Rufus, when you've changed the crew, come to my quarters. We must find another way to enter that walled fortress."

Later Rufus headed to Silva's quarters. When inside, Silva had wine with water served. He opened the map drawn by Joseph. Looking over it carefully, he turned to Rufus.

"The timbers against the wall," he questioned, "would you say they were old timbers?"

Rufus shrugged his shoulders. "I would think them old, sir. They could have been stored there from the time Herod the Great re-enforced the place."

"Very good!" Silva raised one brow.

"Your thinking of firing the timbers?"

"Correct!" said Silva with a wise grin. "I bet the zealots forgot to think about that." He stared at the flickering oil lamp before coming forward with his plan.

"Wait until dark," he began, "then send your men up the ramp. Give them a supply of torches, ones that will burn long enough to ignite the timber gate. Keep shields over the torches so they are not seen."

"Very good, sir."

"If the enemy sees our plan they'll take any risk to dampen our efforts," Silva assured. He dismissed Rufus. He finished his wine and hoped the gods would be with the soldiers in this one last attempt to enter Masada.

Rufus selected his men to do the job of setting afire the timbers securing the entrance to Masada.

When the sky darkened, the men awaited the signal to run the ramp with the fire brands. The soldiers covered each other with shields to hide the glow of the lighted torches. The first torch was tossed and the men dropped to the ground to stay out of sight until the fire ignited. Then more fire torches were released in the same manner.

Silva joined Rufus and the two stood below the ramp watching the scene.

"It's looking good so far," said Silva, giving an approving nod. They stared at the flames shooting high and

Zoheleth

wild in the wind. Once the flames were high, Silva headed back to his quarters. Suddenly he heard the shouts from Rufus who came running to him.

"By all the gods! Look what's happening."

Silva turned. "What is it?" He saw an expression of horror on the face of Rufus. "What are the men doing?"

"They're moving the ramming machine. The wind has blown the flames in its direction."

Silva stood frozen and looked in disbelief. The wind had forced the flames downward. "Have the gods turned from us and given the wind to favor our enemy?" he groaned.

"It looks that way," said Rufus.

"Curse them!" Silva screamed. "What do we do now?"

Both stood open-mouthed and gazing while the hand of fate humiliated them. It was a disheartening event. Silva lowered his head in despair. Suddenly Rufus shouted. This time with excitement.

"Look ahead! Commander!"

Silva's mood turned from exasperation to joy. He saw the wind had changed its course and now the gods favored Rome.

"We haven't lost yet!" Silva announced joyfully. "Send more men up with torches. Keep the fires burning all night!"

Silva returned to his quarters. He thought about tomorrow and what it would bring as he looked at the black night sky changing to a brilliant glowing red. He visioned his men marching the rebels out of their castle in the air and bringing them down to earth. They would go on display for all Rome to witness his victory.

Zoheleth

A LETTER FROM ANTIOCH

While the fires burned the wooden barriers the soldiers guarded the area. They were not visible to the enemy, but ready in case the rebels tried to water down the blaze. In camp, the soldiers relaxed and read their mail from home.

Marcus had received a letter from Nicator. When he and Joseph finished their duties for the evening, he opened it and read aloud to Joseph.

Greetings beloved brother, from Nicator.
God has answered our prayers and you're alive and safe.
What good news when Virgil wrote. He tells me how you have done quite well for yourself. He said you pleaded forgiveness from me. It's not necessary, dear brother. I was to blame for holding back the letter from Martha.
Virgil said you look great! Tall, muscular, and sporting a beard. He said your hair has grown back. Ha! I won't know you when I see you.
Virgil is in Rome and said that Emperor Vespasian is working on an Amphitheater. It will seat fifty thousand people. Can you visualize its size? They'll have mock navel battles right in the arena. Water will be pumped into a water tight pool which will hold ships. The show will be conducted on a water stage.
Virgil had gone to an arena where the prisoners and criminals were made to fight each other. The winner was permitted his freedom. What he saw next made him feel sick. The one who is defeated in the ring, if he's not dead, gets a visit from an underworld figure called the "Ferry Man". This guy, dressed in a hooded cape, delivers a final blow with a mallet to the head of the defeated criminal. Not a pretty sight. I won't linger on this because you've seen enough death in your years with the Jewish wars.

Zoheleth

Vespasian, it is said, has been known to honor the statue of Nero. I suspect he does this to appease the citizens of Rome. Titus is with his father and bears much of the burdens of government. Titus was to marry King Agrippa's sister, but no one knows what happened. The son of Vespasian refuses to marry anyone else. He must still be in love with Bernice.

On my trip into Antioch, I met a traveler who informed me how some Jews attempted to set up camps outside Jerusalem after the Tenth Legion left for Masada. It's my guess these displaced people will always try to rebuild their temple where they believe God dwells.

The traveler was firm in saying how the destruction was a sign given by Jesus. He said it was the end of an age. The world of Judaism, as the Jews knew it. The traveler implied that the hierarchy of Judaism had made it corrupt. He said the Pharisees and Sadducees brought in their laws and used their power to burden the poor. It's a strange twist that the Jewish rebels fought against Rome who burdened them? And the Jews are guilty of placing burdens on their own people!

Now for news about home. When you didn't return, Joseph took me to Pergamum where I met his Christian friends.

I met Mariamne, who became my wife. She's a Christian and we had lots to learn about each other. We fell in love.

Tell Joseph, if you ever see him, that we have a son, Jonathan Sabinus.

I regret mother never learned that you were safe. God spared her until her first grandson was born. We lost her through the night. She slipped away to meet the Lord during her sleep.

Mariamne is anxious to meet you and I know you'll enjoy your nephew. I hope this letter arrives in Masada by the time you get there.

Virgil told me where you were going and I took a chance on sending it to Masada.

Come home to us soon. God bless you, and when you see Joseph say that Mariamne sends her regards.

Joseph listened and his eyes moistened. "Thank God you're safe, Marcus," he sighed.

"I can't believe I'm an uncle. What a great name they gave him." He rolled the scroll and tucked it away in a small box where he carried his personal possessions.

"I must say, Joseph, you've made a dramatic change in our lives!"

"The Lord works in mysterious ways!"

"Why do you suppose Agrippa's sister didn't wed Titus? Do you think Agrippa was against the union?"

"I would think it was Titus' father who would be the one against his son marrying a Jewish woman."

"I can see why," said Marcus. "After all that has happened, I guess it wasn't a wise choice for the son of an emperor of Rome."

Joseph nodded. "Sometimes such a marriage can strengthen the bonds between enemies."

"Do you think it could have worked with Rome?"

"I think as long as there are religious zealots there will never be that kind of bonding."

"You're referring to Masada, here?"

"Right! The Jews would never consent to have Rome rule them again, even if Bernice did become the wife of a Roman Caesar."

"Will it ever end?"

"I think my people will always try to make Jerusalem rise to her original standing."

"A resurrected Jerusalem?" Marcus shook his head. "It's hard to visualize."

"It's happened before, but it will never again rise to its former heights."

"Our Lord sure knew what He was talking about," Marcus laughed. "I'm surprised my brother stayed with Christianity."

"Why does that surprise you?"

"I thought not hearing from me, and the loss of mother, he would turn away from the invisible God."

"When you are most troubled, Marcus, that's when

Zoheleth

our faith is the strongest."

"Do your people have that kind of faith?"

"Many of my people are godly people, but many have turned away from the words of the prophets."

"Speaking of prophets," said Marcus, "while on the cargo ship I learned how John the Baptist claimed that Jesus was the Lamb of God who takes away the sins of the world" (John 1:29).

"Do you understand what it means?" asked Joseph.

"I want to understand," Marcus confessed.

"You must read the letters of Paul of Tarsus," said Joseph. "Jesus is the Lamb of God. The Law commanded that lambs be killed as a sacrifice for the sins of the people. Jesus became our final sacrifice for our sins, instead of using an animal."

"How does that work?"

"Jesus took our sins forever when he shed His blood. The animal had to be killed for the sins of the people every year at Passover. Now Jesus has abolished the need for animals to be sacrificed."

"The temple at Jerusalem, is that where the priest killed the animals?"

"Yes. The priests can no longer slay the animals where they believed God dwelt."

"I saw men looking like priests, when I was traveling here. Who do you think they are?"

"I believe they're the Pharisees. I met with them after I left Antioch. They're the only ones left to teach the Torah. They are traveling through all the cities to keep the Torah alive." Joseph sighed. "The Sadducees and the Scribes have vanished since the destruction of Jerusalem. There must be changes made in the Jewish religious system to keep it alive in the future."

They were interrupted by Thaddeus. "Marcus, Joseph! Come outside!" he called. They hurried to see what was so urgent.

"Look ahead of you! The top of Masada is engulfed in flames!"

"What's happened?" asked Marcus.

"Silva got the idea to set the timbers afire and let it burn all night. We'll be able to mount the ramp tomorrow!"

The three stood in awe when seeing the blaze. The flames sent smoke and cinders into the air with each gust of wind.

"What a spectacle!" shouted Marcus. "Where's your friend, Demetrius?"

"He's stuck on guard duty. Silva wants no one to escape Masada."

"Fire seems to be a final ending for these Jewish zealots," Marcus noted.

Joseph lowered his head and had to agree. "The Lord is not finished," said Joseph. "God's revenge will also come to the destroyer, as well as the ones destroyed!"

"What do you mean, Physician?" Thaddeus, the Roman soldier, challenged.

"Those who take the holy items from the temple have been known to suffer strange trials. There have been times the enemy had to rid themselves of the items."

"Are you saying they're cursed and that Rome will be punished?" Thaddeus accused.

"The holy items have been dedicated to the God of all creation. They don't belong in the hands of pagans!" Joseph defended.

"You speak in riddles, Physician."

Marcus felt the tension and broke in by saying. "One thing different about this fire than the one in Jerusalem is the absence of burning flesh!" He and Joseph walked back to the tent while Thaddeus remained outside.

Marcus was puzzled and asked Joseph. "What did you mean about the holy items?"

"Throughout our history those who stole our holy objects were destroyed by plagues. Sometimes thousands died after such an act."

"Sure sounds weird. Do you think Rome will have a plague?"

"If I know my people, they will never cease praying

for these items to be removed from unclean hands."

"It does sound like a curse," Marcus surmised.

"You could say in the wrong hands the holy items bring misfortunes."

"Why?"

"These objects were used in acts of worship in the holy of holies in the temple." Joseph paused a moment. "You understand as Christians we have no need of holy objects in the worship of God. We walk with the Holy Presence of God with us. God will write His laws in our heart (Heb.8:9-10). At the destruction of the temple building, we now gain access into the heavenly Holy of Holies and no longer need a stone temple. These things were a shadow of what was in heaven."

"It's hard for me to understand the full meaning, but I'm sure your will teach me," Marcus added, "it should be interesting to see what happens to Rome now that they have the holy items."

They decided to get some sleep while the soldiers in the camp watched the glorious flames which promised them a Roman victory, tomorrow!

CHAPTER TWENTY EIGHT
THE FINAL CONFLICT

Before daybreak Eleazar saw the coming doom. The zealots stood watching the dry timbers being eaten away by the fire which burned through the night. The men gazed in disbelief at what they beheld.

"Eleazar," called one man. "Let's flee from here!"

"How?" Eleazar reminded them how the circumference of Masada was fenced in and patrolled by the Romans. He turned away and hoped no one would see his fear. He heard the timbers crackling from the flames which turned them into hot charcoal. Any attempt to use water was useless, he thought, since they were ready to crumble at the first blow of the ram. When the flames first took hold on the side facing outward, it was impossible for them to douse it with water.

The zealots stood staring and began complaining.

"We'll be at the mercy of the Romans soon," one man cried. "Our wives and children will be subject to the Romans' violent pleasures."

"Hold your tongue!" Eleazar commanded. "We have resolved never to be servants to the Romans! We were the first to come against them and we are the last to fight them. God has granted us the power to die bravely!"

"We can creep out while it's still dark and if we meet with Romans, we'll fight them!" suggested one man.

Eleazar disapproved. "What, and leave your families to be brutally used because of our continuous revolts against Rome. We can't leave them here!" He tried to impress upon them his reason. "I know what you're saying, and I know how you feel. But can any man come forth with a better move?"

Eleazar could only see their outline in the darkness. He knew they were not prepared to deal with defeat.

Zoheleth

One man grieved, "God has turned from us. We are guilty of using extravagant means against our own countrymen. We deserve to die!" He shocked his fellowmen. His fear became contagious.

"We may deserve to be punished by God! But I say, not by the Romans!" Eleazar declared.

They agreed, but what could they do? One of the sicarii spoke out. "I suggest that our wives and children die before they are abused by the Roman swine!" He came close to Eleazar and added, "Our children must never become slaves to the pagans! After they're dead, we'll kill one another by mutual consent!" The men began protesting.

Eleazar silenced them. "Have you any better ideas?"

They fell silent in the dark, each man alone in his private fear.

"The only way to defeat the Romans of a victory is to kill ourselves!" said one of the sicarii.

"If we are to die," said Eleazar, "let it not be at the hands of the Romans. We have the power to crush Rome's expectations." A hush fell over the group as the men listened to him. "First we'll destroy all our money," he suggested. "Then, we'll destroy the fortress by setting fire to all the furnishings."

The men seemed to think this was best.

"You have spoken wisely," said a sicarii.

"Then you agree with me?" asked Eleazar. They gave a sound of agreement. "Since you agree, do it now! Send ten men with torches and begin to fire everything that is flammable." They divided and torched the empty apartments one by one.

Not every man agreed with the plan. "We can't allow our wives and children to be killed," they complained.

"You don't have a choice," Eleazar raised his voice. "They'll die brutally when the Romans enter!" He heard them grumbling. "Let the sicarii do the job. They have the skill to kill painlessly and swiftly." He heard their sobs in the darkness. "You men shudder at the thought of death. Are you suddenly cowards? If you surrender now you will go down in history as those who lacked virtue to follow through the decision of death over slavery!"

They groaned again. "We know you're right, Eleazar. We do fear this death, not so much our own. It's the death of our loved ones. We need courage to face such an ordeal. Will God forgive us?"

Eleazar walked over to them. "I want you to remember the men of Jotapata," he asserted. "They didn't fear when it came to their families," Eleazar paused. "Many threw their wives and children over the cliffs. Then bravely followed in a leap to death! We must set an example to others by our readiness to die for our cause."

"How do we know the Romans will be so cruel to our families?" asked one man. "I recall at Caesarea how it was the Greeks who killed the Jews! The Romans never took us for their enemy until we revolted against them."

"Ah!" Eleazar groaned. "You have second thoughts about the Romans? In that case try leaving here and see how long they'll allow you live." He waited for a reply, but there was silence. "Have you overlooked how Silva used our people to do the labor on the ramp. They died in the heat. Have you forgotten how he used their dead bodies in a sling and fired them on the rocks as a threat to us?"

One man spoke out. "It was you, Eleazar, who refused the sacrifices for the Emperor Nero. We were to be a leading example to all nations. Even the pagans came to Jerusalem with the desire to hear and learn about the God we worshipped. You robbed them of God's blessing!"

"Shut up, you fool!" Eleazar responded. "You're quick to blame me. You forget how Emperor Nero claimed himself a god. Did you forget the atrocities our people went through while he ruled?" He hesitated a moment and continued his speech. "Will you brush aside the memories of those who fell into the hands of the Romans, because they wouldn't bow to idols or to the statue of Nero?" He didn't allow anyone to interrupt him. "Do you recall how our people were tortured for refusing to worship idols?"

The men groaned as he went on talking. "Some of

our people were tortured with fire. Others were whipped until they died. Where is your decency?"

Out of the darkness one man challenged Eleazar. "We hear you, Eleazar. Could it be that it is you who fears the Romans? Perhaps you fear what they'll do to you when they get their hands on the leader of the zealot movement?"

"Think what you want!" Eleazar shot back. "I've always stood for freedom, even if it means freedom by death!"

He did worry about being captured by the Romans. As the leader of the zealots, he might have his head removed and placed on a pole to parade through Rome. The fear that his body would be eaten by dogs made him tremble.

"Take pity on your families!" he went on. "Let's rob the Romans from making sport with your families."

The men finally came to terms with the decision. It seemed the only way out. At dawn they could hear the Romans beginning to work the ram through the timbers. They removed themselves to bid a final farewell to their loved ones.

Eleazar stood gazing at the night slipping from the sky. He motioned the sicarii and addressed them.

"Use your daggers now to spare the women and children from disgrace. Kill the husbands who can't kill themselves." They moved swiftly before the women folks were awake.

Eleazar stood near the smoking timbers. He held back his tears when he heard the muffled screams in the distance. He visualized the shocking moment when the women opened their eyes and felt the blade at their throat. He thought about the young ones, some at the breast. He could imagine the children bleeding to death in their beds.

He watched the dawn come quietly before him. The stars faded, except for one which blazed in defiance as though it threatened the presence of dawn. This would be his star. One that made an effort until the end but went out in glory. That star would rise again, but would he? His heart pounded when he heard the screams from the men who apparently put up a struggle with the sacarii. He knew they all must die. He would wait until everyone was dead and then he would choose one who would finish him off.

He smiled to himself when he pictured the Romans finding no one alive. Their defeated commander, Silva, would have no glory of a triumphal parade. He would have no prisoners from Masada to boast his victory! Even the booty would be worthless. He made certain that no Roman would walk away with any objects from Masada. This would be a victory like none before. He remembered how many sacrificed themselves at Jotapata, but Masada, was different. The gold and silver would never be in the hands of the Romans.

How furious Silva will be when he finds nine hundred and sixty people laying dead. Before his last breath he would remember this day and he would die with some satisfaction. It was the second day in the month of May in the year A. D. 73.

Masada was silent like she held a secret. The dawn grew brighter with each moment as Eleazar waited for his man to come and end his life. Together they would go to the private place of worship on this high mountain. He looked to the heaven and whispered a prayer before the last man of the sicarii stood beside him.

In the dark corners of the fortress, two figures were hiding from Eleazar. Unknown to him his count would be short two mothers and five children. There were two wives whose husbands couldn't allow them to die in such a manner. The men who braved their wives and children to be spared. Two men who killed themselves and died knowing that Eleazar wouldn't get his last wish!

Zoheleth

A DAWN OF SURPRISE

The Romans used the battering ram and the timbers crushed with the first blow. The live embers sprayed like an explosion and forced the soldiers back. They had to water down the hot embers. Lines of soldiers sent buckets of water up the ramp until the timbers had cooled and they could proceed with the ram. The final blow brought cheers from the soldiers as the timbers fell to the ground.

Rufus signaled the men to enter the fortress of Masada. Upon entering, something didn't appear right. Not one zealot was present.

"It might be a trap," suggested one soldier. "They're hiding somewhere." A sentinel ran down the embankment to warn of a possible ambush inside Masada.

A scout went forth while Silva and Rufus followed.

"There isn't anyone in sight," said the scout. "I don't like the looks of it.

"Where are the zealots who were eager to fight us?" asked Silva.

Thaddeus presented himself. "I'll volunteer to go and search out the chambers, Commander."

Silva nodded. "It looks like they have set fires to distract us. Use caution, they could be waiting to attack."

Thaddeus walked toward the royal apartments. Suddenly he heard a scream and jumped back, nearly falling. He drew his sword and shouted it was an ambush.

The soldiers ran with their shields and swords ready to strike.

"Wait!" commanded Thaddeus. "It's only women who are screaming."

As the soldiers lowered their swords, one called out, "Thaddeus, they could be the trap!"

Two women were crying hysterically. Their children clinging to them. They had searched the rooms for their

Zoheleth

husbands and found all the dead.

"Save us," one mother begged, as she held tightly to her young. "Please don't kill us."

"I demand you tell us where the men are?" Thaddeus threatened as he placed a sword to the neck of one woman.

"They're dead!" she insisted.

"Stop your lying and tell me where they're hiding and you and your children will go free."

"Look for yourself," she replied. "Eleazar wouldn't allow the Romans to have the final victory."

Thaddeus moved away. "I'm going in," he said to the others. "If I'm assaulted, you know what to do with these women and their children!"

He walked down the steps to the apartments, staying close to the walls. Smoke filled the halls and forced him to move more cautiously when he entered a doorway. He felt his blood rushing and his nerves preparing for the kill. He burst into the room and held his sword to spear the first man. But the room was empty. He stepped further and found a door. His nostrils widened as he tried to breathe. He rushed in and saw what he never expected. His sword fell to the floor when he found the death scene.

The sounds alerted the Romans and they came forward to fight. They too gazed upon the horrifying sight of little children draped in blood. A man lay on the floor with his throat cut. His wife was in his arms and her throat was slit. The scene was repeated in each apartment.

Silva could wait no longer to learn what had happened. He witness the murders and turned to the women with their children.

"Can you give me any idea of what happened here?" he asked as they stood trembling. He ordered his men to get food and water for them. "I mean you no harm," he assured them. "I promise that you and your children will be safely escorted to wherever you want to go."

One mother fell to her knees and kissed his hand.

"Forgive us," she cried. "We had no idea why Eleazar forced our men to come to Masada. We only wanted

Zoheleth

to be with our husbands and have a place to live since we lost our home in Jerusalem."

"I understand," said Silva. "Just tell me why the mass suicide." They began talking freely and both women revealed all that had happened. They told Silva how Eleazar had planned to leave nothing for the Roman soldiers when they entered. Eleazar convinced the zealots to kill their families and themselves with the help of the sicarii. Silva shook his head.

"Who did all the killings?" he asked firmly.

"While we hid, we could hear them as they cast lots. Ten men from the sicarii were to slit the throats of everyone until only they remained."

"Where was Eleazar while this was going on?"

"He chose to remain alive until the last ten men cast lots again. One sicarii was chosen to kill the nine and only he and Eleazar were left."

"Is Eleazar dead?" Silva inquired.

"I saw him heading toward the synagogue with the last sicarii." She pointed to the northern section of the area.

"How did you women escape?"

"Our husbands hid us in an underground aqueduct when learning Eleazar's plans. Our men reluctantly returned to sacrifice themselves. We begged them to change their minds but they didn't want to go down in history as cowards."

"Since you have been cooperative," said Silva, "I offer you the right hand of Rome. You may have your freedom."

They accepted his hand, and the children ran up to Silva and tugged at his leather skirt. He smiled when he saw their faces dirty from sticky figs.

Silva stood outside the death chambers as a deadly silence hung over Masada. The smoke drifted like ghosts haunting a passage of time through the corridors of horror.

His men gave a count of the dead after finding the body of Eleazar and one other man in the synagogue.

The Romans couldn't rejoice over their enemy.

Some even spoke of the courage it took to commit such an act for freedom.

Silva left a garrison stationed at the fortress. He gave orders that if anyone came to claim the body of a relative to allow them to take their remains to be buried. He advised that any of the bodies not claimed within three days were to be burned. He knew how his men felt when deprived of a victory. He pictured what they would do when he left. He visualized the bodies of the zealots being tossed over the walls or taken to the Dead Sea and dumped. Some of his men would allow the animals to devour the remains in the ravine below. War seemed to remove any warmth from the hearts of soldiers, he told himself, as he rode back to his quarters. There was nothing to take to Rome. No trophies or booty, since the rebels had burned everything of any value. Masada stood in the distance smoking like an angry volcano.

Marcus and Joseph cleared the infirmary. There were no casualties since there was no battle.

Marcus asked Joseph where he would be going from Masada.

"I'm going home to Alexandria. My farm lands and my servants await me. My private patients will be overjoyed to have their own physician back. And you, Marcus, what are your plans?"

"I've no special destination. I may return to shipping again."

"I would like you to accept my offer to come with me to Alexandria."

Marcus was somewhat surprised. "I thought about staying with Nicator," he sighed.

"Perhaps the newly married couple need some privacy for a time," Joseph suggested.

"I guess you're right," Marcus sighed. "I've never been to Egypt. Who knows what adventures I'll find there."

"May I take that as an acceptance?"

"You may!"

"I made a promise to your father that I would take

Zoheleth

care of you if anything happened to him." Joseph confessed. "I can keep that promise since I've found you again."

The Roman Legions were ready to march to Caesarea. They loaded the carts with the army baggage which included the timber fencing surrounding Masada, all was packed on ox carts.

Marcus loaded his carts and when finished, he said he would sell all the items.

"I can sell the mules since we're sailing to Egypt," said Marcus.

"I think you should keep the mules," said Joseph. "I'm out of money and we'll be traveling by land."

"You're not out of money, my friend," Marcus replied. "I'm your bank. That means we sail to Egypt!"

"I'll repay you as soon as we arrive in Alexandria." said Joseph. "I'm glad we're sailing. I'm tired, and I want time to talk with you about your future."

"Joseph, we'll have lots of time to talk aboard ship. Now let's leave this sad place."

Marcus sold the kegs, his tent and all the furnishings to the merchants who came along. He kept only a few favorite paintings which he treasured.

On the ship sailing to Egypt, Joseph offered to adopt Marcus as his son.

"Are you serious?" Marcus asked with a wide grin.

"Very serious. I have no children nor heirs. The only thing I ask in return is that you continue your medical education."

"You won't have to insist on that," said Marcus. "I have grown to love the art of healing."

"Good! You'll attend the medical school in Alexandria, the one I graduated from."

"I can hardly believe what I'm hearing," Marcus replied. "I must write to my brother and tell him I have a new father." They laughed and hugged.

"I've always called you son," Joseph said with tears

Zoheleth

in his eyes.

"Father, can I tell you that I love you?"

"All you want." Joseph was overjoyed. He paused and added, "I want you to meet someone who is boarding the ship on the next stop. I've invited them to spend time at our home. I sent a courier before we left Masada and asked them to meet us. Do you mind?"

"I want to know all those you know, if I'm to be a proper son. Who is this we are to meet?"

"They're a Christian family. You'll like them."

The ship docked and picked up additional passengers. Joseph waited at the dock to greet his friend.

"Joseph!" shouted Philippus as he mounted the plank. "God bless you. How are you?" They embraced warmly.

"I'm fine. I see you have your daughter with you."

"This is Julia," Philippus introduced her. "Since her mother died, I take her everywhere with me."

"It's good to see you, child," said Joseph. "But you must excuse me. I see that you're a young lady now."

Julia smiled shyly. Her long dark hair was typical of her Egyptian lineage. She wore a bright colored ribbon tied in the back.

Joseph asked Philippus, "How old is your daughter?"

"She's seventeen."

"I'm sorry to hear about your wife. Please accept my condolence."

"Thanks Joseph. We miss her, Julia and I."

"Come," said Joseph as he led them. "I want you to meet my son."

"Since when did you become a father?" Philippus inquired.

"About two days ago," Joseph laughed proudly. "Marcus has been with me since he was fourteen years old. I've trained him as a medic while we were with the legions. He lost his father in Jerusalem and his mother died recently. He has consented to be adopted."

"You old rouge. Let's meet the lucky fellow."

They entered the cabin where Marcus waited. Joseph

Zoheleth

introduced him. Marcus never expected to meet such a lovely creature as Julia. He fell over his own feet trying to impress her. They spent time on deck while Joseph and Philippus talked over old times. He and Julia had many hours aboard ship to get acquainted.

At night they watched the moon rise over the black ocean. Marcus named all the constellations for Julia. He was well adapted to the sea and knew how each star could direct a ship. Julia was impressed.

When the ship docked, the four headed ashore and Joseph hired horses to take them to his house.

Marcus was thrilled when he saw his new home. It stood like a palace. Servants ran to help them and for several days they held banquets and celebrations for the return of the physician.

Philippus and his daughter were Joseph's guests for several months. During that time Marcus and Julia fell in love and were promised in marriage.

Joseph had the papers drawn for the adoption and Marcus enrolled in Medical School. He studied hard and during school breaks, he aided Joseph with his patients.

The physician had warned him how hard it is for a new physician to get patients, since people desired to have older and more experienced doctors. He told him how he stepped into his father's practice, and he hoped Marcus would do the same.

Philippus was happy about the engagement of his daughter. He told Joseph that Marcus placed another love in the heart of his daughter. Plans were made for the wedding.

After Marcus and Julia married, Philippus came to visit with Julia and his new son-in-law. He sat talking with Joseph one evening after the married couple departed to their quarters.

"I have disturbing news," he said. "I learned that a group of sicarii who escaped Jerusalem, fled to Egypt."

Joseph shook his head. "That's not good." He had his servants pour wine for them. "Have any problems occurred?" he asked.

"They made their way to the temple of Onias with inclinations for another revolution." Philippus said. "They attempted to get the Jews living in the area to revolt against Rome."

"I can't believe what I'm hearing," Joseph shook his head. "I remember the history of the temple of Onias. It was Antiochus, the king of Syria, who came and destroyed the temple in Jerusalem long ago."

"Was that when Onias fled from Jerusalem and came to Egypt?"

"Correct. Ptolemy, the king of Egypt, gave Onias permission to build a replica of the Jerusalem Temple."

"It seemed a kindly act from the king," Philippus noted.

"Ah, kindly indeed. Ptolemy wanted the Jews to flock to Egypt where they could worship freely, and also bring in more revenue to the country. The temple of Onias is a beautiful place," Joseph added.

"You can forget about the temple," said Philippus.

"What are you saying?"

"The governor of Alexandria reported the commotion to Vespasian. The emperor ordered the temple to be demolished to keep down the possibilities of another revolt."

"Will they ever learn?" Joseph cried. "What happened with the sicarii who entered?"

"The Jews were quick to point out the sicarii to the Romans. Six hundred of them were killed along with their families. The Jews wanted to be left in peace."

"This is sad."

Julia and Marcus came back into the room. Philippus walked over to his daughter. "I trust you're having no problems carrying my first grandchild?"

"Father!" she said. "I have two doctors in the house and if Marcus doesn't stop fussing over me and get some sleep, he'll need a doctor!" They laughed.

"My wife thinks I spoil her," Marcus grinned. " I think she thrives on all the attention." He put his arms around her.

"You, Marcus," she said playfully. "Better keep your mind on your studies, instead of me. Joseph keeps a watch over me when you're not here."

Julia bent down and kissed Joseph on the head. "You're the best father-in-law I've ever had."

Joseph laughed aloud. "Since when did you ever have another?" He loved his daughter-in-law and was a happy man with a family. A family he never had. For once he was content with his life.

CHAPTER TWENTY NINE

YEAR A.D. 79

The July evening was warm, but a gentle breeze drifted through the house in Alexandria. The ceilings were high and the rooms spacious.

Marcus sat reading a letter from his brother while Julia bathed their young son, Joseph. The child giggled as Julia dried his small body.

Marcus stopped reading when little Joseph ran naked through the room and right into his father's arms. He laughed when his father caught him.

"Marcus," Julia called. "What's the news from your brother ?"

"Nicator has accepted our offer. He and his family will come to stay with us."

"I'm so happy for you," said Julia. "I'll have the house servants prepare the spare rooms."

Marcus dressed his son for bed. The boy clung to his father's neck as they headed to the front of the house.

"Father," little Joseph asked, "am I going to have playmates living here?"

"Yes, son. Your cousins will be here." He sat down on the divan and stacked cushions behind little Joseph. His son gave him a wide smile. His straight dark hair was dripping from under the towel and his dark eyes sparkled with delight. His skin was a golden brown like his mother's. At times, Marcus thought he resembled the Egyptians' Pharaohs.

"When can we expect your family?" Julia asked as she nestled close to her husband.

"Nicator hopes to be here within seven days, if the winds are good for sailing." He leaned over and kissed his wife. "Have I told you lately how beautiful you are?"

"I love you, Marcus," she kissed his cheek. Little

Zoheleth

Joseph threw himself in the middle and kissed them both.

"I love you," young Joseph repeated over and over. They laughed and enjoyed his ability to speak so well.

"Soon, my son, you will have two cousins whom you've never seen. In fact, I've never seen them."

Young Joseph squealed and hugged them.

"Tonight, my dumpling," said his mother, "you can dream of all the good times you'll have with your cousins."

"Let's sail you to your bed," Marcus said as he held him high and ran. His son screamed with delight. Julia scolded Marcus for getting him excited before bedtime.

"Good night, my son. Say your prayers before we dampen the lights."

"Please, God," he whispered. "Send my cousins here fast." His mother and father kissed him good night and returned to the front room. Marcus rested on the divan and stared at the ceiling. His thoughts were on his adopted father. He thanked God for Joseph, the physician. A pang of sorrow swept over him as he recalled how Joseph's eyesight began to fail, and then he suffered heart problems. He thought about the morning he had gone to serve Joseph his breakfast only to find that he had quietly died through the night. Tears filled his eyes.

Julia interrupted his thoughts. "Darling, what's wrong. Is there something in the letter?"

"Everything is fine," he answered.

"Will you read the letter to me?"

"Of course," he said softly. "I do hope you're not troubled about my family staying with us?"

"My beloved husband, I will love having your family here. We must keep together, Marcus." She paused and looked at him. "As Christians we need each other. You know the times are difficult for those trying to spread the Gospel of Christ."

"I know. Nicator has been very active in teaching the Gospel. At least when he gets here he will have many Christian communities and churches. It will be safe for them to live here." He began to read aloud.

Zoheleth

Doctor Marcus Severus Abtolim of Alexandria;

Greetings from Nicator and Miriamne.
We have been forced into hiding with our children since your last letter. We have considered your offer and decided to accept your generosity. I regret to inform you that our village has been burned and we lost our home.
Christian friends in Corinth have taken us in. Many of us are in hiding since the Romans and the Jews have turned against us.
The Romans look upon us as trouble makers, and the Jews blame us for the loss of their temple, as well as their city.
My concern is for our children, and Miriamne is carrying another child.
Jonathan is now eight years old, and Benjamin will be six. Benjamin reminds me of our father, he's lean and strong.
We want our children to be educated and you did say the schooling is excellent in Alexandria.
We'll sail as soon as we book passage. Our friends are anxious that we get to Egypt to evangelize lower Egypt and Africa. I learned that father has distant relatives in Africa.
There's been an outbreak of plague and hundreds are dying in the neighboring nations. I fear for my family.
Virgil has remained in Rome to teach law. He's married and has a daughter. He said the death of Vespasian has left Rome devastated. The emperor took ill with a fever, but continued to conduct the affairs of state when he should have remained in bed to regain his strength.
Titus, the new emperor, is loved by all. Unfortunately Titus has found his younger brother, Domitian, antagonistic toward him. Virgil said that Titus had offered Domitian to rule with him but Domitian refuses to be second in place. Rumors have it that Domitian has designs to see his brother dead.
Titus never married, but it is said that his friend, Tiberius, rushed to be with Titus right after Vespasian died. They hadn't seen each other in years. Virgil said that Titus

Zoheleth

learned that his former love, Bernice, is living in Pompeii. It is rumored that she had a son by Titus. We don't know if this is true. But Titus is obsessed in finding her, and Rome is concerned for the welfare of their new emperor. They know he searches for Bernice constantly.
Titus sent for Agrippa, her brother, to spend a month at the Flavian Mansion. Maybe Agrippa doesn't know where his sister is, or perhaps he won't reveal it if he does know.
I'm sorry we missed the birth of your son. We feared leaving the home vacant at that time. We're anxious to meet your family. Little Joseph must be four years old now. He and Benjamin should get along well together.
I felt badly when I received your letter about the physician's death. It's fortunate how he adopted you and now you are heir of his estate. You said he paid your way through medical school and now you're treating many of his latest patients. I hope you have gained a few new ones on your own. Mother and father would be proud if they could see you today.
We'll leave for Egypt as soon as Miriamne is over her morning sickness. She's passing her third month and that's when she begins to feel better.
Look for us at the port of Alexandria.
God bless you, Julia, and young Joseph.

"Oh, Marcus, Nicator sounds like a wonderful brother."

"He is. I can't wait until he arrives."

"Who is Virgil?"

"He's a childhood friend of Nicator."

"He's a lawyer?" she asked.

"Yes. His family lived a few miles from our village. I guess I have him to thank for meeting you. It was he who gave me the desire to go to Masada."

"Then I like him," she smiled. "What did Nicator mean about the Emperor Titus searching for Bernice?"

"Titus was engaged to marry her while we were still in Jerusalem," said Marcus. "When they sailed to Rome to be wed, it is said that Titus' father opposed the marriage."

"So what happened?"

"I don't know what really happened. I learned in this letter how he still searches for her. Titus was good to my family after my father was killed. He gave us full Roman citizenship."

"Were you made to worship the Roman gods?"

"I wasn't a Christian at that time. It didn't matter, but being a Roman citizen had its benefits, and still does."

"Do you think Titus will ever find Bernice," she asked with dreamy eyes.

"I have no idea," he answered. "It would appear that Titus is still in love with her."

They sat dreaming together as the evening passed. Marcus thought about Titus and wondered if he would find Bernice and his son, if the rumor was right.

THE FLAVIAN DYNASTY

The aristocrats of Rome gathered at the steam baths, a place where they could discuss matters of business or the latest gossip. Bathers relaxed in heated water and were completely unaware of those who labored underground to heat the water.

Young Lepidus, a relative of the Lepidus who once ruled Rome with Octavian, lay on the table as a slave rubbed him down with oil to scrape his skin.

"Felix," Lepidus called to the man on the next table. "Have you noticed how our new emperor spends very little time in Rome?"

Felix groaned as the slave massaged his back. "I heard that he searches for his one time mistress. What news have you heard?"

"The same! It seems Domitian is eager to take over the position as emperor."

"That horse's rear," Lepidus spat. "We'll all be in trouble when that wet-behind-the-ears paranoid gets into power."

"Too bad about Vespasian," said Felix. "He gave Rome the changes we needed. Titus was very devoted to his father. He's not been the same since his death."

"I agree," said Lepidus as he wiped his mouth on the cloth beneath his head. "You knew Titus years ago. Isn't that so?"

"Yes. I knew him as a boy. He was close friends to Emperor Claudius' son, Britannicus. Titus never forgot his friend. He honored Britannicus by erecting two statues of him."

"Commendable," said Lepidus. "My guess, he'll set up more than two statues of his father." He coughed. "I remember Vespasian bragging about the Arch of Titus which he designed and had built for his son's victory over

Jerusalem."

"Too bad Titus nurses a passion for King Agrippa's sister," Felix sighed. "What some men do for a woman."

"Perhaps he'll find a wife of his own, since his father can't object from the grave."

"He better get one younger than Bernice, she'll be too old to bear him heirs." They laughed heartily.

"I heard how Domitian's wife likes sleeping around. Do you think she has been in Titus' bed?"

"Who knows?" Felix replied flatly.

"It seems she wants to be the wife of a Caesar. Maybe she's not willing to wait for her husband to become emperor."

Felix chuckled. "No wonder Domitian's face has been sour for the past ten years. Do you think he knows of his wife's loose behavior?" Felix got up and wrapped a towel around his waist. "I hear Titus is going to Pompeii. I bet it's not just for a good time."

Both men got dressed and left the baths.

Titus stood on the porch of the Flavian Mansion and watched the children playing in the courtyard. The boys rode two wheeled carts hooked to goats. They raced them like charioteers. Most of the children belonged to his slaves, but he treated them as if they were his own children.

He made his early morning sacrifices to the gods and needed some answers that only the gods could give him. His search for Bernice was leading to dead ends. As he was to leave, an imperial messenger appeared.

"My Lord," he bowed. "A message from King Agrippa. He gratefully accepts your invitation and will arrive tomorrow morning."

"Good," said Titus. "I appreciated his coming to my father's funeral, but I had no idea he would stay in Rome this length of time."

Titus ordered his servants to prepare for the guests. While giving instructions, his brother walked in.

"My brother," said Domitian, "are you expecting

someone of importance?"

"I've invited King Agrippa to spend time with us."

Domitian frowned. "Why, after ten years, you decided to renew your friendship with this king of the Jews?"

"I regret that I allowed the friendship to fade," Titus added. "I know how father was not in favor of entertaining the Jews who once inhabited Jerusalem."

"Father was wise!" Domitian said with a sneer. "Perhaps you should use the same wisdom in your choice of friends."

"What's your problem, Domitian?" Titus asked in exasperation.

"Are you so distant from the problems that you haven't known how the Jews attempt to get back into Jerusalem?"

"I've heard no such rumors," Titus snapped.

"It's not a rumor, dear brother, it's a fact!" His abruptness disturbed Titus. "They gathered enough zealots to form another army to come against our Roman garrisons. Doesn't that phase you one bit?"

"I'm more aware of events than you give me credit for. Perhaps you should tend to your family matters and allow me to tend to the matters of state!"

Domitian turned red. His eyes flared in hatred. He grew indignant by his brother's words.

"When I'm ruler," he said defiantly, "I'll see to it that I prune the family tree of the Jews."

"Until that day, young brother, let me ask. Are you so distant from your personal problems that you haven't seen what's going on under your own nose?" Titus paced the floor like his father before him. "If you don't think I'm running the country the way it should be run, then why haven't you accepted my offer to be equal partners?"

"Oh!" said Domitian as he began to dispute. "You expect me to take the responsibilities of the state, while you run off searching for your whore!"

Titus grabbed him by the tunic. "You ungrateful

self-centered, egotistical pup!" he shouted in his face. "You dare judge me when you seduced a married woman to leave her husband to marry you!"

"Get your hands off me!" Domitian demanded. "You're a weakling. Titus, the darling of Rome!" he mocked.

Titus dropped his hold.

"Are you so sure the Arch that father built to honor you, should not have been in honor of Tiberius, your military informant?"

"If you thought that so, then why didn't you go to father with your complaint?"

"Go to father," he laughed, "and complain against his favorite son?"

"Domitian, you're sick! I offer you to share in the rule, I offer you half the kingdom! Any man in his right mind would accept. Why not you?"

"I won't be second best. I can wait to be emperor and not stand in your shadow!"

"Let's not be enemies. We're blood. We're addressed as Caesars! Please, accept my hand with my apology."

"And if I don't accept, what will Caesar do to me?"

"Just what do you think Caesar would do? I'm your brother. We have no differences."

Domitian accepted his hand. Titus drew him close and hugged him.

Domitian held back his anger. He hated living with his father, and now Titus. He had never been included in the main decisions made for Rome. Always to ride behind Titus. Always to be the last! He left the room and sulked as usual.

Titus was puzzled by his brother's rejection to join him. He walked to his bedroom to change his attire for the evening meal. He never heard her enter his room.

"Titus," she whispered, "are you in need of assistance?"

He spun around and quickly grabbed his tunic to

cover his nakedness. "What are you doing here, Domita?" he demanded. "Didn't you just see your husband leave?"

"I saw him," she smiled slyly. "You should be asking if he saw me."

"Is there counseling you need?" he asked, as he frowned to show his disapproval of her presence. He didn't want her to be found in his bedroom. "You are out of place here, and it's improper for you to enter my private bedroom. You know how jealous Domitian is."

"I wanted to find you alone," she said seductively.

He watched her as she rested herself on his lounge and reach for a fresh peach in a bowl. She bit into it and the juice ran down her chin. She held out the peach and asked. "Care to taste the sweet nectar of the gods?"

"Clear yourself from my bedroom!" he ordered.

She sat up straight but didn't move from the lounge. "And what will big bad Caesar do to me if I remain?"

"Big bad Caesar will have you bodily removed!"

"That might be interesting," she laughed. "I've yet to feel your arms around me, but I'm ready."

He scowled as he headed to the door and opened it. "I have no intentions of removing you myself. My guards will do that for me."

She jumped from the lounge and straightened her gown. She stomped toward him after throwing the peach to the floor. Her face flushed with anger and she pushed the door shut. Putting her hand to his cheek, she said, "I could take away the longing for your Jewess," then, whispered in his ear. "I see the different women entering your bed chambers late at night."

He removed her hand from his face. "You can keep score all you like, but let me remind you that not one of them has been someone's wife!"

"Don't be so sure," she moved uncomfortably close to him. "I have never been refused."

"Except by me," he reminded her.

"You'll change your mind. Perhaps in the dark you will never know who's in your bed until it's too late."

Zoheleth

Her eyes burned with resentment as she opened the door to depart on her own.

"Domita," he said. "You're my brother's wife. How can you expect me to hurt him the way you do?"

"You fool!" she snapped. "Your brother hates you! He even tries to turn the armies against you! How can you not hurt him?"

She threw her arms around his neck. "I need you," she said pleadingly.

He removed her arms and pushed her away. "Don't do this to my brother. I can't return your affections. Forgive me. This can only divide our family and destroy us." He looked into her eyes and saw a beautiful woman. He was always fond of her, but never to take her from his brother. She was desirable and she knew it!

She left with angry tears in her eyes. He was deeply concerned that she would tell his brother that she was in his chambers. He looked out and saw a guard who was in listening distance and knew he heard the conversation. That would be his security. He thought about what she said. It hurt him deeply. He thought about his father and how he didn't like Domitian's lust for married women. He wondered how he would have handled such a situation.

"Tata!" he whispered. His heart was heavy as he dressed and made himself ready to face the public with a smile. A smile which no longer came from his heart. His emptiness would never be filled until he filled his arms with his Bernice.

He walked down the corridor whispering aloud. "A son! A son!"

What had she named him? How much did he know about his father, or did he hate his father for what he had to do? Maybe tomorrow he could get some answers. He was sure King Agrippa would have them.

THE VISITOR

King Agrippa with his guards and his servants had traveled to Rome to pay their respects to the dead Caesar, Vespasian. Agrippa accepted the offer from Titus to visit with him.

"Agrippa," Titus greeted him like an old friend, "it's been a long time since we've seen each other."

"Caesar Titus, your Excellency," Agrippa was diplomatic in his greeting as he bowed. "I wish it were under better circumstances."

"Come, Agrippa. No need for formalities among friends. It's Titus, as always."

"Titus," said Agrippa. "I'm sorry about your father, but may I congratulate you on being the new emperor!"

Titus laughed and led him into the mansion. "Your guards will have their own quarters."

"You're more than kind." Agrippa eyed his surroundings. "Your residence has improved since I was last in Rome."

"You can thank my father for it. As for myself, I would be pleased with a small village house and a good wife."

Agrippa frowned and asked. "You're not married?"

"Agrippa, if I had married, the news would have spread over the world in a matter of days!"

"You must have left many tears on the cheeks of eligible brides." Agrippa tried to laugh, but his thoughts turned to his sister.

Titus led Agrippa to his private quarters for a quiet supper where they could talk freely. They sat opposite each other and said very little during the meal. Titus had forgotten how many years had passed between them until he noticed Agrippa's graying hair. Agrippa had put on weight, and he himself had done the same.

Zoheleth

Titus was still dressed in his black mourning toga.

"Do you like the Greek wine?" he asked Agrippa.

"It's tasty, and I happen to know it's an expensive beverage." He smiled warmly at Caesar.

"How are things in Pella?"

"They're peaceful now. Your father was kind enough to allow Johanan ben Zakkai to set up an academy at Jabneh. He has re-established the Sanhedrin for our people. They keep the Torah active."

"If I recall, it was the year seventy six, my father did that." Titus hedged a bit. "Do you hear any rumors about another revolt?"

"I hear rumors, but you must realize that my people are not easily discouraged. They will always look for a savior to lead them into freedom."

"Do you feel Rome was too harsh on your people?"

Agrippa thought for a moment and made certain not to insult the Caesar. "I think Rome did all she could to allow my people to worship our God without issue."

"I'm glad to hear you say that." Titus smiled.

"Of course you know how the procurators sent from Rome were anything but fair with us."

"I understand," said Titus. "I know how Florus abused your people, and he had a hand in setting them against Rome. You know I promised your sister to do all I could to spare your people." Titus lowered his head. "I never expected the Twelfth Legion to disobey my orders. They randomly set fire to the temple." He watched Agrippa dip bread into a sauce. "We are superstitious about destroying what is holy to others," he added.

Agrippa looked up. "I think my people were expecting one to rule as the messiah," he said. "They could never accept the fact that the one who would rule the world was Vespasian! But the world he would rule was the world of Rome!"

"You mean they expected someone who would rule the world of Judaism?" Titus questioned.

"You could say that, but it was more likely one who

would free them from the yoke of bondage. And they considered Rome as holding them in bondage."

"What was this messiah suppose to do once he came?" Titus asked.

"He would set up his kingdom and the Jews would rule the world."

"I see," said Titus slightly grinning. "What I don't see is how was he to do this without bloodshed?"

"You've a good point. But their hopes have risen again."

"Then it's true there is a conspiracy to take Jerusalem."

"You could say that."

They drank more wine and Agrippa rested back and asked, "I hope I'm not being rude, but I would like to know how your father died."

Titus reached for a few grapes before answering. "He took sick while we were working on plans to rebuild the Theatre of Marcellus. Father did manage to have a new stage built, and revive the former musical performances."

"I heard about that. I also heard that he completed the Temple of Peace."

"That temple began in the year seventy one. My father rose early every morning, even while dressing, he attended to the affairs of the state. People lined up outside his bedroom waiting to present their problems."

Agrippa smiled. "I remember your father's wit. I heard how his remarks, many times, shocked the royal House of Senate. It made me laugh."

"I remember my father not trusting one of his servants. One day the servant told him his brother needed his case heard immediately." Titus grinned while relating the story. "My father thought the man had too many relatives, but he heard the so called brother anyway. After father learned the man was not a brother, but had paid his way to be heard. He asked the man how much he had paid the servant. Father went to the servant and demanded to know how much he charged the man. The servant lied and said it was half the amount. Father put out his hand and said "You can pay me that price, since that man was my brother!" He warned the servant not to do it again."

"Ha!" laughed Agrippa. "Your father was a just man, and most honest in his decisions."

"He was a sensible man. He knew if he forced a criminal to pay large penalties it would cause the man to seek more crime to pay his debts."

"Is it true that he placed a heavy tax on the urinals?"

"Oh, that he did. I complained about it and he tossed me a coin and asked if it smelled. I complained no more."

"Always a sense of humor."

"Did you know Caenus, his mistress, died."

"I'm sorry," said Agrippa.

"One time he found a woman he liked and they spent the night together. He paid her an enormous amount of money. His accountant asked what he should file the sum under? Father smiled and said, file it under Passion!"

"How did he die?" Agrippa repeated.

"Oh, yes. In June he collapsed from a fever. He had dipped himself into a cold river to heal himself. At sixty nine it was not the best idea. He took a bad chill and not long after that he passed away."

"And now you're emperor of Rome," Agrippa said. "Do you intend marry?"

"Didn't Bernice inform you?"

"I haven't seen her in years," Agrippa replied.

Titus felt his heart sink by what he just heard.

"You didn't know how I was forced to send her away?"

Agrippa shook his head. "My sister wrote and said she was taking a voyage to a few foreign countries." He looked at Titus and wondered what really did happen. "She did say how you refused to accept the God of the Jews. Therefore you would remain a pagan whom she could not marry."

"You never learned the truth?" Titus was puzzled.

"That's all she ever said about her departure."

Zoheleth

"My father warned me if we married, she might be murdered."

"Titus, this is the first time I've heard anything like that."

"I regret my decision, but I didn't want some Roman thinking he would put an end to another Jew. I loved her too much. I asked her to wait for me. I promised never to marry until I could bring her to Rome to rule beside me. I can leave Rome to my brother if she desires me to leave here."

"Titus, you should have married and had heirs. My sister is nearly fifty!"

"I have an heir!" Titus declared. "Your sister had a son by me! Tiberius knew this, but promised not to tell her secret until I became ruler."

"You're telling me you left my sister with a child of fornication?" Agrippa was angered.

"I didn't know about it, Agrippa. Honest!"

Agrippa got up from the table. "I don't know what to say."

Titus stood and walked the floor. "I asked you here in the hopes of finding her. I want to marry her, the hell with being an emperor. My brother will gladly take over. He can have my blessings, if that will bring her back to me." He stopped pacing and added, "I swear by all the gods, I'll become who she wants me to become!" Tears blinded him.

"Titus," Agrippa said softly. "I have no idea where she is."

"Tiberius told me she might go to Pompeii after the child was weaned."

"A wild place to lose one's self," Agrippa frowned. "Have you gone there in searched for her?"

"I've sent men there. I've paid large sums for them to seek her out, but no one returns with news of her."

"It sounds like they might not want to find her and bring her to Rome. Have you thought about that?"

"I don't understand?"

"You forget how the Romans still come against the Jews, as well as the Christians. Are you so sure that she would want to be found?"

"I want to be by her side with our child!"

"A child from a Jewish mother?" Agrippa asked cruelly. "How long do you think the child would live?"

"Who would hate my blood that much?" Titus murmured.

"What about your brother?"

Titus said his farewell to Agrippa after a month's stay. He sent gifts along with him and increased his territories to rule to improve their friendship.

Titus' greatest concern was finding Bernice and the child before the plague, which was sweeping the east, found them. Was she and the boy already a victim? He wondered if Agrippa were hiding something? Bernice was known to be very close to her brother. He recalled during their talks, Agrippa referred to a nephew. Had he seen the boy? Did he know more than he was willing to confess? He wasn't sure if Agrippa trusted him to reveal where his sister was living, if she was among the living! He wondered what his next move should be. He could send spies to Pella and watch Agrippa's palace. If his son was there, surely the spies at some time would see the boy. But who could he trust to send? Would they lie to him when they returned?

It was then he planned to go to Pompeii after the grand opening of the Roman Coliseum. He had to be at this great stadium to start the events. Fifty thousand people would wait for his hand to give the signal for the show to begin.

When all the events were finished, he would sail to Pompeii and personally search for Bernice.

CHAPTER THIRTY

CLOUDS OF ASH

Before the games at the Coliseum, Titus went to the Roman priests for the sacrifice of the day. This morning the animal escaped from the altar when it was to be sacrificed. It was not a good sign. Titus fell into a mood which gave him no peace. His apprehension heightened when the sound of thunder was heard and not a cloud in the sky. After the day's events he returned to the palace.

Trajan, his father's friend, entered to speak with him and noticed his despair. "What is it that troubles you, Caesar?"

Titus was looking over the landscape from his terrace. There was an unusual death-like silence in the air.

"I'm not sure I liked the omens these past few days. Even the priests are uneasy," he confessed.

"Caesar knows that omens are not always correct in their interpretations."

"You may think so, but I feel a heavy cloud hanging over me and lowering more every day I stay in Rome."

"Perhaps Caesar needs time to rest from his burdens," said Trajan. "May I suggest that you have the physician, Samuel, look in on you?"

Titus turned to him. "You think I'm sick?"

"I would say you've been looking rather pale lately," Trajan replied cautiously. "You have been in the areas where the plague has struck."

Titus shook his head. "I can't get those people out of my mind. I'm seeing thousands dying from the plague. I've sent all the money I can to help the towns stricken. I don't know how to stop it!"

"Caesar, only the gods can stop a plague." Trajan threw his cape over his shoulder and watched as Caesar walked back and forth. "You should not endanger your

Zoheleth

health by entering the villages which have the plague."

"I must!" he sighed. "You don't understand, I'm searching for someone." He hung his head and fell silent.

"Caesar should use precaution." Titus refused to answer when he saw his brother enter the terrace.

"You sent for me?"

"Yes, Domitian. I want Trajan to witness what I'm about to say."

Domitain's face grew solemn. His dark eyes shifted back to Trajan, who shrugged his shoulders to motion that he too was puzzled.

Titus reached for a scroll and began to read. "I'm appointing you, Domitian, as my heir. It will all be made legal, and the Senate will be given full details."

"Brother," said Domitian. "What is this? I was under the impression I was next in line. Who else would there be?"

"You are aware, little brother, that I may appoint whomever I wish?" Titus looked at him through weary eyes. "There are things which you don't know, and I intend to keep it that way."

"You have me confused," Dominian began grinning. "Have you been in the sun too long?"

"I've all my sanity, brother. I have intentions to take a journey from which I may not return."

"What journey will take my brother so far from Mother Rome that you'll not return to nurse from her?"

"Perhaps Mother Rome wishes to wean her child forever!"

Trajan broke in. "What is it that Caesar is trying to tell us?"

"I'll ask you to not question any further."

"As you request, Caesar." said Trajan. "I stand as a witness that you appoint your younger brother to the throne of Rome!"

Domitian stood motionless. He held back his emotions and asked. "When does Caesar intend to take this journey?"

Zoheleth

"Soon, dear brother," he grinned and added. "Don't use my bed until I'm dead!"

Trajan laughed, but Domitian lowered his head.

"My brother's wishes will be obeyed." Domitian forced himself to salute Titus.

Caesar found it humorous and broke out laughing.

"Don't try saluting again, my brother, you might injure yourself."

Domitian's face turned red. "Am I excused, Caesar?"

"Yes, little brother. Now hurry to your wife and give her the news she's been waiting for."

Domitian departed. Trajan stood shaking his head in disbelief. "Caesar, are you sure you know what you've just done?"

"I know, old friend. The prophesies say my brother will rule Rome!" he motioned Trajan to come closer. "There's something I must tell you. I have learned from the prophesies that your son will rule Rome one day."

Trajan was shocked. "My son?"

"Unfortunately my brother will be murdered during his own reign."

"Caesar, we must do something to prevent this!"

"Domitian will never win the favor of the people."

"What of you, Titus?"

"I have one purpose left in life. I will seek the one I deserted during the most painful time in her life. I don't deserve this luxury while others suffer because of me."

"My Caesar speaks of Bernice?"

"Never reveal this while I live."

"You have my word. Where will you begin your search?"

"I'm sailing to Pompeii!"

"What!"

"What's wrong?"

"Caesar, I beg of you. Have you not heard that Mount Vesuvius in Campania of Pompeii is erupting?"

"You can't be serious?"

"It's true, Caesar. Thousands are fleeing. You must not attempt to go there."

Titus hurried and summoned his guards. He ordered them to have a ship ready for him to leave immediately.

"Trajan," he called. "See to it that my men carry out my orders!"

"Caesar, please!"

"Trajan, that's an order from your imperial Caesar!"

"Yes, Caesar!"

The sea and wind was wild as the ship rocked its way toward the coastline of Pompeii. The crew complained fiercely how they would all be killed by the tidal wave which would follow a volcanic eruption.

Titus stood on deck and saw the volcano shed sheets of fire in the sky. Great puffs of smoke followed with burst of embers shooting so high it endangered the ships nearby. He was forced to order the crew to turn back. Tears streamed down his face, but his crew forged the ship to sail from the dangers of the Pompeii shores.

He was sickened by his thoughts. His throat was dry and the taste of fumes being carried by the high winds were choking those aboard. The August sun stood blackened in the eerie heavens.

Titus had the crew drop him off in Italy. He wanted to stay at the country house where his father died. Trajan requested to join him along with his personal guards.

When they arrived, Titus made plans to help the suffering victims of Pompeii. He gave instructions to one guard and ordered all the holy items from the temple of Jerusalem to be sold. His father had used them to decorate the country house.

"My father should have never kept these items. They're cursed!" he cried out. "I want the money from them to go into a fund for the victims of Pompeii."

"You intend to sell these beautiful items?" asked Trajan.

"Yes!" Titus replied as he poured wine.

Zoheleth

"Caesar," said Trajan. "You look ill. Your skin's red and your eyes bloodshot."

"It's the dust in the air," he said. "But I do feel a little weakened by all the tragedy I've witnessed."

"Why not rest a while?"

"I must rid myself of these things first." He watched the guards pack the items into carts. "I think the God of the Jews is punishing us."

"You're reading into things which you know nothing about," said Trajan.

"Explain this to me. After the fall of Jerusalem, we had a fire break out in Rome which lasted three days and three nights. No one knows what brought it on. Explain it!"

"Fires happen. Titus."

"I have drained all the finances of Rome to help the fire victims, and now this. How can I get money without depleting Rome. I must sell all we have."

"Rome understands," said Trajan.

"What Rome understands can no longer interest me. Get the things on the market and help the people. May the gods help those who haven't escaped Pompeii!"

The sky darkened in the middle of the day. The smoke covered the lands for miles around. The once green meadows of Italy were now resting under a blanket of ashes. The rivers and streams were choked in ashes. The drinking water was contaminated. Ashes covered every animal in the fields and many lay dead from the fumes.

The news grew worse. Titus received word that Pliny was killed when attempting to save the people on the shore of Pompeii. His crew was unable to move the ship to rescue him.

Pliny's young nephew witnessed it. He couldn't reach his uncle on shore due to the height of the fierce waves. Pliny was buried under the debris of trees and houses which were tossed atop him like sticks.

The eruption of Mount Vesuvius sent tons of spewing stones within its lava, uplifting roots of trees, and carrying

Zoheleth

people and animals to their death. It was the worse natural disaster the world had known. Never before had Vesuvius been so violent.

Nothing helped Titus in seeing any good ending to his life. He gave up the hope of ever finding Bernice, that is, if she were in Pompeii.

It took two weeks before he could sail to Pompeii. He found nothing but death. The entire city vanished. Families were killed while they sat at their tables. Some died in their beds, others died at gaming tables. Some poor devils tried digging their way out of the rubble and only their fingertips showed above the ashes.

He ordered the city be left buried beneath the blanket of ash. What was once a lively city, was now the burial ground for the laughing voices of dancers and singers. Their ghosts remained in the mouth of a fiery monster which showed no mercy. The year was A.D. 81, the second year of the reign of Emperor Titus.

After a short stay in Rome, Titus fell ill and returned to Italy to rest. But his fever persisted as he attended to the affairs of State.

Domitian remained in Rome, and Trajan sailed to Italy to visit with Titus.

"Has Caesar regained his strength back?" he asked the physician, Samuel. The doctor shook his head sadly.

"The prognosis is not good," said Samuel, as he removed the mask covering his nose and mouth. Trajan saw a skeleton of a man whose skin was like the ashes of Pompeii. He kept his distance since Samuel warned that Titus may have contracted the plague.

"Trajan," came a weak call from Titus. "I'll never find her."

Trajan saw his Caesar's sunken eyes glazed. Caesar made an effort to raise his trembling body but fell back helplessly.

Samuel whispered to Trajan. "When he dies, you must burn the body!"

"I understand," Trajan replied. He looked across the

room and spoke loud enough for the ailing Caesar to hear.

"May the gods have mercy on Rome if we lose you, my friend." He saw tears on Titus' face.

"I couldn't harm my brother," Titus uttered, "even when I learned that he plotted to kill me, I begged him to be a partner."

"Your brother will handle things," Trajan tried to convince him. "His wife is now by his side."

"Trajan, make your son a good Caesar,"

"I promise to do my best, Caesar Titus."

"I'm dying," he cried. "Promise if you find her, tell her I love her. Ask her to forgive me." With his last breath he called, "Bernice."

The world suffered a great loss that day, September the first, in the year A.D.81. Titus reigned only two years and twenty days. He was forty-one when he died. All Rome went into mourning.

Domitian held a grand burial for his brother. He hated spending all the money, but to keep the favor of the Senate and the citizens, he was forced to do so. He knew how Rome looked upon Titus as their favorite. He saw the people from all nations paying their last respects to the "Darling of Rome".

CLOSING TIMES

In Pella, King Agrippa's servants were packing goods into a caravan heading to Antioch. He had just returned from Rome where thousands paid their last respects to the son of Vespasian, Emperor Titus. After the items were loaded, he spoke to the driver privately.

"Deliver these things to where you delivered them last year. See to it that the people get this bag of gold for the boy's schooling, and here's gold for your services."

"Thank you, King Agrippa," said the driver. "I remember the house. The elderly couple are raising a grandchild."

"Yes," said Agrippa. "They're friends of mine who took the mother in when the boy was three. His mother vanished and no one knows if she's alive, but the family has been the only family the lad has known."

"King Agrippa is most generous," the driver noted. "He's a handsome lad. Perhaps King Agrippa will one day bring him to Pella?"

"Perhaps!" Agrippa sighed. He watched the caravan ride out of sight. "Perhaps!" he whispered as he turned and went back into his palace.

Note: History doesn't inform us of Queen Bernice's life from the time she left Rome. Some rumors say she remained in seclusion at the home of Agrippa. Other rumors have it that she died in the outbreak of the plague. Still other rumors were that she resided in Pompeii when Mount Vesuvius erupted. She may have perished along with most of the city residents.

Marcus Severus remained in Alexandria and led a quiet life as a physician. He was the father of a son and one daughter.

Zoheleth

Nicator Severus came with his family to live in Alexandria after his home was burned and the land confiscated by Rome. Nicator, along with other Christians had been forced to go underground. Nicator sailed with his family to join his brother. Nicator fathered two sons and one daughter.

After several years, Nicator and his family moved to Africa to seek the relatives of Sabinus. Nicator helped Christianize many of the tribes. Other tribes remained as pagans.

History reports that from the line of Severus came one who ruled Rome. Emperor Severus' mother was the Queen of Africa. She ruled successfully in Africa along with her daughter. When Severus became emperor of Rome, the Romans sent assassins to kill his mother and his sister. Emperor Severus was the first man with black skin to become emperor of Rome!

BIBLIOGRAPHY

Josephus, Flavius. The War of the Jews. Vol. I-IV
    Baker Book House, Grand Rapids, Michigan.
Massie, Allan. The Caesars.
    Franklin Watts, N.Y.
Suetonius, Gaius. The Twelve Caesars. Penguin Classics.
Plutarch. Fall of the Roman Republic. Penguin Classics.
Tacitus. The Histories. Penguin Classics.
Maier, Paul. Josephus the Essential Writings.
    Kregel Pub. Grand Rapids, Michigan.
Eusebius. Ecclesiastical History.
    Baker Book House, Grand Rapids, Michigan.
Jesus and His Times. The Readers Digest Assoc.
    Pleasantville, New York.
Potok, Chaim. Wanderings, the History of the Jews.
    Fawcett Crest, New York.
Graves, Robert. I, Claudius. Bl. 2. Claudius the God.
    Vintage International, a division of Random House Inc. New York.

Zoheleth

A History of Private Life from Pagan Rome to Byzantium.
  Belknap Press of Harvard University Press,
  Cambridge, Mass.
Atlas of the Bible. The Readers Digest Association, Inc.
  Pleasantville, New York.
Zohary, Michael. Plants of the Bible. Hebrew University
  Press. New York, London, Sydney.
The Harper Atlas of the Bible. Harper and Row,
  Publishers, New York.
Durant, Will. Caesar and Christ. MJF Books, N.Y.
Downey, Glanville. A History of Antioch in Syria.
  Princeton University Press, Princeton, N.J.
Comay, Joan and Brownrigg, Ronald.
  Who's Who in the Bible, Vol. I and III
  Bonanza Books, N.Y.
Rowell, Thompson. Rome in the Auguston Age.
  University of Oklahoma Press, Norman, Okla.
Chronicle of the World. Ecam Publications.
Dal Maso, Leonardo B. Rome of the Caesars.
  Collana Italia Artistica. Pubblicazione Periodica,
  Rome.

REFERENCE OF PRETERIST BOOKS

Hall, Michael. The Cure for Millennial Madness.
  Empowerment Tech. P.O.Box 40222, Grand
  Junction C0 81504-0222
King, Max R. The Spirit of Prophecy. Living Presence
  Ministries, Farmington, Ohio. 44491.
King, Max R. The Cross and the Parousia of Christ.
  Living Presence Ministries, Farmington,
  Ohio. 44491.
Gentry, Kenneth L. Jr. Before Jerusalem Fell.
  Inst. for Christian Economics, Tyler, Texas.
Stevens, Edward E. What Happened in 70 A.D.?
  International Preterist Association
  122 Seaward Ave. Bradford, Pa.
Melanson, Arthur. The Second Coming-Postponed or

Zoheleth

Fulfilled? Joy of the Lord. P.O. Box 237. Audubon, New Jersey. 08106.

ROMAN EMPERORS

Domitian: Born October AD 51. Ruled Rome from AD 81 until his death in AD 96 at the age of 44.
Galba: Born December 24, BC 3. Ruled Rome 7 months and died at the age of 72.
Otho: Born April 25, AD 32. Ruled Rome for 35 days. Died at the age of 37.
Titus: Born December 30, AD 41. Ruled Rome with his father from AD 69 to AD 79. Ruled alone two years. Died at the age of 41.
Vespasian: Born November 17, AD 9. Ruled Rome from AD 69 to AD 79. Died at the age of 69.
Vitellius: Born September 24, AD 14. Ruled Rome for 8 months. Died at the age of 56
(Emperor Claudius and Emperor Serverus are recorded in history.)

PRIESTS (Historical)

Ananus: Chief high priest in Jerusalem. A godly man and considered most holy. He labored to restrain the wickednes in the city until he was murdered.
Eleazar: Governor and young priest of Jerusalem's temple. Favored the zealots and habored the sicarii.
Hyrcanus: A high priest and king of Idumea. Grandfather to Mariamne, the wife of Herod the Great.
Joshua: Priest in Jerusalem. (Writings of Josephus)
Phanni: Chosen as high priest by the casting of lots.
Theophilus: An evil priest in Jerusalem.

Zoheleth

HISTORICAL CHARACTERS

Asiaticus: Love-boy to Emperor Vitellius.
Agrippa: Herod Agrippa II, King of the Jews.
Bernice: Sister to King Agrippa. Lover to Titus.
Caenis: Mistress to Emperor Vespasian.
Cerealis: Officer of the calvary and friend to Titus.
Epaphoditus: Emperor Nero's secretary.
Florus: Procurator in Jerusalem and instigator of trouble.
Gallus: Governor of Syria and commander of the Twelfth Legion. Dismissed by Nero.
John of Gischala: Son of Levi. A bandit who encouraged an uprising in Jerusalem.
Juncundus: Master of Horse in Florus' service.
Narsissus: Friend of Vespasian and Titus during the reign of Emperor Claudius.
Placidus: Vespasian's Tribune.
Priscus: Camp prefect to Gallus and a traitor to him.
Pudens: An auxiliary man challenged by a rebel Jew.
Pheroras: A respected elder in Gischala.
Sabinus: A black Syrian hero in the auxiliary of Antioch.
Silva: General of the army at Masada and governor of Judea.
Simon: Son of Giora, a bandit with an army of thieves.
Tiberius: Governor of Egypt. Served as military advisor to Titus.
Trajan: Commander of the Tenth Legion.

FICTIONAL CHARACTERS

Adana: Wife to Sabinus. Mother of Nicator and Marcus.
Antonius Salo: An army commander in Ashkelon.
Calpurnius: Elder in the Roman Senate.
Cornelius: Christian friend to Joseph and Drusus.
Demetrius: A Roman soldier.
Doris: Wife of Ebutius, a Roman commander.
Drusus: Christian friend to Joseph the physician.
Ebutius: Commander in the Tenth Legion.

Ezron: An Idumean who enters Jerusalem to fight.
Fabius: Right-hand man to John of Gischala.
Gnaeus: Friend to Emperor Vitellius.
Grates: Brother of Sabinus. Teacher in Rome.
Gratus, Marcus: Young man in the Roman Senate.
Jesse: A Jewish zealot turned informant to the Idumeans.
Joseph Abtolim: Physician from Alexandria.
Julia: Wife of Marcus and mother of Joseph Jr.
Marcus: Son of Sabinus. Educated as a physician.
Martha: Childhood sweetheart to Marcus.
Mattahias: Elderly Jew who escapes from Jerusalem.
Metilius: Roman soldier poses as a leper.
Miraimne: Wife of Nicator.
Mucianus: Officer of the vanguard sent to Rome by Vespasian.
Nicator: Elder brother of Marcus.
Philip: Roman soldier.
Samuel: Jewish physician. Man of wealth.
Terentius, Rufus: Officer of the Roman legion.
Thaddeus: Roman soldier in the Tenth Legion.
Virgil: Nicator's friend. Young lawyer teaching in Rome.

Made in the USA
Monee, IL
28 April 2026

49136489R00246